KT-568-598

Christmas at Rachel's Pudding Pantry

Caroline Roberts lives in the wonderful Northumberland countryside with her husband and credits the sandy beaches, castles and rolling hills around her as inspiration for her writing. Caroline is the Kindle bestselling author of the 'Pudding Pantry' and 'Cosy Teashop' series. She enjoys writing about relationships; stories of love, loss and family, which explore how beautiful and sometimes complex love can be. A slice of cake, glass of bubbly and a cup of tea would make her day – preferably served with friends!

If you'd like to find out more about Caroline, visit her on Facebook, Twitter and her blog – she'd love to hear from you.

f/CarolineRobertsAuthor
🐦@_caroroberts
carolinerobertswriter.blogspot.co.uk

Also by Caroline Roberts

Caroline Roberts

Christmas at Rachel's PUDDING PANTRY

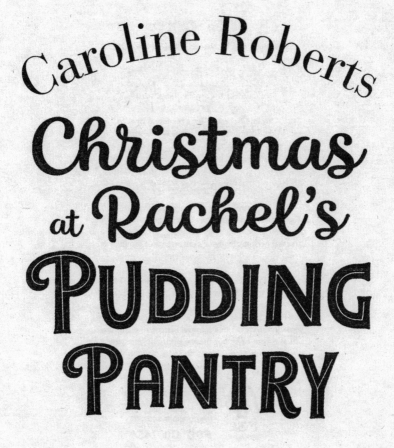

HarperCollins*Publishers*

Harper*Impulse* an imprint of
HarperCollins*Publishers* Ltd
1 London Bridge Street,
London SE1 9GF

www.harpercollins.co.uk

First published by HarperCollins*Publishers* 2019

1

A catalogue record for this book is available from the British Library

ISBN: 978-0-00-832767-5

This novel is entirely a work of fiction.
The names, characters and incidents portrayed in it are
the work of the author's imagination. Any resemblance to
actual persons, living or dead, events or localities is
entirely coincidental.

Set in Minion Pro by Palimpsest Book Production Limited, Falkirk, Stirlingshire
Printed and bound in the UK by CPI Group (UK) Ltd, Croydon CR0 4YY

MIX
Paper from
responsible sources
FSC™ C007454

This book is produced from independently certified FSC™ paper to ensure
responsible forest management.
For more information visit: www.harpercollins.co.uk/green

For Mum and Dad

Winter is the time for comfort,
For good food and warmth,
For the touch of a friendly hand
And for a talk beside the fire:
It is the time for home.

Edith Sitwell

The First Bake of Christmas

*Memories and Mince Pies –
Dad's All-Time Festive Favourite*

As a child, Rachel could walk into the farmhouse kitchen at almost any point during November and December, and if Dad was there on a break from his farm work, he was sure to have a mug of strong tea and a mince pie to hand.

Rachel smiled as she read Granny Ruth's neat handwriting on the page that had long ago been slipped into the 'Baking Bible' book . . .

Buttery Mince Pies:

8oz/225g Butter
12oz/350g Plain flour
3.5oz/100g Golden caster sugar
Pinch of salt
10oz/280g Good quality mincemeat
Splash of sherry
1 small egg
Icing sugar to dust

Preheat the oven to 200°C/gas/fan 180°C.

To make the pastry, rub 8oz cold, diced butter into 12oz plain flour, then mix in 3½ oz golden caster sugar and a pinch of salt.

Combine the pastry into two balls, warming and moulding with your hands – don't add any liquid – and knead them briefly. The dough will be fairly firm, like shortbread dough.

Roll out and cut 12 rounds with an 8.5cm (3½ inch) cutter and 12 rounds with a 6.5cm (2½ inch) cutter. Using a 16-hole non-stick tartlet tin, use the larger rounds to line each hole.

Spoon a heaped teaspoon of the mincemeat, mixed with a splash of sherry, into the pies.

Top the pies with their lids, pressing the edges gently together to seal.

Beat 1 small egg and brush over the tops of the pies. Bake for 20 mins until golden. Leave to cool in the tin for 5 mins, then remove to a wire rack.

Dust with icing sugar before serving.

These will keep for 3 to 4 days in an airtight container.

'These little pies herald the start of Christmas in our household,' Granny had written below the recipe. 'Robert loves to lift up the pastry lid and add a blob of thick cream on top of the warm mincemeat. It melts in so you have to eat it quickly. Delicious! I've even seen him eat five in one go. It's a good job he's a growing lad!'

Oh yes, Granny's mince pies were the best; that crumbly buttery first bite and then the lingering taste of festive-spiced mincemeat. It made you feel like Christmas was on its way . . .

1

Rachel was teetering up a ladder with a strand of fairy lights in her hand.

'Just a touch more to the left, love, that'll even up the loops.' Jill, her mother, was poised at the base of the ladder, keeping it steady and giving directions.

'Okay . . .'

'Careful, now.'

'I'm all right.' Rachel leaned from her perch to give them a tweak. She was used to doing far riskier things out on the farm, not that she would have enlightened her mum about *that*.

Rachel was fixing the twinkly white lights to the guttering of the old barn, ready to give the Pudding Pantry – their new business venture – a festive facelift and a touch of winter magic. From her vantage point, Rachel could see down across the yard and into the farmhouse kitchen window, glimpsing the large pine table and chairs that had been there for as long as she could remember. Memories of Christmases past suddenly came flooding back.

Sitting there on her father's knee, aged about six, the scrumptious turkey dinner now eaten, festive crackers snapped, corny jokes read out and Robert, still wearing his bright red paper hat – now a little skewwhiff – bouncing her up and down boisterously, while singing 'Jingle Bells' loudly. Granny Ruth and Grandad Ken, as well as Grandma Isabel, were sitting there at the table, looking on merrily, with Mum busy at the Aga preparing pudding, scolding him with a smile on her face, telling him that all that bouncing about would make Rachel feel sick after her big meal.

Jill was busy steaming her Christmas pudding ready for dessert, and Rachel, who as a little girl wasn't that keen on the rich fruity pud, was looking forward to a slice of the treat made especially for her and, ready on the side, a Chocolate Yule Log, with thick cocoa frosting covering a rolled chocolate sponge. Rachel loved the little robin that was brought out annually to pop on the top as decoration along with some sugar paste holly leaves.

Smiles and laughter, festive fun and full tummies. Gifts had been given, nothing too lavish but always much wanted – hmm, that might have been the year when she'd got her Jessie doll; the feisty, smart cowgirl from the Toy Story *films. That was the only doll she'd ever asked for, preferring model tractors and farm toys in the main, and soon after, the real things. Jessie was still there upstairs in her room somewhere.*

Oh yes, Christmas at the farmhouse, she remembered the warmth of the Aga, and the warmth of their hearts: the family together.

'Rachel . . . are you all right up there?' Mum's voice broke her reverie.

'Ah . . . yes, fine.'

Life had changed so very much, and Christmas had felt empty these past two years, as though they were just going through the motions. Her father's death had cast a dark shadow over them all, but it was time to recapture some of that festive magic for her daughter Maisy's sake – in fact, for all their sakes.

Life had shifted in ways they could never have imagined, and just this summer they had transformed the derelict stone barn into a gorgeous little tearoom where puddings were very much their 'thing'. Stepping inside the Pudding Pantry, you'd find a counter filled with a mouthwatering selection of Sticky Toffee, Chocolate, Ginger and steamed Syrup Puddings, crumbles galore, lusciously moist Carrot Cake, an Autumn Berry Pavlova, gluten-free banana cake and a selection of home-baked scones, not to mention crisp, buttery shortbreads and frosted cupcakes. Everything was made here at the farm. The Aga in the farmhouse kitchen was always on the go, with delightful baking aromas drifting over the farmyard – guaranteed to make your tummy rumble. They'd had a good start over the summer season, but business in the Pantry had started to slow worryingly during October. It was time to get themselves ready for the build-up to Christmas, and to try and boost trade. The fairy lights were a festive nod in the right direction.

Once again up the ladder, at the far end of the barn now, with the lights all in place, Rachel looked across the hawthorn-hedged fields where their sheep and small herd of cattle grazed happily. The leaves on the trees in the nearby copse were drifting down on the breeze, leaving jumbled heaps of golds and copper beneath them, ready for Maisy to tumble through in her wellingtons with a giggle. Further into the distance, the high moorland hills of the Cheviots rose majestically, bracken bronzed with short grassy banks, rising to purple peaks. This view, this place, held so much of her heart.

Job complete, Rachel climbed back down the ladder. She and Jill looked up, admiring their handiwork, the lights strung in loops along the old stone wall, just under the eaves.

'Well, that's added a bit of festive cheer, hasn't it? It looks really pretty,' commented her mum.

'Yes, just a soft twinkle. I love it. It'll look great as the dusk comes in.'

'It'll not be that long either, the way the evenings are pulling in these days.'

Rachel glanced at her watch. It was nearly three o'clock. 'Blimey, is that the time already? I need to go and fetch Maisy from the school bus.'

Within minutes, Rachel had jogged down the farm track and was standing at the farm entrance, waiting for the minibus to arrive.

She wasn't the only one who was in a rush; Eve came dashing down the lane from her cottage, her dark hair tumbling from its ponytail, in a half-jog. 'Blimey, I got so caught up in making wooden stars and hearts for

Christmas decorations, I hadn't realised the time. I was trying to come up with festive phrases to paint on them . . .' She was panting between words, 'All I've managed so far is "Ho Ho Ho!" and "Merry Christmas" – very original, not.'

Eve was Rachel's closest friend and craftsperson extraordinaire. She made the most gorgeous soft-toy felt animals and children's knits, as well as turning her hand to woodwork, greetings cards, and much more. Crafting was her passion, and in addition to her online Etsy store, she kept a selection of gifts for sale at the Pantry, which had proven popular with their customers. With Christmas on the horizon, it was all go for her with the festive crafting.

'Well, that'll be keeping you busy. Hmm, the wooden hearts and stars sound pretty and they'd be ideal for the Pantry. Do you think you can make enough so we can have some to sell, too? I want to start making the tearooms really festive now. I've just been putting up the outside lights, and some Christmas crafts in there would look great, don't you think? It is October, after all.'

'Ooh yes, I can just picture the barn, with that gorgeous old dresser filled with Christmas gifts. I'm planning on making some pretty tealight holders and hand painting glass baubles as well. Oh, and, I'll soon be making my Christmas knits and toys. So yes, of course, I'll make some extra ones for your display.'

'Gosh, Eve, I don't know how you fit it all in. Superwoman! But that sounds brilliant.'

With that, there came the low rumbling, more like grumbling, sound of an engine pulling up the hill, announcing the imminent arrival of the school minibus. And minutes later, after it pulled to a halt, out spilled Maisy closely followed by Amelia, Eve's daughter and Maisy's best friend. Maisy's attire was typically half-mast, one sock up, one down, with her school coat trailing from her arm.

'Hi, Mummy.' She ran to Rachel, planting an affectionate kiss on her cheek and rounding off with a hug.

'Hey, petal. Good day?'

'Yes, we've been painting leaves and doing prints with them, *and* we've been learning all about squirrels and we're helping to save the red ones.'

'Oh, that sounds good. Did you know that where we live, here in Northumberland, is one of the few counties in England that still has red squirrels?'

'Yes, Mrs Brown told us all about that – and they have *four* fingers and five toes, and their babies are called kittens.'

'Well, I didn't know that,' said Eve.

'And they have no teeth and no hair when they get borned,' added Amelia.

'Hah, they'll look funny little things,' said Maisy.

'Hmm, yes I bet, all bald. Well, you two *have* learnt a lot today,' said Rachel. 'That's great.' It was nice that her daughter was happy and had settled in well in her first year at the local school. 'Time for home then, Maisy?'

'Yep. Has Grandma been baking?' asked the little girl hopefully.

'Oh yes, there's bound to be a little something waiting at home for you.' The smells wafting from the farmhouse kitchen had been delicious as she'd left, so there had definitely been plenty of goodies baking away in that Aga.

Rachel had been covering in the Pantry this afternoon before taking a break to fix up the fairy lights; worryingly, the only custom had been an elderly lady and a couple who'd been out hiking in the hills.

'Yippee!'

They said their goodbyes to Eve and Amelia and set off up the farm track, walking past the field where their small herd of black, Aberdeen Angus cattle were out to pasture, making the most of the late-growing grass. Macduff, the sturdy bull, gave them a stare and one of his ladies mooed. The autumn had been mild so far, but who knew when that might change. Winter could be hard in the Cheviot Hills, as Rachel well knew. Soon enough they'd have to come into the shelter of the cattle shed.

'Can we go and see Petie, Mummy?'

Petie was Maisy's favourite pet lamb from this spring. He'd joined the other sheep out in the fields several months ago, but was still the friendliest of the bunch by far. Maisy (plus Rachel, she had to confess) had a soft spot for him, so much so that when the other male lambs went off to market recently, they couldn't bear to send him. So, he was still here on the farm, even though he was nearly fully grown, full of bounce and cheeky affection. Rachel swore he thought he was a dog at times, chasing about after the quad and their Land Rover, and he loved playing with Moss, the farm's border collie.

'Yes, I don't see why not. We could go and have a check of the sheep before it gets dark.' There had been that bother with the ewes stuck in the fence yesterday, so it'd be good to check the others were all all right and that the fence repair she'd made had stayed sound. 'We could jump in the Land Rover and go before tea. It'll be muddy, mind, so you'd better get changed out of your school uniform and get your wellies on.'

'Yay!'

They popped in to say hello to Grandma Jill, who was now keeping an eye on the Pudding Pantry which was disappointingly devoid of customers. With it being nearly four o'clock, it seemed unlikely there'd be any more. Jill was still baking like a trojan, but the customers weren't there in the numbers they had been over the summer. Rachel might have to have a word. She didn't want to dim her mum's baking enthusiasm, but they really couldn't afford to waste all those ingredients.

Jill was already starting to pack up. 'I'll be across to the farmhouse soon, love. I'll just get tidied here and pop back and check on the crumbles I have in the Aga. Then, we can have a quick cup of tea before I start organising supper.'

No wonder it had smelt so good – Mum's crumbles were divine.

12

'That sounds great. But first, Maisy and I are going out to quickly check on the sheep.'

'We're going to see Petie, Grandma.'

'Ah, how nice. Well, give him a pat from me.'

'I will.'

'We won't be long.'

'That's fine. See you later, then. Oh, here, take a couple of these oat flapjacks with you. You might fancy a little treat whilst you're out and about.'

Rachel rolled her eyes – Jill was unstoppable when it came to feeding them up with her delicious wares – but couldn't resist a smile as her mum popped the syrupy flapjacks into a paper bag.

'Thank you, Grandma.' Maisy broke into a gappy grin, having recently lost her two lower front teeth.

'Cheers, Mum.'

'See you soon, my loves.'

Maisy bounded into the passenger side of their slightly battered Land Rover as Rachel took up the driver's seat. Moss, the collie dog, was in the back, more than happy to join them, and little Maisy was soon chattering on about school and squirrels once more. After a bumpy ride over the fields that made Maisy giggle, they were soon up at the Top Field, where Petie and the hoggs, as the lambs selected for breeding were called, were grazing. Rachel had taken a couple of cobnuts from the lambing shed store to give their fleecy friend a treat. There was no need to call out to him, as he was already galloping across the field to meet the vehicle as they slowed to a halt on the rise.

'Hello, Petie boy!' Maisy was out of the Land Rover in a dash, rubbing his nose and ears affectionately, and feeding him the cobnuts.

The little (well, rather stocky now) lamb was so familiar and friendly. He nibbled happily at the treats. It was lovely to see the bond he had with Maisy, but it had meant a difficult decision a couple of months ago, when Rachel should have been pragmatic and sent him to market along with the others. She just hadn't had the heart to do it, nor to have to explain his fate to Maisy. They'd had enough sorrow in their lives. On this rare occasion, Rachel had let her heart rule her head, even considering the farm's very limited finances.

On a quick drive around, they checked the other sheep, who thankfully seemed to be fine and were keeping away from the fences and out of trouble – for the moment, anyway.

'Can we have Grandma's flapjack now?' a rather hungry Maisy asked.

'Good idea.'

Rachel slowed the Land Rover and pulled up near a rocky outcrop at the top of the hill. They got out and walked up the last of the rise, with Moss at their heels. As they reached the top, Rachel popped Maisy onto a large, flat mossy stone that made the perfect seat, and clambered up beside her. They sat perched together with the sheepdog at their feet.

'Here you go, petal.' Rachel took out the golden-baked flapjacks.

Rachel's first bite was a toffee-crunchy delight that melted in the mouth – scrumptious.

'Yummy!' Maisy announced her approval. 'Ooh, look Mummy, the farm's gone all fuzzy.' Maisy was pointing down to their valley where, sure enough, you could only just make out the dim golden lights of their farmhouse. And there, further in the distance, was the soft glow from the buildings of Tom's farm next door. It matched a soft tender glow within Rachel too.

Since they'd left the house, an autumn mist had swirled in across the lower fields and the stream that ran through the valley, and the view looked as though it was in soft focus. That gentle glowing scene of Primrose Farm made Rachel's heart lift. It had suddenly got chillier so the two of them sat side by side, keeping closely snuggled for warmth, eating their flapjacks. Moss was keeping alert beneath them, on the lookout for the odd tasty crumb that might drop his way.

Dew was beginning to form on the rocks and the grass as dusk crept upon them, the sky deepening to a purply-grey. Rachel was looking forward to heading back down to a warming supper, eaten sitting around the old pine table in the farmhouse kitchen. Mum would be there now, having closed up the Pantry for the night. Rachel could picture the golden-topped crumble puddings sitting there tantalisingly, cooling on the side.

She tightened her arm around her daughter as they

gazed down at their farm. And though Rachel's heart had been shredded these past couple of years – with losing her dad so devastatingly – this legacy of Primrose Farm, though not always easy, warmed her soul. Keeping it going for the three of them, and especially for Maisy and her future, *this* gave her purpose. *This* was home.

2

The next morning, there was the telltale 'fut-fut' of Frank's old Fiat coming up the farm track. Frank was in his mid-seventies, and a real gent. He lived in the nearby small town of Kirkton and he had become one of their Pudding Pantry regulars. Most days he'd appear for his morning coffee by ten thirty and he was always delighted to sample something sweet with it. Jill liked to try out her latest puddings and 'specials' on him, and he was generally most happy to oblige. He enjoyed the cake, chat and company, having lost his beloved wife a few years ago.

'Morning, Frank,' Jill said, smiling as he walked into the Pantry.

'Morning,' Rachel added from behind the counter, where she was stringing a further strand of fairy lights to hang along the till front.

'Hello there, ladies.' Frank doffed his flat cap. 'Now then, what are you pair up to? Christmas lights time is it, already?'

'It is indeed,' Rachel answered. 'We want to make the most of the festive spirit and give the place a bit of sparkle.'

'There's plenty of sparkle here already, what with you two lovely ladies here to greet me.' Frank gave a cheeky grin.

Jill's smile widened. 'Come on in. Now, what can I get you with your coffee today, Frank? Oh, hang on, I've been baking something new this morning, a Gingerbread Pudding. Thought it'd take the chill off these damp autumn days. Fancy giving it a try?'

'Oh, that'll go down a treat, I'm sure.'

'Any cream or vanilla custard with that?'

'Custard sounds delightful.'

'Excellent choice!'

Frank was soon settled at one of the white-painted wooden tables, happily tucking in to his sponge and custard, with the local newspaper set out beside him.

'What's the verdict, Frank?' Jill asked a minute or two later, a trace of anxiety in her tone.

'Well . . . I'd say it's a ten out of ten. Got all those lovely warming festive flavours through it, somehow. In fact, it brings to mind a pudding my mam used to make, back in the day. Though I have to admit,' Frank pulled a wry smile, 'her puddings always turned out a bit on the heavy side, bless her soul. Still, it went down a treat when I was a young lad.'

'Hah, I bet it did.'

'Yes, she used to blame it on the post-war rations, but me and Da knew better. She didn't have the best of teachers, mind. Now then . . .' Frank was off in full story-telling mode. '*Her* mam, Nanna Wallace, lived across on

18

the Scottish side of the border, so she did. Now, she used to make something called a "Cloutie Dumpling". "Clarty Dumpling" me and Da secretly called it. It was a dark-coloured pudding with raisins, currants, and all sorts in. I seem to remember having it around Old Year's Night. It was meant to be a special treat. Well, that thing was like a cannon ball. Don't suppose it was meant to turn out that way. Hah yes, I even spooned some off one day and shaped it into balls for my catapult. That stuff made great pellets.'

Jill couldn't help but laugh.

'Well, we'd better not make anything like that here, Frank!' Rachel pitched in.

'Aye, lass, we'd have to have lashings of custard with it, to manage to get it down. My, it was hard work that pudding.'

'Well, I'm lucky I had the best teacher in my mum, Isabel,' Jill said. 'And, well, I'd be lost without the fabulous Baking Bible.'

The 'Baking Bible' was the family recipe book that had been handed down over generations. It took pride of place on the shelf in their farmhouse kitchen and provided inspiration, recipes and tips, even now.

'That's where the Gingerbread pudding came from, it was one of my old Aunt Elsie's recipes.'

'Well, you're onto a winner there, lass. My taste buds are waltzing.'

'Thank you, Frank.'

Jill then focussed on getting organised for the day

ahead, and began making a batch of fresh cherry and sultana scones in the little oven they had there in the Pantry. Rachel stood wrapping up sets of knives and forks in red gingham checked napkins. They were both humming away to Radio Two, and when one of Jill's favourite oldies, Abba's 'Dancing Queen', came on, they ended up doing a bit of bum-wiggling in time behind the counter, with a dusting of flour spinning around them from Jill's wooden spoon which had suddenly morphed into a microphone, much to Frank's delight.

Rachel then headed out to the customer area to make sure the tables were all set out prettily. She'd bought a spray of red carnations from the flower shop in the village, which she split into posies and placed in the mini milk bottles they had on each table. The red was a blast of colour against the cream stone walls and rustic white furniture. She stood tapping her feet in time to the music – her cheerful wiggle belying the worry curdling in her stomach as she looked out on a near-empty Pantry.

And so began another day at Primrose Farm.

At eleven o'clock sharp, the sound of Tom's quad pulling up came from outside. Rachel couldn't help but grin as he strolled in, his dark eyes smiling warmly beneath chestnut-brown hair that was cut fairly short but still managed to be unruly. He was dressed in his farmyard-stained jeans, green wellies and a weathered Barbour coat.

'Hah, we'll be able to set the clock by you soon. I've

already started the bacon off on the griddle for you,' said Rachel.

'You know me too well. And yes, a bacon roll and coffee it is. Though, I may surprise you one day and order something else. I might live dangerously and have a cheese scone or something.' He grinned mischievously.

Rachel had to admit that eleven o'clock was fast becoming one of her favourite times of the day, seeing Tom stroll in, hungry and handsome in a windswept kind of way after having worked several hours on his neighbouring farm. And, the amazing thing was, that after years of them growing up as children close by – albeit with a bit of an age gap – they were now actually an *item*. A rather wonderful, sexy and caring kind of item. Rachel could still hardly believe it.

She passed him a mug of steaming coffee – strong with a touch of milk and no sugar, just how he liked it – across the counter.

'Cheers, Rachel. Morning, Frank,' Tom greeted the old chap who was still sitting there, browsing his newspaper, with a top-up of coffee to hand.

'Hello, Tom. Busy morning?'

'Yep, I've just put the tups out in the fields with the ewes. And, with this wet weather we've had lately, the fields are getting damned muddy. I've had to pull out a couple of stuck sheep.'

'All fun and games, I'm sure,' replied Frank.

'Tell me about it,' added Rachel. 'There were two stuck in the mud here yesterday morning. They'd got themselves in a right state.' She dished out the crispy bacon onto soft white bread.

Tom took the sandwich and was soon tucking in. 'Delicious, Rach. As always. I'll settle up. Can't stay long, unfortunately. Gotta get back as there's a delivery of bulk feed due in at any time.' He handed his plate and mug back across the counter. 'That was great, thanks.'

'Ah, okay.' Well, that was short and sweet. Rachel couldn't help but feel slightly disappointed.

'Can I see you, later on?' Tom's smile was hopeful and his dark eyes had a rather sexy look about them. Or maybe that was just Rachel's interpretation.

'Yes, I'll try. When Mum's back over in a while, I'll check if she has any plans for this evening herself. She's just nipped over to the farmhouse.' It was unlikely that Jill would be out, but she didn't want to take her mum's babysitting duties for granted. This new relationship with Tom was still very much finding its feet and Rachel felt she was juggling her responsibilities as a mother with it. Tom seemed pretty laid back about the situation, knowing the set up at Primrose Farm, but sometimes what they both *really* wanted was a couple of hours just for the two of them.

Tom leaned across to give Rachel a kiss on the cheek. Rachel caught a whiff of eau-de-sheep and aftershave, which surprisingly wasn't too off-putting.

'Try hard,' he whispered sensually at her ear.

She smiled broadly, feeling a flip in her belly. 'I will . . . but I do need to check.'

She watched him leave, amazed at how this new relationship had even happened, how they'd bridged that gap from neighbours and friends to becoming lovers. Seeing Tom always made her heart soar, and they were getting on so well. But they were at that crucial early stage – where it felt exciting, but also a little bit scary . . .

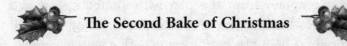

The Second Bake of Christmas

Jill's Toffee Apple Crumble – 1997 and Present Day

In autumn, Rachel used to pick the apples with Dad from the big old gnarled tree in their garden. He'd lift her up in his strong arms so she could reach the fruit, and they'd fill a wicker basket with the large Bramley cooking apples. Mum would keep some to use straight away for her crumbles and apple sauce, the rest they'd lay out on the big kitchen table, the very same table they had now, and wrap them in old newspaper ready to store in boxes under the bottom shelf in the walk-in larder.

Toffee Apple Crumble:

450g/1lb cooking apples
75g/3oz soft brown sugar
60g butter
½tsp cinnamon
For the crumble:
175g/6oz flour
75g/3oz butter, cubed
25g/1oz caster sugar and 75g/1oz demerara sugar

Dice the apples into large chunks and place in a pan with the butter, sugar and cinnamon. Cook gently until the apples just start to soften but are still mostly whole.

Remove apples from the pan with slotted spoon and place into baking dish. Pop the pan back on the heat and reduce liquid by half, stirring with a wooden spoon, and pour over the apples.

To make the crumble, sift flour into a bowl, rub the butter into flour until it resembles breadcrumbs. Stir in sugar keeping a heaped tablespoon of demerara to sprinkle over the top. Sprinkle crumble thickly and evenly over the fruit and press down lightly with the palm of your hand to smooth.

Bake at 180°C Mark 4 for 30–40 minutes until the fruit is bubbling and the crumble golden.

Serve with cream, custard or ice cream!

3

'So, do you think you can make it over?' Tom's toffee-warm voice came through on Rachel's mobile, as she parked the Land Rover outside the farmhouse, making her stomach flutter.

'Hey, Tom, hi. Well, we're still to have supper here. But yes, once Maisy's all tucked up in bed . . . then I'll scoot across.' In fact, Rachel had yet to check with Jill, but her mum hadn't mentioned that she was going out.

'Great, can't wait,' Tom said, and she could hear the smile in his voice. 'So, how's the rest of your day been?' he continued.

'Yeah, not bad. The usual on the farm, and steady away at the Pantry . . . Look, we're just heading in for supper and I've got Maisy with me, so we'll catch up later, yeah?' She was aware of Maisy listening in beside her and Jill was no doubt waiting inside with their meal prepared, having slaved away at the Aga again.

'Ah, okay.'

She could hear the tinge of disappointment in his voice. She wished they could speak for longer too, but it wasn't easy balancing Maisy and her mum's needs with her own.

While remaining cool on the outside, Rachel's heart was already giving little leaps at the thought of spending the evening with Tom – and whatever that might bring. Their budding relationship was still so new and still so exciting that it felt very fragile, like butterfly wings. And, even though they were getting on really, really well, Rachel was afraid they might yet break at any point. She pushed that thought aside – just because things had gone wrong with her relationships in the past, it didn't automatically mean they would now. Not all men were unreliable and selfish like Jake, her crazy first love and Maisy's absent and irresponsible dad, she told herself.

This, with Tom? This was built on friendship, on a steady base of caring and support. They'd known each other for years as neighbours, as farmers – since they were kids, in fact. But it had all changed very recently into something so much more than friends, and that, at times, was hard to comprehend.

'Great, so I'll see you later, then,' Tom added, taking her out of her reverie.

'Yes, that'll be lovely. I'll send a text when I'm about to leave, but it'll probably be around seven thirty, once Maisy's settled.'

'No problem. See you then.'

'Bye, Tom.'

'Bye.'

Maisy was already out of the vehicle and pulling off her wellington boots at the farmhouse porch.

'Was that Tom, Mummy?' she asked, with a serious face.

'Yes, petal, I'm going across to see him tonight.' She may as well be honest.

'Oh.' Maisy paused for a second before adding, 'Can I come?' Maisy got on well with Tom and he seemed to have a soft spot for her too.

'Sorry, not tonight, sweetheart. It's a school night and you need your sleep. By the time we've had supper with Grandma, it'll be bath and bedtime for you.'

'Hah – not fair.' She crossed her arms indignantly.

'Look, we can pop across on the weekend and you can say "hello" to Tom then, if you like,' Rachel appeased.

'Yes!'

'Okay.'

It was sweet that they got on so well, but yet another reason for Rachel to feel anxious. If this new relationship didn't last between her and Tom, how would that be for Maisy? She couldn't risk Maisy getting hurt, couldn't risk another man her daughter had grown fond of suddenly exiting her life. It was bad enough with Jake living hundreds of miles away and flitting in and out when it pleased him – mostly *out*. A small sigh escaped Rachel's lips. Why were relationships always complicated?

She opened the truck's back door and Moss leapt out, following them into the house, hopeful of a warm place by the Aga before having to go out to his kennel in the yard for the night. Rachel leaned down and gave his back a rub, his black and white coat soft and reassuring under her palm, before taking off her boots.

Nothing says home like the smell of baking and a gorgeous aroma drifted under the kitchen door. It smelt sugary-sweet, of apples and mmm, caramel.

'Oh Moss, you're gonna have to stay out here just now, fella.' The dog was banned from the kitchen during Pudding Pantry cooking hours. Everything had to be done by the book for health and hygiene reasons – they couldn't possibly risk getting in trouble with the environmental health agency, and being shut down. She gave the dog one last pat, then hung up her old Barbour jacket on a coat hook in the porch. 'Sorry, mate.'

Maisy was already charging about the kitchen, loudly announcing, 'Mummy's going out. To see Tom. What's for tea?'

Jill looked up. She was busy at the work surface, rubbing butter into flour in a mixing bowl. Next to her was a bag of demerara sugar, no doubt ready to add to the mix and then top her second batch of crumbles.

'If that's okay?' added Rachel politely. 'Sorry, I meant to ask earlier. It'll be later on, after I've settled Maisy to bed.'

'That's fine, love. Well, there's a cottage pie in the oven, and we'll try out one of these for dessert, shall we? There's one batch already made – Toffee Apple Crumbles.'

'I can't wait, it sounds delicious, Mum,' said Rachel with a smile.

'Yum,' grinned Maisy.

Yes, that sticky toffee apple smell filled the kitchen. It transported Rachel back to Bonfire Nights on the farm years ago, back when she was a little girl herself. Dad used to keep old firewood and debris stacked up through the year and then they'd have a huge bonfire out in the yard. There'd be hot dogs with golden fried onions and ketchup. And, earlier in the day, Mum would have dipped apples that were picked from their tree into hot toffee and then let them set on baking parchment. Rachel would have a friend or two over, and they'd watch Dad set off some low-noise fireworks with a 'woosh' of falling stars and colours, dramatic and sparkly as they lit the night sky but without the alarming bangs that would upset the farm animals. Then they'd eat the candied apples on sticks as they stood by the orange, crackling glow of the fire, with the sugary toffee sticking to their teeth and dripping messily onto fingers.

Memories were catching up with Rachel again. It happened all too often these days, the rawness of losing her dad still a haunting feeling within her. Even though it was over two years since it happened, there were still times when she thought of Dad and it suddenly became harder to breathe. There were just so many things here on the farm to remind her. She missed him so much.

They needed to look forwards as well as back, however. Maybe she and Jill could put on a small fireworks event this year, give Maisy a taste of that November magic? Perhaps they could invite Eve and her family along too, and Tom. They might not have much money to spare, but if the two families went halves on some pretty fireworks, then she and her mum could easily cook up some tasty food for everyone – that was their forte, after all.

'You all right, love?' Jill asked.

'Yes, just remembering those fireworks nights we had with Dad,' Rachel shared. 'That toffee apple smell brings it all back.'

'Ah yes . . .' Jill smiled sadly, silently acknowledging their joint grief.

It felt as though the big man himself might just walk back in to the room and take up his old seat by the Aga, holding his 'John Deere' mug of tea.

Sometimes Dad seemed a world away, and sometimes he didn't seem that far away at all.

With Maisy tucked up in bed, and a tummy full of delicious toffee apple crumble, Rachel headed to her room to swap her old jumper for a pretty pink-and-grey checked blouse, teaming it with her best dark-blue jeans. She flicked on some mascara and a swipe of lip gloss – she wasn't the type to worry about wearing much makeup, and her cheeks were certainly rosy enough from working outdoors without needing blusher.

She skipped down the stairs, finding Jill in the kitchen. 'Right, I'm off now, Mum. I'll just be a couple of hours.'

'There's no hurry, love, I'm fine here. I've got an episode of *Emmerdale* to catch up on, and Jan brought me in some magazines the other day, so I can look over those. Might even glance through the old Baking Bible and get some ideas for some warming winter puds to put on in the Pantry as specials in the coming months.'

'Mmm, that sounds good. That crumble was delicious tonight, by the way. Just the thing after being out in the cold.'

'Thanks, love. Hopefully they'll go down well in the Pantry this week. We need to pull a few more customers back in. It's been very quiet lately, hasn't it?'

Ah, Rachel thought, so Mum was more than aware of that too. 'Yes, I've noticed. It's getting a bit worrying,' Rachel admitted. 'I suppose with it being October and out of season . . .' The lack of customers, tourists, and *income*, these past few weeks was a real concern for Rachel, but she hadn't wanted to worry her mum too much, or put a damper on her enthusiasm for the new business. The Pudding Pantry was meant to be *lifting* the farm's struggling finances, but there was no sign of that lately. They were just about keeping their heads above water for now, but they needed a boost over the Christmas period or they'd soon be sinking once more. The very last of their savings from the summer trade had gone into installing a log-burning stove to keep the barn cosy and the customers warm over the winter months. It had felt like a wise investment, but that was it; there were no backup funds at all. And it was still a long while until the basic payment monies would be coming in for the farm.

'Well, it's bound to be quieter just now, I suppose. The summer tourists have all gone. And, remember, we're still getting established.' Jill was trying to look on the bright side. Rachel loved that about her mum – ever the optimist.

'Yes, you're right,' Rachel agreed, trying to sound more confident than she felt.

'Well then, love, don't let me keep you. Get yourself away. Oh, and why don't you take one of those crumbles for Tom? I'm sure he'd like that.'

Rachel stifled a giggle. Ever since a raucous conversation in the pub one night between Rachel and her girlfriends – before she and Tom had become an item – there'd been a standing joke about Tom being 'comforting' like an apple crumble. Her mum was blissfully unaware.

'Will do!' she replied, a wide grin spreading across her face.

4

Rachel drove the two miles between their farms in the dark, along the familiar, twisting hawthorn-hedged country lanes. She felt a touch nervous, her tummy in a bit of a knot, as she neared his farm entrance gate. They didn't get an awful lot of time alone, and though she was desperate to see him, all this togetherness was still strangely new. She *so* didn't want to mess things up. She pulled to a halt, and soon found herself knocking at Tom's farmhouse door, a fizz of anticipation building as she let herself in.

'Hi, I'm here,' Rachel announced.

Tom turned to greet her. He was standing at the kitchen island unit, opening a bottle of red wine. His hair was still slightly damp, as though he'd just got out of the shower. Hmm, just the thought of that sent a little shiver through her.

The house was a large, traditional honeyed-stone building similar to their own. Inside however, the kitchen had been modernised with light-coloured wood units and chrome fittings – a modernisation Tom's ex-wife had insisted on, complaining that the original kitchen was archaic. It wasn't the only thing she'd complained about, so Rachel had heard, with the relationship falling apart after four years. Caitlin had moved back to Newcastle, leaving Tom with a wrecked heart and a large bank loan to buy her out with, so he could keep the family farm intact.

'Hey.' He gave her a broad smile, that reached right through to his deep brown eyes.

'Hi.' Rachel handed him the pudding gift from her mother. 'Crumble,' she said with a suggestive grin.

'Oh, perfect. Can't wait to tuck in . . .' His smile widened cheekily.

Mabel, Tom's Jack Russell Terrier, then dashed to greet Rachel, leaving the warmth of her rug by the stove. She was soon skipping around her visitor's feet, with her tail wagging merrily.

'Hi Mabel, how are you?' Rachel leaned to pat the little dog's smooth white-and-brown patched head.

As she stood back up, Tom took a step forward, taking Rachel into his arms. 'I've missed you.' His lips met hers with a kiss that was tender and oh so promising. The knot in her stomach began to unravel.

'Hah, it's only been a matter of hours.' She made light of it, but she had been thinking about him too. A snatched 'hello' at the Pantry was nothing like spending an evening together. She had a feeling Tom would have liked to meet up more, but life was busy enough and Rachel hadn't wanted to crowd him or appear needy in these early days of their changing relationship. She was still getting used to it herself.

'I know. But still . . .' Tom added, his eyes intense. 'Glass of red?'

'Yes, please.'

They took their wine glasses through to the lounge, where a log fire was roaring away in the stone hearth. It was welcoming and cosy there, with a well-worn plum-coloured sofa set next to a low wooden coffee table. They were soon settled there together, chatting about their respective days. This was just what she needed after being up since six thirty out on the farm, hauling big circular hay bales about, preparing their store of winter supplies in the shed ready for the cattle and sheep, then on her feet all morning and afternoon at the Pudding Pantry. Tonight was a chance to chill out in some rather gorgeous company. She began to feel herself unwind.

Tom was sitting so very close . . . Then the urge to kiss him again hit her. She placed her glass down purposefully and leaned towards him. He didn't need any encouragement. His lips were warm and welcoming, their tongues soon entwined. It was becoming familiar, the way his kiss felt, so tender and passionate. Soon, Rachel's whole body was on high alert, every nerve ending tingling.

Still on the sofa, with their upper bodies pressed so very close, Rachel pushed him down so that he lay back across the cushions. Tom was a tall guy, and as he tried to position himself so she could move across him, his lower legs and feet hung awkwardly over the sofa arm. Rachel looked at his gangly arrangement and giggled.

'Shall we move this fireside?' he suggested with a cheeky, and rather sexy, arch of his eyebrow.

'I think that sounds like a very good idea. We might well end up in A & E otherwise.' Rachel laughed.

They shifted to the rug and lay down by the glowing heat of a crackling log fire. Tom, who was now propped on one elbow, gently pushed a strand of her dark wavy hair away from her face and gazed at her intensely.

'You're beautiful.'

'Oh . . .' Rachel never quite knew how to take a compliment, but she managed a smile.

They kissed again, with warm, wine-tasting lips, and Rachel lay him down, teasing off his shirt, button by button, guiding her fingertips underneath the cotton of his top, and tracing the taut muscles of his chest. She gave a little grin. 'You're not so bad yourself, Tom Watson.'

She loved the maleness of him, his strength, those toned muscles. As a working farmer, he was fit and healthy and she had to admit he looked damned good for his thirty-three years. And, it wasn't all about the exterior, either; Tom's personality was kind and caring too, and in contrast to all that strength, he still had the capacity to be gentle. He'd been a great support to all of them since her father's death. In fact, Rachel mused, as she stroked his chest, trailing her fingertips down over his stomach where the muscles quivered involuntary, the whole of him was a very special combination, and making love with this wonderful man was a joy. She couldn't wait to experience that all over again.

Tom shifted to sit up, his top now off and discarded

across the floor, revealing a very attractive chest above his jeans. He began to slowly remove Rachel's clothing, kissing her bared skin as he went. Down to her under-wear now, he traced his hand along the curve of her waist, her hip, her thigh as she lay on her side. Soon they were both naked in the firelight glow.

The emotions within Rachel were powerful . . . yearning, loving, learning . . .

As they made love, she lost herself to him. And though she hadn't voiced those words 'I love you' lately, she felt it within every bone in her body.

As they lay naked in the afterglow, Tom propped himself up on one elbow beside her.

'Are you warm enough?' he asked.

'Yes, the fire's lovely.'

'And you're okay?' He sounded so caring, checking she was happy, that all of this was right for her.

'*Very*.' She smiled tenderly. This was so beautiful, getting to know every inch of his body, getting to know the real Tom, inside and out.

He moved closer, snuggling up behind her, his arm slipping around her waist, moving on until he found her hand, where he laced his fingertips through hers. Then Mabel trotted in from her kitchen bed and paused, giving them a haughty look.

'Hah, I think she's put out,' Tom commented, though there was a smile through his voice. 'The rug by the fire is usually her spot of an evening.'

Rachel patted the mat beside her. 'Ah, sorry Mabel; will you share?'

The little dog put her nose in the air as though thinking about it, then took up the spot on the rug in front of Rachel and curled up, letting Rachel stroke the short silky fur of her head. Her short tail thumped contentedly in answer.

There were a few quiet moments, where they lay listening to the crackle of the fire. It felt peaceful there, just being together. A world of two . . . and a terrier. Rachel hadn't imagined it could ever be this magical, this close. Her longest relationship having been with Jake, Maisy's father, at aged seventeen into eighteen. They had been so young, naïve, experiencing snatched moments of sex in the back of Jake's car or at his parents' house. It now seemed childish, experimental, as if they hadn't known each other at all.

This was so much more . . . heartfelt, body and soul.

Maybe it was because it was so wonderful, so special, that Rachel's vulnerabilities hit home. She suddenly pictured Tom there with his ex. Had they ever made love here by the fire – they'd lived in this very house for several years, after all? Had he felt all this before? He must have really loved Caitlin once to have married her. Rachel felt a strange twinge of envy for Tom's ex-wife, for what the two of them had shared before, even though it had been over for years now.

'Tom . . . what happened with Caitlin? How did it all go wrong?'

'Ah, let's not talk about that now, Rachel. This is so

nice, let's not think about anything else. . .' He brushed the question off, seeming a little ruffled.

'Oh.' Well, she sure knew how to kill the atmosphere.

'Look, we weren't right for each other. It was never going to last,' he added, matter-of-factly.

That made Rachel suddenly feel sad, lying there with Tom's arm around her. Could they go wrong too? Is that the way things went? But no; she reminded herself of her parent's long marriage, they had been happy . . . up until that last fateful day. She turned her thoughts to Eve and Ben and their secure little family unit. It didn't always have to go wrong.

'And Rachel,' Tom spoke gently, 'it wasn't like *this*.'

She rolled over to face him and they shared a tender kiss. As she finally pulled away, Rachel gave a fragile smile. Oh my, how would it feel not to have him beside her?

The evening passed all too soon; drinking red wine, naked by the fire, with this gorgeous man she had fallen in love with.

Still wearing only her watch, Rachel glanced at her wrist to see that it was already past ten thirty.

Reluctantly, she sat up and began gathering her clothes. 'Tom, I'm going to have to go. I'm sorry, but I don't want to take advantage of Mum's goodwill and babysitting services. And I like to be there in the morning for Maisy, getting her up and ready for school.' There wasn't only herself to think of in all this.

'It's okay, I understand.' He brushed Rachel's cheek fondly with his fingertips. 'You're like the three musketeers,' he said smiling. 'I take on one, I take you all on.' His voice had assumed a daft French twang.

'Exactly,' she beamed. 'Thank you,' she added softly, before kissing him affectionately on the nose.

'Though, I'm sure we could just snatch five more minutes . . .' He gave a sexy grin, before adding, 'I can achieve a hell of a lot in five minutes.'

'I'm sure you can.' She laughed. 'Hmm, well, in that case . . .'

And they were soon back together fireside, in a tumble of arms, legs, lips and hot kisses.

Rachel drove back to Primrose Farm through the indigo dark of the winding lane, her heart still full from their sensual night, her skin still warm from Tom's touch.

The lights were on downstairs and, as she opened the farmhouse door, there was the sound of the radio on in the kitchen. Jill was at the kitchen work surface with a pinafore over her dressing gown.

'Hello, love, did you have a nice time?'

'Yes, thanks.' Rachel still, rather embarrassingly, felt like she was basking in the afterglow. 'Are you still baking, Mum?' Rachel added, surprised to see the late-night activity in the kitchen.

'Oh, I've just about finished, love. And don't worry, I haven't been here all night. I sat and watched my programme after supper, had a bath, and then I was flicking through the old Baking Bible and found this recipe of my Great-Auntie Edna's. I was looking for some warming winter puds for the chillier months, and this seemed perfect. Look, she's even done a little drawing, though I must say those sultanas in the pudding look very like rabbit droppings.'

They both giggled.

The finished article, stood on the side, did indeed look and smell wonderful; a baked sponge in a rectangular dish, with a rich caramel sauce over it. 'Mmm, that looks great. What is it?'

'Sultana and butterscotch pudding.'

'Ooh, delightful.'

The Baking Bible was laid open on the side next to the mixer. There were at least four generations of puddings and bakes recorded there, with the earliest being penned by Jill's own grandmother, Alice. A legacy of bakes and cakes that Jill had brought with her, and since added to, when she had married Dad back in the mid-Eighties and moved into the farmhouse.

'I think I'll put it on as a special tomorrow.'

'Ideal! I can't wait to taste it.'

'Well then, maybe we can spoon out a little portion from the edge to try?'

'Oh yes, go on then. We need to maintain quality control, after all,' Rachel grinned.

Jill scooped some out into a small bowl, spooning over a little of the syrupy caramel-coloured sauce.

Lifting her spoon to her mouth, Rachel's taste buds exploded happily. 'Oh my, that's going to be a hit. The sponge is so light and the sauce is naughty but very nice.'

'Aw, thanks, love.' Her mum beamed proudly.

Rachel loved seeing her mum in good spirits, and farmhouse-kitchen baking was most definitely Jill's happy place. The downside was that Jill was still making nearly as much food as in the busier summer months, 'just in case', and they were starting to waste some now. Rachel knew she should really ask her mum to ease off on the baking, warn her that they couldn't afford to throw things away now that it was quieter. But looking at her mother, happy there in the kitchen, knowing that baking helped to fill a loneliness that Rachel still shared . . . well, she bit her tongue, though she knew she'd have to say something if things didn't turn around soon. In the meanwhile, their friends, family and the postman were benefitting from some rather scrumptious giveaways for now.

Rachel resolved that she would have to put her mind to drumming up some more business, somehow. Fingers crossed, things would turn around for Primrose Farm soon.

She smiled at her mum over the steam of the delicious pudding, and nudged closer at the kitchen side to give her hand a squeeze. 'They're a winner every time, Mum.'

The Third Bake of Christmas

Chocolate Cupcakes with the Cutest of Faces – Maisy's Festive Favourite

Jill's Chocolate Reindeer Cupcakes:

100g plain flour
20g cocoa powder
140g caster sugar
1 ½ tsp baking powder
¼ tsp vanilla extract
Pinch of salt
40g butter
120ml whole milk
1 egg

To decorate: Chocolate buttercream, large milk chocolate buttons, large white chocolate buttons, red and brown Smarties (or similar), cake decorating eyes or mini chocolate chips

Heat oven to 180°C/Gas 4. Mix flour, cocoa, baking powder, pinch of salt, and butter in electric mixer or with handheld electric whisk. Beat until everything combined.

Whisk the milk, egg and vanilla extract together in a jug, then slowly pour about half into the flour mixture.

Beat to combine, then turn mixer to high speed and pour in the remaining liquid and beat until smooth.

Spoon into paper cases to 2/3rds full. Bake 20-25 mins.

Leave to cool before decorating with chocolate buttercream, half a large milk chocolate button for each of the ears, a white chocolate button with a Smartie stuck on for the nose, and the sugar paste eyes (or choc chips).

Extremely cute and very tasty!

5

There was a promising flurry of customers at the Pantry the next morning. By ten thirty, Anne and Irene, two senior citizens from the village, were chatting away, enjoying coffee and shortbread.

'Oh, by the way, Jill,' Irene called across from their table, 'that apple and blackberry crumble I took home last week went down a real treat. I passed it off as my own,' she confessed. 'Well, I didn't exactly lie; I just didn't tell my Ronald that I hadn't made it myself. Anyway, he liked it that much he said I'd have to make it again soon, so I'd better take another one home today.' She grinned mischievously.

'Of course, but this week's crumble is an apple and pear.'

'Ah, not to worry, that'll do nicely. I'll just make out I've been experimenting. He'll be impressed and I'm sure it'll go down as well.' Irene started chuckling.

'Well, that's the way to do your home baking,' added Anne, 'sitting here having coffee and biscuits with a friend, and getting a takeaway bake as you leave.'

'Hah, absolutely, that's what the Pudding Pantry's all about my lovelies.' Jill smiled.

'Oh yes, that's the way to do it, ladies,' Rachel joined in, enjoying the camaraderie.

Two more regulars, Denise and Christine, who Jill knew from the local Women's Institute, called in soon afterwards for tea and cake. Trevor, the postman, stopped by for a takeaway coffee and a flapjack, and then gorgeous Tom for his elevenses. Just picturing last night's fireside activities made Rachel blush bright pink at the counter – she hoped her mum hadn't spotted that and busied herself with the coffee machine.

Tom was in a bit of a dash to get back as he needed to catch up with his farmhand, Jack. 'I'll maybe catch you later, Rach. It was a great evening last night, by the way.' His eyes held hers with a sexy intensity.

'Yes,' was all she could answer, in a pitch higher than normal, remembering all too well.

After a promising morning, the Pantry was disappointingly bare by the time lunchtime swung around.

The slowing of trade nagged at Rachel. 'It's gone so quiet here these past few weeks, Mum, hasn't it?' She stifled a sigh. It had cost so much in money, time and energy to get the Pudding Pantry up and running; they really couldn't afford for it to belly-flop so soon. There was no magic pot of savings to bail them out, no stash of money in the bank. This was it – every last penny was invested in this project. Their livelihoods and future, in fact the whole farm, depended on it.

'I know, love. It is a concern. I don't suppose the takings have been much to speak of, either.'

'No, I doubt we've even covered our costs these past few weeks, to be honest.'

'Now then . . .' Jill placed a reassuring hand on Rachel's shoulder, 'let's not get too despondent, love. Like I said the other day, it's a quiet time of the year for most businesses around here. The tourists are fewer just now. We'll just have to be patient. I'm sure things will pick up again before Christmas.'

Mother and daughter looked about them; there wasn't a soul in the tearooms. It was hard not to feel downcast about it.

'But yes,' Jill continued pragmatically, 'maybe, we do need to get our thinking caps on just now and drum up a bit of interest.'

'No time like the present, then,' Rachel rallied, determined to lift their mood and take some action. 'I'll make us a pot of tea and grab a pad and a pen. Let's smash out some ideas, Mum.'

Sitting down at one of the white wooden tables just a few minutes later, Jill kick-started the brainstorm, 'Well, the Kirkton Country Show, where we had the stall back in the summer, that went off really well . . . so what about finding out about any other shows, or local Christmas Fayres and such like, that might be coming up soon?'

'Good thinking. I'll do some research. Eve might know of any craft events coming up in the area. And, of course, we absolutely need to make the most of the build-up to Christmas here at the Pantry.' Rachel doodled a holly leaf, and a Christmas tree on her pad as she wrote 'Christmas Fayres' down. 'Yes, we can feature a feast of festive flavours, Christmas puddings, mince pies . . .'

'That Gingerbread Pudding went down well with Frank the other day, and oh, what did I used to make for you when you were small? Yes, those little meringue snowmen. They might go down well with the children.'

'They sound good. You used to make reindeer cupcakes too. I remember the noses were chocolate buttons,' said Rachel.

'Hah, yes so I did. Chocolate sponge ones.'

'I used to love those.' Mum's Christmas bakes were legendary. They were a tradition that came out annually along with the decorations. 'Oh, and we can have a festive facelift with our displays on the dressers, with Eve's Christmas decorations and toys for sale. She's already mentioned that she's busy making lots of new things.'

'Great. And I agree, we can really up the ante with our Christmas goodies too; I can make Christmas cakes and puddings for people to take away. I'm sure Brenda at the deli would take some to sell too. I could make up packs of shortbread and those reindeer cupcakes – in fact, there could be all sorts of festive foodie gifts and treats to take away. Folk are busy enough as it is over Christmas, without having all that extra baking to do.'

'Yes, that'd be brilliant. Some great ideas there, Mum. But . . . hmm . . . it's still not much good if we can't get the people here to start with.' Rachel was looking around the empty barn once more. 'We need to step up our promotion and advertising, remind people that we're here. It's like the initial buzz has gone. Though that'll cost, of course.' Rachel took a sip of tea. 'I could design some new flyers. And, maybe we could get a bit of free editorial in the *Gazette*, if I make it newsworthy enough and ask Amanda there nicely.'

'Perhaps we could drop by the newspaper office with a sticky toffee pudding or two, or even better a Christmas Pudding to try?' Jill suggested.

'Hah, that sounds like bribery to me, but it's definitely worth a try.' Rachel smiled at her mother's wily ways.

'Well, at least we have a few ideas to be going on with,' added Jill.

'It's all good, but I just feel like we need something else, something a little different, to make us stand out from the crowd . . . something unique that only *we* can do.'

'But what, love?'

'Hah, I wish I knew! I'll have a think on it whilst I'm sorting out the cattle shed this afternoon. Can you handle the rush in here?' Rachel added ironically, the reality of the pretty but empty space bringing it all gloomily home once more. Empty chairs and empty tables . . .

'I'm sure I'll manage,' Jill answered drily.

'Right, well, I'll be back in time to collect Maisy from the school bus.'

'Okay, pet.'

Rachel finished off her cup of tea and stood up to leave.

'Rachel?' Jill stopped her in her tracks. 'Chin up, love. We'll find a way.'

Oh how her mum's encouragement brought a lump to her throat. Over the past couple of years, it had been Rachel who'd stood strong, Rachel the one to rally Jill, especially through the dark days they'd had, but lately Rachel's own fears were beginning to get to her. There was so much at stake. The future of the farm and their lives here were tied up with the Pudding Pantry. The pressure was really on for it to do well.

'Thanks, Mum.' Rachel nodded, appreciating that prop of support and finding a grain of hope.

No stupendous brainwave hit in the cattle shed, unfortunately. The only thing that came like a bolt from the blue was a large male pheasant who'd decided to take up residence in there, roosting in the rafters and bursting out with a piercing squawk that frightened Rachel half to death. After taking a breather and waiting for her heart to stop hammering – every day brought a new surprise on the farm – Rachel set about splitting open and spreading huge circular bales of straw, ready to bed down the cattle. The time would soon come for them to come in from the fields.

Something unique – something special for the Pudding Pantry. This manifesto kept rolling along in Rachel's mind like the ruddy bales. There didn't seem to be any magic answer, but hey, was there ever?

When Rachel looked at the farm's accounts later that evening, it was obvious that they were still sliding down that slippery slope of debt. Her mood felt black and a headache hung over her right eye. *What was it all for?* All that hard work, the never-ending routine of getting up at dawn, working with the sheep, the cattle, feeding, tending, mucking out, filling in mountains of paperwork – and that was before all the things she needed to do at the Pantry, as well as looking after Maisy. Life was more than a juggle right now; it was a big struggle.

She sighed and took a sip of her coffee. The Pudding Pantry was meant to be the thing that turned it all around and saved them. What if it ended up being the thing that pulled them under?

'Is everything all right, love, you seem a bit quiet tonight?' Jill asked kindly once they'd finished having dinner later that evening.

'Ah, I'm just tired, that's all.'

'Of course.' Jill paused, giving Rachel the chance to talk more if she wanted.

'Oh, Mum, sometimes I just feel like I'm on a hamster wheel, working so damned hard and juggling it all, on the farm, the Pantry, and getting nowhere.'

'It's been a hard couple of years, love. And you've got so much to carry on your shoulders just with the farm. It's no wonder you feel the pressure of it sometimes. We've all been thrown in at the deep end.'

Yes, farm life could be hard, but like most farmers, a bit of hard work had never bothered the Swinton family. It was losing Dad in such a devastatingly tragic way that had left a gaping hole in all their hearts. Much as she'd wanted to, Rachel couldn't just curl up in a ball of grief after it happened, she'd had to keep going for Mum and Maisy, for the farm. And the aftershocks kept rolling with them, like waves.

They had all got up one early spring morning, had breakfast together around the kitchen table, expecting life on the farm to drift along in much the same way as it always had. But that day life was smashed like a raw egg, and their world had been shattered. They were still struggling to find their way.

Rachel gazed absently into the flickering flames of the cosy fire in the living room, her mind elsewhere for a while, taking her back to her childhood days here on the farm, memories of working with her dad, learning the ways of the farm and of the animals. Her voice when she finally spoke was soft, yet filled with emotion. 'It's not just a job though, is it? When I go and stand on the hill above the farm – *our* hill, *our* farm – and I look around at the valley and see our animals . . . Well, this is it, this is everything. It's where my heart is.'

'I know. Mine too.' Jill's voice was tinged with sorrow as well as love.

'Well, then, we battle on, until we've given it every last shot,' Rachel resolved. 'I know I've just got to do my best with the farm work. But we'll try not to be blinkered about it; and if it all gets too much and we're about to go under financially, then . . .' She sighed deeply and looked down at her hands in her lap. 'We'll have to be realistic and look to sell up. But until then, we give it everything we've got, yeah?'

'Yes, absolutely. And it's understandable that you're tired, pet, it's been hectic and you haven't stopped for months. Heaven knows, the farm work's enough on its own. And, even now with the Pantry being slower, you're still on the go, looking for ways to boost business. You need to look after yourself too.'

'I suppose.'

'I *know*.' Jill gave her a stern look.

'Hah, "Your mother is always right",' Rachel quipped.

'Too true.' Jill quirked an eyebrow. 'And Rachel,' her mum's tone became serious, 'don't keep it all in, will you? If it feels like things are getting too much, talk to me, love, tell me. We'll face things together.' They both knew what Jill was referring to; the dreadful circumstances surrounding her father's death. 'It's good that we're talking tonight, but don't feel you've got to carry the load on your own. Don't *ever* be afraid to ask for help.'

'Of course, Mum, and I promise.'

'So, we won't be giving up cowpats, boiler suits and baking aprons any time soon then,' Jill said, resolutely.

'Of course not – and oh, the glamour, hey?'

They both raised a smile, as they gazed into the flickering fire.

6

The weekend rolled around and it was one of those picture-perfect autumn days with golden and russet trees glowing against the fresh, blue backdrop of sky, which was streaked with soft wisps of cloud.

Maisy was helping out around the Pantry. She had her own little pink apron on, with white polka dots, that matched her grandma's, and she seemed happy enough wrapping up knives and forks in napkins. Rachel did worry that her little girl spent far too much time with them working at the Pantry or on the farm. Yet, they didn't have a lot of choice. Yes, Eve would have her sometimes or Granny Ruth might stop by, but otherwise, where else was she going to go?

As elevenses time swung around, Tom stopped by for his Saturday morning coffee break.

'Good morning, ladies. It's a beauty out there, isn't it?' His sunny smile lit the room, as well as Rachel's heart.

'Too right. Morning, Tom.'

'Hi, Tom.'

'Hi, Maisy. I see you're doing a grand job there. I bet you're a star helper.'

'She is indeed,' agreed Grandma Jill.

'Hey, Maisy,' Tom grinned, 'what do you say to a cow if it's in your way?'

'Ah . . . Don't know?'

'You tell it to Mooooove!' He gave her a wink.

Maisy started giggling, then repeated the phrase exaggeratedly, 'MOOOOVE – that's funny, Tom. I'm going to tell that to Granny Ruth *and* my friend Amelia.'

'So, what's on today then, folks?'

'Well, it's just another day here at the Pantry for us,' answered Rachel, 'and we'll just have to see how many people we get in.'

'Ah, well, I have a couple of hours to spare and I wondered if I might whisk you off somewhere, actually.'

'Oh, I'm not sure . . .' Rachel glanced across at her mum.

Jill was quick to respond. 'Go on, get yourself away. Look how quiet it's been; I'll manage just fine.'

True, there was only one couple in, sitting having a shared pudding platter with a pot of tea.

'But, what about Maisy?'

'Well, Maisy can come along too. The more the merrier. Hey, Maisy what do you think?' asked Tom.

'Yay! Where are we going?' She was skipping across the room towards Tom already.

'Well, why don't you choose? I was thinking maybe a walk and then a lunch out, somewhere not too far away. So, what about the woods and a pub lunch, or there's always the beach. What do you fancy, young lady?'

'Can we take Moss?'

'Yeah, why not, and Mabel can come too.'

'Good. Well, we were doing the squirrels at school. We *could* go and see their houses in the woods.'

'Sounds good to me. Rachel?'

Tom turned to face her, his dark brown eyes catching hers with a warmth that made her insides melt. She answered with a broad grin. A little break would be bliss, and with all her recent worries, it might be just what she needed. She felt a tad guilty leaving Mum to manage on her own with the tearoom, but Jill seemed happy to help, and Rachel could always offer to help her mum out another day to give her some time out too.

'Thanks, Mum. I'll make sure we're not out too long.'

'It's no problem, now go off and enjoy yourselves.'

Half an hour later, they were strolling through the woods at Kirkton Burn. They meandered along a slightly muddy path beside a stream which was lined by beech, oak and ash trees. Leaves had been tossed down by the autumn breeze and swept into heaps of gold, copper and bronze. Burnished bracken tumbled in crisp feathery strands alongside.

'Wheee!' Maisy was off, kicking up the crisp piles of leaves with her wellington boots, revealing the soggier heaps that lay beneath. Musky, earthy smells filled the air. And the leaves fell once more around the three of them like autumn-gold confetti.

'Hah, bet I can kick up more than you,' said Tom, challenging Maisy with a grin.

And the three of them started a welly-boot-lifting leaf fight and even Moss and Mabel joined in, dashing around them in daft circles, barking, with Moss trying to catch the odd one in his mouth. Maisy was giggling, and Tom and Rachel leaned against each other, slightly out of breath, at the end of it. Rachel couldn't ignore the burst of happiness spreading in her chest.

They began to walk once more, Maisy moving in close beside Tom and taking his hand. Rachel had to smile, watching them; they were so easy and natural together. Maisy looked up at the trees and asked Tom what a squirrel's nest would look like.

'Well, I know it's called a drey,' Tom answered, 'and it's made out of lots of twigs with moss and such like, and they'll be up high in the branches. I think they're about the size of a football.'

'What about that one?' Maisy was pointing up towards a fork in the branches.

Sure enough, there was indeed a nest in the tree above them. The three of them paused to look up.

'Good spot, Maisy. It might well be, yes. But I'm no expert. It could be a squirrel's nest, or perhaps a bird's.'

'Well, I think it's a squirrel's,' proclaimed Maisy, with a smile. 'I wonder if there are any babies in there.'

'I doubt if there would be at this time of year. It'll be getting a bit cold for them to have little ones. Most likely in the spring.'

'Ah, okay.' Her little girl was taking it all in.

Unlike her real and mostly absent father, Jake, having

Maisy about didn't seem to be a chore for Tom. It lifted Rachel's spirits seeing the pair of them happy together. Tom would make a great dad. An image of her and Tom and Maisy as a family filtered unexpectedly into her mind. Dare she hope that could ever work out one day? But it was all too soon. A little daydream. She'd just enjoy the moment and see where life took them for now.

They enjoyed their pub lunch out at the Black Bull Inn in the little town of Kirkton on their way back. Rachel and Tom tucked into a meal of steak pie with vegetables, while Maisy had a tasty-looking homemade fish finger sandwich. By a cosy log fire, with a glass of red wine to hand and good company, Rachel hadn't felt so content in a long while.

She felt so comfortable with Tom, and seeing Maisy so happy with him warmed her soul. But all too soon it was time to get back – she'd need to help Mum out at the Pantry before going to do the dusk checks on the animals and the farm. Tom had mentioned he had some chores to do too.

Back at Primrose Farm, they unbuckled their seat belts, ready to get out. Rachel really didn't want the magic of the afternoon to end, but life and work had a way of taking over again. Maisy had already skipped down out of the jeep, and was heading into the barn to tell Jill all about her leaf walk in the woods – she'd brought home a few special ones in her coat pocket to show her grandma – and their lunch out, including her chocolate ice cream for pudding.

Tom leaned across the cab of the truck towards Rachel. His kiss was warm and tender and loving, and she *so* wished she could carry this on somewhere else, somewhere very private indeed. But that wasn't to be. Not tonight.

Reluctantly, she drew away, her lips missing his already. 'Thank you so much, Tom. It's been a wonderful afternoon, and I know Maisy loved it too.'

'You are very welcome. She's a good kid.'

'Thanks. I think so too.' She gave a happy sigh. 'Sorry, but I'd really better go on in now and help Mum.'

'Yeah, I ought to get away too.'

Rachel hovered – this moment felt too precious to leave. Just one more brief kiss on the lips, a few more seconds together . . . Rachel moved back towards the scent of his aftershave, feeling the slight scratch of his beard where it was growing in, and meeting the soft fullness of his lips. She lingered there for a few more glorious seconds. Right, she really *had* better go now, or Maisy and Jill would be at the Pantry door wondering what was holding them up.

'Bye,' said Rachel, as she reluctantly pulled away, her voice a little husky.

'See you soon.'

'Yeah. See you.'

She stood and waved, watching his pickup drive off down the track. He gave a chirpy toot on the horn. She'd never felt like this before about a man and it was so good

– but she couldn't deny that frightened her too. She knew just how vulnerable life and relationships could be. Yes, she knew that very well.

7

Sunday had been yet another quiet day at the Pantry. Rachel was still at a loss as to how to get more customers over the threshold. Frosty mornings and November chills would soon be on their doorstep, and though December should bring some welcome pre-Christmas trade, it was likely that the next few weeks would remain slow. And, with that, the farm's bank balance was on a very slippery slope.

The next day at four thirty on the dot, Rachel was standing outside the Kirkton First School gates, her breath misting in the chill air. With a burst of heavy wooden doors, and a blast of chatter, out came the little ones in a rush across the playground, still wearing their gym gear with their coats mostly half-mast over the top.

Suddenly, there was Maisy, with a bounce of blonde curls, dashing forward and waving. 'Aw, that was so good, Mummy. I love Gym Club. We did tumbles with music today.'

'It was fun,' added Amelia, who was close on Maisy's heels, with a sunny grin. Rachel was collecting the two of them today.

This was their second week attending, and they were

so happy with their new after-school club activity. The idea of going to a club seemed different than classroom work somehow. It was sociable, and fun, yet they were still learning.

A club . . . Something about that was starting to oil the cogs in Rachel's mind. What was it that was nagging at her?

'Wowser, I've got it!' she blurted out.

'What have you got, Mummy?' Maisy looked at her quizzically.

'A club. We need a Pudding Club!' Oh yes, something to draw people out to the Pantry on those dull autumn and winter nights. Cosy puddings, in a cosy barn . . . They'd just invested the last of the summer earnings on installing that log-burning stove; it would be perfect in there on a chilly winter's evening.

'But we don't make puddings at school, Mummy.' Maisy had her hands on her hips and was frowning.

'Not at school, petal. At our farm . . . in the Pudding Pantry.'

'Oh, a club for making puddings? But doesn't Grandma Jill do the making bit?' Maisy looked nonplussed.

'Yes, but other people could come along and eat puddings, and maybe learn how to make puddings, have a chat, make new friends, share recipes over a cup of tea.' The ideas were flowing already.

'Could they have cupcakes?' Maisy grinned, catching on to the idea.

'Yes, sometimes, why not? We could have Cupcake

Week, Crumble Week, all sorts.' Rachel's mind was firing now.

'Ooh, that sounds nice,' said Amelia.

'Can I come?' Maisy was starting to warm to the suggestion.

'Oh, well, I think it'll most likely be in the evening, petal.' Rachel imagined an evening might work better as the club would need to be something different from their usual tearoom opening hours. 'So, it would be past your bedtime. But maybe you could come along to the first one, and then we'll see.'

'Okay.'

'Could *my* mummy come?' Amelia asked.

'Yes, of course, if she wanted to. I'll need to speak with Grandma Jill and see what she thinks about the club thing first, but yes I'll let your mummy know all about it if we decide to go ahead.'

They were back at the Land Rover now, the girls clambering in to the passenger side, ready to be belted up. Moss nudged a damp black nose over from the back to welcome them.

Maisy patted his soft furry head. 'Hi, Mossy.'

Driving along the country roads, the girls chatted between themselves as Rachel's mind whirred with this new Pudding Club idea. She couldn't wait to discuss it with Jill. They were soon pulling up outside Amelia's pretty stone cottage, just up the lane from Primrose Farm.

Eve came out to thank her friend for collecting the

girls, just as Rachel was helping Amelia down from the Jeep.

'Hey, sweetie pie.'

'Hi, Mummy.'

Eve took Amelia by the hand, as her little girl announced, 'Mummy, Rachel's making a Pudding Club.'

'Ooh, that sounds fun.' Eve looked at Rachel, her brow quirked with interest.

'You can go too, if you want,' Amelia continued.

'Still in the planning stage,' Rachel explained. 'Need to broach it with Mum, yet. So, I'll tell you all about it soon. It was the girls here who gave me a brainwave.'

'Good, good. Well, maybe we can catch up over a cup of coffee sometime. Seems ages since we've done that.'

'That sounds good. And yeah, I've been a bit snowed under lately. The farm, the pressures with the Pudding Pantry . . .'

'No worries, hun, I know life's fraught at the moment. Same here, we can't catch our breath, can we? But how's the delicious Tom anyway?' Eve asked with a cheeky twinkle in her eye. Eve had had a little crush on Tom for some time now, which she didn't try to hide. It was just a source of light-hearted banter, and she was happily married to Ben after all, so Rachel was happy to go along with the joke.

'He's fine, thank you. Very good in fact.'

'Not *too* good, I hope,' Eve added with a cheeky grin.

'Hah, I'm saying no more.'

'Well, thanks for fetching Amelia. My turn next week.

And let me know when you can drop by, I'll make sure there's some fresh brownies made.'

'Perfect. Oh, and keep the night of Fifth November free. Me and Mum are planning a small fireworks party at the farm. Just something low-key.'

'Sounds good. We don't have any plans for Bonfire Night, so that'd be great. Thanks, hun. Catch you later, then.'

'Cheers, Eve. Bye!'

'Bye, Eve. Bye, Melia,' chanted Maisy, happily waving from her seat in the Land Rover.

Back at the farmhouse kitchen they were greeted by the warming smells of minced beef and onions. Jill was standing at the Aga, cooking supper.

'Hi Mum, we're home. How was this afternoon?' Rachel asked. She'd been out and about on the farm for several hours, checking fences once more along with their farmhand, Simon, so hadn't had chance to look in on Jill before leaving to fetch the girls. 'Did it get any busier?'

'Not a great deal. There was a family and then a couple in. The family were staying in a holiday cottage up the valley, they were nice and chatty. The others were on a day trip from Alnwick for a change of scenery, had some tea and shared a scone between them. Oh, and Brenda from the Deli called, they've sold six puddings this week, so I need to top up the Sticky Toffee supplies there, so that was a bit of good news.'

A bit of positive news, yes, Rachel mused, and a step in the right direction, but it wasn't exactly going to cover the mounting bills.

'Grandma, Grandma! Mummy wants to make a Pudding Club,' Maisy blurted out. News certainly travelled fast when five-year-olds got to know it! And though Rachel was excited about the idea, she had intended to broach the matter a little later on when she and Jill were on their own and would have the chance to chat it over properly.

'Well, that's the cat out of the bag. Thanks, Maisy.' Never tell a child anything you didn't want shared! 'Well, it's just a thought I've had, we can talk about it over supper, maybe.'

'A Pudding Club? Hmm, sounds like it might be quite fun. Something like a cooking class, do you mean?' Rachel was pleased that she'd got Jill's attention.

'Maybe, but nothing as formal as that. We could have puddings to taste, share baking tips, a chance to chat and relax with a cuppa . . . maybe themed nights, even.'

'Okay, but it might be a lot of work. We'll have to think on it, won't we?' Jill didn't sound totally sold on the idea yet.

Oh dear, did it feel to Jill like Rachel was loading more work on to her? She hadn't thought of that.

'Look, I know it's a big ask, and we can chat some more about it in a while. I still need to pop out and do my last checks around the farm.'

'Okay, pet.' Jill lifted a large casserole pot out of the

Aga, resting it on the top as she popped in eight round balls of herby dumplings. 'Supper will be ready in about twenty minutes.'

'That's great.' After baking and looking after the Pantry all day, here was Jill still cooking and caring for her family. Rachel didn't take her for granted, but maybe she needed to show her gratitude a little more often. 'And thanks, Mum. You look after us all so well.'

'Isn't that what mums are for, love?'

'Well, some are better at it than others, I'm sure . . . and you're up there with the best.'

Jill beamed.

'Maisy, do you want to come on out with me?' Rachel asked.

It was already getting dark outside, and the kitchen was a cosy haven. Maisy had her school coat and shoes off and was stroking Moss, who'd sneaked up and joined her on the chair beside the Aga. 'I'll stay with Grandma.'

'Okay, I won't be long.'

Rachel couldn't wait to get the last farm chores done and get back in herself, but she could never rest easy if she hadn't seen for herself that the farm animals were all fine and settled for the night.

Up at the Top Field Rachel's mobile buzzed into life. She stopped the quad.

'Hi, Rach.' It was Tom.

'Oh hi, you okay?'

'Yep. Look, when do I get to see you again? It was

great in the woods at the weekend with Maisy, but I'd love some time just for us too. Can you make tonight? The other evening was pretty special.'

'Yes, it was really lovely.' Her mind wandered back to that sensual night by the fireside at Tom's house. But she'd already promised to go back tonight and chat further with Mum about the Pudding Club idea; they couldn't afford to rest on their laurels with the Pudding Pantry. It had needed energy and a huge commitment to get this business off the ground, and would need even more to make it a success.

'Oh, Tom, much as I'd love to, I can't see you tonight, sorry.'

'Tomorrow?' He wasn't one to give up easily.

The following night was set aside for the mammoth pile of farming paperwork she hadn't managed to get around to today.

'Umm, look, I'll see you at your elevenses.'

'*Is that it?* I can't make love to you over a bacon sandwich in the middle of the Pudding Pantry.'

Rachel couldn't help but laugh. 'Oh, why on earth not?' She was trying to keep her tone deadpan.

'For a start, Frank's false teeth might fall out with the shock, *and* I don't think your mother would approve.'

'Hah, maybe not.'

'I'm serious though, Rach.' His voice softened, sounding so earnest. 'I'd love to see you again soon.'

God, she wanted to see him, to be with him, too, not be stuck under a pile of paperwork, but that wasn't going to keep the farm afloat. Her life seemed to be a never-ending To Do list right now. It was no wonder it was hard to find time to be together. She wasn't young, free and single, like other girls her age might be. Well, she might still be young – twenty-four was hardly ancient – but she was a mother, and tied to a farm and a business. Would Tom prefer a no-strings-attached kind of girl, where every night could be date night? That thought made her feel uneasy.

'Just give me a day or two to get things straight, okay, and then I'll try and free up an evening. I'll see if Mum's all right to look after Maisy, or maybe Eve will step in. We could go out for a drink or something. Or just stay in?'

'All right, I suppose I'll just have to wait. And don't forget our rendezvous at elevenses,' he added more chirpily.

'How could I?'

'See you then.'

'Bye.' She turned off the mobile, and found herself smiling. Amid all the To Dos, the chores, paperwork and bills, Tom Watson was a warm beacon of light. She just prayed he'd manage to stay aglow for her.

'So, come on, tell me more about this Pudding Club idea, then?' Jill asked, as the three of them were sat around the kitchen table with plates loaded with mince, dumplings, carrots and cabbage, fresh from their vegetable patch.

'Okay, so I'm thinking that the Pudding Pantry is already a lovely cosy place to meet up. So, the Pudding *Club* will have to be a bit different. A chance to come in, make new friends, *and* learn something. It'll be about all things pudding and baking, with ideas and recipes, and tastings . . . Ooh yes, we'll have to have a little taster of something delicious from the Pantry to try.'

'We can taste cupcakes!' came Maisy's suggestion with a big grin.

'Hmm, it does sound interesting. So, do we charge for customers to come in? How would it work? We'd have to cover our costs and make a little bit extra ourselves, to make it worthwhile.'

'Of course, we'll have to think about the price. And we'd need to decide on a theme for each week or fort-night, or however often we decide to hold it.'

'Weekly might prove a bit hard to come up with enough rolling ideas, but twice a month might work well,' Jill pondered.

'So, fortnightly then,' Rachel continued, 'with a pudding to taste – something that fits with that session's theme. It'd be great to have a festive one in the lead-up to Christmas, and maybe a recipe to hand out and chat about.'

'Oh well, we can't be giving away all the Baking Bible secrets, you know.' Jill looked rather affronted.

'I know, but just one example, or a twist on one of your classics. Look, say it was Crumble Night or some-thing, then the group could chat about favourite crumble recipes and flavours. We'd have one or two to taste, and of course,' Rachel gave a little wink, 'some more ready to buy to take away at the counter.' Rachel's business mind was firing up now.

'Yes . . . I can see how that might work.'

'Well, I think we should have an ice-cream night,' Maisy added her thoughts on the matter, beaming.

'Oh, now then,' Rachel smiled across at her little girl, 'that might work well. Hmm, "which ice-cream flavours go best with our puddings"? That's a great idea, Maisy.'

'Well done, Maisy. A pudding pairing session.' Jill was smiling too, evidently warming to the idea.

'We could invite someone from the local dairy along for that, and later on we could have other guest speakers.' Rachel was thinking out loud. 'Doing that will give us lots more ideas for the future and pair us with other local businesses too. I like it.'

Maisy beamed proudly, then took up a forkful of tasty carrots.

'Though I do think the ice-cream evening might be something to keep up our sleeve for next spring or summer, when the weather's a bit warmer,' added Jill. 'But, it's a really great idea, Maisy.'

'Hey, what a team!' Rachel made a high-five in the air, and Maisy leaned across to clap it with her palm. 'Well then, we'll think a bit more on it yet, and I'll make sure to cost it out, but I think the Pudding Club has legs, don't you?'

'It's certainly food for thought, love.'

'Yeah . . . well, let's sleep on it and we'll chat more about it at the Pantry tomorrow.'

'Yes, that sounds good. So, young lady, how was your day at school today?' asked Jill, moving things on. 'All you've talked about was gym club since you got back. What else have you been up to then?'

'Umm, we made pictures from leaves. Crunchy ones like we found in the woods, Mummy, and we painted them, then pressed them on to paper so the colour came off.'

'Like a leaf print,' said Rachel.

'Yes. They looked really pretty. We're going to put them up on the class wall.'

'That sounds good,' added Jill.

'Oh! And,' Maisy started pulling an oh-my-gosh face, 'Matthew Timpson wasn't feeling very well. And guess what, Grandma? He was sick in the playground.'

'Oh dear.'

'All over Sarah Scott's shoes! It was yucky and lumpy and yellow and Sarah screamed so loud.'

'Ah, okay, Maisy. Not really suitable dinner table conversation,' Rachel warned, though secretly she was chuckling to herself, imagining the chaotic scene in the playground.

'Poor Matthew,' said Jill.

'Hah, well I'd be really cross if he was sick on my shoes,' Maisy said huffily.

'Yes, but he couldn't have helped it,' added Rachel.

'Well, he could have been sick somewhere else!' That was Maisy's final proclamation on the matter.

Rachel and Jill couldn't help but smile.

Rachel listened to the dinner table chatter with warmth and appreciation for her little family. And with the new Pudding Club plans came a new sense of hope and purpose between them. Though times were still tough at Primrose Farm, the Swinton girls were a team and they were trying to plough forward – they were all in it together.

The Fourth Bake of Christmas

Blackberry and Apple Jam Sponge Pudding – Grandma Isabel's Recipe, circa 1946

This handwritten poem had always been tucked into the Baking Bible as a loose leaf next to a recipe of Rachel's grandmother's:

Autumn days, the sky a blue haze.
Blackberry picking,
Hedgerows thick with brambles,
Watch out for the prickles.
Purple-stained fingers and mouths,
Ripe dark berries sweet with juice,
Baskets laden.
Ready for home, pass on to Mum,
With crumbles, jams and puddings to come!

Recipe:

100g/4oz self-raising flour
Pinch of salt
100g/4oz caster sugar
100g/4oz butter
2 eggs, beaten
2tbsp whole milk

45ml/3tbsp homemade or good quality Blackberry and Apple Jam (or other flavour if you prefer)

Sift flour and salt into a bowl. Cream butter and sugar until light and fluffy. Add eggs a little at a time with a spoonful of flour, beating well until eggs are mixed in. Fold in remaining flour alternately with the milk.

Grease and base-line a pudding basin, add the jam to the bottom. Spoon over the pudding mix up to ¾ full. Cover with buttered greaseproof paper, and secure with string. Using extra string to make a handle for ease of removal.

Steam for 1 ½ to 2 hours in a covered pan of boiling water, keeping water topped up to half way up the pudding bowl sides, until a wooden skewer comes out clean at centre. Allow to stand for 3 minutes before turning out.

Delicious with custard or cream.

8

'Morning, ladies.'

'Hello, Tom,' answered Jill from behind the Pantry's wooden counter.

'Hi . . .' Rachel answered with a slight blush, remembering yesterday's conversation. He was right on time for his elevenses.

'Coffee and a bacon roll, is it?' Jill anticipated.

'Yes,' replied Tom with a grin. 'Though I may well have a little extra something on the side this morning.' He gave Rachel a very cheeky glance.

'And what might that be?' Rachel asked leadingly.

'Hmm, now then, maybe a . . . flapjack.'

'Coming right up,' Jill replied.

Rachel and Tom then burst into a fit of the giggles, leaving Jill bemused. Shaking her head at the giddy pair, she headed to the fridge for some bacon rashers, saying, 'What on earth has got into you two?'

They were still grinning like loons, with the odd splutter from Rachel as she tried to focus on making Tom's coffee, barista-style.

'Ah, young love,' Jill muttered at the griddle pan.

Tom leaned across the counter to whisper in Rachel's

ear, 'I might even have a little crumble waiting for you later on, if I can tempt you away from your chores.'

'Oh, but my paperwork mountain awaits,' replied Rachel matter-of-factly, vowing to keep her promise to herself to get the farm's piling admin sorted, though her body was telling her to ditch it – feeling tinglingly aroused.

'Crikey, my charm must be failing fast – I've never been rejected for a pile of paperwork before.'

'Sorry . . . *soon*, okay,' she whispered. 'Hang in there.'

'I'll try.' He pulled a hang-dog face.

With that, Frank's tut-tutting car could be heard coming up the lane, and the old gentleman was shortly making his way through the barn door.

'Morning, Frank,' greeted Tom first, as the two ladies then chorused, 'Hello, Frank.'

'How are you doing, pet?' asked Jill.

'Not too bad at all, thank you. All the better for seeing your smiling faces.'

That made the women's smiles even wider.

'And morning, young Tom. Farming going well?'

'Yes thanks, Frank. Bit quieter at this time of year, now the harvest's all in, and the cattle haven't yet been brought in for the winter. Can't complain.'

'More time to see this lovely young lady, then,' added Frank with a wink. The news had been out for a while around the village that they were formally an item.

'So you'd think,' answered Tom with a wry smile, followed by a meaningful glance at Rachel. 'She's one busy lady.'

Jill handed Tom his warm bacon roll. He opened the bap, and added a dollop of Brown Sauce on top of the bacon, then tucked in hungrily. 'It's been a long while since breakfast.'

'What can we get for you today, Frank? Coffee, as per usual?' asked Jill. 'Oh, and I've just made a blackberry and cream roulade this morning, you might want to try a slice of that.'

'That sounds just grand, and coffee it is. I'll just settle myself at my usual table.' He liked the one beside the arch-shaped window that looked out across the valley.

'Yes do, and we'll bring it all across in two ticks for you,' added Rachel.

Frank liked to read the weekly local paper – of which Rachel kept a copy for the Pantry guests – and he often brought in his own copy of *The Times* to peruse over his hot drink and cake.

'Right, I'd better be on my way,' announced Tom, soon afterwards. 'We've got some cattle tags to put back in today; they keep losing them out in the fields, so I need to get the cattle herded down to the yard to meet up with my farmhand, Jack.'

'Well, have a good day,' said Rachel.

'Will do.' His tone was ironic. 'It won't be nearly as exciting as your paperwork mountain.'

'Nearly, but not quite.' Rachel pulled a wry face.

'Hah, I might even have to have a look at my own paperwork tonight. Seeing as there's nothing else happening . . .'

'Well, you know what they say, if you can't beat 'em, join 'em.'

He shook his head, yet still managing a small smile. 'Thanks, Jill. See you soon, folks. Take care, Frank.'

Rachel came out from behind the counter to give Tom a peck on the cheek. 'Sorry,' was all she could say, sensing his frustration behind the smile.

'No worries. See you soon, Rach.'

She'd far rather have a carefree flirty evening with Tom than working away yet again, but there were reports to make, records to complete, government checks to fulfil – and no one else was able to do it for her. Why did life have to be so bloody exasperating?

After their lunchtime customers – all six of them – had left, Rachel mooted, 'So, Mum, how do you think we can best go forward with the Pudding Club idea?' She was impatient to move things on quickly, if Jill was in support.

'Well, I do think we should at least give it a try. I have to say, it's been whirring around in my head since you mentioned it – a sign of a good idea in my book. It'll not cost us much to set up, just more of our time. I imagine it'll be something we'll need to hold of an evening?'

Yet another night that Rachel would be tied up and would have to think of childcare. But if it had to be done, so be it. 'Yes, I think that'd work best.'

'So, what do you think we'd need to charge for this Pudding Club?'

'I don't think we should make it too expensive; let's keep it attractive and inclusive, but of course we'll need to make a little bit of money out of doing it, or else there's no point. I'm thinking there are young mums who might want a night out, older people wanting some company, and anyone interested in baking, really. What do you think, say £5 per session? That'd cover a tea or coffee, the puds to taste, and we should come away with a bit of profit for the business too.'

'Yes, that sounds reasonable. Do we hold a club night fortnightly up until Christmas and see how it goes?' suggested Jill.

'So, you're definitely in?' Rachel couldn't help but grin.

'Of course, I'm in. Sounds a lovely idea.'

'Really? I thought you seemed a little cool on it at first.'

'No, I just wanted us both to think it through properly.'

'Aw, thanks, Mum. You're the best, you know that? It will mean another evening of work for us, though.'

'Yes, I realise that, but it does sounds quite sociable. I think we might enjoy it too!'

'We might have to take turns with who hosts it, or ask Granny Ruth across to help with little Maisy.'

'Yes, we can organise that, and I'm sure Ruth would enjoy getting involved. In fact, I've asked her across for supper later, so we can mention it to her then.'

'That's great. Mind you, I have promised Maisy she can come to the first night if the Pudding Club went ahead,' added Rachel.

'So, what date shall we start, and what's the first pudding theme to be?' Jill was sounding quite animated now.

'Sooner rather than later. We may as well get going quickly, to hopefully pick up some new customers. So, what's coming up soon and what puddings can we tie that in with?' Rachel paused and suddenly thought of Bonfire Night and Jill's scrumptious crumble. *Ooh, yes*, something around November Fifth would be ideal. 'This might work – Guy Fawkes, fireworks, and your . . .'

'Toffee Apple Crumble,' Jill finished the sentence for her, with a smile.

'Hah! We could make our first Pudding Club go off with a real bang!' Rachel announced with a huge grin.

Later that day, another autumn beauty with soft sunshine and just a gentle nip of cold, Rachel reached the small row of honeyed-stone cottages where her Granny Ruth had lived since leaving the farmhouse at Primrose Farm herself, when Rachel and her family had moved in, following the long-standing family tradition that the eldest son would eventually take over. She pulled up outside, and walked up the neat front garden path, ready to collect Granny to take her back to the farm for supper with them. The last blooms of a pale-pink rose that climbed the wall beside the cottage door were holding on in the autumn chill. There was a pot of bold deep-purple and yellow winter pansies on the front step to greet any guests. Granny loved her gardening, even though she struggled with arthritis that was particularly bad in her knees.

Rachel knocked on the door and then went on in, knowing that the house would be unlocked and that she was always welcome. 'Only me, Granny,' she called.

There was an intense smell of warm sugary fruits as Rachel entered the kitchen. There was Granny, standing stirring the contents of a large steel pan with a wooden spoon. 'Oh, sorry pet – is that the time? I'm not quite ready for you.'

'No worries. What delights are you concocting here?' Rachel leaned over to take a look at the glossy mixture.

'Jam – blackberry and apple. I'm using those apples you gave me from your tree last week. Thought it might go nice on a fruit scone with some butter.'

'Well, it certainly smells delicious.'

'I've finished one batch of blackberry and raspberry, already. Thought that'd go nicely in the next Jam Roly-Poly I make.'

Rachel was impressed. Despite being in her eighties, her grandmother still loved to cook and nurture. Baking was such a strong influence from both sides of Rachel's family – no wonder she had got the bug.

'Oh, yes.'

'Well, next week, I'll make one of those for you all, too. I know it's one of Maisy's favourites.'

'That'd be lovely, Granny. Just perfect with lashings of creamy custard.'

'Right, well, this just needs to cool a little and then we can pour it into the jars here.'

A row of squeaky-clean jam jars was waiting on the kitchen side. Beside them were squares of red gingham muslin and thin elastic bands ready to cover the lids.

'I'll just nip upstairs and get my things together. I'll not be long; I've already packed an overnight bag.'

'I'll help fill these if you like, while you finish getting ready.'

'Thank you, pet, that'd be grand.'

The old lady came back down just as her granddaughter was placing the material squares over each metal lid.

'Take some back with you, lass, and you can use them in the Pantry.'

'Will do, thanks Granny. I'm sure they'll go down a treat.'

'So, how are you, pet? And how are things going with that nice young man of yours?' Ruth was gathering her coat and shoes.

'Good, thanks . . .' Rachel's voice trailed a little.

'Rightio – but you sound a little disheartened, lass.' Granny Ruth could pick up on Rachel's mood like no one else.

'Oh, Granny! It's just life getting in the way. I'm so busy right now, and me and Tom, well, we get on so well, and it's been lovely, but we don't get an awful lot of time to see each other really. Well, not on our own. I can't keep upping and leaving Maisy and Mum and the farm.'

Granny was nodding, listening.

'I'm worried he might be getting a bit fed up with it all . . .'

'Ah, and have you spoken with him about it?' asked Ruth in a gentle tone.

'Well, not properly, no. It should be pretty obvious how busy I am, though.'

'Hmm, well in any relationship, you need to start by being honest with each other. You've got to be a team. Me and your granda didn't always see eye to eye, but we learnt to talk things through, to come to understand each other. And life's *always* going to be busy for you with the farm and everything else, Rachel, but if this relationship with Tom is worth it, maybe you need to make some time, don't you think?'

'Maybe . . .' Rachel breathed out with a small sigh. 'Thanks, Granny.'

'He seems a good man, Tom. I like him, and it's obvious that he cares for you. Nothing like that waste-of-space Jake you paired up with.'

Rachel grimaced; it was no secret that the intuitive Granny Ruth was far from Jake's biggest fan – not that she'd say anything in front of Maisy.

'And don't be afraid to ask for help, pet. Me and your mum are always happy to help out with Maisy, and where we can on the farm. Don't pile too much on yourself, you're not Wonder Woman.'

'Hah,' Rachel smiled. 'I rather hoped I might be. It'd mean I could get things done a bit quicker. And she does wear one hell of an outfit,' Rachel quipped.

'Well, I'm ready when you are, lass. Shall we head over to the farm?'

'Of course. Mum'll be wondering where we've got to otherwise.'

'Right then, I'll just pop my shoes on. I'll need a seat for that. Here we go, just give me a second.' She sat down stiffly on one of her kitchen chairs. Her body might be struggling, but her mind was still sharp as a tack. She was one of the few people who said it how it was. Rachel admired her for it, even if, at times, the truth was a bit too close for comfort.

Rachel was towel-drying Maisy after her bath that evening when her mobile rang. She glanced at the caller ID: Jake. She gave an inward groan. How did he always manage to pick a bad time? She was trying to settle Maisy, ready for bedtime on a school night. But of course, Maisy's dad would hardly be aware of her routine. Living so far away, he was never really there for her, was he? But, she supposed, at least he was phoning and his promised 'weekly' call could be hit and miss at the best of times.

Rachel wrapped the towel tightly around her daughter to keep her warm, then answered with a gritting of her teeth. 'Hi, Jake.'

'Hey, there. Where's my gorgeous girl? Is Maisy about?'

'Ah, yes, but can you just give us five minutes and I'll call you back? She's just out of the bath and I need to dry her and pop her pyjamas on.'

'Yeah, no worries – although ah, I'm going out in ten, but yeah, if you're quick.'

Hah, ever the doting father.

'Daddy?' Maisy asked, looking excited, bless her. Bloody hell, he did so little, yet Maisy couldn't help that buzz of excitement at hearing from him. His last visit had been back in July, three months ago now, and there was a promised visit for August that had never materialised, much to Maisy's disappointment. Just thinking about the consequences of that day still made Rachel mad.

'Okay, I'll call back straight away,' answered Rachel tersely and she put down the phone. 'Come on then, petal, let's get those PJs on,' her voice softened.

In Maisy's room a few minutes later, with her little girl now dressed in her nightclothes and sat expectantly on the bed, Rachel called Jake back. After saying a brief hello, she passed the phone over to her daughter. Having put the phone on loudspeaker, she sat quietly beside her, monitoring the conversation. Maisy was happily telling him all about school, and her gym club, and about Amelia coming for fireworks night next week with her mummy and daddy for hot dogs. Jake, in turn, said how busy he'd been at work, helping to build people's houses.

Rachel then heard him say that he was missing her. But hey, it was all too easy to say that from two hundred miles away, and then not bother to come and see her. And all too soon Jake said his goodbyes, with an excuse that he was about to go out.

She watched her little girl's sunny face begin to fall as the conversation rolled to a close. It was painful to watch.

'Daddy's got to go now,' Maisy explained to Rachel. Her voice had dropped almost to a whisper. She passed the phone back across.

'Okay, sweetheart.' Rachel placed the mobile to her own ear. 'Hi, it's me.' Her tone was cool.

'Yeah, got to dash. Meeting a mate.'

'Right . . . and don't forget to call Maisy again next week. And, a little earlier might help, not right at bedtime; it can be unsettling for her.'

'Okay. Slapped hands again.' He still managed to sound like a stroppy teenager.

Rachel didn't even bother to respond to that comment.

'See you then, Rach.'

'Yeah. Bye, Jake.' Rachel sighed as she switched off her mobile. Then she turned with an encouraging smile to her little girl. She couldn't let her exasperation show in front of her. 'Let's get you all tucked up in bed then, petal. Shall we have a story?'

'O-kay.' Maisy sounded reluctant, and a frown had formed across her brow. And, just as Rachel had thought, here was her little girl unsettled and upset for bedtime.

'Mummy, when's Daddy coming to see me again?' Maisy was hugging her soft toy sheep that Grandma Jill had given her several years ago – it was still a favourite.

Rachel knew she could only be honest; false promises and lies would only hurt more in the long-run. 'I don't know, petal.'

It broke Rachel's heart to see the look of disappointment that fell across Maisy's face. She gave her daughter a hug and a kiss, before going to the pine bookcase to find her *Floss* book, hoping the sheepdog's story might help cheer her little girl up.

This unpredictable relationship with her dad was so hard for Maisy, and for Rachel. How she wished she could protect her daughter, wrap her fragile heart up in cotton wool, and keep her safe from disappointment. But sometimes, even the love of a mother couldn't do that.

9

It was mid-afternoon, the Northumberland sky softening to a watery blue-grey above the rolling hills. Rachel had just set Hamish, her stocky Scottish Texel ram, out in the field with the Texel ewes. He looked very pleased with himself, given this new freedom. With hormones running high within the flocks, the three Primrose Farm tups had been kept in the sheep shed for the past week to keep them out of mischief. Hamish was now more than happy to find himself in this large grassy area with his very own flock, and he was soon nestling up beside one of his ladies.

The farmhand, Simon, had just set off on the quad to check how Edward and Chevy, the two Cheviot rams, were getting on higher up the valley in the other field, where they had been released earlier that morning. The two flocks had been purposely set well apart to avoid any interbreeding accidents.

Rachel was just having a quick breather, gazing out across the beautiful valley, when her mobile vibrated in her pocket. 'Hello?'

'Rach, hey, you haven't phoned me! It's been days since you dropped Amelia off.' It was Eve, and by the sounds of it, yet someone else irked by her absence. 'So, I've made some cookies, anyhow. You must call in and have some while they're fresh. You are at risk of becoming a farmyard recluse, hun. *So*, is it coffee-break time, yet?'

'Ah . . . Well, I've just finished putting the tups out so I suppose it can be. It'll have to be a quick one, mind, I still have lots to do.'

'No problem, that's great. I'll see you soon then. And afterwards we can walk down and collect the girls from the school bus together.'

Crikey, was it that time already? The days seemed to just fly by. 'Okay, thanks, I'll see you shortly.'

It would be lovely to see Eve, Rachel realised, even if it was only for a snatched coffee break. It was weeks since the friends had met up properly. It wasn't just Tom she hadn't had much time to see lately.

Fifteen minutes later, after a quick catch up with Simon who confirmed all was well with the sheep and rams, Rachel headed across to her friend's cottage.

'Come on in, I'm in the kitchen,' Eve sang out. 'It's the only place with a seat not covered in wool or craft materials just now. It's driving Ben nuts.' Her friend carried on chatting loudly, as Rachel made her way down the narrow hallway. 'I'm on a pre-Christmas craft-making bonanza.'

'That sounds great – hard work though.' Rachel popped her head around the kitchen door, to find her friend dressed in denim dungarees, with a bright flower-patterned long-sleeved tee, her auburn curly hair piled high in a ponytail. Eve was pouring water from the kettle into a cafetière. The aroma of fresh coffee filling the air. Rachel also caught a whiff of the cookies that were smelling divinely chocolatey and looked delightful, stacked on a plate on the side.

'Oh, wow, they look good. And, can I have a peek at what you're making craft-wise? Then I can get some ideas of what we can display for you at The Pudding Pantry for the run up to Christmas. The dressers need restocking and some new and festive things would be fabulous.'

Eve led her through to the dining room while the coffee was brewing. There were piles of grey-painted wooden hearts and stars, and the prettiest dainty wooden angels, strung ready to hang on a Christmas tree. Cute soft-toy animals sat in rows – the hedgehog was particularly adorable – with little Santa hats on and festive bow ties. There were mini Christmas jumpers for babies and toddlers; chunky knits adorned with red-breasted robins, red-nosed reindeers, charming snowmen and sparkly snowflakes.

'Eve, this is brilliant. You're so talented. These must take ages to make,' Rachel enthused, holding up a felt fox dressed in a fabulous waistcoat with holly patterns on.

'Ah, not that long, really. It's just the volumes I need to do to keep up with my online orders that takes the time, *and* I still need to make a load more for a couple of craft fairs I've got coming up.'

'Well, the Christmas soft toys would look gorgeous on the shelves of the dressers in the Pantry, and those tree decorations would be great. I just love the angels. I was thinking of getting a Christmas tree up in the barn fairly soon actually, we're nearly into November after all. Set the scene for the run up to Christmas. What do you think?'

'Oh yes, that'd be lovely. I can just picture it there, with fairy lights twinkling away.'

'So, can you make some extra crafts for us too? Sorry, it sounds like you're super-busy as it is, but I'm sure we'll get some sales for you.'

'Of course, and I've still got more festive goodies yet to make. There'll be wooden coasters with Christmas messages on and pretty tealight holders too. I was even thinking of making some fir wreaths with red tartan gingham ribbons nearer to Christmas.'

'Ooh, they sound lovely. Put us down for one of those. I can just picture it hanging so pretty there on the barn door.'

'Aw, thanks. Right then, coffee time. I've had enough of all this craft stuff for today. My fingers are aching, and my brain's gone to mush concentrating on all the small detail.'

The two friends were soon sitting on stools at the breakfast bar in Eve's galley kitchen with a cafetière between them, two glass mugs ready to fill, and the plate of warm cookies.

'So, where have you been hiding, Rach? You've disappeared, except for the school run, and even then, you always seem to be dashing off.'

Rachel looked down at her hands and shifted uncomfortably on the stool. 'Life's just pretty hectic right now.'

'Yeah, it must be pretty tough, what with the farm and everything to keep going. You have such a full-on life, Rachel, even more so than mine. But, if there's anything you ever want to chat about, I'm here. You can always talk to me, that's what friends are for.'

'Ah,' Rachel sighed, feeling slightly uncomfortable. Should she share how the Pantry was running into difficulties? She didn't want the local community knowing how slow things were. Sometimes that just encouraged the downward spiral. But this was Eve, and Eve was no gossip. Eve had shared her hopes, fears and dreams from as far back as primary school.

'Well, the Pantry is struggling a bit just now, which is a real worry after all the investment we've put in.'

'Oh, that's tough. I had noticed it's been a bit quieter of late when I've called in. But, you know, maybe it's just that time of year. My crafts business slowed right down after the summer, but now I'm on the up again with my Christmas pre-orders. I'm sure you'll pick up soon with the Christmas trade.'

'Maybe. And I know it's early days and we're still getting established . . .' Rachel paused.

'Well, if there's anything me and Ben can do to help?'

'Thanks.'

'And I'll be sure to make you some festive crafts for the Pantry as soon as I can.'

'You're a star.'

'Well, we can't have these cookies going to waste.' Eve passed the plate across. 'I've made some dark chocolate with white choc chunks today.'

The first bite was amazing. They were crisp on the outside and melted in the middle where the white chocolate chunks delighted the taste buds.

'These are divine.'

'Cheers, hun.'

'I might need this recipe for the Pantry. This is taking cookie making to the next level. *Cookies . . .*' she said slowly, in a daft voice, like the cookie monster from Sesame Street.

It took them back to both being little girls, when their friendship had first blossomed and life was always a laugh and carefree.

'Ha ha ha, brilliant, and yes, no problem. I'll jot it down for you.'

'Oh, by the way,' Rachel said, 'we are going to go ahead with the Pudding Club idea that Amelia mentioned the other day. I'm hoping it might help turn things around a bit for us.'

'Oh, fab, tell me more.'

'Well, it'll be a nice thing to do socially, and with it being so quiet lately, we're thinking it might drum up some more interest for the Pantry. Hang on, I've got a flyer here in my pocket. I was trying out some designs on the laptop this morning. What do you think?' Rachel stood up, unfolding the sheet of paper that she'd put in her jeans back pocket earlier, ready to show to Jill.

Eve looked over the leaflet. 'Crumble night, hey.' She had a daft grin on her face. 'Now are you sure that's for the Pudding Club, or is that a night you're planning with Tom?' The old joke about 'comforting' apple-crumble Tom was still rumbling on.

'Stop it, you!' Rachel shook her head.

'Hah, what a way to start.' Eve couldn't stop chuckling.

Rachel felt herself blush, then couldn't help but join in. It felt good to be laughing with an old friend.

'It sounds like it'll be a great night, this club. I'll check with Ben,' Eve continued, once she managed to stop giggling, 'I'd love to come along. I'll give Charlotte a ring, see if she can make it too, and we'll rally some other friends. It sounds like it'll be fun. That's going in the diary, Thursday the 7 November, Pudding Club night. Oh, and are you still going ahead with your Bonfire Night at the farm next week? Can I make anything to help out with that?'

'Well, the food's all in hand. Me and Mum have a few ideas up our sleeves – just keeping it casual. So, if you can bring some small fireworks and a couple of packs of sparklers along, that'd be great. No noisy rockets or screeches, mind, don't want the animals stressed out, just some garden-type ones.'

'Yep, no worries. The girls will love it, I'm sure. So, is the delectable Tom coming along?'

'Yes, of course.'

'And that's all going well?'

'Yeah.' Rachel couldn't help but smile at the mention

of his name. 'Though we're struggling for time to see each other just now.'

'Yes, I bet. Oh, speaking of time,' Eve glanced up at the kitchen clock, 'we'd better head down the lane to collect the girls.' It was already past three o'clock.

'Well, that coffee break flew by. Thanks for asking me round, Eve. It's been really good to chat.' Having seen Granny Ruth and confided in her best friend, Rachel felt as if some of the weight had been lifted. She hadn't realised how much she'd been bottling things up.

'Yeah, I've enjoyed it too. It's been lovely to catch up. And keep me posted on your Pudding Club plans.'

'Will do.'

The girls gave each other a warm hug.

Friends have a way of lifting you, when you didn't even know you were down.

10

With a handful of flyers and a heart full of hope, Rachel was dashing around the small town of Kirkton, spreading news of Primrose Farm's new Pudding Club.

First stop was their staunch supporter, Brenda, at the deli.

'Morning, Brenda.'

'Hello there, Rachel, pet.'

'You couldn't do me a favour and pop some of these flyers on your countertop?'

'Oh, what's this, then?'

'We're starting a Pudding Club over at the Pantry.'

Brenda took a flyer, and began to read it aloud:

'Welcome to The Pudding Club at Primrose Farm
For an evening of fun, food and friendship!
Come along to Crumble Night
on Thursday 7 November
With treats to taste, tea and coffee, and a
chance to chat all things puddings.
There's a small fee of £5, which includes all food
and drink.
We'd love for you to join us.

Best wishes,
Rachel and Jill Swinton x'

Rachel had spent several hours last night on her laptop, planning the first night, then tweaking the poster and flyers for its launch. She hoped the invite sounded friendly and informal, and that they would raise some interest through the coming week and get a nice little group together for the club's inaugural meeting – fingers crossed.

'So, what do you think?' she asked with a little trepidation.

'I think it sounds great. I might have to bob along and take a look myself.'

'Well, you'll be more than welcome.'

'And can anybody go?'

'Absolutely – young, old, experienced bakers, beginners . . .'

'What a good idea. Well, you can certainly put some flyers there on the countertop, and I'll pop one in the window for you, too.'

'Aw, that's brilliant! Thanks, Brenda.'

'Oh, have you heard about Stephanie's new baby? A little boy, 8lb 2oz, born in the early hours of this morning. All doing fine. Joyce was in this morning, made up about it, as you can imagine.'

'Aw, that's lovely news.'

'And there's some new people just moved into the Old Vicarage. Seem a nice enough couple. Just retired. Moved up from Durham way. The Johnsons, that was it.'

Brenda was the eyes and ears of Kirkton village. She had the best vantage point in the high street and a constant flow of customers to keep up to date with. You certainly didn't need a broadsheet when Brenda was around, but it was all done in a friendly manner.

'Oh, and we're running short on your chocolate puddings, so when you're next in town can you bring a few through? And I may as well take a couple more of the sticky toffees too.'

'Great, and I will do. Thanks for your help.' Rachel gave a cheery wave and set off on her mission to flood Kirkton with flyers. After all, nothing ventured, nothing gained.

'You're welcome, pet. Best of luck.'

Next, she spotted Jim parked up at the taxi rank. He'd be sure to see loads of different people on his local travels.

'Hi, Jim. How are you?'

'Hey there, Rachel. I'm good thanks.'

'And the family?'

'Grand. The wee one's already a year now, can you believe it?'

'Aw, I bet he's a little cutie.'

'Aye, he is indeed. Mind, he's off toddling now, so we're in trouble. Nothing in the house is safe anymore. Spent a whole afternoon putting up stairgates and cupboard catches yesterday.'

'Well, better safe than sorry.'

'Aye, indeed.'

'And you're all fine, over at the farm?'

'Yes, thanks Jim. Actually, can I ask a favour?'

'Go ahead, lass.'

'You wouldn't mind leaving a few of these flyers handy on your dash for your customers?' Rachel gave a hopeful smile.

'And what are they about?'

'We're starting a Pudding Club at the farm.'

'Of course, I will, and I'll be sure to spread the word too. My passengers are usually more than happy to chat, so I have sitting targets.' He gave a wink.

'Thanks Jim, I appreciate it. You're a star.'

'It's no bother at all, lass.'

Into the florist's next, where Wendy was busy making up a gorgeous-looking bouquet, with fragrant blooms in pinks and mauves and whites.

'Oh, that's so pretty,' Rachel commented.

'Hello, Rachel. Yes, it's an order for a birthday gift. Can I help?'

'Well, I hope so. I'm sorry it's not an order or anything. I just wondered if you'd mind popping a few flyers out on the counter for me, or perhaps one in the window. Mum and I, we're launching a Pudding Club.'

'Puddings?' she glanced over the flyer. 'Now you're talking. Of course, I'll put a few out for you.'

'Thank you.'

'And how's it going there at the farm for you?' The local community were well aware of the family's background – especially the unexpected grief that had hit them with Dad's death two years ago – and the steps they were trying to take to move on. It meant a lot to Rachel that they always checked in on how she was – the community spirit was well and truly flowing in her beloved little village.

'Well, the new Pudding Pantry started really well,' Rachel was trying her best to sound upbeat, 'but we just need a bit more momentum to get us through the autumn and winter months.'

'Yes, it's gone a bit quieter here too. But I'll soon be getting busy with my Christmas wreaths and such like.'

It really did sound as if they weren't the only ones experiencing a lull in trade then and that was reassuring in itself.

'Thanks, Wendy.' Rachel left a handful of flyers on the counter, beside the till.

'It's no problem at all.'

And on she went to the library and the tourist information office, then she popped one on the village noticeboard by the hall where the Toddler Group was in full noisy swing, and another on the Parish news board by the church. A quick drop by at The Cheviot Café was the final stop. In all, a hundred flyers had been distributed. She felt exhausted, but strangely elated too. It felt good to be *doing* something. And surely somebody would be interested and give it a try.

The Pudding Pantry and the new Pudding Club were also due to get a mention in the local press this week, thanks to Amanda at the *Gazette*. Rachel had made a Sticky Toffee Pudding 'special delivery' to the newspaper offices along with several flyers and a poster. She'd also emailed across some photos of the Pudding Pantry, one with Jill grinning away in welcome behind the counter.

Rachel took a deep breath as she parked back at the farmyard. She looked up at the charming wooden sign Eve had made for their opening all those months ago, when they were starting their new venture, the Pudding Pantry, full of excitement and hope. This was just one more step on the way – the quiet spell hopefully just a seasonal blip – and, a week today, 'Crumble Night', was going to mark the start of The Pudding Club. She popped in to the Pantry and had a quick word with Jill, telling her all about the wonderful support she'd received from across the community.

Next, she needed to get on with some farm work and, once again, there were some fencing issues. While she was out and about with the flyers, Jill had taken a phone call from Mr Mac, their neighbouring farmer, grumbling that there were several sheep on the loose out in the lane, and they definitely weren't his. So, armed with wire, pliers, a hammer and heavy-duty staple gun she drove along the lane, looking for the AWOL sheep. There they were, six ewes, happily munching the grass verge in the lane. She managed to round them up quickly with the help of good old Moss, and got them back into the field.

She scoured the hedgerows and fence to find the weak link that they had escaped from. She soon discovered a trampled area and a gap near the roadside that, on closer inspection, looked unusually like a neat cut in the wires

– odd. Rachel started to pull out and cut away the sharp, broken metal threads that would really be quite nasty should a sheep or other animal catch themselves on it, and then worked on rewiring the fencing lines, pulling them taut and stapling them firmly to the posts which should do the trick. All the while, she was pondering on the nature of the damage. Had someone purposely done it? But why?

A warm voice made her start. 'Hey, there.'

'Oh, hi!' She looked up, surprised to find Tom behind her. She had been so focussed on her task, she hadn't heard him approach.

'Your mum said I'd find you about here. Trouble with escapee sheep?'

'You got it. And see the fence here – come and take a look – I think it's been cut. Usually, if the sheep have trampled it, it just gets pushed down or you find there's a rotten post or something, don't you? But this looks different; I'm sure the sheep couldn't have done that so neatly.'

'Hmm.' Tom's face went serious. 'Is the gate on this field padlocked?'

'Yeah, why?'

'Let's just take a look.'

On closer investigation, it looked as though the gate and the lock had been forced. There were splinters and bashed areas, and the metal chain which roped the two gate sides together had dints in the metal, but evidently neither the padlock nor the gate had given.

'What do you reckon?' asked Rachel, feeling distinctly uneasy.

'This looks like poachers to me – the modern-day sort. Hare coursing and the like for money and so-called sport. It isn't sport, it's bloody cruel. Did you hear anything at all last night?'

'No, nothing unusual, and Moss would have barked if there had been anything near the farm, but I suppose this field's quite a way from the farmhouse.'

'Which is, no doubt, exactly why they tried to get into it.'

'Ah . . .' Rachel was well aware of modern-day poaching methods, often the gangs were more interested in hunting down wildlife, such as deer, than in stealing the farm animals. She'd heard it could be quite intimidating if the thugs got onto your land. But they'd never had any issue with it at Primrose Farm, thank heavens. Up until now . . .

'Well,' Tom gave a frown, 'I heard just this morning that they've had some trouble further up the valley at the Dobsons'. Been a gang with several cars out, driving across their land, hare coursing. Poor bloody hares, they chase them until the dogs get them.'

'Yeah, I've heard of that, cruel bastards. Well, they'll get short shrift if they turn up again around here.'

'Listen, Rach, be careful. If there is any bother, don't do anything gung-ho, and promise you'll ring me straight away? These people aren't nice at all.'

'Okay, will do.' She was already feeling angry that they'd

dared to try to get on to her land, damaging the fences and the gate.

'No signs of them getting into any of the other fields?'

'Don't think so, but I'll go and have a drive about now and see. All the sheep are accounted for, I've already checked.'

'It wouldn't be sheep they were after. We're not in the olden days when poachers were after a rabbit or a trout to help feed their family, or the occasional sheep rustler. No, this is something far more sinister. But at least it looks as if they gave up on it here. Probably drove on up the valley and caused havoc at the Dobsons' instead.'

'They'd better not show up here again,' Rachel warned.

'Let's hope not. Right, well, let me help you finish off here. I'll hold the wire taut while you staple it to the post there,' Tom offered.

Together, they finished the job.

'What's brought you out here, anyhow?' Rachel asked. 'Were you passing?'

'I came to see you, actually.' He looked slightly awkward. 'Well, "if the mountain will not come to Muhammed",' he quoted wryly, '"then Muhammed must go to the mountain".'

'Oh . . .'

'I've brought you some lunch.'

'Oh, Tom, bless you, this is just what I need, I'm ravenous.'

'Well, your mum said you were keen to get those sheep back in and hadn't had time to stop for any. And I seem to remember a really lovely girl making the effort to bring me and the lads a picnic that day we were cutting the hay.'

Rachel smiled, remembering that beautiful day in the summer too, when she and Tom were just starting to fall for each other.

'Now don't get too excited, mind. It's not quite up to your standard,' added Tom swiftly. 'I had already picked you up a couple of chocolate bars at the local garage when I stopped for fuel earlier.'

A man who thought to buy her chocolate? He'd won her over already.

'Oh, and your mum's made you a ham salad sandwich, by the way. Hang on . . .' He went to fetch the food from the pickup, also bringing with him two lidded takeaway coffees.

'Now, that looks good. And *chocolate* did you say, now you're *really* talking. So, what kind is it?'

'A Dairy Milk and a Crunchie bar.' Tom pulled them out of his Barbour coat pocket.

'Yum, and Crunchies are my favourite. How did you know?'

'I didn't. It was a calculated guess. They're one of my favourites too. So, I figured if you didn't like them, then . . .' Tom grinned.

'Hah, so you had an ulterior motive.'

'Absolutely.'

'And there was me thinking you were doing it out of the goodness of your heart.' Rachel smiled. 'Okay, well thanks. Did you know you can make a delicious ice-cream dessert with a Crunchie?'

'No, but I'm sure you as Princess of The Pudding Pantry will enlighten me.'

'Take a good scoop of quality vanilla ice cream, crush up a Crunchie bar and sprinkle it over the top with a drizzle of toffee or chocolate sauce, whichever is your favourite.'

'Sound marvellous.'

'It is. We'll have to try it one day,' she said, taking his hand and giving it a squeeze. And there she found herself talking of their future. They both smiled.

The grass was slightly damp there in the pasture, so Tom laid down his coat for them to sit on. Late October could be chilly both morning and evening, but on a fine day like today, at midday in a sheltered sunny spot, it was actually very pleasant. She ate her sandwich while Tom chatted about what he had on at his farm for the rest of the week. Rachel sat, looking out across the valley, the grass a fading green. Her sheep and cattle dotted around the hillside were grazing contentedly, the trees down by the stream that meandered through the farm were now turning their autumn bronze, their leaves beginning to fall – the ongoing cycle of the seasons and of nature, of life, were laid out before them.

She paused to take a slow breath before forming her next words and looked up into his dark eyes. 'Tom . . . I'm sorry if it seems like I've been shutting you out a bit lately. It's been so hectic and pretty damned crazy here, trying to hold everything together. To be honest, I'm scared that the new Pantry is going to go belly up. That's why I've been frantically putting out posters and flyers and trying to get more publicity and get this club idea off the ground.'

'Well, I have to admit I have noticed I'm somewhere low down the list of late – but you know what? I've always admired your sheer bloody determination.'

Rachel offered him half of the Crunchie bar before continuing. 'It's all been a bit overwhelming, and I've just been keeping going, head down, pushing on because it's the only way I know how. It's what my . . .' She paused, feeling the threat of tears. 'It's what my dad taught me.'

'It's okay, Rach. Look, I'd love to see more of you, but I get it. I get how hard it's been for you all.'

'Thank you, Tom.' A kaleidoscope-whirl of emotion seemed to be swirling inside her.

She leaned in towards him, just as he did the same to her. Tom cupped her chin gently in his hand, drawing her face, her lips to his, in a kiss that was beautiful and tasted of chocolate and honeycomb.

Yes, life at the farm and juggling all that with the Pudding Pantry was pretty overwhelming, but what she hadn't confessed to Tom was just how overwhelming the thought of handing over her heart again was. In the midst of all the happiness was a nagging fear that it couldn't last.

11

It was two nights later, in the dark of the early hours, when Rachel awoke with a start. What the hell was that noise? The security light was on in the yard, and Moss had started barking in his kennel at a pitch of high alert. *Shit.*

Rachel was up and out of bed and at the window in seconds, tugging back the curtain to see what was going on. There was a van, a white transit, parked in the yard with its back doors wide open. Then there was some movement by the tractor shed door. Two figures, in dark clothing and balaclavas, with what looked like wrenches to hand, were trying to force their way in. Moss was now going crazy, barking and growling too.

One of them cursed in a gravelly voice. 'Fucking dog, shut up.'

Rachel's, as well as Moss's, hackles rose. *The bastards. How dare they.* Her anger overtook any sense of fear. *They were not going to break in and steal everything she'd worked for, not everything she was striving to keep going. And if they hurt Moss . . .*

That was it, she was off down the stairs, grabbing Dad's old cricket bat from the downstairs cupboard, just in case. There was Dad's old shotgun too, kept in a locked cabinet under the stairs. Living on a rural farm, you never knew when it might be needed, though she'd never experienced anything like this before. If necessary, a shot into the air might be enough to scare them off.

She fetched the gun quickly, turned the light on in the porch, and stormed out, still dressed comically in PJs and slippers, armed and ready for action. One of the men was swearing at Moss again. *If they even thought of hurting her dad's dog . . .*

'Right then, you bastards, get off my land,' she yelled at the top of her voice, striding angrily into the farmyard in her nightwear.

'Ach, it's just a woman,' she heard.

Hah, just a woman was it. The shotgun was loaded; Rachel pulled the trigger and sent a warning shot up into the air. 'I *said* get off my land!' Her voice was a roar.

The errant pair stood stock-still, their mouths frozen in an 'O' of shock under their balaclavas.

'Shit, shit. Let's go!' They made a panicked dash for their vehicle.

Jill was now at the door, calling out loudly, 'I've rung the police. They're on the way.'

'*And*,' Rachel shouted after them as they scrambled into the van, 'If you dare show your ugly faces around here again, this'll be levelled right at them. Or maybe your balls instead.'

The van's front doors were slammed shut and it sped off with a screech, the rear doors, left open ready for loading any stolen cargo, swinging wildly behind as they disappeared off down the farm track.

Rachel went to check on Moss, who was still barking and on alert, but thankfully he was fine. She undid the kennel and the collie followed her back to the house. Rachel's heart was thumping wildly as she got in to the kitchen.

Jill was there in her dressing gown, looking pale and shocked. 'The police are informed. They're sending someone across as soon as they can, but I expect the buggers will be well away by then. I did manage to get most of the number plate recorded, mind.'

'Well done, Mum. Thankfully they didn't get chance to break in and take anything.'

With that, Maisy appeared, looking dishevelled and confused. 'Mummy, what's happening?'

'It's all okay, petal.' Rachel didn't want to alarm her little girl, and ensuring its safety catch was back on, swiftly lay down the gun that she was still carrying. Luckily, Maisy hadn't seemed to have spotted it. 'It was just a noise on the farm and Moss was barking. Everything's okay.'

'Come on, Missie, let's get you back to bed,' rallied Jill.

Rachel looked up at the kitchen clock: it was past three in the morning. Crikey, she didn't feel like she could go back to bed just yet, herself, with her heart still thumping like a frightened rabbit's. Jill was soon back down in the kitchen after settling Maisy.

'A cocoa, love?'

'Yes, I think so; thanks, Mum.' Rachel realised her hands were trembling.

Her mum put a pan of milk to warm on the Aga. She'd also brought down a fleecy blanket and settled that across Rachel's shoulders. 'That was a bit frightening, wasn't it,' Jill admitted. 'We were lucky they weren't armed themselves.'

Rachel hadn't had time to think about that out there. She had just wanted to protect her family and her property.

'Oh crikey . . . I remember we had a break-in at the barn once years ago. Your dad was up in arms that night too. I suppose it's par for the course in the country, but it's scary isn't it, being just the two of us now,' Jill continued, evidently shaken up by it all.

'Of course. It's bound to be, but no one drives us away, Mum. This is our farm, our land. We've worked hard for this. They can't be allowed to win. They can't go around stealing what our families have worked for all these years.'

'No, I suppose not, love. It's just a shock, that's all.'

'I know, I know,' Rachel soothed. But to think that Maisy was here in the house too. Rachel's heart was still thumping wildly.

Two police officers, a man and woman, arrived within the hour – neither Jill nor Rachel had felt ready to go back to bed by then, anyhow. They were sympathetic as they took a statement, while Jill made them a cup of tea. They said they'd got the part number plate reported and out on the system straight away, but so far there had been no sightings. The van could well be dumped somewhere by now, and the criminals in another vehicle, they warned. They left, after tea and biscuits, advising that another team would be there to do fingerprint checks on the tractor shed doors in the morning. Finally, at four thirty in the morning, it was time to go back to bed for a few hours' kip. But Rachel was still on high alert. She fell into a fitful sleep, the sound of shouting and slamming and the image of shadowy figures infiltrating her dreams.

12

The next day passed in a yawn-filled whirl. Luckily Maisy was off to school as Rachel didn't want her to hear anything more about last night's antics, but she shared the story with Tom at his elevenses. She realised she was still feeling a little shaky, just thinking about it.

'The bastards!' Tom shook his head. 'How dare they. And you're sure you're all right?'

'Yes.'

'You should have rung me, Rach, I would have come right across. You might have needed help.'

'I *really* didn't have time to think, never mind ring. I needed to stop them there and then.'

First the cut fences and now this. Primrose Farm had always felt a safe haven and now it was being threatened. Rachel felt angered and very uneasy.

And the nightmare didn't seem to end there. That very night, in the velvet blackness, Rachel woke from an unsettled sleep, feeling unnerved. The clock in her room told her it was just after midnight. The hairs prickled at the back of her neck as she lay listening. Had she heard something? Maybe it was just the realisation of what had happened last night lingering in her subconscious. After all, Moss was quiet and all seemed still outside. She got up, tiptoeing across the floorboards of her room, to take a look out of the window across the yard, to reassure herself.

Shit. There was a pickup truck parked outside near the tractor shed, but no security light was on. Had it been there a while? It looked familiar, but in the dark, it was hard to tell. After the antics of the night before, she was taking no chances. Rachel crept downstairs to get a closer look, her heart hammering once again, and arming herself with the cricket bat and fully intending to fetch the gun if need be. Would they be brazen enough to try again, or had word got out they were a soft target? Rachel felt the blood pounding in her veins.

She unlocked the door cautiously and looked out, but her movement outside the front door set off the security light, and—

Oh my God! She let out an anguished breath and slumped over, resting her hands on her knees. All was revealed. It was just Tom's truck.

'What the hell are you doing here?' Rachel said, in almost a shout, as she approached the vehicle. 'You frightened the life out of me! I thought they'd come back again.'

'I was just looking out for you.'

'Well, I'm quite capable of doing that myself. I saw them off last night okay, didn't I?' There had been a lot of bravado and a bit of luck in the mix too, but she wasn't going to admit that to Tom. She had, and was able to, protect her own land.

'Yes, well, I just wanted to be sure you were okay.'

'I would be, if people didn't go stalking me at my own property, waking me up,' she fumed. 'Look, Tom, I can take care of the farm fine, whatever happens. I don't need a knight in shining armour. I chased them off pretty damned well myself last night.'

'I'm sure you did.'

'So, I don't need you treating me like some damsel in distress.'

'Well, sorry for troubling you by being here.' Tom sounded put out. 'And, if you must know, I don't think you're a damsel in distress. You're strong and you're feisty and I like that in you, though it's bloody annoying sometimes. I'm here because I care – *really* care about you and your family, Rachel. I want to look out for you, and yes, protect you all.'

Rachel was leaning on the truck's open windowsill. It was getting chilly out there in her PJs and dressing gown.

'Think about it. What if someone came threatening, Maisy, hey?' Tom continued earnestly. 'You'd do everything you could in your power to protect her, wouldn't you? Well, that's what I feel about you – all of you. I'm not going to sit back and let it happen. That's why I'm camped out here in a freezing cold truck. Cos if those bastards return . . .'

'Oh . . .' Rachel's annoyance faded. How could she possibly stay mad?

'It's called love, Rachel.'

And his words brought a huge lump to her throat.

'Come on, get in the truck a minute; you'll freeze out there. I can warm you up a bit,' he added with a cheeky smile.

'Now that's an offer I can't refuse!' Rachel grinned.

He gave her a gorgeously warm hug and they sat for a while together. Two farm warriors waiting for the invasion that, thankfully, on this night didn't happen. He insisted Rachel go off to bed after a half hour, that he was going to sit it out for the night. She brought him out some flapjack and a flask of coffee to keep him going, before heading upstairs, and at six thirty she heard his vehicle start up and drive away.

Tom.

Her Tom.

Her night watchman.

13

With all the ups and downs and night-time dramas at Primrose Farm, the week had flown. Thankfully, there was no sign of a return from the thieves – although it hadn't stopped Rachel lying awake each night, listening out for any whisper of a disturbance.

Now she was finishing her dusk checks of the farm and livestock – having to trim a ewe's foot after she noticed it was limping badly and treating it with her purple spray – and then Rachel rolled in on the quad to park in the yard. She got down, stifling a yawn, and pulled off her green wellingtons in the farmhouse porch. On opening the kitchen door, a familiar smell greeted her – wow, warm toffee, caramelised apple – delicious. Jill was making two large toffee apple crumbles ready for tomorrow, Bonfire Night, and their firework's party at the farm. It would be a welcome diversion from the stressful escapades of the week.

'Hi there, Mum.'

'Hello, Rachel.'

'Looks like you've been busy; those crumbles smell divine.'

Once again, the aroma sent Rachel tumbling down memory lane . . . In autumn, she used to pick the apples with Dad from the big old gnarled tree in their garden. He'd lift her up in his strong arms so she could reach the fruit, and they'd fill a wicker basket with the large Bramley cooking apples. Mum would keep some to use straight away for her crumbles and apple sauce, the rest they'd lay out on the big kitchen table, the very same table they had now, and wrap them in old newspaper, ready to store in boxes under the bottom shelf in the walk-in larder.

There was another tree with eaters on, and they'd fetch some of those in too. They'd be used to make the toffee apples for Bonfire Night, as well as other sweet treats. Rachel loved eating the sticky toffee apples while watching the glittering display – fingers and toes chilly despite wearing gloves, thick socks and boots. The fireworks thrilled the young Rachel with their fizzes and sparkling trails against the black night sky.

Dad would be away in the field next to the yard setting them off. They weren't allowed anywhere near him at that point, nor too close to the bonfire that they always lit out in the yard. He'd adopt his serious voice as he warned Rachel about the dangers. She loved the show, but she was always glad when he came back through the gate safely, and she'd thrust her hand into his big warm palm. Then, after a whirl of sparklers, they'd be ready to head on in for warming mugs of soup, followed by toffee apple crumble and custard, all sitting around the Aga. That was the best finale of all.

Rachel would give anything to hold that sturdy hand right now, to be able to head home and tell her dad about her day, to sit and talk about the farm and their plans, and tell him all about the new Pudding Pantry in the barn, to get Dad's advice, hear his voice. But that could never be.

Her father hadn't been able to cope; the pressures of the farm and its dwindling finances had become just too hard – life itself had become too much. She could only guess at the full reasons, the depths of his illness, and the depression he'd tried too well to hide from them . . . he kept it all shut in, until it blew all their worlds apart. His suicide had been unimaginably devastating. It was Rachel who had found him that dark, dark day. It still haunted her.

Memories were like double-edged swords. They'd start off happy, wonderful glimpses of her dad in their good old days, their life together here on the farm and then the cold, stark reality of what had occurred would surface, because the layers of grief were still there smothering her soul. She knew Jill felt it too.

They couldn't change what had happened, much as they wished that they could. Rachel knew they had to look forward, the other way was just torment. They had to make a future, and that was why, more so than ever, the farm had to work, and the success of the Pudding Pantry was a huge part of that.

'I think I'll make a big jug of custard on Thursday to hand around with the crumbles at the Pudding Club, what do you reckon?' Jill's voice pulled Rachel back from her memories.

'Ah, yes, that sounds good.'

Of course, two days after Bonfire Night was the very first Pudding Club night. It was going to be a busy week.

'These will be another five minutes and then that's them all done. I've made enough for the club night too. I don't want the tops too dark on those ones, just a nice pale gold, as I'll reheat them on the night. I just want to be a step ahead because it'll be a busy few days.'

'Yes, there's a lot on, but you're juggling everything like a hero, Mum.'

'I'm feeling a bit anxious, wondering how it'll go,' Jill confessed. 'How about you?'

'Yeah, I suppose I am a bit nervous too. I've been wondering what I'll chat about for all that time, and who'll turn up. Will the mix of people work? What if they don't get on?' Rachel answered honestly. As well as flashbacks to the attempted break-in, the whole lot had been swirling about in her head for the past two days.

'Well, whoever turns up should have an interest in baking or at least *eating* the baking! And who wouldn't be delighted at that idea?'

'Yeah, that's true. Ah, it'll be fine,' Rachel rallied. 'I think I'll make another crumble to compare, maybe a pear and blackberry, and we can chat about everyone's favourite fillings, that'll start the ball rolling. And I might just have to give our puds for sale a little mention too, before they go home, of course.'

'That's a good ploy, Rachel.'

'That'll give us plenty to go with for the first session, surely?'

'Sounds fine to me. Have you had any more responses to the flyers and posters you've put out?' Jill asked.

Rachel had found even more places to leave her flyers. She'd dropped some in at various B & Bs and Charlotte, her teacher friend, had taken some for her school's staffroom. They'd also had the leaflets set out on the tables at the Pantry all week and several customers had asked about it. They had five bookings for the Pudding Club night so far, which wasn't a bad start – admittedly, two of them were Eve and Charlotte, but one was a young mum they knew from the school, and the other two were ladies from the local WI, who were friendly with Jill and keen to see what was going on. It was a small but positive start, and there was still a week to go. With Amanda's piece in the local *Gazette* due out tomorrow, that might well bring a few more enquiries in – fingers crossed.

Rachel settled into the comfy old armchair by the Aga, with Moss shifting across to rest his furry chin on her feet. Who needed slippers when you had a dog? Her eyelids began to feel heavy. It had been one hell of a week all in all. There was still so much to do, but for now she might just give in to a little ten-minute nap, surrounded by the smells of delicious apple crumble. Maybe she'd dream up some magic solution to the farm's troubles . . .

14

Whizz, fizz and crackle! Fireworks burst into trails of spectacular coloured light across the velvet sky. Maisy and Amelia stood looking up at them in awe and Rachel was enjoying seeing her daughter's face light up as much as the splendid fireworks.

Of course, five-year-old Maisy wouldn't remember the last fireworks night they'd had here at Primrose Farm with her grandad; she'd just been a toddler in a pushchair . . .

Tom and Ben had agreed to go into the empty field next to the farmhouse and set the fireworks off and Rachel, Jill, Eve and Granny Ruth stood wide-eyed in the farmyard with the girls, watching the magical display, all wrapped up in their woolly pom-pom hats, coats, scarves, warm socks and wellies. A smoky tang of gunpowder bursts filled the air and a small bonfire of wood and debris, gathered up from the farm over the past week, burned orange and crackled in the yard.

The crumble was warming in the Aga, and they'd already had a supper of hot dogs with caramelised onions, and mugs of homemade vegetable soup – Jill having made an extra-large batch of soup on purpose at the Pantry that day. They'd cooked the sausages by lantern-light on the BBQ outside, which hadn't had an outing for a couple of years now, and the coals were still glowing beside them.

Rachel's heart was filled with poignant memories of Bonfire Nights spent with her dad, but she was happy, too, that she was recreating that magic for her own daughter. They'd been careful with the fireworks selection, not choosing anything too noisy for the livestock, and Rachel had made sure all the animals were in the fields furthest from the farmhouse. If only Dad could be here now, to see how Maisy was growing up, and making more memories with his family . . .

She glanced at Granny Ruth who stood next to her, looking a bit chilly, despite all her layers of clothing. 'You okay, Granny?'

'Aye, I'm just grand, pet,' she answered, but a cough caught in her throat, wracking her for a short while. When she'd gathered her breath, she added, 'Well then, that was a fine display and didn't the girls love it? I've been watching them as much as the fireworks. But I must say I'm looking forward to getting back into the warm with some of that crumble your mum's made.'

'Why don't you go on in then, Granny? We're nearly done out here anyway. There's just a few sparklers for the girls and then we'll be heading in ourselves.'

'I might just do that, pet. And, Rachel,' she said softly, 'You're doing a grand job here, lass. You and Jill should be proud of yourselves.'

'Aw, thank you.' Rachel gave the dear old lady a hug,

as the whoosh of the next firework went up and off. Those words meant such a lot. With all the juggling on the farm, looking after Maisy, and the downturn in trade at the Pudding Pantry, sometimes it felt that she wasn't doing quite enough. But maybe she *was* giving it her best, and sometimes that was all you could give.

The two men were now nearing the garden fence, wandering through a light film of drifting smoke. Rachel caught Tom's eye, and he broke into a broad smile as she gave the lads a big thumbs up on the fireworks so far. It was a smile that never failed to warm her soul.

Ruth trundled off to the house, as a Catherine Wheel went off in a silver, sparkly arc. Then it all went quiet, until Tom shouted from over the hedge, 'All done. That's a wrap, folks!'

There was a 'Hoorah!' and the small gathering clapped, but then an '*O-oh*,' as the little girls realised the show was over.

'Hang on, girls, look, I have sparklers.' Rachel grinned, pulling out a pack of extra-long ones which Jill lit with a taper, explaining how to hold them safely.

Maisy and Amelia made swirls and circles in the dark air, then Rachel showed them how to write their names or draw smiley faces. Their grins behind the fizzing lights were radiant. After writing 'Maisy' mid-air, her little girl wrote 'Mummy' and then began 'Daddy', though the sparkler fizzled out halfway through the letters of that. Rather like her father's interest in her, Rachel mused wryly. She lit the girls another.

'Hey.' Tom came back to the group, and rested a hand on Rachel's shoulder.

'Hi, that was great. Thank you.'

'My pleasure and we quite enjoyed it, didn't we, Ben? Nothing like letting two blokes loose with a box of matches and a load of fireworks.'

Ben was smiling broadly. 'Yep, we had a bit of fun.'

'Thank you, Tom,' Maisy shouted from behind her sparkly wheel of light.

'Glad you enjoyed it, girls,' Tom replied.

Rachel took out a new sparkler and joined in the fun, writing 'Rachel' and 'Maisy' and then 'Tom' in the air, followed by a big love heart. Tom spotted that and gave her another broad grin.

The girls had a final sparkler each, which after lots of twirls, swirls and laughter, began to burn down to an orange-glowing stub.

'Right, pop those metal sticks carefully in the bucket of water that's over there, girls. It's time to go in for some of Grandma Jill's famous Toffee Apple Crumble,' announced Rachel.

'Yippee!' 'Scrummy!'

Granny Ruth was already settled in her favourite chair by the Aga in the farmhouse kitchen.

'Wasn't that lovely, girls. And well done, Tom and Ben, what a display!'

'Yes, we loved it, Granny,' Maisy enthused, clambering up on to her tweed-skirted lap for a hug.

'Thanks, Ruth,' replied Tom, as Ben stood smiling on.

'Okay, let's get these crumbles out of the oven. And I've got a jug of lovely creamy custard warming,' said Jill.

'I'll get them out for you, Mum, while you sort the custard.'

'Thanks, Rachel, love.'

And they were soon working as a well-oiled team again. A few minutes later everyone gathered around the pine kitchen table, and dipped their spoons into the warm caramelised apple and toffee-crunchy topping, which was a delight for all.

'Oh, Mum, these are amazing.'

'A step up from the basic apple crumble, I must say.' Tom had a wicked grin on his face as he spoke, looking right at Rachel. 'I think I'm going to have to watch my step.'

Eve, who got the joke straight away, started giggling.

'What's funny?' asked Maisy innocently.

'Ah, nothing, it's just delicious isn't it!' Rachel tried to divert her daughter, who didn't miss a trick.

'Crumble is *always* delicious,' said Tom with a wide smile.

'There's a pot of tea made and ready on the table with mugs for all, so help yourselves,' said Jill. 'Oh, I'll pour yours out for you, Ruth. No need to move.'

They all chatted away, the girls still giddy about the magic shooting lights in the night sky. Eve told them all about her latest Christmas themed craft-making, and the craft fayre at Claverham Castle coming up in late November, where she was planning to host a stall.

'Ooh, that sounds good. Do you know, that castle is virtually on our doorstep, and I've never been in?' said Rachel.

'It's gorgeous there and so full of character. I've heard their Christmas Craft Fayre is really popular, so I thought I'd put my name down. After all, we had a cracking day at the Kirkton Country Show back in the summer, didn't we?'

'Yeah, that was such a busy day. Well, if you find out a bit more, maybe it'll be something we can do too. We could have a pudding stall – Christmas puddings? What do you think, Mum?' Rachel was never one to miss an opportunity.

'It's certainly something to look into,' Jill agreed.

It was soon time for Eve and her family to leave. It was a school night after all, and it was past Maisy's bedtime too. They said their goodbyes and thanks, then Jill offered to take Maisy up and get her ready for bed. Rachel and Tom cleared the kitchen together, while Granny Ruth took a little nap in her seat by the Aga; her cough had still been rattling her, bless her.

Rachel then went upstairs to tuck Maisy in. After a short story time, perched on the edge of her daughter's bed, Rachel planted a tender kiss on her daughter's forehead.

'Sleep tight, petal.'

'Night, night, Mummy. I loved the sparkly fireworks. Did you see I drew a unicorn in the sky with one?'

'Aw, I didn't spot that one, but it sounds lovely. They are a bit magical, aren't they?'

'Super-duper magical.'

It was lights-out time in the lilac-painted unicorn-themed bedroom. Rachel hoped her little girl would be able to settle after such an exciting night. As she slowly closed the bedroom door, she saw Maisy's eyelids beginning to droop already – maybe her fears were unfounded.

'Right then, shall I get you home, Ruth?' Jill offered, as Rachel came back down to the kitchen hub.

Ruth no longer drove, and relied on them for lifts to and from her little cottage on the far side of Kirkton.

'Yes please, pet. That'll be grand.' She had another coughing bout. 'Ooh, goodness.' She held a hand to her chest for a second. 'Well then, I think I'm ready for an early night.'

'You need to get that cough checked out, Ruth,' Jill warned, 'Get yourself an appointment booked with the doctor. It's been hanging around for a while now.'

'I can take you down to the surgery, Granny,' offered Rachel.

'I'll be fine, don't you worry about me, lass. They can't do anything much about a cough. They don't like dishing out antibiotics like they used to. It'll run its course soon enough.'

'Well, I suppose. But don't let it get any worse. Or I'll be booking the appointment for you myself,' added Jill. It was said in a friendly manner, her daughter-in-law was just concerned, after all.

'Aye, pet.' Ruth raised herself to stand, seeming a little out of breath, and gathered her woollen overcoat. 'Bye,

Rachel. Bye, Tom. It's been a grand night. So lovely to see the little ones faces all lit up too.'

'Yes, it was.' Tom smiled warmly.

'See you soon, Granny. Take care.' Rachel gave her a warm hug.

'You too, pet.'

Rachel could see that her Granny was getting older, and a bit frailer, and that touched her heart.

The Land Rover was soon heading off, and with Maisy tucked up in bed for the night, it was the first time Rachel and Tom had been on their own all evening – for days, in fact.

'That went off well. Thanks for all your help with the fireworks.' Rachel finished washing up the last mug and moved from the sink to give Tom a 'thank you' kiss on the cheek.

'Hmm,' he murmured appreciatively as he shifted his lips to meet hers, his tongue cheekily parting her lips.

That sparked something and, within seconds, Rachel had pressed Tom, still with tea towel in hand, up against the wall next to the Aga as the kiss developed. Soon it was making her tingle all over. He tasted of apples and crumble and there was a whiff of bonfire smoke on his clothes. It was a sexy combination.

It was already warm there by the stove, and things were definitely hotting up. It was amazing how a kiss could reach your fingers and toes . . . and all kinds of other places.

'Now then,' Tom pulled his lips away for a second, 'if you keep on doing this to me there may well be more fireworks about to set off.' He grinned mischievously.

Rachel couldn't help but notice the firm heat that was hardening against her thigh. She pulled back a little, smiling. 'Ah, well now, we can't do anything about *that* this evening. Maisy's upstairs and Mum's due back any time. So, you can think again, matey.' She laughed, glancing down at the raised crotch area of his jeans.

'She's not back yet, though . . .' He quirked an eyebrow.

Rachel laughed again and hit him playfully with the tea towel. 'Nope, no way! Can you imagine her walking in on us all coupled up in front of the Aga – literally?' Memories of their fireside tryst just a couple of weeks ago were making her nerve endings tingle even more, despite her efforts to be restrained.

'Now, don't make me think about things like that, when I'm meant to be getting rid of this . . .' They both looked down – there was no sign of anything subsiding just yet. They couldn't help but laugh.

'I'll be batting it down with a wooden spoon in a minute,' Rachel jested.

'Ouch! Mind you, even that sounds interesting.'

'Weirdo!'

'Now just shush and stop making me think of all these scenarios, when I can't do anything about it.'

With that, there was the telltale crunch of gravel out in the yard, and the bright flash of headlights. Jill was back.

'Oh shite, now what do I do?' Tom pulled a panicked

face. How were you meant to greet your girlfriend's mother with a hard-on in full salute?

Rachel was giggling away as she moved back to the sink and pretended to still be washing up as Jill came in through the kitchen door with a cheery 'hello'.

'Hi,' Tom managed in a slightly higher tone than usual, grabbing the tea towel from the side and strategically positioning it.

'Oh, hi Mum.' There was a smirk over Rachel's face.

Jill, who hadn't seemed to notice the kitchen kerfuffle, merely said, 'Well, that's Granny Ruth back safe and sound. I'm a bit worried about her cough, mind. She needs to look after herself.'

'Yes, let's hope she gets better soon.'

'Thanks so much for all your help this evening, Tom.' Jill turned to look at him. 'It was an exciting night, wasn't it?'

'Very exciting.' His voice was slightly strained.

'Yep, we're just finishing the washing-up.' Rachel's eyes were glinting with laughter as she caught Tom's gaze.

'Oh thanks, love, but you needn't have done all that. I could have helped.'

'It's fine, we soon cracked on with it, didn't we, Tom. Lovely crumble, by the way,' Rachel added naughtily, having to bite her own lip, to keep the giggles in.

'Thanks, yes, that turned out well. I think it'll go down well at the Pudding Club,' said Jill.

'It certainly will,' Tom managed, his voice now an octave lower than usual.

'Well then, if we're all done here, we may as well go through and relax in the sitting room?' Jill suggested.

'Oh, yes,' said Rachel chirpily.

Tom coughed. 'I'll join you in just two ticks.'

At that, Rachel's giggles spilled over, until she was in tears.

Jill gave a confused smile, 'Crikey, I'm not sure what's the matter with you pair, but it's nice to see you smiling, anyhow.'

The Cheshire cat grins continued – it definitely wasn't appropriate to enlighten her!

Rachel quickly nipped upstairs to check on Maisy, who was flat out, sound asleep in her bedroom. Then, she sat down on the sofa beside Tom to watch the late evening news. Jill was in the armchair near the roaring fire.

'Right then,' Jill announced with a yawn, after the headlines had finished, 'I'll get myself off to bed, can barely keep my eyes open. It's been a long day.'

Rachel had a feeling she was trying to give them some space. 'Okay, night, Mum. And, thanks again for all the special food tonight.'

'Glad you all enjoyed it.'

'Goodnight, Jill,' added Tom.

After the door closed gently behind Jill, Tom gave Rachel a cheeky grin – obviously hopeful of carrying on where they'd left off an hour or so before.

'Nope, don't even think about it. I meant what I said about the wooden spoon,' Rachel quipped. Despite their joking about, Rachel knew it would feel all wrong with Maisy and Mum about. What if either of them came downstairs for some reason? Rachel knew she wouldn't be able to relax. 'You'll just have to put up with some old-fashioned kissing and cuddling.'

And, sure enough, just a few minutes and several hugs and kisses later, that was enough to get the full salute back in place again. All fully clothed, of course.

'You could always come back to mine?' suggested Tom, ever hopeful.

'Not tonight, Tom. Sorry, I need to be here with my family.'

'O-kay. I'll have to save this for another time, then.' He managed a frustrated smile.

'Ha, I'll look forward to it.'

'And make sure you bring your wooden spoon with you.'

And they were chuckling with laughter again, before finishing with a very sexy goodnight kiss.

Firework night indeed.

15

'Welcome! And here we have the splendiferous Toffee Apple Crumbles made by Jill to taste at our first-ever Pudding Club! How does that sound? Too much, Mum?' Rachel was carrying a tray of crumbles, ready to warm through at the inaugural Pudding Club tonight. She was testing out how to begin presenting the evening.

'Hmm, it's a bit OTT, love. Just be yourself,' said Jill. 'I did tell you I took a call this morning for another booking, didn't I?'

'Yes, but I was dashing out at that point to meet Simon at the cattle shed. We're getting ready to bring the cows in soon. So, who was it, anyone we know?'

'Someone who'd spotted the flyer in the Deli. It was a man. Says he works at the care home for the elderly in Kirkton. Daniel, yes, that was his name. He sounded nice enough on the phone. Quite new to the area, likes to bake a bit, apparently, and looking for some tips.'

'Well, that sounds good, and a mix of age ranges, and men and women will be great. So, after we had the mention in the newspaper and the two bookings that came from that . . . I think that'll take us up to nine now, plus the two of us and, of course, Granny Ruth, who's keen to be there.'

'Hah, a baker's dozen – oh no, that'd need to be thirteen,' said Jill.

'Well, if we count Maisy in, who I've had to promise can stay up for this one, we will be.'

'Perfect.' Jill clapped her hands together, 'I'm sure we'll get on just fine, and we'll find our feet as we go.'

'Well, these puddings look and smell gorgeous anyhow, so I'm sure that'll sway things in our favour.'

'Absolutely.'

They knew they had to keep thinking positively and believe in themselves. Would they be able to pull it off? The proof, of course, would be in the pudding . . .

The evening rolled around quickly. Rachel wanted there to be a different ambience for the Pudding Club – as the November nights drew in, she envisaged it to be a toasty haven from the outside world; a place where people could escape and enjoy the warmth and glow of new company. She'd set out some tealight candles on the dressers, as well as lighting a couple of lamps. The log-burning stove was glowing cosily and she'd pushed two tables together to make one big area for the group to gather, ideal to get everyone together and hopefully chatting. An informal and friendly atmosphere was what she was trying to achieve, so fingers crossed it would work.

With just a quarter of an hour to go, Jill came in after collecting Granny Ruth. 'Ooh, this looks nice, love.'

Maisy was helping, setting out cups and saucers carefully on the countertop ready for the arrival of their guests. 'Hello, Granny! We're nearly ready.'

'Aye, and doesn't it look lovely in here, lassies,' said Ruth, taking in the softly-lit barn with the Pudding Club table set out with tasting spoons and a little posy of pink carnations set in a milk jug at its centre. 'Oh, and the twinkly lights outside look good too – very welcoming. Aye, you're doing a grand job here as always. Now then, is there anything I can help you with, Rachel?'

'No, but thank you, Granny. I think we're about ready, so take a seat. We'll be making some tea and coffee shortly, as soon as our guests arrive.'

'That's fine, pet. I'm in no rush.'

Rachel stood at the counter, taking in the Pantry in front of her. They had come so far with this project already; the barn looked so pretty, transformed like this, with its natural stone walls brought back to life, gently glowing in the candlelight, the cosy wooden tables, the new kitchen area and counter, the chandeliers. Maybe this was just the last push they needed to really get this business off the ground.

First on the scene, just a few minutes later, were Charlotte and Eve. 'My goodness, what is that divine aroma?' Charlotte was grinning as she strolled in.

'Hah, it'll be Mum's toffee apple crumbles warming in the oven,' answered Rachel.

'Ooh, I can't wait to test those out,' said Eve. 'I purposely had a small portion of supper, so I could make the most of the tastings here. Hello, Maisy, how are you sweetheart?'

'Good, thanks. I'm a helper-outer tonight.'

'Oh, how exciting. And I'm sure you're doing a really great job.'

'Yes, I've got all the cups ready for drinks,' she said proudly. She loved being a part of everything. And she was delighted to be having a late night on a school evening, by special permission.

Next to enter were two young mums, Hannah and Kirsty, who hadn't booked, but who often called in at the Pantry with their toddlers for morning coffee and cakes. Rachel knew Hannah from the school gates, as she had an older child too.

'Hi, Rachel. Hello, Jill.'

'Lovely to see you here, girls,' said Jill warmly.

'We've managed to escape. Sorry we didn't book in, but we weren't sure if we could sort the childcare. But the other halves are in charge of the kids for the night. So, we get a bit of a time out – bliss.'

'Oh yes, we made it sound very educational, so they thought we weren't just out for a jolly.' Hannah winked.

'As long we go home and bake something new and scrumptious through the week, I'm sure the family will be happy. We're looking for inspiration,' added Kirsty.

'Well, that's what the club's all about,' answered Rachel with a smile. 'So, I'm sure you'll find some. And if not . . . we have some great puddings to take away.' Rachel winked back, as the ladies grinned.

'That's us sorted then,' said Hannah.

'Okay, I'll pop the kettle on and make some tea and coffee while we wait for the others to arrive. What would you like?' Jill offered.

The two women replied and then sat down next to Eve and Charlotte, starting to chat straight away. There was a nice friendly atmosphere in the room already, phew.

Next in were husband and wife duo Nigel and Pamela, who said they were keen bakers and had travelled the fifteen miles from Alnwick to find out all about the new pudding club that they'd read about excitedly in the paper. Then, two of Jill's friends from the local WI appeared.

Last to arrive, and just a couple of minutes late, was Daniel, the gentleman who worked at the care home, who'd spoken with Jill a couple of days ago. He was tall and broad (Rachel thought in a comfy-looking way, as though he enjoyed his food but might also do a little exercise too). He looked to be in his late forties, with a silvery-grey short beard and closely cropped hair.

He gave a warm smile. 'I'm sorry I'm a little late, I do hope I've not held you up.'

'It's no problem. We were just getting settled in and introducing ourselves,' answered Jill. 'Can I get you a tea or coffee to start with?'

'A coffee would be perfect. Milk and one sugar, thank you. I just had to stay on with one of our residents who was having trouble settling.'

'Ah yes, you work at the Little Oaks Care Home, don't you?' added Jill.

142

'Yes, it's a nice place there, and a great team to work with too.'

'Well, that's good. Do find yourself a seat and I'll bring the coffee over in two ticks. We'll be making a start shortly.'

Brief introductions were made around the table, with Rachel setting the ball rolling. 'Hi everyone, and thanks so much for coming along to the Pudding Pantry for what I hope will be a fun and inspirational, as well as tasty, evening. So, a big welcome from me and my mum, Jill.' Rachel's fingers were trembling slightly on the sheet of notes that she'd made for the evening, but Jill glanced at her with a supportive nod and encouraging smile, and she began to relax a little. She briefly explained their background and how they'd converted the barn this summer to begin their new business venture. Then she finished with, 'Please let us know what you're hoping to get from the Pudding Club, and any suggestions on how we can go forward are most welcome. And, I hope you enjoy this evening!'

Jill's Toffee Apple Crumbles were the first out for the taste-testing, served in pretty fluted white china dishes, with creamy custard for those who wanted. It was met with hearty approvals by way of 'Yum', 'Delicious', 'Gorgeous', 'Love it', and 'I need this recipe now!'. This was followed by Rachel's Pear and Blackberry Crumble, which again was met with a round of appreciation and enthusiasm. The guests animatedly discussed the crumbles they'd sampled, with Granny Ruth talking happily with Daniel, and Maisy carrying across a fresh jug of milk for the teas.

'You're doing a fab job, Maisy,' said Eve. 'I think you deserve extra pocket money for this.'

'Yes, I do too,' she grinned. 'I'll ask Mummy in a minute.'

Gathered back at the table with a fresh brew to hand, Rachel soon had the group's attention once again. 'So, we've had a couple of tastings and you've all now got Jill's fabulous recipe sheet for her Toffee Apple Crumble, so, what are *your* favourite crumble recipes? Any hot tips or tantalising or unique flavour combinations?'

'Rhubarb and Ginger,' suggested Denise, one of the WI ladies.

'Oh yes, we have that here at the Pantry sometimes, it's a lovely warming combination with a touch of spice,' said Jill.

'I tried a Damson and Apple Crumble once, that was nice,' added Christine.

One of the young mums joined in, which was great to see. 'I made a Raspberry and Chocolate Crumble once and that was *so* good.'

'Ooh, sounds amazing,' said Charlotte. 'I'm not that adventurous, just the usual apple crumble for me.'

'Oh yes.' Eve winked at Rachel at that point.

Rachel was in professional mode and somehow managed to keep her cool. She'd have words with her friend later, mind.

'Apple and Blackberry's my favourite,' piped up

Granny Ruth. 'Just like my own Granny used to make, back in the day. And, going blackberry picking as a child was the best bit, sampling as you went, with sweet juices running down your chin and purple-stained fingers.'

'Hah, yes. Maisy, you like doing that, don't you?' added Rachel. They'd been out bramble picking earlier in the autumn to boost supplies for Grandma Jill's baking – several bags of blackberries were still in the freezer – and Maisy had loved it.

Unfortunately, Ruth had a coughing fit then, and politely made to leave the table.

'Here, I'll fetch you some water, Granny.' Rachel got up to get a glass for her.

After taking a sip, and coughing a little more, the old lady excused herself, 'I might just head over to the house. It was lovely to meet you all.' She seemed embarrassed at causing a fuss.

'Lovely to meet you too, Ruth,' said Daniel kindly, who'd been sitting beside her. 'You take care now.'

'Well, I always like a gooseberry crumble,' Pamela, the wife of the couple from Alnwick then said. 'Nice and tart. With a big blob of thick cream.'

'It's delicious, I can vouch for it,' added her husband, Nigel, with a proud smile.

'Ooh, yes,' Eve commented.

'I tried to make a spiced pear and almond once, and that was good,' said Daniel joining in.

'Oh, I do like the sound of that,' Jill said animatedly,

who'd now taken Ruth's seat next to Daniel. 'You'll have to give me the recipe sometime.'

'Of course,' he answered, chirpily.

Rachel looked around the vibrant group. It was brilliant that the first club night had started off so well, and that everyone seemed happy to join in and make the most of the experience. Hopefully, they'd all enjoyed themselves so far.

'So, on to toppings. Any suggestions?' said Rachel, hoping to keep the conversation flowing.

'Custard, cream,' WI Denise said.

'Ice cream!' Maisy found her moment.

'Good old-fashioned vanilla ice cream, I'd say,' said Christine.

'Yes, that's always lovely, but you could experiment with different flavours depending on the crumble filling,' suggested Jill. 'Like a nice butterscotch with the toffee apple we had today, or ginger ice cream with your rhubarb crumble.'

'Ooh, you're making my mouth water *sooo* much,' confessed Eve.

'Hah, yes there's even a bead of drool on her lower lip,' Charlotte teased, then creased with laughter.

Rachel glanced at her watch. Wow, the time was flying. 'There's only fifteen minutes or so left, so I thought we might chat about what *you* want from the club. Are there any suggestions for future themes, baking workshops, or particular puddings you'd like to taste? I do have one or two ideas, but I'd love to hear your thoughts.'

She gave the group a few minutes to think on it and to chat amongst themselves. A collaborative, inclusive club – that's what Rachel wanted. A safe haven where everyone could get away from the world. Tea was poured and fresh coffee was gurgled in the new 'fandangled' machine as Jill called it.

Maisy was now sitting next to Eve, with a milky hot chocolate in front of her, sleepily propped on plumped-up cushions, bless. It was past eight, an hour later than her usual school-night bedtime, but she was fighting her fluttering eyelids determinedly.

'We've three more sessions up until Christmas,' Rachel said, 'as we'll be holding the Pudding Club bi-weekly, on the first and third Thursdays in the month. I was thinking a Christmas Pudding night might work well, maybe for the first week in December, so any suggestions for the other two evenings would be really welcome.'

'Ah,' one of the young mums raised her hand tentatively, 'I'd really like some help with easy pudding and baking ideas for over the Christmas season. I'd love to be able to make some nice home-baked treats for the family that don't take forever or need a heap of costly ingredients.'

'Yes, that sounds a great idea,' agreed Christine, from the WI.

'Foolproof festive bakes then, yes,' piped up Jill enthusiastically, her mind no doubt already mulling over what recipes might work for that.

'Yep, I always intend to bake for Christmas and then I get stuck for ideas, or I'm in a whirl of last-minute gift

147

hunting and present wrapping and then, oops, it's Boxing Day before I know it,' added Charlotte with a sigh of frustration.

'Okay, so that sounds a really good idea,' said Rachel, knowing this was her moment to promote some extra business for the Pantry too. 'And on that note, after every session there will be the chance to buy any of the puddings and bakes we have here, to take away too. We'll make sure there are plenty of the puddings we'll be tasting on the night, as well as our other goodies.'

'That sounds wonderful,' said young mum, Hannah. 'Scrumptious.'

'Can I pretend I made them myself?' asked Charlotte, cheekily.

'Well, I'll not let the secret out,' grinned Rachel. 'So, any ideas for the next session . . .?'

'What about a tart night?' suggested Eve, before bursting into giggles and realising the connotation of what she'd said. 'I mean, as in Treacle Tart, Bakewell and such like.'

'Lemon tart, French Apple tart,' added Daniel.

'There'd be lots to chat about with that,' continued Jill.

'Hah, as long as we don't have to dress up for it,' added Christine with a naughty glint in her eye. 'Stockings and suspenders anyone?'

Nigel nearly choked on his tea just then, while Dan blushed and gave a wry smile.

'Or, we could be "Passionate about Pavlova" for another night?' said Kirsty.

'Love it! These suggestions are marvellous. Thank you.'

'Well, we could run with Eve's idea first and have "Taming the Tart" for next week,' said Jill mischievously.

'Do you think we can get away with that poster-wise?' Rachel was laughing, yet slightly concerned, thinking about the older generation in the village area who might be affronted.

'Why not? As long as we mention puddings somewhere in the flyer. It'll certainly attract attention. Yes, "Taming the Tart" – treacle, apple and lemon. Come along to the Pudding Club to find out more,' said Jill with a mischievous smile; she was obviously enjoying this evening. It was so lovely to see her relaxing and that twinkle back in her eye. Rachel knew how hard she worked, trying to keep everything together.

'Tart Week it is then, in a fortnight's time,' declared Rachel.

'Can we book in for it now?' asked Kirsty, 'I'll get my Steve lined up for babysitting duties straight away.'

'Yes, of course.' Rachel was delighted. 'I'll get the diary out right away.'

And even before the group started to pack up and head away, she had five bookings for the next session, with the other attendees promising to check their diaries.

Coats were gathered and several takeaway crumbles and some chocolate brownies were bought as the various guests made to leave.

'Thank you, it's been a delightful evening,' said Pam, 'Well worth the trip. I'll mention it all to my friends in Alnwick this week.'

'Thank you so much for coming,' said Jill.

'Goodnight, and thank you,' Rachel called out.

'You did brilliantly,' said Eve, giving her friend a big hug. 'I knew you could do it. It really was fun.'

'Amazing crumbles, too,' added Charlotte. 'Sam'll love the Toffee Apple one I've bought, so that's pudding sorted for Sunday dinner already. Perfect. My kind of baking!'

'Catch you soon, ladies,' chanted Eve, and off went Rachel's friends with a jolly wave.

'Shall we have a five-minute breather before we clear up? Go and have a quick sit down in the kitchen by the Aga with a brew? I don't know about you, but I feel shattered,' admitted Jill.

'Hah, I think someone else is shattered too.' Rachel pointed across at little Maisy, who was slumped to one side in her chair, eyes closed, and her mouth slightly open. 'Yes, let's head back over, get this one to bed, and we can see how Granny is too. She really doesn't seem herself with that cough.'

'Yes, I hope she's all right. She'll be ready for home, I'm sure. And let's not worry about the washing-up just now, Rachel. It's been a long day. I can do it in the morning.'

'Okay, and thanks for everything, Mum, – for all your support with the Pudding Club.'

'No worries, we're a team. I'm pleased it went well, it was a good night,' added Jill.

'Yes, and a really great start for the Pudding Club,' Rachel agreed, with a sense of relief and a pinch of joy. 'What a lovely group too.'

Jill and Rachel gave each other a happy high five behind the counter of the Pantry.

'Well, there's one little girl and one old lady back at the farmhouse to get home and safely to bed. Time to go.'

'Yep.' Rachel scooped up Maisy in her arms, who stirred but then closed her eyes again. Rachel walked carefully out and, while Jill locked up for the night, turning the big metal key in the old barn door, she stood poised on the sill, her arms heavy but in no way burdened with her child. *We did it, Dad*, she spoke silently to herself, looking up at the old converted barn. Tonight was another step on the way back up.

The Fifth Bake of Christmas

Mary's Black Forest Gateau – 1975

Frank's Memory:
It was our tenth wedding anniversary. It had been such a busy day at work and I walked in, shattered, to our house . . . it smelt rich and sweet of chocolate and something more, I couldn't quite think what. I had some flowers and a card with me, I hadn't forgotten. Anniversaries were always special to us.

So, there was my Mary in the kitchen, putting the final touches to a gateau, a Black Forest Gateau no less. She knew it was one of my favourites, but she'd never made it for me before. It was chocolate sponge with juicy dark cherries – that was the other ingredient of course – and lightly whipped cream, an absolute delight. She was a wonderful cook, my Mary, bless her soul. I swear that was the best cake I ever did eat . . . made with real love that one.

16

A few days later, and Rachel was still riding high on the success of the inaugural Pudding Club. Nothing could dampen her spirits – well, except that right now there was a mysterious woman sitting at table three in the Pantry, looking her way . . . in fact, *staring* at Rachel. She was finding the whole thing a little unnerving and was trying to occupy herself behind the counter.

The lady must have been in her early thirties and had straight dark hair that fell sleekly beneath a navy beret, to just below her shoulders. The fingernails that grasped her coffee cup were polished in a fuchsia pink. Rachel had a vague feeling that she recognised her; but she didn't look at all like a local, not even like their usual holiday-makers.

As she caught Rachel's eye, her glance was cool. Rachel couldn't put her finger on it, but she felt uneasy. She raised a smile as she would for any customer. In response, the woman's mouth gave a twitch at the corners, giving the barest trace of a smile back.

Rachel busied herself tidying a nearby table of its empty cups, and she felt mightily relieved when Frank strolled in.

'Hello, Rachel pet.'

'Hi, Frank. How are you today?'

'Grand pet, just grand.'

'That's good to hear. Usual coffee?'

'Yes, indeed.'

'And can I get you any treats?'

'Well, what have you got to tempt me with today?'

'There's a coffee and walnut cake that Mum's made fresh this morning, or a spiced plum crumble, the usual selection of scones, shortbread, and a chocolate and cherry pudding. I can recommend that one – I had a taste last night and it was delicious.'

'Well, I can't go wrong with that then. Pop a blob of cream on it, pet, won't you.'

'I will indeed.'

'Hmm, it sounds a bit like a black forest gateau. I don't suppose you remember them . . . bit of a Seventies thing. My Mary used to make that cake for special occasions. Really lovely it was.'

'Yes, I have heard of that, actually. I bet it was a real treat back then.'

'Indeed.' And he went a little glassy-eyed, no doubt thinking back to those happy times with his wife.

Frank was served and soon settled at his table near the window, newspaper spread out beside him. He put a thumbs-up sign as he took a mouthful of the rich chocolatey pudding. Jill, who was busy in the little kitchen piping swirls of frosting on to vanilla cupcakes, grinned as she spotted him.

'Another triumph, Jill,' he called across.

'Thanks, Frank.'

Although her instincts were telling her to duck behind the Pantry's counter, Rachel risked a sneaky glance across the barn. The dark-haired woman was still there, giving her yet another cool stare.

Who could it be?

Oh God, she was getting up now. Rachel saw her leave some coins on the table top, presumably enough to cover her coffee bill, and, keeping her head low, she headed towards the exit.

'Thank you,' Rachel called after her, to be polite.

There was the smallest nod of the woman's head as she kept on going – she evidently wasn't in the mood to chat.

Miss Beret trotted out on her high heels. Oh yes, they were black stiletto ankle boots, no less. She was *definitely* not from around here; much more practical footwear was needed in the countryside. Stilettos were kept for party nights only, and even then, rarely.

'Oh, I'd better fetch those cupcakes out of the oven. They must be about done,' Jill said distractedly, wondering where she'd dropped her oven mitts.

Rachel stood, watching the woman leave. She lowered her voice: 'She was a bit odd, wasn't she?'

'Who, darling?' Jill looked up. The mitts now in her hands. 'That woman, the one on her way out . . . she kept staring at me from the table. Like a bit too much.'

'Oh, I didn't really catch that. I was too busy keeping an eye on the timer for my cupcakes.'

They stood and watched the woman step through the barn door, dark hair swishing beneath her hat, stiletto heels clip-clopping into the yard.

'Hmm, there's definitely something familiar about her.'

'Oh, do you think she might have been someone official? You know, like Environmental Health or something, undercover?' Jill asked with a crease in her brow. 'Checking us out?'

'Now, there's a thought.' It had definitely seemed like they were being checked out about *something*.

But the council employee theory didn't quite ring true with Rachel. The woman just seemed that bit too glamorous.

'Crikey, I did wash my hands and all that, didn't I? But maybe I should have had my hairnet on, mixing up those cupcakes.' Jill had a moment of panic.

'I wouldn't worry too much, Mum. Who knows why she was here? Might just have been a simple coffee break, after all. I don't suppose we'll ever find out.'

'Well, I hope I'll not get us into trouble.'

They weren't to find out for a while, but the mystery woman did spell trouble, although not quite as either of them might have imagined . . .

17

The following day, after a quick bite of lunch in the Pantry, Rachel headed out to meet Simon and the vet in the yard. It was time for the four-yearly TB testing, and while the vet was in, they were going to get the cows' pregnancies checked at the same time. One by one, the animals began to filter through. There was plenty of mooing and the odd stubborn antic from some of the cows, who Rachel treated gently but firmly, guiding them into position.

'Come on, Ethel it's fine,' Rachel encouraged. Most of her cows had a name, especially the ones who'd been with her for a long time. There was Panda, with her black-and-white patch eyes, as well as Morag, Iona and Flora, to name but a few. Each of them had their own distinct personalities – and Rachel had loved getting to know them over the years.

Rachel's mobile suddenly started ringing. 'Sorry Ethel, bear with me,' Rachel said to the cow who was now in place in the 'crush' and waiting patiently.

Caller ID: Jake. *What the heck did he want now?*

'Hi,' she said, rather tersely.

'Hiya, Rach. How's tricks? How's Maisy?'

Bloody hell, Maisy's dad calling for a little chat was all she needed right now. A yard full of cows, the vet in, and Jake on the bloody phone. His timing, as always, was impeccable!

'She's fine. Look Jake, this really isn't a good time.'

The vet now had his arm right up Ethel's rear end for the pregnancy check and she gave a disgruntled moo.

'Well, yeah, just quickly; we were thinking that we want to come up and see her.'

We? Rachel was confused. But ah, maybe he wanted to visit with his parents, yes, Maisy's grandparents, that would make sense.

'Can I chat to her? Is she about?' Jake asked.

Rachel really needed to get back to the task in hand, though Simon and the vet seemed to be managing fine for now. 'Jake, she's at school.' She resisted the urge to say *Duh*! 'She'll be back in an hour or so. Look, I'll give you a call back later. I've really got to go. We're sorting out cattle and I've got the vet with me.'

'Righto. Well, yeah, call me back. I want to talk to her.'

Rachel gritted her teeth and had to fight the urge to lob the mobile into the farmyard. Bloody Jake, as oblivious as ever.

After they'd hosed down the vet – yes literally – they herded the cattle safely back out to the field for their last week of freedom in the pasture before winter kicked in. Rachel had a quick chat with Simon, went back to the farmhouse to get herself changed, and headed over to the Pantry.

There was Maisy, back from school after being dropped off by Eve, happy as a lark and chatting away to Grandma Jill, who was wrapping up and covering the remaining cakes for the night. There were some customers in too; a couple who were sitting near the log burner, finishing off a pot of tea, and happily spooning away at what looked like a Sticky Toffee Pudding.

'All been okay, Mum?'

'Yes, fine pet. How did you get on?'

'Job done. Fingers crossed on the TB results coming back all clear, but I haven't seen any nasty signs, so I'm feeling hopeful.' This was always a tense time, waiting for the results and hoping to goodness that the dreaded disease hadn't hit their precious cattle herd. 'And,' she continued, 'the good news is that fifteen of our sixteen cows are pregnant. Not sure what happened to poor old Panda this time, but that's a pretty good result. Macduff's still going strong, bless him.'

'Hi, Mummy. Look, we've made some chocolate muffins ready for tomorrow.' Maisy gave a big grin. 'And I'm allowed to take one home for after tea.'

'That sounds good. Did you help ice them?'

'Yes, Grandma put the swirly icing on and I sprinkled them with the chocolatey bits.'

'Lovely. And how was school? Did you do your reading check today?' They'd been practising a lot lately, and Maisy's reading was really coming on.

'Yes, and I'm doing "brilliantly", so Mrs Brown says.'

'Great. Oh . . .' Rachel suddenly remembered her

promise to call Jake back. 'Your daddy phoned a bit earlier; we need to call him back.'

Maisy's face lit up. 'Can we do it now? Do you think he's coming to see me? He said he would soon.' She was still desperate to spend time with him, however lackadaisical he was with her. It touched and burnt Rachel's heart.

'Maybe.' Rachel didn't want to make any promises on his behalf, until she'd ascertained exactly what his plans were.

Her little girl placed the plate of muffins down carefully, then raced across to Rachel to get the phone. 'Come on, ring him then, Mummy.'

'Okay, okay.'

Rachel stepped out towards the barn entrance to get a little privacy.

'Hiya.' He picked up immediately – that was a first.

'Hi, it's me, calling back.'

'Okay, so have you got Maisy there?'

'Yeah, she's here.'

'Great, can I talk with her then?'

Rachel passed the phone over with a feeling of anxiety. Maisy's emotions were something to be toyed with as far as her father was concerned.

'Hello, Daddy!' Maisy sounded so excited.

Rachel could hear her little girl's half of the conversation, chatting about going to Eve's for tea after gym club in the week and making chocolate cupcakes with Grandma for the Pantry. Maisy's voice lifted. 'You're coming to see me . . . soon?'

Maisy was then grinning away shyly, nodding, with the odd 'yes' in reply. Then she offered the phone back to Rachel animatedly. 'Daddy wants to speak to you. He's coming to see me!'

Bloody hell, why did he have to tell her that already and get her all wound up again? It had better not be more false promises. They'd had enough of that back in the summer; there was one nightmare occasion where he had failed to turn up completely and Rachel was always the one who had to pick up the pieces and sort out the emotional mess left by his absence. It wasn't Maisy's fault, bless her, but being let down tended to mess you up, especially when you were only five. There was, in fact, more chance of the real Father Christmas turning up, Rachel thought wryly.

'Hi, it's me again.' Rachel's tone was cool.

'Yeah, so we'll be coming up this weekend.'

'*This* weekend?' So soon. Did he never consider her feelings?

'Yep, why not? Got a couple of days clear. I'm just sorting out a B & B.'

'Oh blimey, okay, I suppose we can work it out.' She didn't really have a lot of choice in the matter by the sounds of it. 'And Jake . . .' She turned away from Maisy, her voice low but emphatic, 'don't you *dare* let her down again.'

'Nah, course not, what do you take me for?'

He sounded far too bloody flippant for her liking.

After finishing the call, Rachel realised she was meant

to be seeing Tom this weekend too. But she really needed to stay around to see how Jake and Maisy got on. She wasn't prepared to let Maisy go waltzing off with her irresponsible prick of a father, without the chance to veto him and his plans. There was no way she could go out for a romantic lunch now; she'd never relax even if she did. Trust Jake to mess up her weekend. So, lunch out was going to have to wait for another day, damn. She was trying her best to make time for her new romance, but life just kept getting in the way. She wasn't looking forward to breaking this particular piece of news to Tom, either.

18

Rachel couldn't get to sleep. It had been an uppity kind of day. It had been busy with the vet, and she knew she'd be anxious until the results on the cattle came through. Dad had been around for the last four-yearly check – what if things had gone wrong on her watch, that she'd been the one to let TB into the farm? Then there had been Jake's bloody call and his imminent arrival no less. And when she'd called him to break the news, Tom had been really disgruntled to find out she was letting him down over the weekend. She hadn't been able to explain everything very well, she knew, and it had come out a bit wrong, and she'd ended up getting frustrated with him for not understanding. But her brain had been mush by that point – and how the hell could you put all that into words? Years of being let down left you on your guard, and she needed to protect her daughter, that was the bottom line. But she hadn't been able to voice that very well. Tom had been disappointed about the cancelled lunch date, and accused her of coming up with a load of excuses for not seeing him. 'Aren't relationships about spending time together?' he'd said accusingly.

The bedroom clock tick-tocked away on the wall and

Rachel could hear the rustling of the trees in the wind outside, the odd hoot of a barn owl. Her eyes were staring fixedly at the ceiling; her mind firmly awake.

But as she lay there, thinking about all the chaotic mess, she came to realise it wasn't Tom she was angry with; what he'd said rang true and what she wanted more than anything was to feel his strong arms around her, to show him how much she needed his patience and his love. Ironically, just to be with him.

Could she go now? Sneak across to the next-door farm? Steal into his bed? She'd have to come back in the early hours, be here at the farm for the morning routine – she didn't want to upset Maisy by being absent; her little girl had enough on her plate to deal with. Mum was here with her now if there were any unexpected problems, and she'd leave a note by Jill's door and another in the kitchen saying where she'd gone – she'd have her phone and could be back in five minutes if need be, but Maisy slept well generally. She lay listening and all was quiet in the house.

Would Tom think she was a little bit crazy turning up out of the blue at eleven thirty at night? But she missed him like an ache, right then. Silly, as he was only a few miles away. Was he lying there, thinking of her too, wishing he could hold her in his arms? Or, was he still cross with her?

Wide awake now, she flung off the covers, slipped on her jeans and a T-shirt, plus a warm fleece. She tiptoed downstairs, grabbed the keys to the Land Rover, started it as quietly as she could and drove slowly away. She didn't put the headlights on until she was halfway down the track; the moonlight was bright and she could see safely enough.

Her heart was beating faster as she got nearer to Tom's farm. The lane was quiet at this time of night, just the glorious sight of a majestic barn owl and its swoop of white wings as it flew from its perch on a fence post and out across the road ahead of her, a safe distance in front of the vehicle. It was beautiful.

She turned at the entrance to Tom's farm, her heart racing a little, and was soon pulling up beside his house. The farmhouse was all in darkness; he must have gone to bed. She felt a little uneasy about her plan now. Would he think her late-night appearance odd, or might he be grumpy at being woken up? This little act was so out of character for her . . . Oh well, she was here now, and there was only one way to find out.

The door was locked when she tried the handle, so she knocked, gently at first. But still there was no sound from upstairs, and no lights going on, not even Mabel barking from her kitchen bed, which was odd. Hah, she'd have to revert to throwing stones at his window – how very *Romeo and Juliet*. She knew which was his bedroom from the rare, wonderful nights she'd spent there.

'Tom, Tom,' she called from beneath his room. Nothing. She aimed a small pebble, launching it but not too hard, hoping to goodness she didn't actually break the glass. Perfect. A direct hit; she'd always been a pretty good shot. Still no movement. Honestly, that man must be sleeping like a log.

Was he actually in there? She felt a slight tightening in her stomach, a weird thought entering her brain. Could he be sleeping somewhere else? But no, not her Tom, there had never been any mention of another woman since his wife left him. *His wife . . .?* She poo-pooed the thought immediately. They'd been separated for ages. She was just being silly. 'Tom!' she shouted louder now, and launched one more pebble.

Come to think of it, where was his pickup? It was usually parked outside.

Well, there was no use freezing her butt off out here. The night air was chilly and Rachel suddenly felt very lonely. She waited another minute. No lights, no sounds. Tom didn't seem to be in, or if he was, he wasn't interested in answering. Her excitement deflated like a popped balloon. Where was he at this time of night? Her fears and uncertainties began to grow and rear their ugly heads. Loving someone left you oh so vulnerable. She decided it was time to go home. Back to her cold, lonely bed.

19

It was Saturday, and Jake's big arrival at Primrose Farm was imminent. As the minutes on the Pantry clock passed tick by tick, Rachel could feel a knot of tension balling up within her. It didn't help that she hadn't yet had chance to quiz Tom as to his whereabouts the other night. In some ways, she was terrified to find out the truth. Was the matter best left alone? Anyhow, there were other pressing concerns right now.

Maisy was all excited, skipping about the barn and then looking in and out of the big doors, just in case. She had insisted on wearing her best dress for the occasion. Apparently, they were going out to the cinema in Berwick-upon-Tweed, and then having some fish and chips somewhere along the coast.

Would he get here on time? Was he still bringing his parents with him? Rachel mused. Jake had said about eleven o'clock, but Jake being Jake . . . A whirl of questions and worries spun in Rachel's head. She was glad when Frank came in to take her mind off things.

'Morning, Frank.'

'Hello, Rachel. And how are you today?'

'Oh, fine, fine,' she lied, keeping a brave face on it.

'Hello, Frank. My daddy's coming to see me today.' Maisy waltzed confidently over to him.

'Well, that's a good thing. And I must say, you are looking very pretty in that frock, young lady.'

'Thank you.' She gave a little curtsey.

Soon afterwards, a navy saloon car pulled up outside – no grey van this time. Out stepped Jake and . . . *what*? From the other side of the car came a rather petite and glamorous-looking young woman. It was hard to tell her age. She had full makeup on and her blonde hair was swept back in a chic ponytail.

'Hi, Rachel.' Jake was smoothing back his dark blonde hair and stretching out his legs a bit. 'That's some journey.'

Rachel found herself still staring at the woman. Who on earth was this, and why was she here? Did this week have any more surprises to throw her way?

'Hi, I'm Chelsea.' She took a step forward, and gave a cool smile. 'Oh, and this must be Maisy. Hello, poppet.'

Maisy ran up to them and then stopped, suddenly unsure of herself and how she should be with them. 'Hi Daddy, hello . . .'

'Chelsea,' the woman repeated her name. 'I'm Daddy's friend.'

Daddy's friend . . . as in *girl*friend? The penny was dropping. And he hadn't thought to say! Rachel began to fume. But the 'we' on the phone, ah yes. Was that all he thought they needed to know? This was a huge leap for Maisy – yet someone else for her little girl to get to know, who'd probably disappear from Jake's life in a nanosecond, never to be seen again. And how would this woman be with Maisy? What if she was unkind, or mean? Had she even had any experience with children?

Maisy quite rightly seemed a little hesitant, hanging back next to Rachel for a second.

Then Jake opened out his arms to her. 'Come here then, give your dad a hug.'

And there she was in his arms, with Chelsea smiling on, playing at happy families already.

'Oh, she's a little sweetie, Jake. Look, she has your eyes too.'

Did she? Rachel was getting riled. She had always thought Maisy looked far more like her, except for the blonde hair. She'd credit Jake with that, but her eyes . . . *really*? They were green, like Rachel's, Jake's were blue-grey.

With that, a clucking of free-range chickens moved in around Chelsea's feet. They seemed fascinated by the sparkly jewels on her bright white – oh yes *white* – trainers. They began merrily pecking at the glittering glass gems on them.

She squealed in panic. 'Get those things off me!' and jumped back, but her feathered friends were in hot pursuit. 'What are they even *doing* here?'

'It's a farm,' Rachel answered coolly, trying to keep the smirk off her lips. 'We keep animals here.'

'Oh, and they smell horrible.' With that, one pooped right on the previously clean white toe of Chelsea's right shoe. She tried to scuff the creature away. 'Jakey! Help me.'

Jake moved in, rather ineffectually, making them flap

and squawk momentarily, and then the birds resettled just a metre away from Chelsea's feet again, their beady eyes trained back on her trainers.

Maisy let out a giggle, and Rachel gave her a little nudge in the ribs. Even though she found it all highly amusing herself, she didn't want them to set off on the wrong foot today.

'Come on then, Maisy, let's get away from here. Are you ready for your day out?' Jake said, already shifting towards the car. 'Do you like the film *Frozen*? We're going to watch the sequel at the cinema.'

'Yesss!' Maisy clapped her hands with glee. 'I love Anna, and Olaf is so cute. I can't wait till we get some real snow so we can make a snowman.'

Rachel frowned. Hah, *really*? That was the film she'd planned on taking Maisy to as a pre-Christmas treat. So, that was *their* special afternoon out scuppered. Grrrr.

'And I bet you like popcorn and ice cream too.' Chelsea had recomposed herself somewhat, despite the chicken shit on her shoe, and reached out a well-manicured hand towards Maisy, showing perfect pink nail varnish. Rachel was sure her own nails probably had some baking dough or mud or possibly animal excrement under them, and certainly hadn't seen any varnish since she was about eighteen.

Maisy was nodding away happily now. 'I love ice cream.' Her little girl walked across and took Chelsea's hand, which felt weirdly like a betrayal, but Rachel quashed the thought. Of course she wanted Maisy to feel comfortable with them, yet she couldn't help feeling all gnarled up inside. You couldn't buy love on one day out with sweets and popcorn. You had to be there for your kids, coping with all the tough stuff, as well as dishing out treats.

'Right, well, we'll be heading off,' Jake said.

'Oh, hang on, you'll need her car seat.' Rachel started to make her way to the Land Rover.

'No need, we've already got one in,' Jake called out. 'It's for Kelvin, Chelsea's lad. He's seven, so we can easily adjust the straps. It'll be fine.'

Rachel stood there, gobsmacked. So, Jake struggles to make one phone call a week to his own daughter and all the while he's playing happy families with someone else's kid? Rachel fumed. Jake had the power to rile her within seconds at the best of times, but he was excelling himself today.

'Are you serious? So, you can play dad to another child and you hardly remember to ring up your own daughter? That sucks, Jake.' She stopped herself before she really started shouting, spotting Maisy looking across at her with confusion all over her face.

At least it meant that Chelsea might have a bit of experience and would know how to look after a child of five, she supposed. Chelsea herself was wisely keeping quiet at this point – and covertly looking over her shoulder for any more roaming chickens.

'Well, have a nice day, petal. Be a good girl, now,' Rachel rallied.

'I will, Mummy. Bye.'

Maisy was smiling once more, and that was how it should be, but boy, was this hard. Rachel's daughter was holding a stranger's hand. She knew she had to let her little girl go; she needed to get to know her daddy and spend time with him.

Rachel looked on as they put Maisy into the car and strapped her in. She had to smile and wave as she watched them drive away, yet all the while her heart was aching.

'All right, love? I know this must hard for you.' Jill was standing at the Pantry door, waiting to see her back in. She placed a caring hand on Rachel's shoulder. 'So, he's turned up with a new girlfriend in tow.'

'Yeah, and it stinks, Mum. She has a little boy that Jake must be helping to look after and yet he's never had time for his own child.'

'Oh, pet . . . Look, why don't you go back over to the house for a little while? I'm fine here, it's not that busy.'

'I think I might, if that's okay.' A little time out was what Rachel needed.

This called for some serious baking. If her head was pounding and her heart was sore, then she needed some baking therapy. In times like this, her go-to was chocolate brownies, comforting to bake and comforting to eat.

She put her country music on – she'd got the country bug from years of listening along with her dad. His favourite was Kenny Rogers' 'Islands in the Stream' and she could picture the two of them now, singing out loud and dancing in this very kitchen. She gave a sigh. Fathers could certainly vary, but she had to concede that at least Maisy was beginning to get to know hers, even with his many flaws and foibles.

Rachel began weighing out ingredients, mixing and stirring. The dark chocolate aroma soon filled the kitchen. She mixed up a double batch, one lot for the Pantry and one to keep for themselves. Brownies would be a lovely treat for Maisy to come home to, she thought. Once they were baked and cooling on the side, Rachel went back over to check on Jill. The Pantry wasn't very full and still didn't need two of them working. Rachel's head started drifting to what Maisy would be doing now. Would she be getting too high on sweets? Would they be patient with her? Listen to her chatter kindly? Know the wriggly, crossed-leg signs when she needed the loo?

Rachel was in need of a friendly ear and took out her mobile. A fellow mother would understand.

'Eve, I'm going nuts here. Maisy's out for the day with her dad and I can't stop worrying about her. She's probably fine and happy somewhere, eating ice cream and goodness knows what, but all I can do is think about her.'

'Oh, hun, that must be so hard. Especially when he hardly knows her, really.'

'Argh, don't remind me.'

'Sorry.'

'And, there's only a new bloody girlfriend on the scene too.'

'Really? Is she with him?'

'Yes, and he hadn't even thought to mention her, or the fact that she was coming.'

'Oh gosh, typical Jake. So, what was she like?'

'She seemed okay, I suppose,' Rachel conceded. 'A bit of a townie. Very glam, just his type, I'd imagine.'

'You were glam once.'

'Hah, thanks, I like the *once*.'

'Well, we've all changed.'

'It's farming life; doesn't merit manicured nails and false lashes really, does it?'

'Nah, not really. Listen, do you wanna come around? Have a glass of something to take the pain away?'

'I have tried baking the pain away. I have just-baked brownies cooling on the side.'

'Your dark chocolate ones?'

'Yep.'

'Well, that's it then, you *must* come around. There's no question about it. I've got two of those mini prosecco bottles in the fridge. They're my emergency rations. Do you fancy one?'

'Well, I think this might class as a bit of an emergency.' Rachel was very tempted. But, should she use the time to call over and see Tom? They'd left things on a bit of a sour note when she'd had to cancel their lunch trip. She could ask where he'd been the other night too. But all she really wanted right now was a friendly ear, and someone who understood the background to her relationship with Jake, and why she was feeling so tense today.

'Come on, get yourself over here.'

'Okay, I'm on my way.'

Rachel called in to let Jill know that she was popping over to see Eve and that she'd be an hour or so. She'd still be back in plenty of time to help out at the Pantry if need be and for Maisy's arrival home – Jake had said it would be around six o'clock.

'That's a great idea,' said Jill, 'And yes, I'm fine here. You go and see Eve. It's no bother at all. Better than two of us strumming our fingers on the counter waiting for the big rush.'

Ten minutes later, the old friends were sitting on stools in Eve's kitchen. Eve popped open the mini bottles, a welcome sound, and poured the golden bubbly into flutes.

'Oh, I *so* need this today.'

'And I need *those*.' Eve pointed to the plate of chocolate brownies that Rachel had brought with her.

'It's just been one of those days. And then, when Miss Glamour Puss turned up, out of the blue . . .'

'Yeah, I bet that was a moment. Hey, did you know that stressed is desserts spelt backwards?'

'Really?' Rachel sat thinking about it, and it was. 'Oh yes, of course!'

'That makes absolute sense, doesn't it?' added Eve. 'When stressed, what you need is dessert, it's simple.'

'Hah, yes,' she said, reaching for a brownie and taking a big chocolatey bite. 'I know I should be happy that

Jake's made the effort to come up and see Maisy, but I can't help but worry about her. It always mixes Maisy up when she sees him again. And then there's this new woman. If it doesn't work out, it's someone Maisy's got to know and maybe like, for nothing. And then, what if it really does work out between them? What if she does stick around? Will they want to see more of Maisy? Make her part of the family there, maybe even try for custody? Oh yes, I didn't mention that part, she has a little boy already so she's used to kids.' It all came pouring out, Rachel's thoughts spiralling dizzyingly.

'Hey, one step at a time, Rach. Slow down. Just breathe. It'll be fine, I'm sure.'

'Oh, Eve, but what if it really came to that? I couldn't bear it. Jake might want me to send her down there for weekends or something, like pass the parcel.'

'Look, I can understand your fears, but aren't you jumping the gun here, Rach? They're just having a day out. He's never been that bothered about having Maisy to stay with him before. So, try not to worry too much about something that might never happen.'

'I know, but that's easier said than done.'

'You've done a brilliant job bringing up Maisy, and then look at Jake's track record. No court in the land would favour him above you.'

'No, I suppose you're right. I'm overreacting, aren't I?'

'Another brownie will help get this into perspective. And I could always open another little bottle of prosecco to share. What do you think?'

'I think you are the best friend ever. Thank you.'

'You, my lovely, are most welcome.'

Rachel sat at the farmhouse kitchen table, tugging at a hangnail on her thumb. The clock was ticking away on the wall mockingly, already showing two minutes past six. She'd completed the farm checks, helped Mum to tidy up the Pantry, and on her way back from Eve's earlier she'd also tried to call and see Tom, her chat with Eve having calmed her somewhat and helped to put things back in perspective. Rachel felt far better able to explain the Jake scenario with Tom and to make an apology for being brusque with him about the lunch date; she might even have found out why he hadn't answered the door that night, but frustratingly he was out. She caught up with his farm help, Jack, who said he'd gone off to the merchants in Alnwick to pick up a tupping harness, as the local store had run out.

The hum of an engine and the crunch of gravel under tyres came from the yard, and Rachel was up and out of her chair like a shot.

Maisy soon burst in through the porch door. 'Mummy! Look, I've got a real Olaf!' She thrust a cuddly toy towards Rachel, with a happy grin. 'Chelsea bought it for me.' She turned to glance coyly at Jake and Chelsea who were following her across the yard.

'Well, that's lovely, isn't it,' Rachel tried her best to keep her tone light. 'And the film was good?'

'There was singing and dancing and snow, and Olaf

was so cute in it. And I had chocolate ice cream *and* popcorn.'

'Brilliant.'

Other than being a little hyper from an overdose of sugary treats, she did seem to have had a good day, thankfully. Rachel managed to smile and to politely ask Jake and his girlfriend if they'd like to come in, despite her inner scowl.

'Ah thanks, Rach, but I think we'd better crack on.' He looked at Chelsea who was nodding vigorously and almost jumping out her skin as Moss padded across the yard. 'Got the B & B to check in to yet. Need to find a nice place for supper too.'

'So, are you back to see Maisy tomorrow?' Rachel knew she had to clarify so Maisy knew what she'd be doing.

'Ah, well the thing is . . .' He looked sheepish. 'Well, me and Chels have plans, actually.'

'Ri-ight.' Evidently plans which didn't involve five-year-old girls. Rachel felt Maisy's disappointment, seeing her daughter's face drop. Bloody typical! No doubt a cosy romantic day for the two of them was on the cards. And she'd given hers up for him and his paternal visit, the twat. So that was it, day trip done, the duty visit and daddy-time was over.

Maisy hugged Chelsea and then Jake at the threshold to the farmhouse before they left, holding on to her daddy extra tight.

'Missing you already,' he called out, as he strolled to the car. 'I'll ring you, Maisy. Like we usually do, yeah.'

Grrrrr, was rolling through Rachel's mind. 'Don't you forget,' Rachel warned, taking her little girl's hand protectively in her own, 'And every week, like you promised.'

'All right, all right, no worries.' He looked irritated by Rachel's comments, swatting them away like flies.

'Bye, Rachel, nice to meet you. You've got a lovely little girl there,' Chelsea added, giving her a small smile. She seemed to have genuinely got on well with Maisy, and Rachel was thankful for that.

The comment brought a lump to her throat. 'Thank you.' Yes, she did, and she had done a damned good job of bringing her up. Jake really had played no part in that.

For the second time that day, Rachel watched the dark blue car drive away down the farm track. And this time she had her daughter's hand safely in her own.

The Sixth Bake of Christmas

Lemon Be-Ro Rich Biscuits and Jill's Biscuit Christmas Tree

Jill's old Be-Ro book (40th Edition) sits tucked in the back of the Baking Bible.

Use the Be-Ro recipe for lemon rich biscuits, or alternatively make a shortbread dough. Cut out into star shaped biscuits of varying sizes, from small to large. You will need at least three different sizes of star cutters, or you can buy sets specially made for this.

Once baked, allow to cool and then ice with either white or green water-icing. Stack into a Christmas tree shape using three large, two medium and two small stars or triangles, or ever-decreasing which you can buy as a set. Use any spare icing to stick them together, making the star points stick out at differing angles. Drizzle with a little extra white icing and decorate with edible silver or coloured balls to replicate Christmas baubles.

20

In the Pudding Pantry the next morning, a far-from-lazy Sunday, Maisy piped up, 'Mummy, *we* need a tree with lights and sparkle and pretty things on. They've got one at school now, in the hall.'

Rachel and Jill hadn't got around to putting up a Christmas tree in the Pantry as yet, though Rachel had been wanting to. Time seemed to be flying, it was already the second week in November, so it really was a good time to up the ante with the festive decorations in the barn. This, she realised, would also be an ideal diversionary activity for Maisy, who was already asking when she'd next see her daddy, and what was he doing today. Soft toy Olaf had gone to bed with her last night, and was sitting on the counter at the Pantry right now.

'That sounds a brilliant idea, Maisy. In fact, I think we should head out this morning and see if we can find the perfect tree. What do you reckon?'

'Yes!' Maisy clapped her hands together with delight.

Having a farm and land of your own meant you didn't have to go out and buy a tree at a garden centre or such like. Oh no, you went out armed with your saw to your very own copse and found a pine tree of the desired height and general look, then you cut it down. It certainly made it much more fun, and it was an annual ritual that Rachel used to love doing with her dad.

After explaining they were about to go on Mission Christmas Tree and checking that Jill was happy to cover the Pantry for a while, the two of them wrapped up warm in coats, hats and scarves, and set off walking in their wellingtons across two fields – Rachel carrying the necessary tools. Moss was happy to be part of the expedition too and the trio headed to the copse on the hill.

It was a crisp, frosty day, with a sky of baby-blue, the grass a little ice-crunchy underfoot and their breath was misting as they strolled. This morning there'd been a thick layer of ice on the water troughs around the farm and Rachel had had to go around cracking it with a heavy stone, so the animals could get a drink. Winter was upon then.

It was the first time Rachel had taken Maisy with her to choose the tree. Last year, Rachel had gone quickly and without much ado on her own to cut down a small fir for their living room, letting Maisy help to decorate it, trying to muster a little Christmas spirit. The year before they were really struggling with the prospect of Christmas and hadn't got around to having a tree at all, with it being the first Christmas after her father's tragic death.

Rachel climbed the fence that enclosed the small wooded area, then lifted Maisy over. Moss managed an agile leap to join them. Then the pair of them stood looking up, scanning the Christmas tree candidates.

'Now, we can't have one that's too big, Maisy. It has to fit in the barn without touching the roof and remember that we also have to be able to pull it home.'

'It has to be a prickly one, doesn't it, Mummy?'

'Yes, they call it a *pine* tree, that's right.'

And prickly was too damned true – the garden centre ones were specially grown so that the needles were much softer on the skin. A wild pine, however, was lethal – as she'd learnt as a child. Rachel had brought her heavy-duty gloves and made sure Maisy had her woollen ones on so they were armed and ready for the mission.

'Hmm . . .' Maisy was contemplating the various trees above them seriously.

'Let's have a little walk about and check carefully, so we get the best one,' suggested Rachel.

Ten minutes later, they'd scoured the small copse. It had a mix of deciduous and pine trees of varying shapes and sizes. Walking and looking up at the same time had made them both a bit giddy, so they paused for a few seconds. Moss lay down by Rachel's feet.

'Soooo, decision time. Which one do you think?' Rachel asked.

Maisy dashed forward, past a small pine tree and pointed at the next one that stood behind it. It was somewhat taller than Rachel had anticipated – the ones they'd taken for the farmhouse in the past had been around seven feet high and this one must be nearer to ten. But, Rachel mused, the barn was tall, and the tree would certainly make an impact. Why not? It would please Maisy to have her first choice.

'Okay, yes. That one looks pretty good.'

On closer inspection, one side was a little bushier than the other, but that was often the case with a natural tree.

'Mummy, does it hurt the tree?' Maisy asked as Rachel got her saw to hand, ready to start cutting.

'No, no, it can't feel it, petal. This one won't be able to live any more, once it's cut down, but we can always plant another one, and sometimes the extra space means the other trees near to it will get more light and air and they will get to grow better.'

'Okay.' She nodded happily, appeased.

'Right then, I need you to stand out of the way, just over here by the fence with Moss.'

Rachel began to saw low down into the trunk, the jaggy needles of the lower branches digging uncomfortably into her face as she worked. The air was filled with the smell of fresh, zingy pine, suddenly reminding her of Christmases past – standing watching her dad fell the tree *she* had chosen, with her excitement mounting at the thought of all the festive decorations and Christmas yet to come. She had never imagined back then that he wouldn't be here with her still.

She took a deep breath of the cold air and made herself concentrate on the task to hand. The sap was sticky on her glove as she gripped the trunk with one hand. After a short while she could feel the trunk begin to give, and she called out to Maisy, 'Stay right there!' There was a little creak as it gave way, and 'Woo hoo! Timber!' called Rachel, then it fell, bouncing with a blast of fresh pine aromas to the ground.

'Yay!' shouted Maisy.

'Okay, so we'll get it back, and we'll need to find a crate or pot to put it in, and then we'll go and fetch all the Christmas decorations and make it pretty.' The decorations were stored up in the loft of the farmhouse somewhere – there'd be a mix of old and new. 'Hmm, maybe we can get Auntie Eve to bring across some of her lovely handmade decorations to put on it to sell at the Pantry, too.'

'Ooh, can Amelia come and help put all the sparkly things on?'

'The tinsel and baubles?'

'Yep, and the twinkly lights.'

'Yes, that sounds a nice idea. I'll give them a call when we get back, see if they want to come over. And we could have hot chocolates in the Pantry with Granny Jill to warm up before we start.'

'Ooh, yes!'

They began their walk back, Rachel dragging the tree behind her making a trail through the frost, with Moss barking at it both animatedly and suspiciously, as though it were something to round up.

'Grandma Jill, Grandma Jill, we've found a good one!' Maisy was shouting excitedly, as she reached the barn door.

'And a big one,' Rachel followed up with a wry smile. Despite being used to heavy manual work on the farm, her arms were aching from dragging the tree back. It seemed to get heavier with every step. She'd abandoned it outside in the yard.

'We're going to ask Amelia to come and help too,' said Maisy.

'To decorate it,' added Rachel by way of explanation.

'Super.'

'And we need hot chocolates to warm up – pretty please.' Maisy gave her most charming smile.

'In you come, then, you're letting out all the warmth.' Jill ushered Maisy through.

'But we need to bring in the tree.'

'We'll leave it outside for now, petal,' said Rachel.

'Oh, but I wanted to show Grandma.'

'Yes, but we need to find something to put it in and fetch all the decorations and the fairy lights yet. It'll be best left outside until then.'

'O-kay. Well let's ring Amelia's mummy straight away.' Maisy was on a mission.

After sipping warming hot chocolates in the Pantry, served Grandma-style with whipped cream and chocolate flakes crumbled on the top, Rachel headed across to the farmhouse to find the Christmas decorations. She knew they were boxed up in the loft, so she got out the stepladders and a torch and made her way up.

After a bit of poking about, there they were, three

slightly dusty, brown cardboard boxes marked 'Christmas' in Dad's handwriting. The lid on one of them was open so she pulled out strands of silver tinsel and found a pack of baubles, and then the ancient angel that used to sit on the top when she was a little girl. She remembered that it had been Granny Ruth's. Yes, Dad used to pop her on his shoulders so she could reach the very top. She trailed her fingertips over his writing on the box.

'Oh, Dad.' He should be here, getting ready for Christmas with them, looking forward to all those special times with his family. Memories made him feel so close, and yet so far away, always out of reach. 'Miss you,' she whispered aloud, feeling that familiar pang in her heart.

Well, this wasn't getting her very far; Maisy would be waiting at the Pantry, no doubt along with Eve and Amelia by now. When she'd phoned a little earlier, Eve had said they'd be delighted to help, and they were going to set off as soon as she'd gathered some of her craft decorations together. Rachel gave an emotional sniff, took a deep breath, and then moved the three boxes to the edge of the large loft hatch. Hmm, it'd be a bit tricky on her own, but if she took it slowly, she should be able to manage the stepladders one box at a time.

She ferried the boxes over to the Pudding Pantry and was delighted to see Eve and Amelia already there, sitting at a table, chatting with Maisy. Eve and Rachel were soon manhandling the rather enormous tree into place in the far corner of the barn, setting it upright into a huge terracotta garden pot full of stones and earth. With a bit of tweaking and pieces of kindling jammed down the trunk on one side, they straightened it and it just about reached the top of the stone wall.

Maisy was already opening up boxes and clapping her hands with glee, pulling out glistening strands of tinsel in silver and gold, and boxes of baubles. Amelia found Granny Ruth's angel for the top, and some silver beads.

'Hold fire, you two, and go gently with all that – some of it's very old and delicate. And before we put anything else on, we need the fairy lights arranged. Let's find them.'

The two girls and their mums dug around in the Pandora's box of Christmas decorations. 'Is this them?' Eve pulled out a green wire strand with little glass bulbs all along that was wrapped around a piece of card.

'Yep, and let's get them tested first, before we pop them on.' Rachel remembered that magic rule from the time when her dad had them strung on the Christmas tree in the living room of the farmhouse, with tinsel, baubles – the full works – and the magical moment of switching on, and . . . nothing. When they had looked closely, a couple of bulbs were smashed and that was it – an unravelling of tinsel and baubles, a trip to the hardware store with a rather grumpy Dad, plus a herd of disgruntled cattle whose hay delivery was late.

Rachel gently unwound the lights and plugged them into a nearby socket. Phew, they lit up with a warm-white glow that gave a gentle twinkle. *Perfect.* She was beginning to get in the festive mood herself.

Frank was now in the barn for his late morning coffee

and sitting watching, delighted with the festivities. 'You're doing a grand job, girls,' he called from his seat, as they began draping festoons of tinsel over prickly branches.

'Thank you, Frank.'

'Cheers. Would you like to join in and help?'

'No thanks, lassies. I'm more than happy sitting here watching the proceedings. Let the little ones have the fun decorating.'

'It'll look a dream once we've finished,' said Eve, holding Granny Ruth's slightly battered but beloved angel carefully.

'It'll be *sooo* pretty, I just know it,' added Maisy, beaming.

Lights and tinsel were now on and glass and glittery baubles were carefully positioned on the outstretched branches, plus a selection of Eve's handmade, grey-painted wooden stars and hearts. The tree was laden by the time the girls had finished. The 'less is more' mantra was not applicable to five-year-olds, with an Aladdin's cave of Christmas decorations to hand, and hey, why not? This Christmas tree was big and bold and beautiful.

They stood back to admire their handiwork. Then Rachel did the grand lighting-up ceremony, counting down, 'Three, two, one!' She was ready at the electric socket and click!

A twinkle of lights, making the baubles and tinsel shimmer even more, were set against the dark green of the pine.

'Wow-ee! I love it,' exclaimed Maisy.

'It's so pretty,' gasped Amelia.

'Hurrah. Fantastic, well done, ladies,' shouted Frank from his seat.

'Well, I think that calls for hot chocolates and cookies.' Jill came across, smiling broadly. 'It looks lovely, girls.'

Moss was lying down just outside of the barn door, looking in, bless him. He was banned from coming in to the Pantry, and knew the drill. But even he gave an excited 'woof' before laying his head back down. He knew if he waited there long enough, Jill might cave in and provide a tasty titbit – a corner of cheese scone was one of his favourites.

There was the tree Maisy had chosen, twinkling away in the far corner of the Pudding Pantry, giving a soft glow to the old stone walls of the barn. Eve brought in more of her crafts from the car and filled the wooden dressers with festive gifts: handmade cards, wooden plaques and coasters, stylish Christmas decorations in silvers, whites and greys, cute felt animals, her knits – chunky jumpers with Rudolph and funny-faced farm animals with Santa hats on. The barn had come alive today in a gorgeously festive way and looked truly wonderful. There was a happy glow amongst the customers there too, as well as the friends who now sat together with their special marshmallow-melted hot chocolates and melt-in-the-mouth choc-chip cookies.

Later that evening, once Rachel had finally managed to settle Maisy – who was back to chattering on about

Daddy Jake and Chelsea his friend – Rachel crashed on the sofa next to the roaring fire in the living room. Jill was nestled in the cosy armchair beside her. Combined with the turmoil of Jake's arrival, today's decorating festivities – though lovely – had brought back so many childhood memories, and Rachel was feeling that familiar ache of loss inside.

'You all right, love?' asked Jill.

Rachel gave a small heartfelt sigh. 'I've just been thinking a lot about Dad again, today,' she admitted, 'what with getting the tree and everything. I used to go and do that with Dad. Oh, Mum, he should still be here with us all. See Maisy growing up . . .'

'I know, love. And yes, of course all those traditions bring back lots of memories, don't they? Watching you go out and get the tree and Maisy's little face so excited about it . . . it caught my heart too. There's not a day goes by that I don't think about your father.'

'I miss him so much, Mum. And – and I feel cross with him too. If only he could have talked to us back then, been able to share the load.'

'I know, pet. But we can't go back and change the past or what happened.'

'No, but it's such a shame and a bloody waste. He was a good farmer, a good man. A *really* good dad. Argh, when I see that waste of space, Jake, who's meant to be a father, it's so obvious my dad was a great dad, up until his last crazy decision. I just want to be able to reach out and hug him.' Rachel brushed away a tear from her cheek. 'Then sometimes I want to shake him and tell him what a silly bugger he was being that day, and ask him what the hell was he thinking? If only we could have told him it'd be all right, that we'd work it out together somehow.' Her voice softened, the words trailed to a close, as the lump in her throat thickened.

There was a tear in Jill's eye as she gently said, 'I know, love, me too.'

'It's extra hard at Christmas time, isn't it?' said Rachel. 'Too many memories.'

Jill gave a sniff. 'Yes, but we need to keep going for Maisy, and make Christmas special for her too. It's very hard, I know that, and we've had two tough Christmases already, but let's put our energies into the here and now, pet. What's done is done. We go forward from here, yeah?'

'Yes, of course. It just gets you sometimes; something happens, or there's a smell, a trigger, and it all comes crashing back down on you.'

'I know, love . . . Hey, do you remember that time when Dad had to dress up as Santa for the kids at the First School and the suit was too tight?'

'Oh yes, I do.' Rachel couldn't help the grin that was quickly spreading across her face. 'Yes, I was there helping out that day. He'd put on a bit of weight since he'd last had that suit on, and when he bent down to get a gift from the bran tub there was loud rip and his underpants were on show.'

'Yes, and I'd kept telling him to throw that old greying

pair away too, and guess which ones he was wearing that day?!'

'Well, I remember Mrs Peters looking mortified, bless her, and the children were all giggling. I seem to remember she had to try and fix it with safety pins.'

'Now that could have been a disaster waiting to happen too!'

Mother and daughter now had tears of laughter mixed with their tears of grief.

'Oh, Dad, you silly man.' Rachel suddenly became serious again. 'Oh . . . are we doing the right thing, Mum, staying here, trying to keep Primrose Farm going? Working all these hours? It doesn't seem to be getting any easier.'

'Will it be any easier anywhere else? The memories aren't just here, pet. They're with you, in your mind, your heart. Can you really imagine living anywhere else?'

'Well, I see Maisy growing up, doing the things I used to do as a kid, like helping me with the sheep and choosing the Christmas tree today, and you know, I can't quite picture her anywhere else. But sometimes it's just so hard and it's as if we're paddling in circles just to keep afloat.'

'Yes, it's been a difficult few months. You're worn out, pet. That's understandable; it's been such a hectic time and you haven't stopped. Even with the Pantry being quiet, you've still been on the go looking to boost business, starting the Pudding Club and all that.' Jill said all this with an air of caution, knowing she was riding near to the mark in telling these home-truths to Rachel.

'Hmm, I suppose,' her daughter agreed reluctantly.

'And, as far as the farm is concerned, I think you already know the answer to that, Rachel love.'

They both gazed at the flickering fire for a short while, lost in their own thoughts. The farm was their everything. It was the only place they ever wanted to call home.

'Well then, I think it might be time to head up to bed.' Rachel yawned.

The two women stood and gave each other a warm hug. As Jill pulled gently away, she said, 'Onwards and upwards, pet.'

'To the moon and back,' Rachel said, remembering the books about the Nutbrown Hare that her dad used to read to her as a little girl and that she read now with Maisy.

Jill nodded, remembering too. She put an arm around her daughter. 'Your dad would be proud of you, our lass.'

21

The next two weeks whizzed by and the second Pudding Club night was suddenly upon them. Remarkably, all of the group had returned, bar one of the young mums whose toddler had fallen ill and needed looking after. And there were also two new members, one of whom was Frank. Having heard how well the first meeting had gone, and encouraged by the fact that there were two other gentlemen in the group, he had decided to come along and give it a try; the other was a certain Vanessa Palmer-Pilkington, notorious village gossip, member of the local Women's Institute, and stirrer-upper extraordinaire.

Rachel had groaned aloud when Jill had told her about taking her booking, but they couldn't exactly say no. It was an open and friendly group, after all. But there was history there – namely an ongoing battle of the bakes, since Rachel's carrot cake had pipped Vanessa's, claiming second prize at the Kirkton Country Show, pushing hers down to third place. The indominable V.P.P. wasn't one to forget that easily.

As club night started, the excitable group was sitting around the big table once again, making their greetings. Vanessa introduced herself as an *experienced* baker, longstanding member of the Kirkton village community, and 'feline entrepreneur'. Jill nearly choked on her tea at that point – she did, in fact, run a small cattery. The two other WI ladies who had come along last time raised their eyebrows exaggeratedly, having heard it all before – *many* times.

Who she was trying to impress, Rachel wasn't sure, as most of the people there knew of her anyway. Mind you, she had sat herself very closely beside Daniel, who – to give him credit – was persevering well with his chirpy manner and friendly chat. Oh my goodness, yes, she was actually batting her eyelids at Daniel now, while Frank was taking his turn to introduce himself to the group, admitting that he wasn't much of a baker but was willing to learn, and was looking forward to the tastings very much.

'Well, thank you, everyone,' Rachel addressed the group. 'That's great. So, tonight as you know is Treacle Tart Thursday.'

'Tart week,' Eve blurted out with a giggle, 'Sorry, I've been waiting to say that all day.'

Rachel grinned, 'Well, yes, tart week it is. And tonight we'll be sampling Jill's Treacle Tart, and I've also made a French-style Lemon Tart for you to try.' She'd been quite pleased with the way it had turned out, actually. She'd never been much of a pastry chef, happier baking cakes and cheesecakes, but with a few tips from Jill, it certainly looked the part. However, the proof of the pudding was in the tasting, as she well knew, and they hadn't cut into it as yet.

'Well then, let's have some teas and coffees first,' offered Jill, 'Let me know who'd like what and I'll get them made. And then it'll be spoons at the ready!'

'Can't wait,' said Charlotte, eyes bulging at the two delicious-looking tarts Rachel had now set down on the table.

'They look amazing,' added Eve.

'Delightful,' said Frank. 'What a way to spend an evening. I'd just be home alone right now, watching something on the television.'

'I'll fetch the jug of cream, ready to go with them, for those who like,' said Rachel.

There were lots of positive comments as Jill's treacle tart was tasted, even Vanessa reluctantly admitted it was 'good'. It was served slightly warm so the filling was meltingly sticky and toffee-treacle scrumptious. Rachel handed the recipe sheet out for those who wanted to try and make it themselves at home.

'Well, I already know how to make a good treacle tart,' Vanessa pronounced. 'It's not exactly rocket science.'

'Oh well, some others here might be glad of the recipe and some baking tips,' Jill said, batting the comment away. 'We're not all *Bake Off* contenders,' she muttered under her breath.

'Hmph,' spluttered Vanessa. 'Oh, by the way, how's your neighbour, Tom?' she turned to ask Rachel pointedly.

'Fine, thanks,' answered Rachel, certain there was something behind this.

'Well, you do know his wife Caitlin's back on the scene.'

What do you mean? burned on Rachel's tongue, but she knew the old bat would be up to no good with her meddling games. Instead, Rachel interjected coolly with, '*Ex*-wife,' to clarify.

Vanessa raised her eyebrows nastily, 'That's what they all say! Yes, I saw her in the village just the other day.' She left the words hanging leadingly.

Maybe that was the woman in the Pantry a few days ago? The one who was staring and acting shifty? She'd quiz Eve and her mum later as to Caitlin's appearance. She really couldn't remember much about her, as it was several years since Tom's wife had left the neighbouring farm. And Rachel was too busy getting on with life and a new baby back then.

She took a deep breath to compose herself. All that quizzing could come later; for now, she needed to concentrate, and next it was the turn of her very own lemon tart.

Slices were plated, spoons raised and mouths filled. Vanessa was the first to launch into commentary, with the others being far too busy enjoying their first mouthful. Actually, the first thing Vanessa did was frown, and then she looked deadly serious as though she was a judge on *Masterchef* or something. The lovely ambience within the group from week one was destroyed as she started. 'Hmm . . .' She jotted something down on her notepad, as though she were scoring it points, low points by the scowl on her face.

There were 'Oohs' and 'Aahs' from the others, and a

'Delicious!' from Daniel, which made Rachel smile, but then Vanessa went into food critique gear, as she began to launch into her verbal missile attack. 'Oh no, no, it's way too sharp. The pastry's not as crisp as it could be, and there's a stodginess about the filling.' She had a nasty glint in her eye as she spoke, which intensified as she saw Rachel's shoulders slump.

'Well, that's a bit harsh,' Frank countered sweetly, bless him. 'I think it's delicious. It's not meant to be too sugary and the cream counterbalances the tartness perfectly.'

'Bloody hell, who does she think she is?' Eve grumbled next to Rachel. 'Greg-Bloody-Wallace? Actually no, he loves a pudding and he'd never be that rude,' she added in a loud whisper. 'Anyway, you can tell she has a sweet tooth from her expansive waistline.'

'I think it's nice to have the variety between the two puddings,' said Kirsty, one of the young mums from last week. 'Some sweet like the treacle and others tart like the lemon. I like it. Not so heavy after a main meal, either.'

'Thanks,' said Rachel, beginning to feel slightly better, after the initial onslaught.

Daniel nodded in support. 'I think it's just right, Rachel. A crisp and short pastry base, nice lemon filling and I really like the addition of the grated lemon rind through it. Lovely.' He took another bite, and then added, 'Perfect, in fact.'

Aw, how lovely that the group had rallied in her defence; Rachel felt a tear brimming in her eye.

Vanessa's pinched face looked far sourer than the lemons in the tart at that point. Before they had chance to chat about other tarts fillings, favourite recipes and suchlike, the old dragon got up to leave. 'Well, this seems to be a place for chit-chat more than serious baking. I thought it was meant to be some kind of Masterclass.' She scowled at Rachel and Jill. 'I haven't learnt anything new or useful at all. I'll not be back.'

There was an audible sigh of relief from the rest of the group as she strode out of the Pantry door.

'Thanks heavens, for that,' said Frank.

'Who on earth was *that*?' Daniel asked Jill, with a grimace.

'What a woman. I've seen her down in the village, I'm sure,' said Kirsty. 'Yes, I remember now, she told off my little boy, Jack, down by the playground in the park for "squawking" too loudly. He was only upset because he'd just fallen over.'

Rachel was shaking her head, still annoyed by Vanessa's stirring about Tom's ex-wife, she was now riled that the woman had been so rude and scathing about her baking. 'No doubt, she'll be spreading the word about my dreadful lemon tart all around the village, tomorrow.' *And spoiling our good reputation*, she added silently. Agh, that woman could really wind her up.

'Hah, and *we'll* spread the word about how delicious it was,' said Eve indignantly. 'And remember, there's nine of us!'

Rachel had to smile at that.

'More tea anyone, and *chit-chat*?!' added Jill brightly, with a mischievous grin.

'Absolutely,' said Daniel, giving Jill a supportive smile.

'Hear, hear,' said Frank, as the others added, 'Yes, please.'

'Anyone for seconds? There's a little more of both tarts left if anyone would like?' Jill offered.

'Marvellous.'

'Oh, yes, please.'

'It'd be rude not to!'

It was wonderful to see that nobody else was in any rush to go, and the ambience had lifted no end with the old bat's departure.

The Pudding Club had been created to help raise some funds for the Pantry business but already Rachel could see that it was becoming far more than that. It was a place for the community to meet up and already there was a sense of belonging. It was a little haven of friendship and a tonic for the soul.

The Seventh Bake of Christmas

Auntie Jean's Treacle Tart

Golden and warming, a gorgeous treat for those autumn and winter months. Auntie Jean, Grandma Isabel's sister, always used to serve it with custard back when Jill was a little girl. Nowadays, Rachel prefers her mum's version served warm with a dollop of vanilla ice cream melting down over it. Perfectly divine!

Recipe:

Shortcrust pastry made with 175g (6oz) flour
50g (2oz) fresh white breadcrumbs
225g (8oz) golden syrup
1 tsp finely grated lemon rind
2 tsp lemon juice
Beaten egg to glaze

On a floured work surface, roll out the pastry. Use to line a 20.5cm (8 inch) pie plate. Trim any surplus pastry from the edges.

Mix the breadcrumbs with syrup, lemon rind and juice. Spread over the pastry to within 2.5cm (1 inch) of the edges. Brush edges with cold water.

Cut remaining pastry into thin strips and arrange in a criss-cross pattern over the treacle filling. Press the strips down well on to the pastry edges. Brush with the beaten egg.

Put the plate onto a baking sheet and bake at 200°C (Gas Mark 6) for 30 minutes until pastry is golden.

Serve with cream, vanilla ice cream or custard.

22

Daniel seemed in no hurry to dash away and stayed for a while at the end of Pudding Club, chatting with Jill and offering to help her wash up the cups and dishes.

'Thank you, that's very kind,' Jill accepted gratefully.

The two of them were chatting amicably as they worked in the kitchen area, and once Rachel had cleared everything from the table, she said, 'Is it all right if I go back across now, Mum? See how Maisy's been with Granny Ruth?'

'Of course, love. We're nearly done here.'

'Thanks, Mum. Night, Daniel, and thanks for staying back to help.'

'It's my pleasure. It's not as though there's anyone waiting at home for me. I'm really enjoying the club, by the way, it's been great. A nice mix of people too, well, *mostly*,' he added with a wink. They knew exactly who he was referring to.

'Aw, thank you.' Rachel was smiling as she left the barn. It had been a good night, despite Vanessa's meddling. And it was lovely to have Daniel on the scene and to see him getting on nicely with Mum.

Granny Ruth had Maisy all tucked up in bed by the time Rachel got back across to the farmhouse, and was eager to know how it had all gone. Rachel filled her in.

'Oh, that sounds wonderful pet. Except for that damned Vanessa woman – she's trouble that one, all right. Though it sounds like she won't be coming back any time soon, and good riddance. So, where's Jill?'

'Ah, just finishing tidying up. She'll be over in a minute. Daniel – you'll remember him from last week – offered to help wash up and they were nearly done when I left.'

'Oh, right.' Granny smiled softly, not making any further comment.

'So, Maisy's been fine?'

'Yes, the little poppet went down lovely for me. No bother at all. We had a bit of a read, and a chat, and that was it. When I looked in on her half an hour ago, she was sleeping soundly.'

'That's great. Thank you, Granny. That's really helped me out tonight. The Pudding Club definitely needs two of us at the helm and I don't want Maisy up too late on school nights, if I can help it.'

'It's no problem at all, pet, any time. And, I was thinking: I'll be making my Christmas puddings soon. I know it was mentioned as an idea last week, so why don't we go ahead with a Christmas Pudding Club for next time. It'd be just the right time to be making them, with "Stir-up Sunday" being in late November. I'd certainly be happy to say a few words and share the recipe for my Whisky and Orange Christmas Pudding.

It'd take some weight off your shoulders if I helped out with a session, too.'

'That sounds a great idea, Granny. Very festive, and I'm sure it would be popular.'

'Well, that's sorted then. I'll dig out my old recipe, and check it over. Then maybe you could type it up on your laptop thingie for me to hand out on the night.'

'Of course, I will.'

'Good, that's settled then.' With that, Ruth's cough came hacking back, wracking her for a few seconds.

'Oh Granny, your cough's still not gone.' Rachel quickly went to fetch her a glass of water. After passing it to her, she rubbed her back to soothe her. 'It's still troubling you?'

'Aye, pet.'

'And did you go to the doctors?' Rachel could imagine her stubborn Granny holding off from doing that.

'In fact, I did.'

Well that was something. 'Good, and?'

'Like I thought, there's nothing much they can do. Didn't want to give me antibiotics and said to take some honey lozenges and keep an eye on it. Honey lozenges! Hah, a drop of whisky in a hot toddy is the best thing. I've been having one each night.'

'Well, whatever works best, I suppose.'

'It certainly helps you sleep.' She gave a cheeky wink.

'Well, as soon as Mum gets back, I'll take you home.' Rachel was aware that Granny would be getting tired and in need of her bed. 'Or you can stay over here if you'd rather; the spare room's always made up for you?'

'I'd rather be back in my own bed, tonight, pet. So, anytime when you and Jill are ready, that'll be grand.'

'Of course.'

Jill was soon back over, with a smile and a spring in her step. 'Well, that went off well, didn't it? Once we saw old V.P.P. off, that is. What a misery, that woman is.'

'Hah, yes, I was telling Granny all about it, before. I was just about to head back and drop her home now that you're here.'

'I'm a bit tired,' Ruth explained.

'She's done a great job with Maisy. Fast asleep in bed.'

'Once a mother, always a mother. I haven't lost the knack.' Ruth smiled.

And it was true, you never stopped being a mother, no matter how old your children were.

Rachel made sure she gave her granny the biggest of hugs as she dropped her off and saw her safely in to her cottage.

'Now, what's all that for?' the old lady asked, surprised by the extra show of affection.

'Just because! Sleep well, Granny. And watch that cough. I'll pop round and see you soon.'

23

A large cardboard box on legs was coming through the Pudding Pantry doors.

'Can you give me a hand here, Rach? Think I've tried to carry too much at once.' The stripy navy-and-white tights below the box belonged to Eve, who seemed to be carrying an absolute mountain of crafts.

'On my way,' Rachel called laughing. She dashed from behind the counter to help take the bulky box and place it on the floor. It was laden with wooden stars, hearts, table decorations and glass baubles, rabbits, foxes, hedgehogs, sheep – all of the soft toy variety, and much more.

'My Christmas crafts for your dresser displays,' Eve announced.

'My, someone has been busy!'

'Too right, I haven't stopped for days – been burning the midnight oil making all these.'

Rachel pulled out the cutest felt black-and-white cow, which had the most gorgeous Christmas pudding jumper on. 'Ah, I adore him. And that jumper! Do you think you could make me a big one. Wouldn't that be ace here at the Pantry in the run up to Christmas – a real Christmas Pudding jumper?'

'Of course I will!'

'I'll pay. I know just how busy you are.'

'Maybe just enough to cover the materials. The rest you can pay in coffee and puddings, that's only fair.'

'Sounds a good deal to me. So, do you have time for a coffee now?'

'Just a quick one, yeah. That'd be great. Then I'll have to get back and make the most of the last couple of free hours before Amelia gets home. I've got a stack of orders to make up by the weekend.'

Rachel set the machine to go and the rich coffee aroma filled the air. 'You know, I'll always have Amelia if you need. You've helped me enough with Maisy over the years.'

'Might well take you up on that some time, hun. Me and Ben are like ships in the night just now. I think he's starting to get a bit cheesed off, in fact. Says I'm a victim of my own success. But whilst the orders keep coming in, then I have to keep making. I can't let anyone down on their Christmas gifts, can I?'

'Well, it's brilliant you're doing so well, but yes, I can understand that'd be hard, and it's not as though anyone else can make them for you. It's your craftmanship that makes them so special. You're so talented, Eve.'

'Thanks.'

Rachel passed her a cup of frothy flat white, no sugar, just as Eve liked. The Pantry was quiet and the two tables in were already served, so Rachel took a few minutes out to sit with her friend.

'And everything okay with you and Tom?'

'Mostly, yeah . . .' Rachel's voice trailed.

'Come on spill, what is it?'

'Again, a bit like you two, we're finding it hard to get time to see each other these past couple of weeks. And he just seems . . . I don't know, a little bit cooler. I can't quite put my finger on it.'

'Ah, don't tell me your loved-up balloon is deflating? You two are the hottest things out. I'm counting on you pair to keep my faith in romance alive.'

'Ah, well . . . real life getting in the way and all that.' Rachel was trying to make light of it, but she was aching inside, wondering if things really were beginning to change between them.

'Actually . . .' Eve started and then stopped herself, as though thinking better of it.

'What?'

'Well, I don't know if this is anything really, but well, there was a car turning into his farm yesterday and the woman driving it seemed familiar – had long dark hair. I knew I'd seen her before. Then it clicked. We went to a BBQ there years ago, in fact I think I was pregnant with Amelia at the time, so there was everyone else on the beers and there was me stone-cold sober. I'm sure the woman was Caitlin.'

Rachel went quiet. Tom's ex. So the rumours were true, she really was about.

'Yeah, so everyone was merry except for me,' Eve continued chattily, 'and Caitlin actually, who had such a sour look on her face all night. But then, I think that wasn't long before they split up.'

'Did she like wearing stilettos?' Rachel asked. The jigsaw was beginning to take shape.

'What? That's a bit of a weird question, Rach. But come to think of it, yeah, I think she did. They always made her look a bit out of place. I mean, who wears stilettos around here?'

Rachel took a sip of coffee, trying to figure out her emotions.

'What? What is it?' Eve sensed her friend's unease.

'I think she must be back. You think you've seen her, old V.P.P. spotted her, and I think she's been here at the Pantry too. There was this woman who came in, acting strangely – I knew she looked really familiar but it was hard to tell with what she was wearing, and I think she might have dyed her hair since I last saw her too. Did Caitlin have family up this way, who she might be visiting?'

'Not that I know of, hun.'

'Hmm, I wonder what she's up to? Why is she going to Tom's farm?'

'No idea. Maybe a little trip down memory lane? Some people manage to stay friends after a break-up.'

Tom had said it had been a very acrimonious split, but had he been telling her the full story? He always seemed to clam up whenever Caitlin was mentioned.

'But what if it's more than that, Eve? They were married for several years, after all.'

'Well, I think you're gonna have to ask Tom that question yourself, hun. He's the only one who can answer it for you.'

Rachel really didn't know how to even start a conversation like that.

'Hey, don't worry. I'm sure there's some innocent explanation. There could be loads of reasons behind it. Or maybe it's just someone who looks like his ex.'

'Hah, that's even worse. A glamorous lookalike on the scene, without the background of breaking his heart.'

'Well, I'm sure you two will be just fine. I've seen the way he looks at you, Rach. There's no denying that. And remember, you're the one he's seeing now.'

'Yes.' Rachel nodded, trying to hide the mound of insecurities that were building inside her.

Just then, a couple with a toddler came in and asked if they had a high chair. Rachel took a deep breath and got up to fetch the one they kept there. Eve said she'd better be off anyhow, and set off with a cheery wave, 'Catch you soon, hun. And remember, I'm here whenever you want to talk, okay?'

'Yeah, thanks Eve, bye.'

Eve might have gone, but the conversation stayed with Rachel, leaving a distinctly uncomfortable aftertaste. If Caitlin had just been visiting, why had Tom not said a word about it? What was he hiding?

The Eighth Bake of Christmas

Granny Ruth's Whisky & Orange Christmas Pudding

This is the sheet typed by Rachel and handed out at the Pudding Club . . .

Recipe:
250g dried mixed fruits
175g ready-to-eat stoned dates, chopped
85g dried cranberries
1tbsp freshly grated root ginger or ½ tsp ground ginger
Grated zest and juice of 1 large orange
100ml/3 ½ fl oz whisky or Grand Marnier
100g butter, room temperature
2 large eggs, beaten
50g self-raising flour
85g fresh white breadcrumbs
1tsp ground cinnamon
85g walnuts

Walnut topping and sauce:
100g butter
100g light muscovado sugar
50g walnuts
50g dried cranberries
1 orange

3tbsp whisky or Grand Marnier

Put the dried fruits, dates, cranberries and ginger in a pan with the orange zest, juice and whisky or Grand Marnier. Warm gently for 10 minutes, stirring occasionally. The mixture should look sticky.

Lightly grease a 1.3l/2 ¼ pint pudding basin, and line base with a disc of greaseproof paper. Beat the butter, sugar, eggs and flour together until light and creamy, then stir in the cooled fruits, breadcrumbs, cinnamon and nuts.

Spoon the mixture into the pudding basin, cover the bowl with greaseproof paper and foil, and tie on securely with a string. (It's also wise to make a string handle or use a long strip of folded foil to put under the basin and up the sides to lift it out with.) Place basin in a large pan and carefully pour in boiling water from a kettle so it comes halfway up the bowl. Cover and steam for 3 hours, topping up the water every now and again.

Leave to cool, and keep in a cool place for at least one week before using.

The sauce can be made up to a day ahead. Melt the butter and sugar together in a pan. Tip in the walnuts and cook, stirring for a minute or two. Add the cranberries, orange juice and whisky, and simmer until bubbling, rich and syrupy. Cool, then chill until needed.

To serve: Steam the pudding for 1 hour to warm through. Warm the walnut sauce. Turn out the pudding, peel the lining paper from top and pile the nuts and cranberries from the sauce on top, spooning over the rest of the sauce. Decorate with holly leaves and a dusting of icing sugar.

A real festive delight!

24

The weeks rolled on in a haze of frantic activity and darkening winter nights. It was time for Pudding Club round three and Granny Ruth was still keen to take the helm this time around. Eve had offered to have Maisy to stay overnight, so the three Swinton ladies could steer the festive proceedings together.

Ruth was ready fifteen minutes before the start time, eager with all her ingredients set out neatly on the counter for her hands-on 'Stir-up Sunday' session (on a Thursday evening, of course, to fit in with the club night.) Rachel had put out yet more posters and flyers, and they'd had a fabulous editorial piece on Primrose Farm and the Pudding Pantry's journey so far – with a special mention of the new Pudding Club and its Christmas Pudding night – in the *Gazette* again, so Rachel and Jill were hoping that there could be a further boost to club numbers.

First to arrive were Denise and Christine, and they'd encouraged two more from the local WI to come along – they'd heard about the antics of a certain Vanessa Palmer-Pilkington at the last session and, now that she was definitely not coming back, thought it an ideal time to join in. They were introduced as Eileen and Judith. Brenda from the Deli had made it along too.

Then a young woman shyly approached the barn door. 'Ah, excuse me, is this the right place for the Pudding Club?'

'Absolutely,' welcomed Jill, 'Come on in. I'm Jill, and what's your name, pet?'

'Alice.'

'That's a pretty name. And do you live nearby?' She hadn't seen her before.

'Just down in Kirkton. We only moved in a few weeks ago.'

'Oh, that's lovely. You'll find it's a friendly little village. And coming along here's a good place to start; it'll give you chance to meet a few people.'

'And eat lots of pudding, of course.' Rachel smiled. 'Hello Alice, nice to meet you. I'm Rachel, Jill's daughter, we run the Pantry together.'

'It's gorgeous in here,' said Alice, as she looked around her.

The wood-burning stove was lit, the Christmas tree was looking gorgeously festive in the far corner, with a string of extra fairy lights now hanging along the top of the refrigerated display counter twinkling away softly.

'Thank you,' answered Rachel, with a warm smile.

'I've always loved baking,' Alice commented, then she seemed to go a little shy again as the two young mums, Hannah and Kirsty, came in through the doors.

'Hiya.'

'Hello, all. We're so looking forward to our Christmas Pudding session.'

Granny Ruth beamed at the head of the table, ready to take control of the evening.

Daniel was next to stroll in. 'Sorry, I know I'm cutting it fine, had to stay a bit late on my shift at the care home. Staff illness.'

'Ah, well at least you made it,' Jill said brightly.

They waited a few more minutes to give anyone else a chance to arrive, but there was no Frank this week, as he'd had a bit of a cold and wasn't feeling like coming out on a chilly evening, saying that he'd buy a Christmas Pudding from them soon. The couple from Alnwick were back; they were looking forward to some Christmas Pudding tips and a bit of inspiration. And Charlotte whizzed in at the end, telling them all about her crazy day at school – she hadn't even managed supper – so it was going to be Christmas pudding for tea for her. Rachel laughed and said she'd make hers an extra-large portion. The group took up their seats, a grand total of twelve. Not bad at all.

Rachel was glad to see the young mums were chatting with Alice. She caught a little of the conversation as she started getting the hot drinks ready, hearing Alice say that she had a baby boy. Kirsty mentioned the local playgroup being good, and it was nice to see Alice being made to feel welcome. It was always difficult being the new one.

After serving out teas and coffees, Rachel stood up at one end of the table and rapped a spoon to get the group's attention. "Okay, well it looks like we're all here. A big warm welcome to the Pudding Club or should I say the Christmas Pudding Club. There are a few newcomers tonight, so if we briefly go around the table and say our names, that'd be great.'

Introductions were made, then Rachel added, 'Well, tonight, I'm handing over to my wonderful Granny Ruth, as she has far more experience in Christmas Pudding making than me, and she has a very special family recipe that she'd like to share with you all.'

There was a small round of applause and Ruth stood proudly at the head of the table, ready to start cooking.

'Well, hello everybody, lovely to see you all. I have to confess I feel a little like Mary Berry standing here with all my ingredients. I've been around a while too, like the fabulous Mary, though I don't think my hair is quite as coiffed or my bakes quite so amazing.'

A ripple of laughter swept through the room.

'I have eaten my fair share of Christmas Puddings in my time,' Ruth continued, 'and this particular one was handed down from my mother with a tweak or two added of my own. I'll go through it step by step, but my granddaughter, Rachel here, has typed up the recipe for you, so you needn't worry about remembering every detail, as you'll have it to take away with you.' Granny smiled. 'Now then, being brought up near to the Scottish Borders, this recipe has a nip or two of whisky through it and a lovely touch of warming orange – ideal for a chilly winter's night.'

'Ooh, sounds lovely,' commented Eileen from the WI.

'Do we get to taste it?' asked Hannah.

'Of course, there's one I made earlier.' Ruth was now in *Blue Peter* presenter mode. 'Well, two in fact. I didn't think you'd want to wait the three hours or so until this one steams, and then wait another week to let the flavours work through.'

'Ooh, great.'

'Can't wait.'

'That's good news; my tummy's rumbling with you just talking about it,' said Charlotte.

'Now then, before we start on the cooking and tasting, I want to tell you a little about the traditions of "Stir-up Sunday".'

Rachel went around topping up everyone's tea and coffee cups, while Granny Ruth chatted away confidently. It was lovely to see the old lady so relaxed in front of the group – she was a natural.

'So, does anyone know how and why it was named?'

'Well, I know it's traditionally the last Sunday before Advent,' said Denise.

'That's right, pet. Our good old home cooks spent the Sunday before Advent stirring up their Christmas Puddings. There's actually a phrase that was used in the Anglican church service on that day: "Stir up, we beseech thee, O lord, the wills of thy faithful people." Well, being busy Mams and all, I reckon the women churchgoers that day were busy planning how to get ahead with their Christmas cooking, and thinking of the never-ending "to do" list we all have this time of year, while they were in church.'

'Hah, yes.'

There were nods of agreement and empathy from around the room; the build-up to Christmas was always a hectic time.

'So, as soon as they left the church, they'd be cracking on with their Christmas preparations and mixing and stirring their figgy puddings and suchlike, so "stir up" stuck in their minds. And Stir-up Sunday it became!'

'Hah, yes. That must have been it,' said Brenda.

'Mind you, if Vanessa was here, Stir-up Sunday might mean something else indeed,' added Denise, obviously fed-up with that dratted woman's antics.

The group were smiling away, smitten with Granny's raconteur style, and more than happy that meddling Vanessa had kept her promise to stay away.

'Now then,' Ruth continued, 'we used to have a tradition at home where everyone in the household would take a turn at stirring the pudding, for a bit of extra luck. Does anyone else do that?'

'Oh yes,' answered Christine. 'My old mam used to do that. I remember standing on a stool to give the mix a stir as a little girl. I still get my granddaughter to do that now, in fact.'

'Aw, that's sweet.'

'And my Nana always insisted that we stir from west to east,' said Pamela, 'to echo the journey made by the wise men.'

'Any other traditions or memories of Christmas pudding making from the group?' asked Ruth.

'Well, we always put a sixpence in the mix,' said Daniel. 'My ma made a lovely pudding.'

'Yes, we did that! It was considered lucky for whoever found it. We do that still, but it's a pound coin nowadays,' added Brenda.

'Hah, we *used* to do that, back in the day when I was little,' said Jill with a chuckle, 'That was until Auntie Hilda choked on it one year. If it wasn't for Uncle Henry and his Heimlich manoeuvre, it might have been a very *unlucky* sixpence indeed! We never put them in after that!'

'Ooh, well we'll have to be careful. Don't want any trips to A & E over Christmas,' said Brenda, pulling a worried face.

'Right, shall we make a start and I'll tell you all the ingredients I have here?' Granny proceeded with her best Mary Berry impression. All the fruit items were listed and tipped into the big bowl, with a generous splash of whisky and the juice and finely grated rind of an orange no less. The mixing bowl was then passed around the table for 'stirring up'. Everyone took a turn, and it was a lovely tradition to be following to make the first ever Pudding Club Christmas Pudding.

There was a conversation about which other alcohols might be used in the mix, the favourite being brandy, with the group interested in tasting how the whisky and orange combination would turn out.

'Well, generally, I like to give these puddings a good few weeks to stand to really enhance all the flavours, but I do have those samples I made last week for you to try in a minute, so it'll give you a good idea on the taste.'

Jill, in the meanwhile, had beaten the butter, sugar, eggs and flour together, and then the fruit mix was added to that, for another stirring session. The smells wafting from the bowl were delicious.

'Just the aroma says Christmas, doesn't it,' said Ruth, sniffing the air.

'This is like "pass the pudding" – I love it,' smiled Alice, who looked very happy within the group, which was heart-warming for Rachel to see.

'Now then, I have my pudding basin ready, greased lightly, with a circle of baking parchment in the bottom, so it doesn't stick.' Granny Ruth took up again. 'Spoon the mixture in, like so, and cover with more greaseproof or baking paper and a layer of foil and then tie that on securely with string.'

'Oh, and my top tip at this point,' added Jill, 'is to make a strip of folded foil that you put under the basin, like so, and bring up around the sides so you can use it as a handle to lift the pudding in and out with.'

'Genius, Jill,' Daniel grinned.

'So, this'll need to steam for around . . . Oh excuse me.' Ruth was then rattled by her tickly cough for a short while. She moved politely away from the group, as Rachel got her a seat and a glass of water.

'Just bear with us a second,' said Jill.

'No worries at all,' said Brenda, speaking for the group.

They all chatted between themselves for a minute or two, until Ruth came back over, with her apologies. 'So, you'll need to steam the pudding for around three hours. Leave to cool, and it'll keep in a fridge or a cool place for up to four weeks, or you can freeze ahead.'

'That's a great recipe, thank you.'

'Oh, hang on, I haven't quite finished yet, there's a walnut sauce to make to go with it.' Ruth went through the method for this, with a nip of whisky, orange juice and cranberries, as well as the delightful walnuts. It all turned into a syrupy sauce, which Jill warmed on the stove in the kitchen area behind the counter. 'This is my own personal tweak, and makes a great topping for the pudding.'

Granny had one of the puds she'd made earlier warming through in another pan. She carefully turned that out to great effect on to a white dish, adding a hearty drizzle of the nutty, fruity sauce, and fresh holly leaves to decorate.

The crowd gave a round of applause.

'Wonderful, Ruth,' said Jill.

'Thank you, Granny, it looks and smells amazing,' said Rachel. 'Are you okay, now?' she added as an aside.

'Of course, pet. Just that silly cough. I'm fine now.'

Spoons and dessert bowls were at the ready for the moment of truth – the tasting. Ruth was holding her breath.

'The proof of the pudding, Granny!' said Rachel, as they were all about to dive in.

There was a second or two of silence, and then lots of 'Mmms' followed by 'Divine.' 'Love the rich fruit and spice flavours.' And a comment from Charlotte, 'Ahh, I'm in pudding heaven right now.'

Ruth grinned widely, looking somewhat relieved. 'Thank you, and thanks for being such a lovely audience.'

'You were a superstar, Granny. I reckon the BBC will soon be on the case looking for a new baking queen.' Rachel grinned.

'Don't be daft, pet.' She batted the idea away, but she was still beaming broadly.

'A natural,' added Daniel warmly.

As the club night came to an end, Daniel and Jill chatted as the group were beginning to gather coats, hats and scarves ready for the journey home.

'Jill has some of her own special Christmas puds on the counter for sale, and I do believe Granny Ruth's Whisky and Orange will soon be featuring in the Pudding Pantry selection too. Thanks for coming everyone, and next time we meet will be the last session before Christmas, so it's all about easy Christmas bakes and cakes, ideal for the family and any last-minute extra guests,' said Rachel to the departing crowd.

'That sounds great, thank you.'

'Lovely night.'

'Brilliant.'

'I'm definitely going to try Granny Ruth's recipe out.'

'See you soon then, everyone.'

There was a scraping of chairs. The barn door opened

and a draught of chill November air came blasting in as the club members drifted out in small groups, still chatting away. The two young mums gave a cheery wave as they left, with Alice by their side, sharing tips on weaning.

'Pureed apple and pear, that was always popular with my two,' Rachel overheard Kirsty saying. 'You can freeze any extra you make too.'

'Thanks, I might start with that soon. He's nearly six months now.'

'Yeah, that's about the right time,' added Hannah.

A new friendship group within the club was forming. It was so lovely to see the Pudding Club putting a smile on people's faces.

Daniel was the last to head off, saying his goodbyes to Ruth and Jill. Rachel spotted a warm smile pass between him and her mum. *Now what was that about?* Rachel couldn't dwell on it for long, preoccupied with seeing people out of the door, but this was something she'd come back to later . . .

Oh, wasn't it lovely to see baking bringing everyone together? The Pudding Club seemed to have just the right ingredients.

25

With the club guests now gone, the three Swinton ladies sat down for a quick breather before tackling the clearing up.

'Granny Ruth, you were a triumph! Thank you so much for helping tonight,' said Rachel.

'Oh, I enjoyed it, pet. What a friendly bunch they all are, too.'

'Yes, it seems to be working out really well,' added Jill. 'I'm so glad you twisted my arm on this idea.' There was a lightness to her tone that hadn't been there for a long time. It seemed to Rachel that the Pudding Club wasn't just a tonic for their guests. 'Would you like to stay over tonight, Ruth, to have a bit of company and save the journey back?' Jill continued.

'Thank you, Jill, but no, I'd rather get back to my own little cottage this evening, if you don't mind. This cough's been niggling and the last thing you need is me spluttering away and keeping you awake all night.'

'We could look after you – we wouldn't mind,' said Rachel.

'Thank you, but I'd rather get myself tucked up in my

own bed with a little tot of whisky. That's as good as anything.'

'I'll take you home then, Ruth, I expect you'll be tired after that marvellous cookery display,' offered Jill.

'Thanks.' Another nasty coughing bout ensued and Ruth gripped the back of a chair to steady herself.

Rachel was really worried about her granny now. This cough didn't seem to be getting any better. Though she was mentally a strong and feisty lady, she *was* in her eighties and her body was understandably getting older and frailer. 'I'd get yourself back to the doctor, if I were you, Granny, if that doesn't start clearing soon. In fact, I'll take you down to the surgery myself.'

'We'll see, we'll see. A good night's sleep will help put me right, lass, that's probably all I need.'

Rachel decided she was going to keep a closer eye on Ruth from now on. There was an independent and stubborn streak among the Swinton ladies and Rachel was determined that Granny wasn't going to adhere to that, above the importance of her health.

With Ruth and Jill out of the door, and Maisy over at Eve's, Rachel, unusually, had the farmhouse to herself. All was quiet, too quiet. She sat for a while at the kitchen table, thinking of Christmas to come, reflecting on the year they'd had, and hoping to goodness she could pull off this Pudding Pantry business venture. Without thinking, she wandered upstairs and found herself standing at the wardrobe in her mum and dad's room.

She opened the heavy wooden doors and rummaged along the rail. There it was. An old, well-worn jumper of Dad's. She pulled it out and took a long, slow sniff. His aftershave still lingered there, just. But more than that it was the smell of him. Dad.

She held the pullover tight, felt its woolly softness against her cheek, then closed her eyes. And the tears flowed . . . She'd been bottling so much up of late. At the best of times, she found it hard to share her emotions; even allowing herself to feel this deeply made her so uncomfortable. Emotions scared her. She was the one who kept things together, who fought for the family and the farm. But every now and then it had to find a way out, and here by herself, just for this short time, she could allow the tears to come.

'I'll do it for you, Dad. We'll show 'em. The farm *will* come good again, *and* the Pudding Pantry. I'll not let Mum and Granny and Maisy down.'

It was a heartfelt promise.

When Jill got back from dropping off Ruth, she seemed a little quiet, as though something was on her mind.

'You okay, Mum?'

'Oh yes, fine pet. It was a good night, wasn't it, and a really nice bunch of people that come along. I really look forward to seeing our club members now.' She looked a little thoughtful and quickly switched the conversation. 'Well, let's hope Ruth can shift that nasty cough of hers. She really isn't herself just now, is she? Though she did a fabulous job taking the helm tonight. She's a natural, a local Mary Berry for sure.'

'The Christmas Pudding Queen,' added Rachel with a grin.

They both chuckled.

26

It was a week later when strange things started to happen.
Jill had taken several orders over the telephone for
Granny Ruth's 'special' Christmas Puddings. She'd been
using Granny's recipe and had made a dozen of the
Whisky and Orange ones since the Pudding Club night,
which had already sold, but there were now orders
coming in thick and fast for them.

That morning, with another batch made, a couple
arrived for coffee and cake, insisting they take home two
of the special Christmas Puddings they'd heard so much
about. Jill thought perhaps it was Pamela and Nigel, the
Pudding Club attendees, who had told them about it, as
they lived in that neck of the woods too. But within a
half hour there were yet more orders coming in on the
phone. Jill decided she'd have to get cracking making a
further batch later that afternoon to try and keep up.

'It's odd, isn't it, all this sudden interest in Ruth's
Christmas Puddings?' Rachel commented.

'Well, we won't complain,' replied Jill.

'Absolutely. But do you think she's been talent spotted
and they've had her doing a cameo on *Saturday Kitchen*
or something?' Rachel jested.

'Who knows, with Ruth – she's always been a bit of a character.'

They gave Granny a quick call late that morning, to see how she was feeling and mentioned what was going on with all the orders. The old lady swore she knew nothing about it; what with her cough, she had hardly left the house since the Pudding Club night.

Oh well, it was all to the good. Perhaps word had got out about how nice they were and maybe it had coincided with people getting organised in time for Christmas, Rachel mused.

A further three calls that afternoon, and that was it, supplies were all out. Now they found themselves taking *future* orders for collection as soon as they were ready.

'It is odd,' Jill said to Rachel that evening, over a production line of dried fruits and whisky and orange zest. 'I'm not sure what's going on, but word has got out about Granny Ruth's Christmas Puddings, and they seem to be the "in" thing. I've not known anything like this from our first few months of trading. Brenda's told me she's even had people calling in at the Deli today, asking for the "award-winning" Christmas Pudding made by Ruth.'

'Maybe it's just a pre-Christmas thing. We haven't had this time of year yet to compare with, have we? Might just be seasonal.' Rachel was trying to reason it out. 'But hey, long may it last. Our takings are *way* up this week.'

'Well, that's brilliant. I just hope I can keep up with all these orders.'

'Here, let me help,' offered Rachel. 'What do you need doing next? Can I weigh out the flour and sugar for you, or something?'

And they worked together, celebrating the six steaming pans of Christmas Puddings in the making with a well-earned cup of tea thereafter.

The root of the mystery came to light the very next day. Frank was in the Pantry as usual, catching up on the week's papers.

'Have you seen this, ladies?' He suddenly shot up out of his seat, with the local *Gazette* still in his hands. 'Look! You've won.' He seemed delighted.

'Won what?' Rachel, standing behind the counter with Jill, was completely baffled.

'The Christmas Pudding Tasting Panel. Here in the paper. Yes, look, Granny Ruth's Whisky and Orange Pudding has come out tops. You've won the award for best Christmas Pudding. Didn't you know?'

'No! No idea, I've not had chance to look at the paper this week. I've been too busy making Christmas Puddings, in fact.' Jill started chuckling, the penny dropping.

'And it's been all go on the farm,' added Rachel. 'Let's see then, hand it over.' She was eager to check this out.

She and Jill laid out the paper on the countertop and peered closely at the newsprint. There was a picture of Granny Ruth's Pudding, all wrapped in Eve's latest design; a holly print material with the Pudding Pantry tags on and red silk ribbon, and then the panel's description:

'Deliciously moist, with zingy orange and a warmth of whisky running through it. Particularly enjoyed the syrupy walnut and cranberry topping. Ideal for Christmas day!' And nine out of ten was awarded (yippee!), the next one was marked as an eight and two more came out at only five and six, one of them being a leading supermarket brand.

'We've only gone and done it!' squealed Rachel. So, the second lot of puddings she had delivered to the *Gazette* recently, as a thank you for their promotion of the Pudding Club, must have inspired the paper to run a competition. A little goodwill had gone a hell of a long way this time.

'Congratulations,' said Frank, with a wide grin. 'Well, I always knew you had something special here. You deserve it.'

'Well, Granny Ruth deserves it,' said Rachel. 'I need to call her up right away. She doesn't know anything about this either.'

'Oh yes, we'll have to let her know. It's her recipe, after all,' agreed Jill.

'Granny, hello. Have you heard?' Rachel was on her mobile straight away, with Frank and Jill listening in.

'Heard what, pet?'

'You've won an award for Best Christmas Pudding in the local *Gazette*.'

'Well, I never,' came Ruth's shocked tones from the phone on loudspeaker. 'Well, my neighbour Jean's just here . . .' There was the sound of footsteps and a door opening. 'Hang on, she says she's called in with a news-paper clipping for me. So, it's all true, then. I can't believe it. What an honour.'

'You're famous, Granny, and so's your Whisky and Orange Christmas Pudding.'

'Maybe I will have my Mary Berry moment after all.'

Rachel could tell her grandmother was grinning away at the other end of the phone.

'And you definitely deserve it.'

Rachel was out in the yard the next morning, collecting the still-warm eggs in her wicker basket, ready for Jill's next round of baking. The air was fresh and cool and there had been a touch of frost on the ground when they woke. Things were looking up, and Rachel had an extra spring in her step as she carried the eggs carefully back to the kitchen. Mind you, there were only about two dozen here – the hens would never keep up with the amount of pudding orders they were getting. They'd have to start buying some extra ones in at this rate. But it was a very good problem to be having.

The next few days were a whirlwind of Christmas Pudding orders, and there were several new customers calling in at Primrose Farm for tea and cakes, to see what this 'award-winning' Pudding Pantry was all about. Business had never been so good. To keep up with demand, Rachel and Jill were baking every night till the late hours. On the down side, it had meant that Rachel had hardly had chance to catch up with Tom lately. They'd had a few snatched phone calls and a brief hello over his elevenses the day before yesterday. But she suddenly realised that she hadn't seen him since, and that was unusual. She didn't have time to dwell on it, but it made her feel a little churned up somewhere deep inside.

Granny had offered to come in and help with the pudding production line too, if need be, but Rachel had heard her coughing over the phone and told her they were managing fine. It sounded as if Ruth still needed some rest and a bit of TLC. Rachel promised she'd pop by with some soup, fresh ham and eggs, and a pudding from the Pantry as soon as she got chance. As well as making sure her grandmother had some hearty food to hand, she wanted to see for herself how the old lady really was. The pudding success was brilliant – but Ruth's good health was the most important thing.

27

Rachel was determined to give the Pudding Pantry every chance of success, so even with the upturn in trade from Granny's Christmas Puddings there was still no resting on their laurels. Before the flurry of extra orders had started, she'd managed to get a stand next to Eve's at the Claverham Castle Christmas Craft Fayre, and she was really looking forward to it.

The Land Rover, laden with puddings, arrived at the huge wrought-iron entrance gates of the castle. Even though the castle was located in the countryside just six miles away from Primrose Farm, she had never actually stepped inside.

Tom – who she'd managed to finally speak to, albeit briefly, the night before – had offered to bring Maisy along later, as she was singing carols with the Kirkton First School Choir here this afternoon. It would have been a very long day for her, otherwise. She was to stay the morning with Grandma Jill, plus Jill's friend Jan, and Granny Ruth, who had insisted on helping at the Pantry despite her niggly cough.

Rachel still hadn't broached the enigma of Caitlin's apparent return with Tom. Life was busy and complicated enough right now. She was also waiting for the right moment, and a snatched hello in a phone call, or over an elevenses cup of coffee in the Pantry was not the time or the place.

So today, puddings were on the brain once again. Rachel's boot was filled with Christmas Puddings, Sticky Toffee Puddings, Sticky Chocolates and Ginger. They'd decided to keep the selection simple and festive. All the cartons were wrapped in Christmas-inspired material, with a bold holly pattern on the Christmas puds, and angels, stars and snowflakes on the others, along with pretty ribbon ties and tags – all thanks to talented Eve, and a production line with Jill, Maisy and Rachel packaging them up yesterday evening.

The castle's grand driveway was undeniably awe-inspiring as Rachel drove on through. Tall, grey-gnarled trees lined each side of a wide, gravelled road. She felt a bit like royalty driving in. She had heard that kings had stayed there in the distant past. Mind you, she reminded herself, she was here in more of a serving capacity. As she reached the castle itself, she saw a huge grey-blonde stone building, five stories high, with crenulations and towers – the works! – and there were several cars and vans parked in the half-moon-shaped arrival area. The place was already buzzing with activity, with stallholders ferrying goods up the old stone steps like little ants, in and out with boxes, bags, gifts, crafts . . .

Rachel parked and thought she'd get her bearings and

find out where her stall was before starting to move her puddings. She walked up the castle steps, past a flaming torch propped on the wall like something out of *Game of Thrones*, and continued in through the huge, solid wooden door. She stumbled on an entrance passage before coming out into a large, stone-flagged courtyard, with stone steps that made their way up to the main interior of the castle. A woman was working away, intent on her task, busy weaving ivy, pine and holly branches along the balustrades. Rachel realised she knew her; it was Wendy from the florists in Kirkton.

'Oh, hi, Wendy, look at all this, it's incredible.'

'Rachel, hi. Have you got a stall here today?'

'Yes, they've managed to squeeze the Pudding Pantry in at the last minute.'

'Well done. Should be busy; last year's event was a big success.'

'Sounds promising. Well, I'll not keep you. That floral weave looks beautiful.'

'Thank you.'

Rachel then gazed up at the castle walls, the evidently once-grand steps. It made you wonder who had walked those same steps in years gone by. Who had lived there, loved there, centuries ago? Well, this country pad was *way* bigger than Primrose Farm and would certainly take a bit of looking after – but what a legacy it'd be.

'Stunning, isn't it.' A tall dark-haired man, who looked to be in his early thirties, appeared at her shoulder. 'I'm Joe, by the way.'

'Hi, sorry, I was in a little world of my own there, for a minute.'

'Come on up. I imagine you're here for the Craft Fayre, yes?'

'Yes.' She followed him up the main steps.

'You're doing a great job, as always, Wendy, thanks,' Joe added, with a smile.

Rachel followed Joe inside the castle. 'This is the Great Hall, where the main action is today. You'll find all the stalls are in here. Now bear with me, I'm sure Ellie will be around here somewhere and she'll be able to put you right.' He glanced around him.

Rachel, in turn, looked around the hall they were in. It was a gorgeous and extremely large stone-walled room with two massive fireplaces, and a long mahogany table that ran down its middle, laid out with mediaeval-looking pewter candelabras and ivy-and-holly entwined festive table decorations. In one corner of the room was a huge pine tree, which made the Pantry's one look miniscule.

Two gentlemen were orchestrating the tree decorating. 'Malcolm, no . . . just a little more to my left. *Left* . . . that's my right. Okay, stop, stop.' The gentleman up high in a cherry picker managed to place a large silver star right at the top. 'That's perfect. Bellissima, darling, thank you.'

Around the edge of the hall, stalls were already taking shape, with everyone setting out their wares. There were jams and chutneys, woodworking, a cake stall from the Castle Tea Rooms, Christmas cards and wrap, scented candles. It was all go.

Rachel was feeling a little nervous. Would anyone want to come to *her* stall? Everything looked so impressive. As yet, there was no sign of Eve. They were to have adjoining stalls, as far as Rachel was aware. She could do with the familiar sight of her friend right now.

'Oh, Ellie, over here,' Joe called out. 'I've found a waif and stray out in the courtyard. Sorry, I didn't catch your name . . .?'

'It's Rachel – from the Pudding Pantry.'

'Oh, hi Rachel.' Ellie came striding over and extended her hand, giving a warm smile. She was tall with a mass of thick, dark-blonde hair, which was pulled back into a loose ponytail, the odd tendril escaping prettily. 'Lovely to meet a fellow baker, and I've heard all about these award-winning Christmas puddings. I must get one to try. I run the Castle Tea Shop, so I love a bit of baking myself. It's been all go, mind, this past week, getting enough made for the tea rooms and this Fayre.'

'Tell me about it.' Rachel grinned. 'Our poor old Aga's been groaning under the strain of constant pudding steaming and baking for the last two weeks.' Rachel had also been quite concerned that the farmhouse's cooker was going to give up on them altogether at one stage. Now, that would have been a disaster.

'Hah, I bet. Well, I have your place ready over here, just near the window, so if you'd like to follow me . . .'

They walked across to a row of tables that were set alongside latticed-windows, overlooking the rear castle gardens.

'So, this is you, next to Eve's Cottage Crafts.'

'That's great, thanks. Eve's a close friend, so that works well.'

'Ah, lovely. Well, if there's anything else you need just find me, or Joe – my husband – who you met as you came in. I have a million and one things still to do before we officially open at eleven, so I'll have to dash. I hope you have a really good day.'

'Thank you, and you too.'

Wow, what a setting for a Christmas Fayre. A real mediaeval castle hall with old tapestries, pewter cups, huge white candles entwined with ivy. Oh, and look, there was a Santa's grotto being set up, all red tarpaulin and fuzzy-white fake snow, with a large wooden reindeer standing beside it. Joe was there, busy moving the wooden barrels of wrapped gifts into place, with a little toddler-sized helper now alongside him by the looks of it. 'Hang on, Jack, you can't open them yet, mate!' His voice carried across the hall, as the toddler was obviously about to help himself. Aw, Maisy would love that when she got here later.

She and Amelia were both coming to sing 'Carols in the Courtyard' with the Kirkton School choir here at three and, after some initial apprehension, Rachel was starting to look forward to the day. It would be good to catch up with Tom for a while later, too. They'd been too distant of late.

Right, she'd better get out to the Land Rover and get her puddings in and her stall ready. As she headed towards the main entrance doors, catching gorgeous festive smells of pine and cinnamon on the way, she spotted Eve coming in, laden with various cardboard boxes and bags.

'Over here,' Rachel called across. 'Hang on, I'll come and help.'

She took a large box from Eve, before it toppled out of her friend's hands.

'Oops, think I've overloaded myself, thanks. Ooh, wow, it looks wonderful in here. Glad we booked up this one.' Eve propped her various goods and boxes down on the tabletop, and looked around her. 'I feel like I've been transported back in time.'

'I know, isn't it fabulous?'

'Definitely. It was Emma from the Chocolate Shop – we met her at the Kirkton Show back in the summer – who told me to try here. She has a stall today too. She's been doing this Fayre for a couple of years now, said it was a popular one.'

'Oh fab, and yes, I remember her, she was lovely.'

They helped each other to unload and set up, and soon both stalls were ready. Eve's crafts looked delightful with her wooden decorations resting on mini-tree stands that she'd made herself and sprayed with shimmering white paint. There was a terrific selection of her toys, festive knits, table decorations, picture frames, plaques, coasters and more. The midnight oil must have well and truly been burned again for Eve.

'Your stall looks stunning, Eve, like a Christmas fairy-tale tableau.'

'Aw, thanks, hun. And yours, my love, is a Christmas platter of pudding perfection!'

Rachel made her way down to the 'Teashop in the Castle' to grab a couple of coffees – a caffeine hit was much needed after this morning's early start.

'Well, best of luck, hun.' The two friends pretend-clinked their takeaway paper cups.

Rachel glanced at her watch. 'Doors open in half an hour.'

'Yes, not long now. Ooh look, there's Emma and her gorgeous chocolate stall across the way. I might have to nip and get a few bits for my mum's Christmas parcel.' Eve went over and was soon chatting animatedly. Emma then waved at Rachel, who headed across.

'Hi, there, Emma. Isn't it amazing here? What a cool place,' said Rachel as she joined them. 'Thanks so much for giving us the nod.'

'Oh my, look at all these divine chocs, Rach.' Eve was practically drooling.

The rich smell of cocoa drifted from the stall, which was laid out so prettily with gold and silver boxes and ribbon-tied bags of chocolates and fudge. Rachel couldn't resist choosing some treats for Jill and Granny Ruth, and some white chocolate stars that would be ideal for Maisy's Christmas stocking.

'Well, have a good day both of you,' said Emma, handing them their chocolate gifts. 'Here's to lots of sales and success!' She grinned and they made their way back to their own stalls with a little trepidation. After all the hours of baking and crafting, they both hoped this event would prove to be worthwhile and give their fledgling businesses the boost they needed.

They needn't have worried; customers flowed in from eleven o'clock and both Rachel and Eve made several sales straight away – result! The next few hours flew by. A constant stream of visitors came through, lots of them asking for Granny Ruth's famous Christmas Puddings, and checking that they *were* the ones mentioned in the local paper. The other flavours were proving popular too and Rachel was very glad they'd gone all out this past week with the extra baking.

Eve seemed to be doing equally well with her crafts, which was brilliant. The ten-pound notes were building up nicely in the cash tin and the stack of puddings was going down. With the takings flowing nicely, Rachel began to feel hopeful that she might be able to get Maisy some nice Christmas gifts after all.

Tom arrived at the Fayre after lunch time with Maisy. Her little girl came bounding across the hall to give Rachel a hug.

'Hi, petal. All ready for your singing later? You look very smart in your uniform, I must say.'

'Yes, Mummy.'

'Hello, Tom.' Rachel looked up, finding herself feeling a little awkward. Concerns over Caitlin's reappearance were still fresh in her mind, and their lack of time together of late seemed to have placed a distance between them. 'Thanks for bringing Maisy across,' she added, aware she was sounding far too polite.

'It's no problem.'

A customer then nudged in front of Tom to muscle in on one of Ruth's Christmas Puddings.

'We'll just go and take a look about.' Tom moved out of the way, reaching to take Maisy's hand in his own. 'It was three o'clock for the carol singing wasn't it?' he checked. 'I'll be sure to get her to the group well before then.' He glanced down at the little girl. 'Don't want you to miss your moment, do we, Maisy?'

'No way. We have been practising at school all week. Can we go look at the big tree, Tom?'

'Of course, that's our next stop.'

'Thank you.' Rachel managed a smile, then turned to serve the next customer.

She looked up, wishing they hadn't had to dash away, and then began to lose sight of them in the crowd. She hoped so much that she'd got this wrong about Caitlin, whatever it might be.

A busy spell followed on the stall, and Rachel had to focus on the task in hand. Keeping her smile up, chatting with everyone about the various pudding flavours, and offering a little taster plate for people to try. With fab friend Eve calling across, now and again, 'I can vouch for them, they're utterly delicious!' if anyone seemed to be dithering about buying. Forty-five minutes later, Tom reappeared with Maisy who was beaming as she held up a rather gaudy plastic doll. 'Look what I've got from the Grotto, Mummy! Father Christmas let me choose it.'

'Ah, very good.'

'Yep, we've been to see good old Father Christmas,' confirmed Tom. 'He was a bit gruff and grumpy, I must say,' he whispered to Rachel, then more loudly, 'You enjoyed it, didn't you, Maisy?'

'Yes, he's going to be a very busy man soon. Got the whole wide world to do,' Maisy chirped.

Rachel smiled and gave Maisy a little pocket money to go and choose something from the stalls and off the pair of them went again, Maisy weaving her hand through Tom's. It was lovely to see her little girl and Tom getting on so well. Her mind inevitably drifted back to the circling rumours of Caitlin's reappearance in the village . . . she so hoped that it was nothing to worry about.

It was starting to get dusky and chillier outside in the courtyard, and the carol singing was due to begin so Tom came back into the hall to warn Eve and Rachel.

'Go on you two, get yourselves outside quickly, they're nearly ready. I'll keep an eye on the stalls for you. Go and watch your girls.'

'Are you sure, Tom?' asked Rachel.

'Absolutely, and I'll see if I can charm a few more sales for you.' He gave a wink, as the two ladies gathered themselves swiftly, popped their coats on, and nipped away.

As they stepped out into the darkening grounds, with flame torches lit on each side of the courtyard, it looked so magical. The girls and boys were gathered ready, all excited. Maisy and Amelia stood side by side, looking so smart in their uniforms. Their hair had been brushed and tied back with a festive addition of silver-sparkly tinsel wrapped around their ponytails.

They found a good vantage point to watch from and Maisy caught Rachel's eye and waved across with a big grin on her face, just as the chords of an old piano started up. As 'Away in a Manger' started, Rachel felt a proud surge of maternal love and a tear caught in her eye. The sweet young voices filled the frosty air. This was what Christmas Carol singing was all about, festive and magical. They followed that with 'While Shepherds Watched' and rounded off with a rousing 'We Wish you A Merry Christmas' to great applause. Mrs Brown and the children took a little bow at the finale, before the classmates were allowed to go back to their families.

'That was wonderful, Maisy . . . and Amelia. Well done the pair of you.' Rachel's voice was warm with emotion.

'The singing was beautiful,' added Eve. Rachel wasn't the only one feeling a little choked, she spotted the glint of a proud tear in Eve's eye.

'Shall we head up to see if there's any cupcakes left on my stall, then girls? Or do you think Tom's sold the lot, by now?'

Back in the hall the crowds were thinning as the customers started to drift away, and the stallholders began to pack up. The girls found a cupcake each from the dwindling supplies and sat behind the stall on plastic chairs, munching away, looking a little jaded now that the excitement of the day had passed. Rachel thanked Tom, wishing they had time to *really* chat, but there was still so much to do.

Emma caught Rachel's eye and gave a big thumbs-up from across the way, so it must have been a successful day for her chocolate stall too. One or two more puddings were sold, but the hall soon began to empty out and Joe came by each stall to thank everyone for attending.

Soon the Land Rover was loaded with the table stand, plus Eve's 'Pudding Pantry' sign that her friend had created for the Kirkton Show, and the almost-empty cool boxes with just a few puddings left, and not a single one of Granny Ruth's; in fact, Rachel had taken orders for four more to be collected from the Pantry on Christmas Eve, as they'd quickly sold out.

Trying to stifle her yawns, Rachel drove the few miles home along the country lanes, following Tom's truck with Maisy in. She was feeling tired but happy. She couldn't wait to tell her mum about their successful day and all about the stunning castle at Claverham. And despite the tight knot of anxiety in her stomach, she also couldn't wait to catch a few minutes alone with Tom. She needed to put a stop to all the questions running riot in her head – even if the answers were ones she couldn't bear to hear.

28

'Granny Ruth, Granny Ruth!' The next morning, Rachel was straight round to her granny's little cottage; she'd held her promise to keep a close eye on her. She couldn't deny that she was worried. She stood for a few minutes, knocking repeatedly and calling out, but there was no answer.

Rachel started to feel very uneasy now.

The cottage was unlocked, so she went on in. The house seemed unusually quiet. There was often the hum of the radio on or the television, or perhaps the kettle boiling ready in the kitchen. But today all was eerily still.

'Granny?' Rachel called again, and she checked the downstairs rooms just in case. There was no sign of her grandmother in the living room or kitchen. Had she gone out and left the door open? It wasn't unheard of. Rachel climbed the narrow stairs, her concern mounting with each step.

'Granny Ruth?'

'Here, lass,' came a frail, gravelly voice from Ruth's bedroom.

Finally, thank goodness. Rachel relaxed a little, though from the sound of her voice, Ruth didn't sound that well.

Rachel poked her head around the bedroom door and there was her grandmother all tucked up in her double bed, which was unheard of at ten o'clock in the morning. Ruth was always up with the lark, despite her age. Her favourite response to questions about that being, 'What do I want to be lying around in bed for? Life's short enough as it is when you get to my age so I'm not going to waste it.'

'Are you all right, Granny?'

'Aye, just a bit tired this morning, pet.'

She looked awfully pale and frail there lying under the duvet, with one arm resting on the top, the so-thin skin showing the blue veins beneath. Rachel was floored for a second; this strong feisty old lady, who always seemed so resilient, was today showing all of her eighty-one years. Had she been doing too much, trying to help them out yesterday at the Pantry? They should have realised, Rachel felt awful.

'I did try and get up, made myself a cup of tea, but—' Ruth was suddenly wracked with that nasty cough. She pulled a tissue away from her mouth and Rachel spotted some blood in the mucus.

'Oh, Granny!' She leaned over and gently tested the temperature of Ruth's forehead with her palm. It was boiling hot and felt very clammy. Rachel was now definitely not prepared to take any risks; this had gone on too long already. The doctors' surgery in Kirkton would be closed with it being a Sunday, so she decided to take her directly to A & E. 'You've a temperature. There's blood coming up too, so at the least it's a chest infection. You're not well at all, Granny. Enough's enough. We're getting you checked out in a hospital.'

'I'm all right. There's no need to fuss, pet.'

But with that, Ruth was taken by another coughing fit.

'You are not all right at all. I'll fetch you some paracetamol to get that temperature down a bit then we're going to get you dressed, and I'm driving you to hospital right away – no ifs or buts.'

'Oh, pet, no!' But she knew the game was up, that her granddaughter was right.

'Come on, let me help you, Granny.'

Rachel had her dressed and down in the Land Rover within fifteen minutes. She phoned Jill to briefly explain what was happening as they headed for the Borders General Hospital. On the fifty-minute journey, Rachel chatted away to keep Granny occupied – about Maisy and the farm and the Pantry, and of course Ruth's award-winning Christmas Pudding stealing the show at the Christmas Fayre yesterday – which drew a smile from the old lady. Ruth dozed part of the way and seemed forgetful and not herself at all. She twice asked where they were going, bless her.

After a two-hour wait in A & E and eventually being taken for X-rays, Granny Ruth was tucked up in a bed with crisp white sheets on the women's ward. She looked even frailer in this alien and clinical environment.

'Maybe I did leave it a bit long, pet,' she conceded.

'I'm sorry.' She began coughing up the mucus and blood once more. Rachel rubbed her back as the old lady arched over, trying to ease her pain. Her cough sounded so raw and uncomfortable.

'Well, you're in the right place now. They can get you sorted out. You'll be just fine.'

There had been mention of pneumonia, and they were waiting for a consultant to get the final analysis from the blood tests and X-ray.

'Aye, well, I've had my life, pet. And, despite the troubles these past two years, on the whole, it's been a good one. If this is my turn . . . well, much as I'll be so very sad to leave you all, I'm not going to live forever.' Ruth was propped up, looking awfully pale even against the white hospital pillows.

'Now don't you go talking like that, Granny. Getting all morbid on me. Of course you're going to get better! You'll live to a hundred.' Rachel was clasping her granny's hand fast. She looked so damned frail there.

'I just feel so tired right now, pet. And, come now, Rachel, that's nature's way, and well you know it, lass. As farming folk, we see it all the time. Death follows life . . . spring, summer, autumn and winter. It's just the way of the world.'

Rachel found that she couldn't speak. She couldn't imagine a world without Granny Ruth and her wise counsel in it. The old lady was just feeling weak. They'd soon fix her up, get some antibiotics pumped in to her.

'Crikey,' the old lady continued, 'I'm stiff enough in

the mornings as it is, if I live even another ten years I'll be creaking, or I'll have seized up altogether.' She managed a cough-filled chuckle. 'You've got the farm now, you and Jill and Maisy – and despite everything that happened with your dad, I know you'll do a grand job of taking it forward, lass.' She managed a gentle pat on Rachel's arm. 'You *are* already. And you'll soon be teaching young Maisy how to farm – if that's what she wants, mind; you never know, she might turn out to be an astronaut yet.'

They both smiled at that.

'And then *you'll* be watching her set off in to space,' Rachel took up. 'Please, Granny, don't talk like this any more.' Rachel couldn't contemplate losing her granny yet. It was way too soon.

'Just let me finish what I need to say, pet, just in case . . . Look, I'm proud of you. I know you'll do what you can to keep it all going because Primrose Farm has a special place in all our hearts.' Ruth's eyes looked distant yet warm, as thoughts of happier days filtered through her mind, memories of her life there with Rachel's grandad and dad.

'It is a special place, Granny, and I will do everything I can to keep the farm, of course I will. But you're not going anywhere just yet, not if I can help it. We need you back there to help with all those Christmas Puddings. There's a zillion new orders since that Craft Fayre at the castle.' Rachel knew Granny liked to be useful, to have a role to fill, maybe knowing this would help her recovery.

'Who else is going to keep us on the right track with your Whisky and Orange Pudding?'

'Aye, well there is that, pet.'

'And we *absolutely* need you home and well in time for Christmas day.'

'Well, I wouldn't mind one more Christmas, to see Maisy opening her gifts and everything.' Ruth was suddenly wracked with another coughing bout. Rachel held the hospital's grey cardboard sick bowl in front of her, just in case, until the bout passed and then handed her granny a plastic cup of water to sip.

'Well then, that's settled. You just *have* to get better, Granny. There's nothing else for it,' Rachel said, trying to smile through misty eyes.

29

Jill had arrived at the hospital by the time the consultant came round. Tom, who'd kindly brought her across, politely said he'd nip outside for a breath of air at that point. Good friend Eve had stepped in and offered to look after Maisy while they were all away.

The consultant, Mr Andrews, approached Ruth's bed. 'So, Mrs Swinton, that cough of yours has taken quite a grip. It is pneumonia, I'm afraid. So, we're going to put you on some strong antibiotics, and we'll keep you in at least overnight and see how you're getting on. Okay?'

'Yes, that's fine, doctor.' Ruth began spluttering once again; just talking seemed to set it off. 'Oh my,' she said when she'd gathered her breath, 'will this darned cough ease?'

'In time, yes, the antibiotics should help, but it may take a couple of weeks to settle.'

'Oh, I see,' she answered stoically, resting back on her pillows.

Rachel knew that pneumonia in the elderly could be dangerous, but didn't want to alarm Granny any further. Once the doctor had had a bit more of a chat and answered the couple of questions Jill and Ruth had, he left their cubicle but Rachel nipped out after him, wanting to have a word out of Ruth's earshot. 'Excuse me, Mr Andrews, just how serious is it? Can the pneumonia be life-threatening for someone of my granny's age?' She needed to know what they were dealing with, what they might yet have to face.

'It can be, yes.' He looked serious for a second, and rubbed his grey-bearded chin. 'But, if we can get her fever right down and the antibiotics really kick in, well, then I believe she should make a good recovery, though her lungs could be a little weaker in the future. But let's see how she gets on overnight, shall we?'

'Yes – and thank you.'

The lights suddenly seemed too bright. The air too stuffy. Granny had Mum with her for company, so a breath of fresh air and a glimpse outside called Rachel. The hospital was such a clinical environment, way out of Rachel's comfort zone – no one in the family had ever been really ill. Up until the end, ironically, Robert had never had a day sick in his too-short life.

As she reached daylight and the grassy area of the hospital grounds, Rachel spotted Tom pacing about across the field, obviously talking on his mobile. She headed his way, suddenly feeling in need of comfort and a hug.

As Rachel approached, Tom appeared quite agitated. Whoever was on the other end of that phone was really winding him up. He had his back mostly to her, so he hadn't spotted her as yet. From the glimpses she got of his face, his jaw was set and he was shaking his head in frustration. This was no ordinary phone call. Rachel had rarely seen him angry like this in all the years she'd known him.

They'd never managed to have their one-to-one chat last night after the Fayre, what with unloading the truck and Mum and Maisy being about. And when they finally had a glimpse of five minutes alone together, Tom had got up and said he had to leave as he'd promised to visit his parents for supper.

But here, now, someone was really riling him up on the phone. What was going on?

He looked up, saw her, and still he had that frown etched across his face.

She could hear him saying tersely, 'Look, I'm going to have to go.'

He caught Rachel's eye, looked a little awkward, and then switched his mobile off, shoving it into his pocket.

'Who was that?' Rachel asked with trepidation.

'Ah, it's nothing.'

It didn't *seem* like nothing. Far from it. But, Rachel had enough on her plate right now so didn't carry on probing.

Tom stood beside her, still looking tense, shoulders hunched, his brow creased. So much for getting a reassuring hug.

Suddenly, he seemed to realise that he needed to snap out of himself for Rachel's sake. 'Sorry,' he said, and he managed a small smile. 'How is she?'

Rachel didn't know how to put into words her fears about Granny Ruth. Yes, she should get through this okay now, but her lungs might be damaged or weakened. And that brutal truth had hit her hard: her granny was getting older and frailer – she really was only human after all. Rachel bit back the tears as her emotions threatened to swamp her.

'Come here.' Tom's arms were open. There would be time to talk afterwards, to discuss what the doctor had said.

She stepped forward into his embrace. For now, there were no words, just this comfort, this closeness, the feeling of Tom's arms around her, when she needed it the most, his warm breath at her ear, as she rested her head against his shoulder. And her world found its axis again.

Ruth remained in the hospital for two days, while they monitored her, checking that the antibiotics seemed to be working and easing her symptoms, and taking a further X-ray before she left. The consultant warned Jill and Rachel that it might take some time before she felt herself again – tiredness being a major factor.

'That's lots of TLC needed then, Granny. And you're going to have to listen to us and rest up a bit.'

'Hmm, I suppose,' Ruth replied gruffly.

It was with a huge feeling of relief that Rachel got her into the Land Rover to take her granny back home to her cottage – she had refused absolutely to stay at the farm, determined to keep as much independence as possible.

There was a regular rota of visitors once Ruth was installed back at home, with old friends from Kirkton, plus Rachel and Jill and little nurse Maisy, taking turns to bring her hot meals and pudding treats. Her cottage was a buzz of activity much of the time, which kept Granny amused, though she did have trouble staying in bed to rest.

'Makes me feel even worse,' she moaned. 'All cooped up in there. I can rest as well in my armchair and I get to see the view, or the television.'

There wasn't a lot of resting going on, Rachel was certain. In fact, she was often up and putting the kettle on for the guests who had come to help out and were meant to be looking after her!

'I think I might have to make a few more of those Christmas puddings too. I mean, I'm famous, now. Everyone will be wondering where the new Mary Berry's gone, won't they?' she quipped.

There was no point in arguing with her, Rachel mused, and it was hard keeping a Swinton woman down at the best of times. And perhaps keeping busy meant that the dear and feisty old lady was starting to find her feet again.

With Christmas approaching, that was at the top of Rachel's wish list.

30

Whoever said 'never work with children and animals' was *so* right.

Before Granny Ruth had been taken to hospital, Maisy had come home buzzing with the idea that Petie could play a starring role in the upcoming nativity at school. Maisy was to be one of the shepherds, and the idea had sprung to full-blown life in her mind.

Dashing off the school bus a couple of weeks ago, she'd called out excitedly, 'Mummy, Mummy! I'm going to be a shepherd and Petie can be my lamb for baby Jesus.'

'Hold fire, what's all this?' Rachel tried to slow her daughter down and get some more information.

'Yes, and I'm an angel,' said Amelia proudly.

'So, does Mrs Brown agree you can bring in live animals for the show?' Rachel was still trying to check if this was right.

'Yes, of course,' Maisy said, as though it was common knowledge and her mum was being daft. 'She said James brought his donkey in, last year.'

'Well, let me think about it, and I'll double-check with the school, all right?'

Petie had, in fact, been trained to the harness, as

Simon, their farmhand, had wanted to put him into the Alwinton Show earlier that autumn as a fine example of the Cheviot breed. And knowing Petie, he'd do anything for a cobnut, so he should follow a bucket with ease. Rachel's mind was already beginning to ponder the practicalities of the request.

But what Rachel hadn't factored in was fresh hay in the manger and a crowd of friendly-looking spectators . . .

It was the evening of the nativity play at the Kirkton First School, and they were waiting in the wings of the school hall. Petie, the now rather large lamb, was in place next to Maisy and the two other five-year-old shepherds who were suitably attired in their checked tea-towel headwear and converted white-bedsheet outfits (Eve had proven very handy with her sewing machine when a panicked Rachel had called around, thrusting a costume disaster at her, offering to bribe her with sticky toffee pudding as payment).

Grandma Jill, Granny Ruth – who had insisted on coming out because she 'wouldn't miss Maisy's play for the world' – Tom, Eve and Ben were sitting out front in the audience, but Rachel had stayed in the wings wanting to make sure Petie didn't miss his cue and that he was behaving himself. And so far, so good. The bucket of cobnuts was proving a hit and was keeping his attention just now.

Mary and Joseph had got to the stable in the story and were getting settled. The angels had been and it was soon to be the shepherds' turn, just before the wise men played their part. There was a moment of panic when Maisy announced she needed a wee 'bad', so all three of them, including Petie, had to make a quick dash to the bathroom, and after a quick signal to the headteacher they held off the shepherds' entrance with an extra chorus of 'Oh, little town of Bethlehem'.

Just as they were getting back, Rachel spotted that Mrs Brown, who was on piano, was turning the hymn sheet, and from the first three chords chiming across the hall, she knew they were about to launch in to 'While Shepherds Watched' at any moment. It was time to hand the bucket, harness lead and lamb across to Maisy.

'Good luck, Maisy and Petie,' she whispered proudly, yet with a hint of trepidation.

'Thank you!' Maisy was beaming excitedly as she stepped onto the stage with her two compatriots plus Petie. Rachel decided to stay and watch from the wings to save any kerfuffle disturbing the other parents en route to her family.

And it all started well. The shepherds walked across the stage with a very obedient Petie, who followed Maisy and her cobnut bucket beautifully. The scene was set: Mary, Joseph, the three shepherds, a child in a cute cow costume, a large toy donkey – probably brought back from Spain as a holiday memento – and real sheep, Petie. Aw, Rachel even had a little tear in her eye as Maisy spoke her one line. 'We are the shepherds, come to visit the new baby.'

The manger had been filled with lovely fresh hay and Baby Jesus was then placed in there by Mary as 'Away in a Manger' began. Which was when Petie got a whiff of the hay – and that was it. He lunged forward, and Maisy lost her grip on his lead rein as he took a big mouthful of the hay, toppling Baby Jesus out of the crib and across the stage, where he landed in a heap exactly on the words, 'Laid down his sweet head'.

'Oh sweet Jesus,' was what slipped out of Rachel's mouth at that point.

Petie then paused and looked out to see what looked to him like a field full of people in front of him. His curiosity piqued, and with a mouthful of hay still to finish and a few strands poking out of his lips, he duly leapt down from the stage (sheep can be surprisingly agile when they want to be!) and into the audience. Pandemonium ensued for a short while as he galloped merrily up and down the walkway and then in amongst the seated parents and children. Tom finally managed to catch him, grabbing him firmly by his halter, while Rachel left the shelter of the wings, bolted across the stage, and dashed up the aisle to join him and the errant sheep.

At that point, shepherd Maisy was standing on the stage with her mouth open, aghast. Mary had retrieved Baby Jesus from the floor and was rocking him, and the rest of the cast were giggling away. Maisy's teacher Mrs Brown, on piano, had gone white, and the headteacher Mrs Stewart was calling for calm.

Just when they thought it was all over, Petie's triumphant

grand finale was to poo on the floor in the middle of the aisle of the school hall, much to the amusement of the crowd who were no longer able to stifle their laughter. Even Jill and Granny Ruth, who hadn't been sure whether to laugh or cry initially, had tears of mirth streaming down their cheeks as Rachel and Tom and naughty Petie began to make their exit.

Rachel was mortified, muttering, 'Sorry, sorry everyone,' desperate to get the wayward beast back out to the car park and into his trailer and fast. Never, never again! she vowed.

And so the old piano fired up and the traditional nativity play came to a swift end with a rousing carol of 'The First Noel', which strangely sounded very like 'Oh hell' in Rachel's frazzled mind.

'Well, that was an experience!' Tom couldn't stop his laughter.

'Bloody hell. I knew I shouldn't have let her talk me into it.' Rachel was still burning with embarrassment, wondering what the teachers were thinking.

They got Petie safely into the trailer and then they collapsed in the front seats of the Land Rover, where even Rachel had the curve of a smile on her lips, beginning to see the funny side of it.

Several minutes later the school doors opened and a flurry of people came out. Rachel and her family regrouped.

'Oh Mummy, Petie was *sooo* naughty.' Maisy was still a little in shock from the unexpected sequence of events.

'Do we just go, or should I go back and apologise?' Rachel was still somewhat concerned about the trail of nativity disaster Petie had left in his wake.

'Why not call the school tomorrow?' Jill suggested. 'When the dust's settled. I borrowed a dustpan and brush and I've already cleared all the poo up from the aisle, so there's no real damage done.'

'Only to Mrs Stewart's pride. She didn't look too happy,' commented Ben with a wry smile.

'Oh dear, oops.' Rachel groaned aloud, still trying to take it all in.

'Let's make a swift getaway,' said Tom, 'and get this bad boy back in his field!'

'Blimey, I nearly wished he'd gone off to you-know-where with all the others!' Rachel was still feeling mortified.

'And miss *that*? Never.' Eve was still laughing. 'Ah, my ribs are sore!'

'That was brilliant, lass.' One of the wise men's dads came up and gave Rachel a friendly pat on the back. There was now much chatter and laughter in the school yard as the crowd spilled out.

'Best show yet,' came another comment from the parent of one of the older children.

The very next day, the school introduced a strict policy that no live animals were to be allowed to take part in any future performances. Rachel made her very apologetic call to the headteacher while Petie and his antics grew famous in the Kirkton area, and there were many comments in the coming weeks when Jill or Rachel were out and about in the town that that had been *the best* nativity play ever. There was even a video clip doing the rounds that Mr Stewart, the headteacher's husband, had taken of the event – he was apparently thinking of putting it up for *You've Been Framed* – though Mrs Stewart had reportedly given him short thrift and banned him from doing so.

This was definitely a Christmas that Rachel wouldn't forget in a hurry.

31

Rachel needed to buy a birthday card and a small gift for one of Maisy's school friends as there was a children's party coming up at the weekend. She thought she might as well nip into town before collecting the girls from gym club. Jill had closed up the Pantry a little early as it had been a bit quieter this afternoon; a downpour of rain seemed to have kept most of the customers at home so Jill said she had a couple of errands to run and mentioned that she was going to pop to see her friend, Jan, for a bit of a catch up.

Rachel was halfway up the high street, heading for the newsagents, and was passing The Cheviot Café when she stopped in her tracks. There was Mum – but it wasn't Jan she was with – it was Daniel from the Pudding Club. They were sitting in the corner table near the window, chatting away and looking very cosy indeed. Rachel didn't know what to think. Had Mum lied to her? Pretended to be seeing Jan?

Rachel suddenly felt awkward, and then had a real gut-churning twist of emotion. It just seemed all wrong, Mum meeting up for cosy chats with another man. What about Dad? What about their marriage? And why all the secrecy? Was this the blossoming of a new romance? It felt very much like a betrayal of Robert's memory.

Rachel stood for a few seconds, in shock, taking in the scene. Well, they weren't quite holding hands, but they seemed to have eyes only for each other – they hadn't spotted her at all. They looked very comfortable in each other's company. Oh, how could she be laughing and chatting away with another man when Dad was lying in a cold grave in the churchyard down the road? Rachel felt queasy. She had to get away from here and fast. She'd pick up the card and gift another day. She strode back down the street, back to her Land Rover, and then sat in the driver's seat for a few minutes, staring blankly out of the windscreen and going nowhere, feeling a bit shell-shocked.

Surely Mum should have told her if they were meeting up, mentioned it, even if it was just for a friendly coffee or something? Did this mean there was more to it? Had she and Daniel met up before this? All sorts of thoughts were whizzing through Rachel's mind. She let out a sigh. She'd quiz Mum later, see if she was keeping something back.

For now, she needed to calm herself, and go and collect the girls.

But the sight of Mum and Daniel together filled her mind as she drove off. A flurry of emotions were spinning in her gut as she parked near the school gates.

* * *

Later that evening, with Maisy in bed and Rachel and Jill sitting watching TV in the front room, she could hold back no longer.

'So, er, did you have a nice time with Jan this afternoon?'

'Ah, yes, fine thanks, love. It was nice to have a bit of a girly chat.' She seemed so calm. It was odd. She'd never put her mum down as such an accomplished liar.

'Oh . . . r-right.' Rachel glanced at her, to see if anything might give her away, but Jill's face was a mask. It was quite unnerving.

She evidently didn't want to say anything about meeting up with Daniel. Rachel bit her tongue, and kept quiet. She wanted time to think this through.

They carried on watching TV in silence, but this new knowledge began to fester inside Rachel. They had always been so close, she and Jill, so open about everything. This seemed all wrong, and though Rachel tried her best to hide it, it began to wedge a distance between them.

The Ninth Bake of Christmas

WI Denise's Easy Festive Fudge

Recipe:

1 can condensed milk (397g)
A large knob of butter
400g good quality melted chocolate (dark, white or milk)
Icing sugar to hold
Additional ingredients such as: crumbled Christmas pudding, cranberries, rum-soaked raisins

Melt the milk, butter and chocolate carefully in a microwaveable bowl in short bursts of around 20 seconds, stirring each time. Stir in a dessert spoon or so of icing sugar to hold.

Add in your dried fruit or crumbled pudding (cranberries work well with white chocolate, Christmas pudding with dark) and stir gently through to mix.

Spoon into an 20cm (8 inch) square tin, lined with greaseproof paper and allow to set for an hour. Cut into bite-sized squares.

Ideal to pop into small bags tied with a pretty ribbon as festive gifts.

32

The next morning dawned frosty and very cold. The skies above Primrose Farm were a shocking, clear blue, with a mere drift of wispy cloud and Rachel was trying not to dwell on what she had seen yesterday; after taking Maisy to the school bus, she had headed out on the quad and got on with her farm work, spending a fair while trying to break the ice on the water troughs for the sheep out in the fields. The water pipes to the cattle shed, where the herd were now sheltered for the winter, were frozen too and if it didn't thaw out soon, they'd have to bring fresh water in for the animals in huge plastic tanks on the back of the trailer. Yet another job to add to her load. They were a week on from the nativity play antics and the Swinton ladies were steamrolling their way towards Christmas.

The Pudding Pantry was full of festive cheer – there were only ten days left until Christmas, after all, and just as they'd prayed, the customers wanting to sample the Swinton's delicious puddings and bakes kept on coming. They had another fifteen Christmas Pudding orders in, and as well as making those they still needed to stock up the Pantry shelves for the regular flow of customers looking to enjoy a pre-Christmas treat out, as well as those wanting to take something home for the family or to keep for store cupboard Christmas supplies. The fairy lights were twinkling, the coffee machine gurgling, and Jill and Rachel had been baking like trojans last night and this morning. They still needed to work as a team, so Rachel kept her emotions in check and had said nothing about having seen her mum with Daniel.

Rachel got back from her rounds on the farm to launch herself into making two Bailey's Irish Cream cheesecakes, and a cherry and whipped-cream filled chocolate roulade. Jill had already baked some steamed gingerbread puddings, full of festive spice, and a large apple and cinnamon crumble.

Frank was in for his morning coffee just after ten thirty, and today he fancied some of the gingerbread pudding with a swirl of citrus cream. A sudden rush meant that all the tables filled at once, with a queue forming for Christmas Puddings orders. Bless him, Frank even chipped in at one point, carrying across a tray of tea and scones to table nine, and clearing table six to help them out.

Tom arrived for his elevenses bacon roll, stopping for the quickest of chats, and grabbing a coffee to take away as he was going back to sort out the mounting pile of the farm's paperwork and e-mails. Hmm, that reminded Rachel – her current admin was waiting on the 'to do' pile. But there was only so much multitasking you could do in one day!

'Sorry, Rach, I've really got to dash. I'm waiting on a call from the bank too.'

Rachel well knew how tense that kind of a call could be and gave an understanding smile. The counter and a whole host of customers kept them apart, but her skin tingled for his touch. It had been far too long since they'd had chance for an evening together, just the two of them. It felt like they were dancing around each other just now, and it felt a nervous, hesitant dance. The family had been about after the nativity play, and she'd never had the chance to talk to him after the Christmas Fayre event. So they still hadn't yet managed an honest chat. Was he still hiding something from her?

'Okay, we'll catch up soon.'

'Yeah, of course.' He headed off, striding out, tall and handsome, with her heart in his hands. She pulled herself back to her Pantry customers. It was a hectic time and though Rachel and Jill were both tired from weeks of early starts and late finishes, it was wonderful to see a real swarm of Pudding Pantry customers enjoying the ambience in the barn, sitting by the cosy log-burning stove, and tucking into their home-baked delights there. The counter was a festive treasure trove of mouthwatering cakes, bakes and puddings galore. Their dream for the old barn had truly come alive before them. They really were, thankfully, starting to turn their fortunes around.

It was already turning dark outside and four o'clock rolled around quickly. Maisy was now with them in the barn, as Rachel had dashed down on the quad – only just in time – to collect her from the school bus. It was now freezing and very frosty out; the ground had remained solid all day, with its white-gilded dusting. Rachel and Jill started to pack up, as there was only one couple remaining after the rush.

After the last customers had gone, Rachel offered to go across and cook supper. There was some ham and local cheddar left and she'd thought she'd make some omelettes for them. It'd be good to give Jill a bit of a night off too, as her mum tended to take on the bulk of the home cooking.

'That'll be nice, thanks pet. Well, I'll finish off here. We're nearly done, anyhow. You go across and take Maisy.'

'Okay.'

Rachel had got Maisy settled in front of the television after spending some time reading her school book with her. She'd chopped the ham and grated the cheese, ready for the omelette fillings. She'd even peeled some potatoes ready to boil. Moss was laid out by the Aga, enjoying its warmth, after being out in his kennel for the day. They should be making the most of a quieter evening and looking forward to Christmas together as a family, but Rachel's heart was full of unease over this new development with Jill and Dan. And what irked the most was the fact that her mum had been lying to her. They *didn't* keep secrets from each other – it just wasn't the way they worked. Not until now, anyway.

Once Maisy was in bed, Rachel kept herself busy in the kitchen, doing her accounts and then making a carrot cake for the Pantry the next day. She liked to try and contribute to the Pantry's baking, but the real truth tonight was that she really couldn't face sitting down, watching TV with her mum and pretending that everything was okay.

Once the cake was in the oven, Jill came through, a look of concern shadowing her face. 'Rachel, what is up with you? You've been quiet for days now. There's something you're not telling me, for sure.'

That was it, Rachel broke. 'There's something *I'm* not telling *you*, Mum? Don't you think it's the other way around?' Rachel answered pointedly.

Jill stayed silent.

'Mum, you don't need to lie any more; I *know*. I saw you together.'

'What are you talking about?'

'You and Daniel. All cosied up in The Cheviot Café last week.'

'Ah.' Jill looked a little taken aback.

'So, it's all right, you can carry on your little affair, make it public now if you like.' Rachel couldn't stop her tone sounding acerbic.

'Look, I'm sorry, I was just trying to protect you, love.'

'What from? I'm not a child. I'm not five like Maisy. You should have let me know what was going on. That you and Dan were meeting up. Not let me catch you at it and pretending all the while that you were seeing Jan.'

'Hang on there! *At what*?' It was Jill's turn to be affronted. 'If you mean having a coffee together, then that's the sum of it. And yes, if you must know, I do enjoy Daniel's company. But there's been nothing sordid or scheming about it.'

'So why all the secrecy? You even told me you were seeing Jan that day?'

'Yes, and I did see her. I called there, but she had to nip out unexpectedly soon after and then I called into town to see if Brenda might want any more of our puddings, so I'd know what I'd need to make next. That's when I bumped into Daniel.'

'So, it wasn't planned?' Rachel was softening, but still struggling to get her head around it.

'No, it wasn't planned – and I didn't mention anything to you for exactly this reason. Why stir things up, when I don't even know how I feel about it all myself, or if it's going any further than a cup of coffee? Yes, okay, I admit it, I do like Daniel, but it's very early days. And you know what, Rachel, I do have a life of my own! I don't actually have to tell you every little detail.'

'It was a shock, Mum, seeing you both like that, I didn't know what to think. And it looked like far more than a friendly chat.'

'Okay, so we are getting on well, we were having a good time. But I don't need to be justifying my actions to you. You're sounding like a stroppy teenager, Rachel.'

They were both getting fired up now.

'Well, thanks. Can't you see this is hard for me too? Seeing you with someone else. And what about Dad?'

'Rachel, love, your dad's gone and I'm betraying no one. You're making a big deal about nothing.'

'So, Dad dying is *nothing* now?' It was all spilling out. Rachel's hands were on her hips.

'Don't be so damned silly. You're putting words into my mouth and making the whole thing into something that it isn't.'

With that, Maisy appeared around the sitting room door, yawning and looking anxious. 'Mummy, why are you and Grandma shouting?'

Shit, they'd woken her up.

'Oh, sorry petal, it's all right. We were just chatting about something. Everything's fine,' Rachel reassured.

It was all far from fine. It was a mess.

'Sorry, love. It's nothing to be worried about,' added Jill.

'Come on, I'll take you back up to bed.' Rachel got up and took her little girl's hand, glad to get out of the room and its echoes of blame and accusations. She couldn't bear to look at her mum's face as she went.

Rachel hated arguing with Jill, and it hardly ever happened because they were so close. But this went deep. Was there really nothing to be worried about, or was this a rift that wasn't going to heal?

The Tenth Bake of Christmas

Rachel's Irish Cream Cheesecake

This is one of Rachel's all-time favourite cheesecakes – it's very easy to make and involves no baking as such!

Recipe:
175g digestive biscuits
70g unsalted butter
275g full fat cream cheese
150ml double cream
200g condensed milk
4 x 15ml spoons (tbsp) Irish Cream liqueur
8-10 large chocolate chips/chocolate curls or chocolate coffee beans to decorate

Crush the biscuits with a rolling pin, or whizz in a food processor until evenly crushed.

Melt the butter in a pan, add biscuits and stir through to mix well. Spoon into a deep 20cm/8inch flan dish (one with a push-up base or clip side release would be ideal). Press into place with the back of a dessert spoon around the base and sides of the dish. Chill in the fridge whilst you do the next step.

Place cream cheese in a bowl, add the cream and condensed milk and beat until thick with an electric hand whisk. Slowly add the Irish Cream and beat again lightly to mix through.

Chill in fridge for at least 2 hours.

Decorate with your chocolate garnish at equal spaces around the outer circle area, ideally one garnish per slice.

Serve with friends!

33

Nothing more was said on the matter the next morning. There was still a strong air of tension and both Rachel and Jill were afraid they might fire up the argument again, so they let the dust settle and forged on with their busy lives.

That evening, the last Pudding Club of the year was about to go full steam ahead with Rachel and Jill at its helm. Staying as professional as ever, no one would have guessed they'd had a big falling out just the night before.

There was Rachel, in her Christmas Pudding jumper that Eve had made especially for her, and Jill was sporting a Frosty the Snowman knit. Her gorgeous friend, bless her, had even made Maisy a jumper with the exact face of Jill's Rudolph Cupcake on. They were apparently one of Amelia's favourites too, and they'd taken one home. She'd laughed as she told Rachel she had the perfect model, though Amelia was most put out when she was told she couldn't dive in and eat it straight away. As a special treat, Maisy was allowed to stay up late tonight and join in at the Christmas Jumper Pudding Club.

Rachel had sent a message out on the club's e-mail loop to advise members to come in their favourite festive pullovers to celebrate the 'Club before Christmas'. Even Frank had made the effort and was looking very dapper with a Santa Claus tie and matching waistcoat.

'Where did you get that ensemble, Frank? It's fabulous,' said Jill.

'Oh, I've had it for donkey's years. Found it lurking in the back of the wardrobe. I was amazed it still fitted, to be honest. The old tummy's not as trim as it used to be.'

'Hah, it's all these puddings you've been eating,' Rachel jested.

'I know, I keep saying you two are a bad influence.' He gave a broad smile.

The theme this time was Easy Christmas Bakes, and as Rachel's Bailey's Cheesecake was one of her favourite go-tos – and be honest, who doesn't like a tipple of Bailey's Irish Cream over the festive season – she'd made that for the taste trial. With no actual baking involved, it was quick to prepare, the filling dead easy to whip up, decorate, chill and serve. She managed to make two of them whilst serving solo at the Pantry and it was going down very well with the pudding clubbers.

'Oh my, I *need* this recipe.'

'Dreamy,' said Eve, who was sporting a bold Robin Redbreast knit and now had a glazed look on her face.

'This'd work well after a fancy dinner party. Not that I tend to give many of those nowadays with a toddler in tow,' Kirsty said, smiling from above her Father Christmas pullover.

'Perfect for a girls' night treat.'

'Oh yes, though I might just eat the whole thing myself – it's delightful,' agreed Christine.

'Scrummy, it's like the poshest Angel Delight-style filling that's a bit naughty with Irish Cream in,' Charlotte raved, fittingly sporting a sparkly angel jumper.

'Well done, Rachel,' said Daniel, who was wearing a Fair Isle Rudolph knit that his mother had apparently made for him several years ago. He gave a thumbs-up of approval and – although she knew he was in no way to blame – Rachel found that she couldn't quite meet his eye.

They drank tea and coffee, and Rachel also had a plate of buttery pastry mince pies for them to dive into. The conversation then turned to other easy bakes and crafty shortcuts they kept up their sleeves for busy family times and emergencies.

'Cheat's trifle,' said Eileen. 'Buy in some good custard, madeira sponge, cream, raspberry jam and fresh raspberries and the obligatory splash of sherry, of course.'

'Excellent.'

There was a Choco-o-nana trifle suggestion too by Kirsty, a banana and chocolate custard dream by the sounds of it, which Rachel noted down – Maisy would love that.

'Well, I make Christmas Tree Meringues. Just add a little green food colouring to your meringue mix, and when they're just baked, sprinkle on a few hundreds and thousands, and fix a little sugar star to the top from those

293

sprinkles packs. So easy and pretty. The grandchildren love them,' added Christine.

'Ooh, they sound great.'

WI Denise mentioned a gorgeous-sounding micro-wavable chocolate fudge recipe that you could add all sorts to, to make festive gift bags or hand out with a coffee as a little treat: dark chocolate and Christmas pudding, white chocolate and cranberry, were her family's two favourites. Yummy.

'And I make lots of shortbread as gifts for Christmas time. If you cut them into star shapes, and add a little sugar dusting as they cool, they look so pretty.' This was from Pamela, the lady from Alnwick.

'Oh, that reminds me of the star biscuit Christmas tree I make,' added Jill. 'The star cutters come in various sizes, and if you stick them together, smallest at the top, sandwiched with green icing they make a fabulous biscuit Christmas Tree. You can break them off one at a time to eat.'

The group were really inspiring each other, and there were so many great suggestions and so much chatter that Rachel was able to sit back for a while, relaxing with her cup of tea and just soaking up the ideas and camaraderie.

The last suggestion from her friend Charlotte brought a big smile to her face. 'Coming to buy something at the Pudding Pantry is *my* emergency backup,' grinned Charlotte. 'Honestly, I love what you've done here. It's brilliant.'

Despite it having been the most hectic of weeks – and,

in all honesty, dragging herself out to the Pudding Club had seemed a chore today after all the drama – Rachel was so glad she had soldiered on and made the night happen for everyone. This group felt like a lovely support team already.

The evening was rolling to a close.

'So, what's next for the club night? Something for New Year? Diet puddings?' Dan's crinkled cheeks showed that he was jesting.

'There's no such thing,' countered Jill. 'And if there is, they should be banned. Puddings are there for a treat. A little of what you fancy . . .'

'Never did anyone any harm,' Daniel finished her line, his grey eyes smiling warmly.

'Here, here,' said Eve.

Rachel looked across at her mum and Daniel sitting cosily side by side and suddenly felt like the third wheel. This was so hard. She could barely watch them together. Throughout the evening she had tried to avoid speaking with Daniel directly. She didn't want to be rude, but knew it was the best way to keep her emotions in check.

The group began to disperse, laden with takeaway Christmas Puddings and other delights – Charlotte's easy bakes, courtesy of the Pudding Pantry, proving popular – along with their cheesecake recipe sheets. They all wished Rachel and her family a Merry Christmas, sending special wishes on to Granny Ruth for a speedy recovery.

Daniel was again the last to leave. He came across to have a few words with Jill and offered to help out at the

Pantry in the coming days, should she and Rachel need an extra pair of hands, saying that he had a couple of days off coming up before Christmas.

'I'm sure we'll be fine,' Rachel answered rather coolly, just as Jill replied, 'Oh, that's very kind.' Her mum gave Rachel a look, as if to say she needed to buck up.

Rachel busied herself with the clearing up, yet found herself on high alert, sneaking the odd glance at the pair of them. Jill, too, looked a little uncomfortable.

Where was this going? Was it just friendship as Mum had mooted, or were the pair of them already feeling a little more than that? It was just so disconcerting that Daniel was keen to spend more and more time with her mum. Rachel knew, on a wholly selfish level, that her ill-feeling was to do with Dad. But how could Jill forget about him?

After helping to clear some coffee cups, Daniel thanked them for tonight, saying he was really enjoying the group and was picking up some great baking tips. He didn't seem such a bad guy, in all honesty . . . Rachel gave a small sigh. She should be pleased that Mum was finding a new friend, but she couldn't help but feel odd. It was as though it marked the start of something new for Jill, a moving on. It highlighted the ever-crushing reality that Dad was never, ever coming back.

She stepped out of the barn, into the cold dark night, looking up at the stars through teary eyes. Was Dad there, looking down at her? She liked to think so; it was the only comfort in these changing, uneasy times.

34

The next evening, Rachel was settling Maisy into bed after bath and story time. With Christmas fast approaching, her daughter was taking longer to go off to sleep, asking a million and one questions about the *real* Father Christmas.

'How does he do the whole world in one night?' Maisy enquired, with eyes wide.

'Magic powers,' was Rachel's answer to that one.

Rachel wished she'd had some of those magic powers herself this week with all the multitasking needed to get everything done on the farm. Her own Christmas preparations were all too feeble at the moment, too and she still had to finalise a couple of gifts for Maisy – Amazon would be getting a browse and an order hit this evening, for sure.

'Is my daddy coming to see me for Christmas?' Maisy was sitting up, propped against the pillows.

'Oh . . .' Jake had made no mention of intending to visit any time soon in his recent phone calls. To be honest, her ex arriving for Christmas lunch would be the last thing Rachel would want, but of course Maisy would be hoping to see him. It was a special time of year, a family time, and he was her daddy, after all. 'I don't think so, Maisy.'

Her little girl's face dropped.

'He's got lots of things to do where he lives now, and it's a very long way away.' Rachel tried to ease the feelings of rejection that might well be hitting Maisy right now.

The reality was that Jake would probably be spending Christmas with the new girlfriend, Chelsea, and her little boy who was just two years older than Maisy. Ironic really, Jake didn't have time for his own child but he'd no doubt be playing happy families with little Kelvin, or whatever he was called. She kept all that to herself, of course.

'I'm sure he'll come and see you again when he can. Now then, it's time to get to sleep, petal. Shall I read you a little bit more of your storybook, just a page or two?' That might take Maisy's mind off her missing Daddy and into a place where sleep might come more easily.

Maisy was nodding.

'Great. Now, where were we?' They were soon lost in adventures of fairies and dragons and princesses. Unfortunately, Rachel's eyelids were beginning to droop before Maisy's, her nonstop days catching up on her.

'Night, then, lovely – Mummy's going to have to go and bake some more puddings for the Pantry.' There was no letting up quite yet. There was still another load of Whisky and Orange Christmas puds to create for orders that were to be collected tomorrow. Granny Ruth had really started something, she thought wryly. Thankfully,

Granny's cough had eased a lot over the past few days, and the old lady seemed as though she was back on track to enjoy all the Christmas festivities with the family. So, some Christmas wishes did come true after all.

With eight Christmas puddings steaming gently away on the top of the stove, Rachel had a rare couple of hours to spare. She could look at the mounting pile of paper-work, or she could go and see Tom. The latter option was by far the most appealing, though it filled her with some trepidation too.

With all the issues at the Pantry and the crazy-busy Christmas run up, Rachel had still only seen him briefly, just glimpses when they were with other people, or a quick hello as they passed on the road. He had called in once or twice for his elevenses, but it was hardly the place for a heart-to-heart in the middle of the Pantry, or for her to ask the burning question about Caitlin's mystery reappearance.

So she thought she'd go and surprise him; hopefully they could clear the air, have a deep and honest conver-sation. And she could only hope that Tom wasn't about to drop any bombs on her. Anxiety churned in her stomach.

She knew that she should nip up to Jill's room and let her know of her plans to pop round to Tom's. She made to go up the stairs, before swivelling quickly back. She just couldn't quite face her yet – residual anger about her mum's sneaking around with Dan still swilling around in her mind. No, she'd just slip out. Maisy was sleeping soundly and she wouldn't be long anyhow. She did however leave a note on the kitchen side.

Rachel jumped on the quad, enjoying the cold wind racing through her hair as she raced around to Tom's farm, excitement and a little anxiety mounting inside. She was determined to find out the truth about Caitlin. Surely there was bound to be some simple explanation? And then they could put it behind them and look forward to a slightly less hectic time after Christmas. She prayed that would be the case.

When she arrived, Rachel knocked, waited a few seconds and then let herself in when there was no greeting at the door. 'Hi Tom, it's just me,' she called.

There he was, on his mobile, pacing the kitchen, his voice strained and raised. 'I don't see the point in all this. Not now!' He glanced up and spotted Rachel then. 'This really isn't a good time,' she heard him say and it was like a rerun of the call he had taken in the hospital grounds. He looked irked. Should she go? Perhaps this wasn't the best time to visit after all. But she'd been so looking forward to seeing him, and clearing the air.

Rachel managed to catch his eye, and mouthed, 'I'll just . . .' as she gestured towards the hallway, heading through to the living room to give him a bit of space.

Who was that? Could it be the same person who'd been bothering him at the hospital that day? Was there something up? Tom was rarely riled. He coped with all sorts on the farm, and in all the years she'd known him, Rachel had never seen him particularly wound up about anything. He just got on and dealt with things, calmly, that was one of the things she admired most about him.

A few minutes later he came to find her in the lounge.

'Sorry about that.' His jaw was still tight. He seemed tense, frustrated.

'Everything okay?' she asked cautiously.

'Ah, it's nothing.'

'Tom, whatever it is, it's not nothing. Something's bothering you. Can I help? Tell me about it. I feel like you're keeping something from me.'

He shot her a dark look. 'Just leave it, Rach.'

Rachel knew when to back off. But whatever was behind this, it felt all wrong. The room filled with tension. Her old fears were resurfacing.

'Glass of wine?' he offered.

She stood silent, unsure whether to leave or stay put. Finally she acquiesced. 'Okay.'

He went off, back to the kitchen, where he poured two glasses of red. Rachel followed him through, not knowing how to handle things. He passed her a glass and took the biggest glug from his.

'So, what's been happening with you?' he asked, obviously deflecting.

'Ah, pretty hectic. It's been full-on at the Pantry, making a mountain of Christmas puddings – honestly, all I can smell is whisky and bloody orange. Oh, and I called in to see Ruth earlier too, who thankfully is on the mend, though it seems to be a slow job. It's like I'm nurse, nanny, chef, cattle and sheep handler, all rolled into one.' She chuckled, trying to break the layer of tension.

Rachel took a stool at the island unit, her feet throbbing after yet another day on them. She shouldn't complain; the cash till was full, and the bank balance finally looking creditable. Financially, they were on their way back up, but physically, boy, was she knackered. And what with the Mum/Daniel scenario and now all this with Tom . . . well, her emotions were frankly all over the place. Even after just two sips of wine, she felt like she could sleep for a week.

'I'm glad to hear Ruth's on the mend.'

'Yes, she's coming on pretty well. They did say it'd take a while, having pneumonia at her age, but her cough is way better. She's just a bit weak still, but she's back pottering about at home. She was baking goodies for the church Christmas fete when I called in earlier.'

'Sounds like you can't keep her down. But that's probably a good thing.'

'Yes.'

The conversation was polite, too polite. It was as though they were skirting around something much bigger. There was definitely an elephant in the room, one they were both afraid of approaching.

'And Maisy, well, she's a whirlwind of Christmas excitement,' Rachel continued.

'Hah, I bet.'

'So, there's just over a week to go until the Big Day

and I can't wait to just stop, close up the Pantry and stay home for a few days. That'll be bliss.'

'Aren't you doing a big Christmas dinner for everyone, though? It's hardly as if you'll be putting your feet up.'

'Yes, but it's family and friends, and we'll all muck in. There's no real pressure with that. You are still coming, aren't you?' The unsaid was that something had changed between them, that he might have changed his mind.

'Ah . . . yes, of course . . .' He didn't actually sound that sure. 'Just one sec, if you'll excuse me a minute . . . I really need the bathroom,' he explained as he walked out of the room.

Damn, she'd just been about to start her apology, promise she'd find more time for them to be together. Rachel took another sip of the mellow wine. She'd talk about it when he came back through. He seemed to have calmed down a bit now so perhaps they might have a nice hour or two together, after all.

A few seconds later, his phone, which he'd left on the side, started buzzing.

Could it be the same person? The one who was riling him?

The phone was there, just within reach . . .

Rachel paused, then picked it up, felt it vibrate in her hand.

She saw the caller ID.

Caitlin. Tom's ex.

* * *

'I think I'd better go, actually,' said Rachel, swiftly finishing off the last of her wine as Tom got back from the bathroom.

He looked at her bemused. 'What? You have to leave already? You've only just arrived, Rach.'

'Yeah, well, Maisy was a bit unsettled as I put her to bed.' It was a necessary white lie, then she added, 'And Mum really needs an early night.' It was just a quick hello.' Rachel stood up to leave.

'Well, okay, I'll see you about soon then.'

'Yeah,' Rachel answered, unable to hide the sadness in her tone.

Is this what they had come to? How quickly love and relationships could change, like autumn leaves they fall and wither. It was just a week before Christmas, one that she'd been looking forward to for so long. And the new frostiness between them was so very hard to bear.

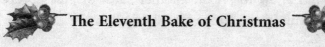

The Eleventh Bake of Christmas

Chocolate Coconut Snowballs

Songs of snowflakes and eyelashes . . . The Swinton family can still be found sitting around watching The Sound of Music *re-runs at Christmas! It was one of those Christmas classics that brought the whole family together, fireside, with a large tub of Quality Street chocolates and homemade chocolate coconut snowballs. Ruth and Jill had even been known to sing along rather loudly after a festive sherry or two.*

Recipe:
220g (about ½ can) of condensed milk
8oz (240g) desiccated coconut
2 tbsp icing sugar
100g good quality dark or milk chocolate

In a bowl, mix the condensed milk, coconut and icing sugar together with a wooden spoon.

Shape into small balls and rest on greaseproof paper.

Melt the chocolate, either in a bowl over a pan of simmering water, or very carefully in short bursts in the microwave. Dip the balls into the chocolate, covering well, and allow to set on another sheet of greaseproof paper. Chill in the fridge for 10 minutes.

These make perfect snowball-shaped treats. Enjoy!

35

It was still dark outside, early morning, as Rachel fumbled for and then squinted at her phone. It was ten to six. Something had woken her. Had she heard a noise? Was it Moss barking? There it was again. That was definitely Moss. All had been quiet since the night of the burgling thieves, but the long dark winter nights were always a concern, at times providing cover for those looking for trouble.

It was probably nothing, maybe an owl or fox that had perhaps swooped or scuttled too near Moss's kennel. She'd better get up though, check it out. Her bedroom was cold, the central heating not yet on. Her bare feet nipped as they touched the wooden floor, toes searching for slippers in the dark . . . there they were. She slipped her feet in.

She didn't turn the light on, could see better looking out from the dark of her room. She shifted the curtain across. There was no security light on in the yard, but there was a strange glow through the air. A soft white whirl. Snow.

Oh . . . the first snows of winter. Rachel felt that child-hood excitement rising inside. There was always something magical about that first snow. Maisy had been waiting for this moment. Should she wake her? Dash out to play with her before she had to get ready for school? Who knew, this might be the only snows they'd get? Snow could go as soon as it came in Northumberland. Rachel wrapped herself up in her dressing gown, resolved to wait a little while and see if it carried on. After all, it was still very early. She didn't want Maisy nodding off at her school desk.

Ten minutes on and there was enough snow on the ground to make snowballs or a very small snowman. That was it; they might not get their moment again this winter. Rachel pulled on her thermal underwear, woolly socks, jeans, a warm fleece top. She'd put on some waterproofs over that downstairs. Then she went to Maisy's bedroom.

'Maisy, petal. Wake up.' Rachel gently shook her shoulder.

'Ah . . .' Maisy blinked her eyes open. 'Is it time for school, did I sleep in?'

'No, petal, something magical is happening. Look.' She pulled the curtains back.

Within minutes they were out in the yard in their waterproof overalls and wellingtons, with Moss now frolicking about too. The falling snow cast enough light in the deep-grey morning air for them to see, their eyes soon adjusting. Rachel opened her mouth to feel the cold melt of it on her tongue, just like she used to as a child.

They made snow angels in the back garden and a cute little snowman with dark stones for his eyes and mouth, and a couple of twigs for arms. Snowballs flew between them next, until they began to feel numb frosty fingertips, and were blinking snow off their eyelashes.

Jill came to the door then. 'What on earth are you pair up to out here in the dark? What's all the rumpus?' Then she looked around her. 'Ah!'

'It's snow, Grandma! We've been making snow angels, and Moss has been our snow dog!'

He too was covered in half-melted snowballs.

'Ah, I see.' Jill couldn't help but smile. 'Well, you snow angels need to get in and get warm and get ready for school.'

'Aaaw . . .' Maisy pulled her lip down.

'That's right, petal. Time's up,' Rachel agreed. 'Hopefully, it'll still be here when you get back after school.'

'I bet it won't.' The little girl folded her arms crossly.

'Well, at least we didn't miss it,' soothed Rachel.

'No, we didn't, did we?' Her arms loosened. She looked up at Rachel from snowy lashes. 'Thanks, Mummy. That was so fun.'

'You're welcome, my little angel.'

Sometimes the simple, happy things that came for free in life were the best.

Their two body prints, little and long, lay beside each other in the snow, touching hands with gorgeous sweeping angel wings.

Rachel and Tom's relationship, however, was undeniably complicated, and not particularly happy, at this moment in time.

He caught up with her later that same morning, as she was filling the wooden feeding troughs out in the snow-dusted fields with sheep nuts, carrying and pouring out sacks of the stuff from the back of the Land Rover. The pregnant ewes would need all the extra nutrients they could get in this weather and the animals nudged in hungrily beside her.

Tom pulled his quad to a stop.

'Hi,' she said softly, turning to greet him.

'Hey, what happened to you last night? You just upped and left,' he said, launching right in. 'What's going on, Rach?'

She hadn't yet had chance to explain or ask her burning questions. And now here *he* was, being grumpy with *her*. Perhaps it was Tom who had some explaining to do. She remembered how she'd felt, seeing Caitlin's name appear on his phone. It still stung. His ex was back in his life in some capacity and he was lying to her about it.

Tom's indignant stance as he got off the quad set her off.

'I've been worried sick, Tom. First, Vanessa, in the village said Caitlin's been back on the scene, and then Eve thought she saw her driving into your farm the other day. And all these phone calls. I saw the Caller ID when I was at your house. What's going on, Tom? Are you seeing her again?'

'Whoa, now hang on there, Rach! So, you'd rather listen to tittle-tattle from that old bat in the village than talk to me? Come on, Rachel, what do you take me for?'

Rachel really didn't know what to think. Her fears had built and burrowed away inside her these past few weeks. But she needed the truth. And there was something else on her mind. '*And* I turned up to see you one night. It was late, past eleven thirty. I just wanted to be with you, spend a couple of hours with you, but there was no one home. No truck, even.'

'Okay, so when exactly was this?' His brow was furrowed.

Was he just getting ready to form his alibi?

'It was a Friday, maybe a month ago. What was I supposed to think, Tom? When you weren't there? And then hearing that Caitlin was back on the scene?'

'Jeez, so you put two and two together and made about a hundred! Well done, Rachel. It sounds like the night I was out in a cold, wet field until past midnight. One of my calves had got his leg snagged up in a wire fence. It was in a right panic and making the injury worse. It took me a while to unravel it, the poor little chap, and his mum was going ballistic. It was the mooing that had woken me up. So, if you'd have just asked me about it, instead of stewing on it for bloody weeks and making up your own daft bloody theories . . .'

'Oh.' So, she'd got that one way wrong. 'Is he all right now?'

'Thankfully, yeah. Got the vet to him the next day and he had to have a few stitches put in.'

'I see.' That took a lot of the wind out of her sails – but Rachel was still left wondering if there was any truth in any of the rest of it. Why was his ex hanging about? Making persistent phone calls?

'And Caitlin?' she pursued.

'I really don't believe this. Have you no trust in me at all?' Tom was getting irked. 'I thought we had something really good going on here, Rach.'

'Me too – and we do!' That's why she was so bloody afraid to lose it. Was she just bulldozing her way into doing that anyhow, with her doubts and insecurities?

But he still hadn't told her the truth about Caitlin and what she'd been doing back here.

'Has she been here? I don't think Eve was hallucinating. And someone came into the Pantry who was really staring me down, it was pretty unnerving, Tom,' she wheedled away, unable to help herself.

'Wow – *really*. Look, I don't need or want to go into every detail of my messy marriage and shitty divorce, and we've got to have some trust between us, Rach. If you're happy to believe some old gossipmonger ahead of asking me properly, then I don't think we have much of a future, do you?'

With that, he jumped back on the quad, revved the engine and did an about turn. Leaving Rachel spattered in a spray of sleety mud standing staring after him, her heart in tatters.

36

Rachel was sitting with Granny Ruth in the warm glow of her sitting room by the open fire. She had called in the morning after the scene with Tom with some fresh eggs, a homemade minced beef and onion pie that Jill had just pulled from the oven, and some vegetables picked from their veggie patch, including a glossy dark-leaved cabbage. They needed to make sure the old lady was eating well during her ongoing recovery.

'How are you feeling today then, Granny?' Rachel asked.

'On the mend, pet, on the mend. The cough's nearly away and I'll be back up and on my feet all day in no time.'

'That's good. I knew you'd come through stronger than ever.'

'And how are things with you?'

'Fine, thanks . . .' Rachel's voice trailed away miserably.

'Are you sure about that? What's the matter pet?' She gave her beloved grandchild a kind smile.

'Oh Granny, I've had a bad falling out with Tom.'

'Oh dear. Well then, I think this calls for a cup of tea and a slice of Jam Roly-Poly. I'll go pop the kettle on.'

She went to stand, but her knees were still weak and a bit wobbly.

'Let me go. You stay here and keep warm by the fire.'

'Thanks, pet. The pudding's in the fridge. Cut yourself a good slice and warm it in the microwave for a few seconds. It'll be even better then.'

Five minutes later, she passed Granny a cup of tea and settled herself back on the sofa with a generous bowl of Blackberry Jam Roly-poly. But then she found herself feeling a little queasy.

'Oh, Granny, there's something Tom's not telling me, to do with his ex. I know she's been back in the village, at his farm.'

'And have you asked him about it? Given him the chance to explain?'

'Well, I tried, but he's like a bear with a sore head just now. It all got a bit heated and out of hand. We had a row, and he stormed off.'

'Hmm, well, in any relationship, honesty is the best policy. Me and your granda had some right ups and downs when we were younger, but in time we learnt to talk things through, to come to understand each other. Life will always throw you curveballs, pet, but if this relationship with Tom is worth it, then you need to work through them – together.'

'Yes, maybe . . .' She spooned some of the comforting jammy pudding into her mouth.

'Look inside your heart, lass. It'll tell you if it's worth fighting for.'

Rachel breathed out with a small sigh. She already knew the answer to that, but did Tom feel the same way?

'Thank you, Granny. You always know what to say. What would I do without you, eh?'

37

With only five days to go until Christmas, the weather took a turn for the worse. Snow was pummelling down outside Primrose Farm's kitchen window, there was already a thick layer mounting on the sill, and a chill wind was roaring around the house. This wasn't the pretty, magical dusting of two days ago, no, this was a blizzard, and if it kept on going like this it'd spell big trouble for their sheep out in the fields.

A concerned look passed between Rachel and Jill, with memories of a past harsh winter and the spiral of events thereafter.

Mother and daughter hadn't exactly put their differences aside since their blowup, and things were still pretty frosty between them, but they were trying to be civil – for Maisy's sake, at least.

'It's worse than they forecast, isn't it,' said Jill, her brow furrowing.

'Yes, it'll be starting to drift out there,' answered Rachel.

It was still early, only breakfast time, and Rachel was standing finishing her coffee. But she was well aware she'd need to get out to feed and check on her flock very soon. There was no time to waste and the longer she left it, the harder it would be to get through to them.

'Can I build a snowman? A big one this time?' asked Maisy innocently.

'Not just now, petal. This is a storm. The wind is wild and raw so it's no place to play.'

'Oh.' A shadow crossed her little face; she could hear the warning in her mum's tone.

Looking out, the sky was a metallic grey between the furious flakes of white. It looked as though it was dusk, even though it was only eight thirty in the morning.

'I'm going to have to go out and check on them soon. I can't just leave them, Mum.'

'I know.' There was a flicker of fear in Jill's eyes, however.

'What's wrong, Mummy? Is something in trouble?'

'It's the sheep, Maisy, they're all out in the fields with little shelter. I need to make sure they are safe and can get to their food.' She didn't add that if this kept going the likelihood was that drifts would form that could bury them. The animals would huddle by the hedgerows and that shelter would eventually become their tomb as the snow drifted higher, covering them.

'Oh, can I come?'

'No, Maisy, you need to stay here with Grandma.' Rachel's voice was firm.

'But what about Petie? Is he in trouble too?'

'He might be, but that's why I need to go out and check.' There was no point lying to her little girl. These snowstorms had happened before and Rachel knew she had to get out to check where the sheep were, to find any that might already be buried under the snow, and to clear a safe pathway for them to get to their hay and feed.

Maisy went quiet, her lip beginning to wobble.

'Are you sure you'll be all right up there on your own?' Jill asked with concern.

'We don't have a lot of options, do we? Simon will never get through if it's as bad as it looks out there and you need to stay here with Maisy.'

'All right, yes, well at least you've had a quick coffee, so something warm inside you at least. But what about breakfast; can I cook you some eggs, toast?'

'No, I want to get on, Mum. Time is of the essence.'

'Well, here, take a couple of flapjacks with you.' She wrapped up two of the biscuits in cling film and passed them across. 'And I'll make you up a flask too. The kettle's already boiled.'

'Okay, thanks.'

Jill's insistence on keeping her fed and watered seemed like a small olive branch.

'And make sure you put an extra layer on under your waterproofs, and take the weatherproof gloves and a hat.'

With that, Rachel's mobile phone buzzed in her pocket: Tom. Their recent row still burned in her mind. She answered, feeling a little hesitant.

'I'm out on the hill.' The line was poor and she could hear the rush of the wind. 'Some of my sheep are already stuck. I'll come and help you with yours next. It'll be better with two of us. The farm lads can't come out, the roads are thick with snow and hard to pass already.' He was being pragmatic, the farmer instinct taking over despite their argument. There were bigger issues afoot here right now.

'Okay, well, I'm just ready to come out myself. Where are you? I could come and help you first?'

'I've taken the tractor up the Top Bank. If you go steady, it's okay getting up. You'll need your shovel and a long stick with you, though.' The line went a bit crackly then.

'Okay, I'm on my way.'

She took a few more glugs of hot coffee, located her gloves, hat and some rope, popped her waterproofs on over her clothes and grabbed the keys for the Land Rover – the quads were no good in this weather, sinking easily. The Land Rover was sturdy and she'd been out in thick snow in it before.

'Be careful, Rachel.' Jill was anxious, but trying her best to hide it from Maisy.

'I will.'

Rachel gave Maisy a quick peck on her forehead.

'Make sure Petie's okay, Mummy.'

'Will do. And Mum, it'd be great if you can have some nice warm soup ready for when I get in.' She knew Jill would feel better having a task to do.

'Of course. I'll get making some right now, we've plenty of vegetables in. Maisy, you can help me.'

'Then can we make some cupcakes, Grandma?'

'Yes, why not? That sounds a good idea.'

They were meant to be opening the Pantry today, but there was no way anyone was going to make it in, not without a snow plough, so a bit of baking wouldn't go amiss – help keep the spirits up.

'Right, I'm away.' Rachel was keen to get out there and face the elements.

'Don't take any chances out there.' Jill gave Rachel's arm a gentle pat.

'I won't,' Rachel replied, but she also knew she needed to do whatever it would take to save her flock and the farm's livelihood. 'I've got my mobile with me, but the signal may not be that great with a storm blowing, so try not to worry. I've got Tom with me, remember. We'll be fine.'

'Take Moss too, he might be able to help. He used to go with your dad . . .' Jill's voice trailed away.

'Come on then, Mossie. Let's go, boy.' The sheepdog was up and off the mat by the Aga in a second, bless him.

Rachel grabbed her wellingtons then braced herself as she opened the farmhouse's door. The snow blew almost horizontal at her, icily blasting her bare cheeks. Blimey, a balaclava might have been more suitable. She climbed into the Land Rover with Moss leaping in beside her, and set off stoically into the storm, realising too late that she'd forgotten the flask of coffee. Well, she wasn't going back for it.

With the windscreen wipers on full, she headed off down the farm track, making her way to Tom's land. Visibility was poor and with a sudden shunt of snow from the roof of the Land Rover covering the whole screen, for a second or two she couldn't see a thing. She braked gently, took a slow breath, and then set off once more. The road was already thick with snow, maybe a foot or more deep, but the vehicle kept going, and thank heavens for the hawthorn hedges which marked the route.

Rachel knew there was a track to follow up the bank to where Tom had told her he was working, but on reaching the field as she turned off from the lane, it was evident that the track had disappeared under a blanket of snow. She just hoped her trusty Land Rover could cope with the incline through the snowfall. The good thing was that it wasn't too icy, and in the main, except for where it had drifted, it wasn't yet too deep. The Land Rover whirred on and thankfully had enough traction to keep going steadily forward up the bank.

Dad's voice was coming through loud and clear in her mind as she concentrated on driving: 'Treat her gently in the snow, now, lass. Handle her properly and she'll come through for you. Imagine there's a bucket of water you don't want to spill in your passenger footwell, so no harsh breaking or accelerating.' Dad had taught her to drive all the farm vehicles – his calm, steady tuition with her still. In snow like this, she knew she had to keep the momentum up to maintain the climb as the bank steepened.

And there, ahead of her, through the constant flurry of snowflakes battering the windscreen, was a glimpse of the blue of Tom's parked tractor. Rachel pulled up slowly alongside and gently braked. She jumped out, grabbed a shovel and her long, flexible stick, already knowing that the task in hand might be a grim one.

There was Tom in a hi-vis yellow jacket, carefully working away with a shovel and his hands at a drift that had formed against the hedge.

'Tom.' The word was stolen by the rush of the wind up there, a biting easterly. 'Tom!' she raised her voice.

'Hey, I think there's several under here. I'm missing twenty in all. I've already dug out a couple.'

Rachel started to shovel away beside him. Moss was soon on the case a bit further along the drift, suddenly digging with his paws frantically, and sure enough, when Rachel came across and pushed her stick gently down at that spot, it touched a firm but giving object.

'Over here, Tom.'

This was a matter of life and death – they didn't know if they might be too late already. The poor ewes could have been buried all night, the drift was that high here, at over eight feet deep. Seeing this, Rachel was worried about her own flock too. She'd need to get back over there, as soon as possible. But there was safety in numbers in this weather, and two could work quicker than one. When they got this lot out, then they'd head back across to Primrose Farm.

It was a hard, physical job, digging, finding that warm

woolly head and shoulders, and then heaving the sheep out, over and over again. Tom had already made sure there was plenty of fresh hay out yesterday on seeing the forecast, and had scattered it in regular heaps across the field.

Still digging, still finding fleeces beneath the snow, Rachel began pulling a sheep out that seemed lifeless, its limbs limp, heavy. It was heartbreaking. 'Sorry, Tom, this one's already dead.'

'Ach, let's just keep going. Place her by the stone wall there for now.'

Rachel clawed away snow with her gloved hands to tug out another that had been beside it. It kicked as she pulled. 'This one's okay, it's alive.'

'That's good.'

Seeing this made her feel torn, but she had her own farm and animals to think of and she could hardly bear to leave them any longer. 'I need to get back to my own flock, Tom.'

'Aye, I understand. Come on, let's move over there now.' Tom was prepared to leave his flock to help Rachel out. Farming was full of difficult decisions.

But there were sheep here, too. And some that must be alive. Moss was still digging away, despite now being covered in icy snowballs all over his coat and she changed her mind. 'Hang on, Tom, let's work quickly, let's finish this drift at least.'

'You sure?'

'Certain.'

Fifteen minutes later, they left a huddle of rescued sheep with a cleared area of snow and a pile of hay, in the knowledge that they would return the next day for the four that had sadly perished. It could have been worse. They had lost thirty in one bad winter's storm at Primrose. That memory weighed in her mind as she drove carefully down the bank, feeling the back end of the vehicle drift at one point, but managing to correct it with some gentle steering. She hoped she wouldn't come to regret helping Tom out first, but it would have been risky to go out on her own, with no one knowing quite where she was.

Her flock were over two fields, luckily in the lower valley at this time of year. She couldn't get there soon enough, but knew there was to be no daft rushing, not when driving in the snow; the last thing she needed was to get herself stuck.

She had to dig out the snow with a shovel, just to open the five-bar gate to the first field. Once in, and with Tom soon behind her in the tractor, she tried to make a rough head count, which was difficult in the driving snow, as there was no way she could see the whole field at once. About thirty were gathered by the feeding troughs, and on a check around, another dozen were huddled in an area by the hawthorn hedge. She was relieved to see a further twenty or more in the far corner of the field. That meant around twenty were missing in this field. On one side of the field was a stone wall and this had a large snowdrift along it, which had formed into a wave-like shape.

'Let's go, Moss.' She'd parked alongside one of the deepest drifts, trying to remain positive and focussed; they just had to work steadily through. She set to, immediately poking down the long stick, over and over. Her hands were cold, her heart sinking when she repeatedly couldn't find the right spot. They were wasting precious time. She knew Petie was in this field too, and she hadn't spotted him in any of the safe huddles. It was like looking for a needle in a bloody haystack.

Suddenly, there was a shout from Tom. 'Here, Rachel, over here!'

She and Moss made their way across, leaning hard, battling against the wind. Just walking was difficult, with snow coming over the tops of her wellies now, but that was the least of her worries. They began shovelling as quickly as they could, shoulders and arms aching, then digging gently as they neared the level where the sheep should be. As they got further down, they used their hands to dig away the snow, Moss sniffing and working beside them. As she uncovered the first woolly face, Rachel cleared the snow from its nose and mouth, tears in her eyes. A shudder, a breath. It was alive.

'Thank God,' she muttered, 'thank God.' These hardy, beautiful animals, *her* animals.

Again and again, they pulled them out and began digging once more, no time to rest or catch your own breath. Then, there was one that was lifeless, tucked right down alongside the wall, and another beside it. Dammit. They'd saved sixteen now, two dead, another two . . .

where? Each side of the hole they'd dug out was empty. There was no sign of little Petie. Exhaustion and the bone-nagging cold were beginning to kick in too.

Moss ran up to Rachel, barking and circling her. Then he dashed away, looking over his shoulder, but was lost to her in the snowfall. 'Slow down, hey, Moss.' She began to follow, but the heavy swirling snow was a whiteout just then. Thankfully, the dog came back to her side, tail wagging, eager, impatient for her to follow. And she did.

Moss began barking where a drift had formed under a tree in the hedge-line.

Tom came alongside them. 'Let's go.' They were digging in tandem once more, Rachel trying her best to ignore the biting ache in her shoulders and back.

'Oh.' There was a damp, heavy fleece beneath her gloved fingertips. She pulled the little mite out. 'It's Petie.' He seemed so very still. 'Oh no, Tom.' *How on earth would she tell Maisy?* She rubbed away the snow from his mouth, his nose, and rubbed his cold body, wrapping him in her coat. Moss licked his black-patched face, and by some miracle, Petie gave a little shudder.

'Oh! Come on, Petie.'

He was weak, but he was still alive – just.

'I've got the other one here, she's fine,' said Tom. 'I'll set some more hay out here for you, and I'll clear a path around the food for the animals. Go and get Petie home, Rachel; he's got a chance if you get him to the warm now.'

'What about you?' She didn't like to leave Tom out here. It was wild and harsh.

'I'll finish off here, then I need to go back and see if I can get the last of my sheep out. I'm still missing ten or so and I can't just leave them – another night of this and there'll be no hope for them.'

'I'll help; I'm not leaving you out here on your own, Tom.' She was cold and damp and aching, but she couldn't leave Tom, not after all the help he'd just given her. Just two sheep dead from her flock in these conditions was a bit of a miracle, and all thanks to Tom's hard work and stalwart attitude.

'You need to get Petie home, Rachel. And you need to get back to Maisy and your mum. Go home, Rach, you've done really well here, but you'll be shattered.'

'But Tom—'

'I mean it.' He suddenly sounded stern. 'Look, Petie needs your help. He might not make it, otherwise. Go! I'll just be ten minutes here sorting out some feed for the sheep. I've a bale on the tractor spike, and then I'll give it another half hour or so back at my farm. I just want to recheck that field where we were before, okay?'

'Let me help you.' Rachel felt so torn.

'Go – *please.*' His look was intent.

'Well, ring me . . .' She began to cave as she looked down at Petie, battling for survival in her arms, the gorgeously naughty lamb they'd all grown to love. 'Let me know how you're getting on. And come back to ours as soon as you're done out here. Mum's making soup.'

'Okay, that sounds good. I'll see you soon.'

'Shall I leave Moss with you to help out?'

The loyal farm dog had been so good, tracking the scents of the buried sheep.

'No, it's okay, and I've a feeling he'll want to follow you home. He could get lost in the snows himself.'

'Yes, I suppose.' Snowflakes were sticking to her eyelashes as she spoke and the wind was weaving wildly around them.

'Honestly, I'm fine. I've done this before, in other winters. Get going.'

'All right. Take care.' She left reluctantly, carrying Petie, looking over her shoulder at the last, to see Tom nod purposefully at her.

Moss followed Rachel back to the Land Rover and jumped into the passenger footwell. She laid Petie on the seat, covering the lamb with an old rug that she always kept in the back. She set off hesitantly, giving Tom a wave, whilst sending out a silent prayer to keep him safe in this wild weather. She hated leaving him out here on his own. She drove away slowly until the swirling snow and the white track ahead was all that filled her vision. But – despite the complications and arguments of late – it was Tom that filled her heart.

38

Parking at the farmhouse, Rachel realised there were no lights on, just the glow of a candle from the kitchen window. Dammit, the electric must be out, the lines down in the blizzard winds. At the door, she shouted out to Jill for help while she carried the poor bedraggled mite that was Petie in, ready to warm him by the Aga, followed closely by faithful Moss who was at her snow-filled, wellington-booted heels.

'Oh, thank goodness you're back, Rachel!' Jill looked relieved, then took in the bundle in her daughter's arms with a frown, just as Maisy came running across in the half-light.

'Mummy, what is it? Who's poorly?'

'It's Petie, pet.' She felt a catch in her throat. 'It's okay, I think we can get him better. He needs warming up and a nice quiet, gentle time just now. So, sshh. No shouting.'

'Okay, but can I see?'

Rachel knelt down by the Aga – even with the electric off, that was still warm and toasty being oil-fired, thank heavens. She began to loosen the rug around the small lamb so his little face showed, all damp curly wool and half-closed eyes. He looked so weak, bless him.

'Oh, my Petie!' Tears started streaming down Maisy's rounded cheeks. 'He won't die, will he, Mummy?'

'Not if I can help it.' Rachel tried to smile soothingly, but felt the weight of the harsh winter elements in her bones and on her shoulders, and all she could think about just then was Tom.

Back to the crisis they faced here and now; the sheep feed and Lamlac was over in the shed, a battle of a walk away, so Rachel remembered an old tip of her grandad's and asked her mother to warm up some evaporated milk for Petie – normal cow's milk wasn't suitable for sheep.

'And what about you, Rachel, you must be freezing cold too?' Jill's tone was anxious.

Rachel hadn't realised it, but she was shivering, with the snow now melting down into her socks in her boots, around her cuffs and down her coat collar. She was rubbing Petie with the blanket gently, soothingly, trying to get his circulation going.

'Let's get some of that soup I made down you,' Jill said. 'I've kept it warming on the stove here for you.' She suddenly stopped, registering. 'What about Tom? Where is he? Did he go back home?'

Rachel shook her head. 'He made me leave him, Mum. I didn't want to. He helped with all our flock, then said he needed to get back to his. There were still several missing in the drifts.' She didn't want to say more, for fear of alarming Maisy.

'Oh, good Lord.'

'I've made him promise to ring us and to come straight

here afterwards.' But thinking about it, the mobile signals would be crap; they were dreadful at the best of times, let alone with a snowstorm going on.

'Okay . . .' Jill tried to contain her fears.

'When did the electrics go out?'

'About an hour ago. I had the candles ready, just in case.' They'd experienced power cuts many a time in this kind of weather, the overhead power lines which they had out here in the rural areas often freezing and blowing down.

'Why don't you go and get changed, love, get some warm clothes on?'

'In a minute. I'll just try Petie with a little of this milk, get him started . . .'

'All right, pet, it's ready now. I'll pop some in Maisy's plastic bowl she had as a toddler and we can see if that works for him.'

'I can help, Mummy.'

'Yes, I think Petie would like that.'

Maisy sat nursing her grown-up pet lamb with warm milk and gentle cuddles. It was heartwarming to see and Rachel prayed he'd make it through.

Twenty minutes later Rachel was dressed in dry warm woollens, with jogging bottoms and fresh socks, sipping a mug of soup.

Maisy was still cradling little Petie, stroking his woolly head, and softly singing him 'Away in a Manger' with a few ad lib words and several repeats, from her nativity play. The poor little sheep was now a million miles from his naughty drama queen self.

He'd managed a little of the sweet milk, and a little nibble of raw cabbage that Jill had found for him, and was resting. Only time would tell for this little chap.

Meanwhile, there was no way Rachel could rest. She'd tried Tom's mobile to reassure herself that he was okay, but as she feared, there was no answer, just an engaged tone as if there was no signal getting through. But it hadn't even been half an hour since she arrived back. He might just walk in the door any minute – cold, damp, tired and longing for a hug and a mug of soup.

As the time crept on, though, Rachel began to feel very uneasy. It was past two o'clock now and daylight would be fading (what dim daylight there was) in another hour or so. You really didn't want to be out in this weather in the dark.

Concerned looks passed between Rachel and Jill. Rachel kept checking her watch and the window, hoping for the rumbling sound of Tom's tractor and the re-assuring beam of its headlights. She was pacing the kitchen.

'It's no good, I can't hang about any longer, Mum. Something might have happened to him.' Rachel couldn't bear to wait. She couldn't take that risk. They'd already lost a father, a husband.

'Mummy, don't go! Look what happened to Petie out there.' Maisy was looking quite distraught.

'I know. But, that's why I need it go, petal. In case Tom's in trouble. I'll be okay. I really need to find him.

He might just need some help with one more sheep and then we can both come home.'

'I s'pose.' Maisy was biting down hard on her lip.

'You stay with Grandma and make sure Petie's doing fine.'

With that, the sheep's eyes fluttered open.

'See, he needs you here. Try that song again, I think he likes that one.'

'Okay.'

'I won't be long,' Rachel looked at Jill, 'hopefully. And if I get any signal on my phone, I'll keep in touch.'

'All right. Don't take any chances though, please.'

With no time to waste, Rachel grabbed her waterproofs, hat, her now soggy gloves and wellingtons and then headed back out, taking Moss once more, heading straight for Tom's field.

As she concentrated on the few snowflake-filled metres she could see ahead, there was a voice in her head, chanting, 'Let him be all right, please let him be all right'.

Instinct took her back to the field where they had started, guessing at the best track to take. The Land Rover started sliding at one point but she stayed calm, letting it roll back a little and then took another run up at the hill at a steady but smooth pace. The wind was howling hauntingly up here.

There! Over there. Rachel could just make out the blue of Tom's tractor parked at the brow of the hill. Thank heavens, he'd be somewhere nearby and she'd make him come away. It was time to give up, go home and get warm. He'd done all he could and more by now for sure.

The wind battered the door of the vehicle as Rachel tried to climb out, howling and blasting it with snow. No wonder the poor sheep were struggling up here. But the forecast was for it to ease tomorrow. Moss was on her heels as she began trudging along the hedge-line, figuring Tom would be here somewhere, still digging out the drifts.

'Tom, Tom!'

Moss began barking too.

She walked along the length of the top wall by the drifts, snow biting at her cheeks and dimming her vision. The world was a whirl of icy grey and white.

'To-om!'

No sign. The tractor engine was cold and the vehicle covered with snow. It hadn't been moved in a while. She pulled out her mobile and tried to phone him. A glimmer of hope as she saw it had service – but a couple of rings and then it cut out. Now there was no signal. Bugger.

Where the hell was he?

She made a search of the field, scanning the ground, the heaps of snow for a glimmer of colour, of clothing. Had he fallen, hurt himself? She called his name over and over, the sheep bleating with her from their huddled groups where they battled for shelter.

Nothing. *If he wasn't here, then where was he?* She could try his farmhouse – had he just gone home, exhausted, got into bed? Something told her no; he'd promised to go to Primrose Farm. He knew she'd be worried. Might he be tending an injured animal? Checking on his cattle in the sheds? But he must have walked from here and there were no footprints left to follow, the blizzard having swept away any trace. But he'd brought the tractor back up here, and there was a fresh bale put out for his herd, so where was he now?

'Tom? Tom!' The wind stole her words.

Think . . . *Why would he leave the tractor?* If he couldn't get it started – they were sometimes dodgy in extreme weather and the diesel could freeze – then he'd have to leave on foot. She climbed into the cab; the keys were still there, and tried turning the engine on . . . nothing, no response, no life in the engine at all. That explained one thing, but left a horrible question: where on earth was Tom now?

Stay calm, Rachel. Work it out. What would she do in the same circumstances? She'd head home on foot and his farmhouse was nearer than hers. She got back to her Land Rover, calling Moss in, who was more than happy to get out of the harsh elements. She set off, windscreen wipers on full, the foreboding sky darkening around them, and drove slowly, scanning all sides as she went. A skid took her adrift at one point, her heart in her mouth as the vehicle slowed to a halt just a few yards from a stone wall at the bottom of the field.

She then had to get out of the vehicle and dig out the back wheels with her shovel because they were spinning. She was cold to the bone after doing that and so tired.

But she wasn't heading back until she found Tom. She'd keep looking. Now on the track to Tom's farm, still no sign. The farmhouse door was unlocked, but he wasn't at home or out in the barns. Shit, shit, shit!

She made a call to Jill from Tom's landline, to let her know where she was, and that she was okay.

'Oh Rachel, thank goodness. Where are you? Have you found him?'

Bugger, so he wasn't there either. Her heart dipped.

'No, not yet. So, he's not turned up there?'

'No, I'm sorry.'

'I found the tractor. He'd left it. I think it had stalled. Oh, Mum . . .'

'Shall we come out? Help you look?'

'No! No Mum, you need to stay safe there with Maisy. I'll retrace my steps, try again. I'll find him.' She sounded way more positive than she felt.

'Go steady, love.'

'Will do. Okay, I'd better get going again.'

'Keep me posted, pet.'

'Yep.' She put the phone down with a sigh.

Should she call the emergency services? Would they even be able to get out here in these conditions? Probably not in time. They were miles from any police station or ambulance depot, and how the hell would they get up here in this snow, anyhow?

She was in this alone, there was no way she would endanger Jill or Maisy in this weather. With no time to waste, Rachel plodded back through the deepening snow to the Land Rover where Moss was still waiting, and headed back along the same track she'd come down on, just in case.

'Come on, Tom. Where are you, my love?' Please, dear God, let him be all right. She was beginning to get seriously worried now. If he was injured and laid up in this weather, hypothermia would soon kick in. The stupid row they'd had two days ago seemed futile. Her world felt on a dangerous precipice. Moss gave an empathetic whimper from the footwell beside her, as though sensing her fear.

She had just found this amazing, heart-soaring love with Tom and she wouldn't lose it now, she couldn't.

'I'll find you,' she vowed.

Driving slowly, with the Land Rover tyres slipping here and there, her eyes scanned the landscape through swirls of snow. Still no sign.

Perhaps she could try Mr Mac, ask him to come along in his tractor, help her to look? He was a grumpy old bugger, but he might just rally to arms for a fellow farmer. He was probably the only other person who could get out in this and who knew the lay of the land. She looked up his number on her mobile. *Sod it,* this was an emergency, any help she could get was worth it. She saw one bar of signal on her phone, slowed the vehicle and dialled. But there was no answer, not on his landline nor his mobile, damn, though she left a brief message on his voicemail.

What if she didn't find Tom? He could have wandered anywhere, got confused, be lying with the snow heaping up on him like poor Petie. Panicked thoughts began to fill her mind. She pushed them aside abruptly. Tom was strong, he knew this landscape, understood the power of this weather. Though the vortex of fear in her stomach kept whirling, she kept it at bay. *Focus*, Rachel, *focus*. She followed the track back towards Tom's tractor and the field they'd been in, moving slowly, lowering her window, scouring the landscape and calling, calling. Then she continued, heading further up the valley, along what she hoped was still the track, the snow even deeper here, the darkening sky a thick grey soup behind the swirling flakes of white. She hoped to God that she didn't get stuck herself, but there was no turning back for her now.

'Tom! Tom! Are you there?' she yelled through her open window, snow hurtling in at her. She tooted the horn.

And the memories of calling for Dad on that fateful day were strong and foreboding, clutching at her soul . . .

Keep going, Rachel. You'll find him. Granny Ruth's sensible voice was suddenly in her mind, spurring her on.

I am. I will.

But should she turn back, try elsewhere on the farm? Why would he be up the valley this far? She'd have to find somewhere to try and turn the Land Rover, which would be tricky in all this snow. The last thing this situation needed was two of them stuck out here.

There! What was that? She squinted, trying to focus. Ahead . . . a glimpse of clothing? Something yellow? A figure stumbling. Surely no one else would be mad enough to be out here on a day like this. She pulled up, leapt out with Moss on her heels. Oh God! 'Tom!'

It *was* him. He was staggering, snow stuck horizontally to his clothing, his face, his lashes. He looked ashen. He was heading the wrong way up the valley.

'Tom! Hey, it's me, Rachel.' There were tears in her eyes as she stopped him and took him in her arms.

He seemed confused, looking at her blankly for a second or two. 'Gotta get back,' he muttered.

'I know. Come on, you're okay. You're safe now. Let's get you in the truck.'

And then he seemed to register. 'Rach?'

Moss was criss-crossing behind the two of them, herding them back to the vehicle.

'It's all right, Tom. You'll be okay now,' she reassured. She guided him to the truck and helped him in to the passenger seat. Moss took his place at his feet and gave his hand a welcoming lick. Rachel could see that Tom was shivering uncontrollably. He could well be hypothermic. She tucked a rug from the rear of the truck around him, managed a six-point turn in the snowy lane, having to stop and dig out the tyres with her shovel at one point, insisting Tom stay put, and they set off.

Tom seemed rather dazed and weak. 'Got lost . . .' was all he could say.

'It's okay, I've found you. We're going home.' And she couldn't wait to see the steading of Primrose Farm. She concentrated on the blur of track ahead.

'Sorry,' he added a few minutes later, seeming to register a little more.

'No need. Oh, Tom, I shouldn't have left you out here.' Guilt began to bite, mixed with relief. He'd insisted, yes, but it was no place to be left alone.

'Did we save them . . . the sheep?' It was as if his short-term memory was struggling.

'Mostly, you saved nearly all my flock. Thank you. Thank you so much.'

'Oh . . . good. That's good.' He seemed bone-tired, shivering still. He closed his eyes. Moss's nose nudged the hand he had rested in his lap as they made the last leg of the journey.

A rumbling noise came from ahead and a daze of headlights – a big green tractor that she recognised as Mr Mac's. It paused ahead of them in the lane and he jumped out, coming across to the Land Rover.

'Aye, you've found him. Thank heavens for that.' The old man seemed genuinely concerned and relieved to see Tom in the vehicle. 'I tried to call you back, and then your mam answered at the farm. This is no weather to be out in. How is he?'

Tom wasn't answering, he was so sleepy.

'He seems hypothermic. We need to get him home and warm.'

'Ay, let me turn about and I'll make a clear track for you, lassie. I've got the snowplough on.'

'Oh, thank you. Thank you.'

'Nay worries. Grand he's back wi' ye. Let's get you all home then.'

Rachel smiled. Tom wasn't quite out of the woods yet, but this show of human kindness, that her grumpy neighbour was there when it mattered, suddenly made her feel teary. She wouldn't let on, of course, wiping a little droplet away as Mr Mac turned to go back to his tractor.

The journey was swifter with a clear road and a big green tractor to follow, all the way back to Primrose Farm. Mr Mac helped to support Tom inside, where Jill was ready in the candlelight, with warm towels, and fresh clothes she'd found in Dad's side of the wardrobe that she hadn't yet been able to bear to throw out.

Maisy looked on, concerned at first, but came over to give Tom a big cuddle once his wet clothes were changed. 'Tom, you are very brave. You saved Petie – thank you.' She climbed onto his lap carefully and gave him a gentle kiss on the cheek. He opened his weary eyes and she pointed to Petie who was there beside the Aga too, wrapped in an old blanket and snoozing contentedly now.

'Oh, that's good. So the little chap's okay?' A little colour had started to return to Tom's cheeks.

There were mugs of warm vegetable soup for everyone, and bread that Jill had freshly baked. Mum liked to keep busy in a crisis and baking was her go-to, so the mixer had come out whilst they still had electric this morning and Rachel and Tom had been busy battling the elements up on the fells. Rachel spooned some of the soup into Tom's mouth and his eyes caught hers with a tired but tender look of love and gratitude.

Tom was soon sleeping soundly in the chair by the Aga. It looked odd and yet kind of right, seeing him sitting in Dad's clothes, which were a little baggy on him.

'Well then, I think the lad'll be fine now.' Mr Mac looked across, almost fondly, at the sleeping figure too.

Rachel knew that he didn't have any children and had lived at his farm alone since his wife died over ten years ago now. Rachel had never asked about the fact he had no family because it felt like prying, and knowing the grumpy nature of the old chap she'd probably have had her head bitten off. But from the look in his eye just now, perhaps he'd always wanted a son of his own.

'Close call that one, mind,' he continued, 'up on those hills in this weather. But I know what it's like when it's your animals at risk. Right then, well, I'd better be on my way.' Mr Mac stood up from his place at the kitchen table, ready to go.

'Thank you so much, Mr Mac,' said Rachel, standing too.

'Aye, well, it's what anyone would do in the circumstances.' He sounded gruff, like he didn't want any fuss.

'Here – I'm sure you'll be glad to take some warm soup and sandwiches back with you for your supper this evening. And what about a sticky toffee pudding and a nice slice of Christmas cake?' Jill was already ladling soup out for him into a Tupperware dish.

'Aye, well, that'd be grand.' His tone quickly softened.

'And, once we're open again in the next couple of days, do call in at the Pantry,' Rachel added. 'There'll be a lunch or two on the house for you.'

'Well, thank you, lassie.'

A few minutes later, with Tom still sleeping soundly, Mr Mac took the food bundle with a grateful nod, and was back to action and his usual grumpy self. 'Aye, I'll clear the lane with the plough as I head back, now that the snow's starting to ease off. Make a track for you and the others further up the lane. Some daft buggers have no idea how to drive in the snow.'

'Ahh, this is the best way of warming up.' The sound of Tom's voice was a welcome relief as he and Rachel lay close under the duvet in her double bed later that evening.

Maisy had been tucked up in her room an hour before and Rachel and Jill had made a sleeping area for Petie out in the porch, clearing the boots and wellies and covering the stone floor with an old blanket, so they could keep an eye on him overnight.

They were all exhausted as the dark took hold outside. The snow had finally stopped and the winds had eased. A relieved hush fell over the farmhouse and Rachel was more than ready to have an early night.

Rachel had crawled in, naked, beside Tom, yearning to feel the warmth of his skin next to hers. She didn't like to think how close she had come to losing him. She traced a finger across his brow and down his cheek, over the slight stubble on his chin. 'Thank God you're all right,' she whispered. She couldn't hold back the tear that had formed in her eye. It dripped down her cheek. A tear of relief, of love.

She held him tight to her then, pressing her body against his warm skin, and she sighed deeply, the fraught emotions of the day still with her. She snuggled her face into his chest and murmured, 'I was so afraid, Tom.'

'It's okay, I'm here now. Just got a little chilly that's all.' His voice was still a little frail.

Trust him to make light of hypothermia.

He stroked the top of her head softly. He still seemed weak, but was over the worst.

'What a day,' Rachel whispered.

'Uh-huh, it certainly was.' He sounded so tired.

She lay beside him, feeling the steady beat of his heart beside her, as she gently stroked the contours of his chest. She wasn't sure if he was beginning to fall asleep once more, but spoke anyhow, 'I love you, Tom. So much.'

'Love you too, Rach . . . thanks . . . for not giving up on me.'

Her heart was full to the brim. Their recent argument dimmed into insignificance. She couldn't imagine ever being without him now, didn't want to. Today had brought them far too close to that.

'I'd never give up on you, Tom.'

39

Rachel left Tom in her bed the next morning to rest up and recover from the trials of yesterday. She was pretty shattered herself, but there were sheep and cattle to tend to on both farms. Jill offered to go along and help out, as it was unlikely anyone would make it through to the Pantry today – unless they came by sledge! – but Rachel wasn't sure what the snow and terrain would be like, and as it would mean Maisy would have to come along too. She didn't want to risk an accident with her precious family in the truck.

'I'll be okay, Mum, you stay here with Maisy, and Tom's still resting upstairs. I'll just crack on,' she answered stoically. 'There's bound to be a few weak sheep out there after that storm. They'll be needing extra feed and nutrients.'

Rachel wrapped up warm and headed to the store in the lambing shed, filling the back of the Land Rover with sacks of feed and some mineral blocks, Moss keeping her company. It was heavy work, and her arms were still aching from digging out the drifts yesterday, but she put her back in to it and carried on.

She made a little pen up in the shed for Petie, as already the porch was getting messy with sheep poo, much to Maisy's amusement! If she could manage to get the tractor out later, Rachel mused, she'd get some more silage and hay out to the fields on both farms too. She wanted to check the lay of the land and the driving conditions first though.

This was the harsh side of farming, when the winter weather could be so cruel, and the risk to life and your livelihood very real. And yet, up on the hills just ten minutes later, emptying sacks of feed into the wooden troughs for the hungry sheep, with the snow clouds now gone and a glow of morning sun forming a silvery-blue light over the white-snowclad landscape, this place could still take Rachel's breath away.

The next day, with the roads cleared, and the snow on the fields melting to slush, the Pudding Pantry was getting busy once more. Word about Granny Ruth's famous Christmas Puddings and the new Pudding Club at their quaint country tea rooms was spreading like hot cakes. With only a few days left until Christmas Day, the Pantry was a hive of activity, with orders coming in thick and fast, customers queuing for tables discussing the terrible snowstorm, with puddings galore being eaten amid excited chatter about the Christmas break. Being stuck in the farmhouse for a couple of days with the bad weather meant Jill had caught up with more baking and stocks were holding up well for now, though there'd be more late nights and early mornings at the Aga yet, to keep up with demand.

Tom was now back on his feet, if a little tired, and very much back to work.

He and Rachel finally caught up with each other over a cup of coffee at Tom's farmhouse, when Rachel called in on her way back from delivering puddings to the Kirkton Deli.

'Hey, you okay? You look shattered.' It was Tom's turn to be concerned. He could see just how exhausted Rachel was. He stepped closer, and moved a strand of hair that had fallen across her eye. 'I'm sorry, I know I added to your workload, being out of action for the last day or so. Just when there was so much more to do on the farms. Thanks for all your help with that.'

'No worries, it was just what I had to do. You'd have done the same for me if the boot was on the other foot, I'm sure.'

He nodded. 'Can I help now? Is there anything I can do?'

'Well, most of it's pudding mayhem, and I'm not sure if that's your forte,' she smiled.

'True.'

'Yeah, the Pantry has gone a bit crazy. You'd think there was going to be food rationing or something after Christmas.'

'Well, I can certainly help with your farm work, give you a bit of breathing space.'

'Aw, I appreciate that.'

'I bet you'll still be soldiering on though, wearing yourself out.' He was getting to know her foibles. She wasn't one to accept help easily, her sense of pride and determination being so strong. 'You know, you need to slow down, Rachel.'

'But there's so much to do right now. I can't just stop. It's never-ending.'

'Okay, I realise that for the next few days you've just got to knuckle down, get Christmas out of the way. But then maybe you need to look at how you organise it all, try doing things another way? Think about it, do you really need to open the Pudding Pantry every single day? You're piling so much pressure on yourselves.'

Rachel knew he was right. Was she strong enough to keep carrying such a heavy load? Could there be a different way?

'Slow down, my love,' Tom continued, his voice gentle. 'Not for me, but for yourself. These past two years have been so tough for you. You still need time to heal, to find a way forward.'

Their eyes fixed with a depth of shared understanding. He had been there too. He had seen what had happened back then. That day when her father had chosen to end his life. Life had felt like a battle ever since, but maybe she didn't have to struggle on alone.

Rachel nodded. It was time to think about how to move forward.

'Rachel, about Caitlin . . .' Tom suddenly looked deadly serious.

Rachel swallowed slowly. So, this was it. Did she really want to know the truth? Might this be the end for them?

She stayed silent, afraid that if she spoke the emotions would crack in her voice.

'Okay, so yes,' he continued, 'it's my ex, Caitlin, who's been calling.'

Rachel felt her heart contract. It was suddenly hard to breathe.

Tom took a sip of coffee, before continuing, 'She has been here, you were right. She's out to get more of the farm, claiming it wasn't a fair split, that she's had a raw deal. She's got a new solicitor in on the case and everything.' He rubbed his forehead, agitatedly.

'Oh, Tom!' And there Rachel had been imagining there might be some romantic element behind this; she felt so stupid now. But oh God, the implications for Tom and his farm . . . Rachel knew all too well the dread of losing your home, your land, your livelihood, the place that was so precious to you and your family.

'She hated the bloody farm here and farm life, that's the shit thing,' Tom continued. 'I gave her money for half the house and a decent payout. It was all agreed and finalised, supposedly, in the divorce settlement.'

'So, why's she coming back on the scene now?'

'Probably out of cash, spent it all. How the hell did I even fall for someone like that?'

'Well, we can all make mistakes, especially with relationships.' Falling for Jake hadn't exactly been Rachel's best move in life.

'I'll have to mortgage the farm even more, or sell off some land, if she gets this agreed and I already had it mortgaged to the hilt to buy her out. Damn it, I can hardly even afford the solicitor's bills to fight the bloody case, right now.'

'Oh Tom, this is so stressful. But it's been years now; surely, she can't have any further claim? And what timing, too, right on the run up to Christmas! Some Merry Christmas from your ex, that is.' Rachel was angry on Tom's behalf.

'I think she's planning on giving herself a nice Christmas present – a chunk of *my* farm. Or the money from it, anyway.'

'Bloody hell, that's so not fair.' Caitlin sounded like a right bitch.

'Hah, well, not that Christmas has been much of an exciting time for me lately,' Tom admitted.

'Hmm, I know that feeling, with Dad gone . . .' The spark had gone out of the festive season for her too. But this year they had been trying so hard to make it magical and to try to enjoy it again, for Maisy's sake. 'Look, maybe it's not the easiest of times for either of us, but you will still come to ours for Christmas dinner, won't you?' Rachel paused to give Tom time to consider. 'On one condition, that is – you have to promise not to sit there all sour-faced like Scrooge!' She gave a cheeky smile, relieved that they were still okay. However tough the circumstances with Caitlin, they could support each other now, not be driven apart by it.

'Hah, yeah, and yes, of course, I'll still come. That'd be really nice, Rachel. Thank you.'

Granny Ruth had been right: relationships had to be built on honesty. They shared a warm, tender smile and Tom came across to stand beside Rachel, placing a hand on her shoulder. His touch soothed her. She turned to put her arms around his waist, resting her head on his chest. Maybe, as long as they had each other, they could find a way through the maze that was life, and what it seemed to constantly throw up at them. Amidst all the chaos, the prospect of sharing their first Christmas together was a good one.

40

There was a welcome calm in the weather over the next couple of days and the snow had gone. Thankfully, Petie made a good recovery and the remaining animals on the farm appeared to be doing fine, with no further casualties. The customers were still flocking to the Pudding Pantry, eager to take a little time out in their busy Christmas schedules for a festive treat, and to purchase some extra goodies to take home to their families. Granny Ruth's Whisky and Orange Puddings were still selling out hard and fast.

Christmas Eve was soon upon them, and the Pudding Pantry was in full festive swing; carols were playing on the radio, the tree lights were twinkling away, with the coffee machine gurgling in the background as an array of delicious puddings were warmed, served and spooned. There were orders being collected for Ruth's award-winning puddings, along with Jill's Chocolate and Cherry Puddings, Rachel's Irish Cream Cheesecakes, Pavlovas, and Chocolate Yule Logs to name but a few. Mince pies were munched, along with Danish Pastry Cinnamon Swirls, and Maisy's new favourites, festive cupcakes with Rudolph noses, teamed with creamy-topped hot chocolates.

Having wished for weeks for more business back in the autumn, Rachel wasn't about to complain, but her feet were certainly throbbing and, with a queue of customers snaking past the counter, there was no sign of having a sit down yet.

Glancing up for a second, Rachel took in how lovely the barn looked, with its festive decorations, Eve's gorgeous crafts and the Christmas tree, a little sparser on needles than when she had first put it up with Maisy, but still twinkling merrily with its lights and baubles. The pretty chandeliers, chosen by her friends, were sparkling above them too, giving the old stone walls a golden glow and there was excited chatter as children wondered if they'd get their Christmas wishes and families discussed if it might well be snowing again by the morning.

Star helper Maisy was helping to serve, and Daniel, who had repeated his offer to help, had thankfully come in today too. He was busy clearing tables and washing up. Rachel had to acknowledge he'd been a bit of a godsend in the circumstances. It really was a team effort today.

The light started to fade outside as the afternoon rolled on; it was now past four o'clock and Jill was still on her feet, serving. Rachel noticed she was slowing however, and looked awfully tired.

'I'll help to finish off here with Rachel. I'm in no particular rush,' offered Dan, coming over.

'Thank you, Daniel.' Jill gave a smile.

'Yes, we'll manage . . . go on, Mum,' said Rachel pressing.

'Hah, I know where I'm not wanted,' Jill jibed, as she began to gather her things. 'Don't stay too late, Rachel. And thank you, Dan,' she added with a small smile as she made her exit.

'I'll stay and help Mummy too, Grandma.' Maisy skipped on up to her at the door.

'Good girl.'

Maisy really was on her best behaviour today. She'd heard all about, 'You'd better be good . . . you'd better watch out,' and she knew that Santa Claus really was coming to town very soon.

'We'll see you in a while, Mum.'

'Thank you, love. And Dan, have a marvellous Christmas, and thanks again for all your help today. You've been a godsend.'

'You're welcome, that's what friends are for. And it is Christmas, after all. Have a lovely Christmas yourself, Jill. Be sure to take some time out and enjoy the break.'

'Thanks. Oh, and Daniel . . .' Jill paused, looking almost shy. 'If you get chance, why not call by for a Christmas drink with us? Any time.'

'I'd like that, thank you.' Daniel gave a warm nod.

Rachel felt a beat of unease, but quashed it, realising she needed to find some Christmas spirit within herself. Daniel had been kind enough to help today after all.

After Jill had left, the till kept on dinging, and they must have done well today. This was well worth the sore feet and backache. Rachel was *so* looking forward to a big mug of tea, a cosy chair and the frisson of counting the takings, but there were a million things yet to do back home and they were all going off for the Christmas Eve carol service in Kirkton too, a tradition never to be missed by the Swinton family. And later, there were gifts to wrap once Maisy was in bed, and the veggies to prepare to get a head start on tomorrow's Christmas feast. Wow, just thinking about all that made Rachel's head spin.

'Can I take two of the Christmas puddings? I've quite a crowd tomorrow.' A woman's voice pulled her back to the here and now.

'Oh, yes, of course. Maisy, do you want to fetch two of Granny Ruth's specials for me?'

'Yep.' Even Maisy had to stifle a little yawn. She'd been a little star, helping today. Rachel felt a bit guilty – they hadn't had time to go out and play and do Christmassy things for themselves yet. But tomorrow and Boxing Day would be their time to spend some proper family time together.

The next two customers bought the last Yule Log and Christmas cake, then a family who'd been in having hot chocolates, came to the till to pay and spotted the very last Christmas Pudding.

'Oh, is that the pudding we saw in the local paper?

Do you remember, Kenny, the one that won the award?'

'Yes, it is indeed,' answered Rachel proudly. 'Made to my granny's own special recipe.'

'Oh, we'll take that one, please.'

So that was it. They were all Christmas Pudding'd out.

The final customers of the day left just before five, wishing them all a 'Merry Christmas' as they headed off with big smiles and happy tummies. Daniel and Rachel swiftly cleared the tables, washed up the last bits and pieces, then Rachel leant against the countertop, exhaling a loud, 'Phew.'

'Well, that was busy,' said Daniel.

'Yes, thank you so much, Dan. I really don't know how I'd have managed without you.' Rachel was extremely grateful for his help. She still felt uncomfortable about the situation with him and Jill – but had she been wrong in judging him so harshly, she wondered?

She took out fifty pounds from the till to pay him for his work but he shook his head and wouldn't accept a penny.

'Are you sure? But you've worked so hard.'

'I wanted to help . . . and to make sure Jill didn't overdo it. Though I fear she might have done that, anyhow.'

'Hah, yes. We can be rather determined, us Swinton ladies.'

'I'm beginning to find out.' He grinned.

As he wouldn't accept any money, Rachel gave him the last Sticky Toffee Pudding as a gift.

'Well, thanks, that'll go down well with my mam. I'm sure.'

'Have a lovely day tomorrow. And thank you *so* much for all your help today.'

'You're welcome. Happy Christmas to you all. Hope Santa's good to you, Maisy,' he added. 'You've certainly been a very good girl today. Have you asked for anything special?'

'I wanted a mini quad bike, but Mummy says that might be a bit tricky for Father Christmas to bring down the chimney, and he might think I'm too young.' Rachel was raising her eyebrows at Dan, across the top of Maisy's head. 'So, I said a Twister game and some sweeties.' Maisy gave a cheerful smile.

At least she was sticking to her latest ideas, Rachel thought with relief, as any last-minute changes at this point would be nigh on impossible to fulfil.

'Well, that sounds fun. I do like a game of Twister.' He gave a wink. 'Right then, I'll be on my way. Have a lovely time all of you. Happy Christmas and bye.' Daniel set off towards his car.

'Bye, Dan. Merry Christmas!' Maisy was waving from the barn door. It was pitch-black outside and a chill breeze blew in.

So, that was it, the last shift before Christmas was completed. Rachel turned off the coffee machine, switched off the chandeliers and the fairy lights on the Christmas tree, just leaving the pretty outdoor lights to twinkle from the barn eaves. The dream of this spring really had become a reality. The Pudding Pantry had been born. And wow, what a shift it had been. They were now going to enjoy a much-needed break.

Rachel took Maisy's hand. 'Ready then, sweetheart?'

It was time to go home, across the yard. Tom had said he'd call by and head along to the Christmas Eve Carol Service with them this evening. Granny Ruth, with Mum, would be meeting them there, any time soon. Then they'd all head back to the farmhouse for an easy supper and start preparations for the big day ahead. But first, a huge mug of tea and a sit down by the Aga was calling!

41

'Merry Christmas, Dad, love you,' Rachel whispered as she stood, holding Maisy's hand tightly, by her father's graveside. How she wished he could still be here with them; sitting at the big table in the farmhouse kitchen tomorrow, celebrating Christmas with his family. If only they could turn back time . . .

'Happy Christmas, Grandad,' chanted Maisy, which touched Rachel's heart.

He wasn't ever going to see her little girl grow up . . .

Rachel had taken a bunch of red carnations, gathered from the posies in the Pantry, and now she laid them down on her father's grave. Maisy then stepped forward to place her Christingle ribbon-decorated orange, that she'd kept from the last day at school, by the headstone, asking her mum to light the little candle on it. There were also three white roses, tied in a green satin ribbon, laid there on the grave. Had Mum already been, or Granny Ruth?

'I want Grandad to have a special light, so he doesn't feel lonely,' Maisy added seriously.

Rachel suddenly found it hard to breathe. How had all this happened to them? How could life, that was at times so beautiful, be so damned cruel? She was conscious of Tom, standing back by the church gates, giving them their time.

It was cold there in the churchyard. Rachel liked to pay her respects every now and again and to mark his resting place, but to her, Dad . . . well, he was everywhere as memories within her mind – on the farm, in the hills around them, in the lambing shed, in the places he had been so many times, in the things he had touched, not just here in the churchyard.

The starting notes of 'Silent Night' rang out on the slightly cranky organ, filling Kirkton church. The congregation stood up to sing, with Maisy, Rachel, Tom, Granny Ruth and Jill, lined up in their pew. It was chilly in there; you could even see your breath as you sang, but being local they were familiar with the cold interior of the centuries old stone church and knew all about wearing two pairs of thick socks, stamping your feet a bit, and layering up with thick jumpers and warm woollen coats. They were all primed and dressed for the occasion.

The church was important to the local community, a place to celebrate and a place to grieve. And everyone was gathered here tonight, on Christmas Eve, a night of tradition and of celebration. There were farmers and friends, there were young and old. Eve, Ben and Amelia were there, and some members from the Pudding Club, including newcomer Alice and her family – Rachel had made a point of saying hello to them as they found their seats. Just across from them was Jim, the taxi driver, Brenda from the deli and her husband – blimey, there was even Vanessa Palmer-Pilkington. Rachel drew a truce, for tonight only, and even managed a small smile at the old bat.

The congregation sang together and said their prayers, with everyone looking forward to a day of rest and celebration tomorrow. Rachel found herself feeling grounded, a sense of peace settling on her. The service came to a close with a blessing from the priest, and a 'Merry Christmas' to all. Friends and acquaintances wished each other 'Happy Christmas' as they milled out of the church into the cold, frosty air.

Back at Primrose Farm, Rachel nipped upstairs to take off one of the extra layers needed for church. On her way back to the hubbub of the kitchen she was drawn by the glinting coloured lights of the Christmas tree in the sitting room and decided to take a few moments out.

She picked up a stray bauble from the floor where it had dropped and placed it carefully back on a branch, trying not to let the needles drop. The fire was on in the hearth and the lounge looked just the place to curl up with a sneaky tipple of Baileys Irish Cream, but there was work still afoot. Maybe tomorrow.

Christmas Day was almost here; another year almost over. Dad's photo smiled at her from the mantlepiece, the pull of emotions ebbed and flowed within her. Memories rose, Christmas traditions, the past and the present . . . the future. Maisy, Mum, Granny, the farm and the Pantry. There was Tom, too, in this new equation.

She knew that life could never be the same again without Dad, but tonight she had a feeling it could be a happy place again once more. And, with a lot of hard work and a little luck, the future for them would be right here at Primrose Farm.

After a chaotic hour of food prepping for the big day and getting Maisy ready for bed, Rachel and Tom found themselves alone – miracle of miracles – in the kitchen. Rachel had really enjoyed this evening with Tom by her side. It was Christmas Eve, a special, magical time. She realised that she didn't want him to go.

'Can you stay tonight?' Rachel asked, almost shyly. She realised the significance behind her suggestion – Tom had only stayed at Primrose Farm, her family home, a handful of times.

'Here?' Tom clarified, with a small yet hopeful smile.

'Yes . . . I'd like that.'

'And what about, Maisy? You were always a bit anxious . . .'

'Well, maybe it's time. And, she'll be so excited tomorrow that it's Christmas morning and that Father Christmas has been, you probably won't get a look in, anyhow.' Rachel grinned, imagining the likely scenario. She moved in closer. 'And I'd so like to wake up with you on Christmas morning. And,' she whispered in his ear, 'I'd rather like to make love with you on Christmas Eve.'

'Right, I see.' Tom gave a daft grin back.

She sensed the frisson of anticipation run through him.

'Well, in that case . . .' Tom started.

'It'd be rude not to,' finished Rachel with a wide smile.

'Exactly.'

And they closed the conversation with a very gorgeous, leading kiss.

'Where are the carrots, Mummy? We need them for Rudolph and his friends.'

Maisy was out of the bath and prancing about in her new festive pyjamas, that had a cute red-nosed reindeer print. It was well past her usual bedtime, but excitement for the big day tomorrow had given her second wind, and there were of course certain routines and traditions yet to be fulfilled . . . after all it was 'The Night Before Christmas'.

'Yes, and Father Christmas likes a drink of whisky,' the little girl stated.

Oh, she'd remembered. There was a tug inside Rachel's heart just as Jill looked up catching Rachel's eye. Yes, that had always been the way. A mince pie, a nip of whisky and carrots for the reindeer, all set out on a little wooden tray on the table by the fire. Of course, it was Rachel's dad who had enjoyed the whisky and the mince pie.

'Of course, petal, I'll go find the whisky bottle,' Rachel responded, setting off for the kitchen, where she knew there was a little left over from the mammoth Christmas

Pudding making session of last week. A head and heart full of her own childhood memories suddenly appeared – she could picture her dad coming in after a hard day on the farm, sitting there by the Aga in the chair that Granny Ruth liked, mug of tea in hand, toes warming by the stove. Hah, she used to hold her nose sometimes and complain about the whiffy, cheesy smell of his damp woollen socks. Boy, she'd give anything to have him back here, smelly feet and all. To climb on to his lap for a cuddle like the good old days. For him to be there with them all tomorrow carving the turkey for Christmas Dinner, with Maisy running about showing him all her new gifts. A lump lodged in her throat.

Right then. Stop right there, Rachel Swinton, pull yourself together, Maisy needs to see you happy and cheery, Rachel rallied. She located the whisky, took a deep breath, and headed back to the living room, where she found one of Dad's cut glass tumblers in the cabinet.

'Here we go. Shall I pour it out? Just a small one, mind. Santa's got to drive his sleigh, you know.'

'Yes, we don't want him crashing,' Maisy added seriously.

'Oh, and we need the list, Maisy. Where's your special Christmas wish list that you wrote out the other day?'

'I know, I know. It's in my room.'

'Well, it's time we sent it up the chimney.'

'Yes, yes.' She scampered off up the stairs, returning a few minutes later, clutching her neatly-written note that she'd decorated with glitter and stars and snowmen.

Rachel used to do this same ritual with her dad every Christmas Eve. He'd light the corner of the Christmas list with a match and hold it carefully above the fireplace where the draught of the chimney would take it up and away, as Rachel sent it off with a silent Christmas wish. And, guess what, the list had always worked, the gifts delivered with love.

The flame flickered, the paper soon catching alight and curling, then off and up it went. Maisy watched it go then squeezed her eyes closed for a few seconds – making an extra wish, no doubt.

'Thank you, Father Christmas,' the little girl said aloud.

Rachel went to settle Maisie, who was finally starting to get sleepy after two full readings of *'Twas The Night Before Christmas* and *The Snowman* in bed. Rachel tucked her down under the duvet, with Olaf the snowman by her side, and gave her a big kiss. 'Sweet dreams, petal.'

'Mummy,' she whispered, 'I wished for some real snow so we can make our own really big snowman tomorrow. The stormy snow was too bad, so we never got to make him, and the first one was really little.'

'Ah, well, we'll have to wait and see what the weather does, won't we.' Hmm, well, that was one present she couldn't wrap up and deliver.

'It's time to go to sleep now, Maisy, or Santa won't be able to come.'

'O-kay.'

Rachel well knew that it might take her little girl some

time to drift off, however. Granny Ruth, who was staying over, had retired to bed early too, happy to be propped up against plump pillows with her book and her knitting for a while.

Tom had nipped back to his farmhouse to collect terrier Mabel, who was going to come over for the evening, and also to have a last check on his farm and see that all was well with the cattle in his shed.

When Rachel came back down to the living room, Mum was sitting quietly, gazing at the fire. She seemed thoughtful, quiet.

'All okay, Mum?'

'Yes, of course, love,' she replied, but her tone had a trace of sadness though it.

'You sure?'

Jill nodded, but then, after a pause, added, 'I dropped by the churchyard earlier, on my way to fetch Granny Ruth for the carol service. Had a few words with Dad.'

'Ah . . .' Rachel had seen the three white roses laid against the headstone. It *had* been Mum who'd left them.

'Well, I knew we'd all be busy tomorrow.'

'Oh, I'm sorry, Mum, you must be really feeling it today.'

There was a pause as they both watched the orange flames flickering in the grate.

'We went to visit Dad too, me and Maisy, just before the service,' added Rachel, after a while.

'Oh, did you, love? Thank you.'

'Yes, Maisy wanted to take her Christingle orange for Grandad.'

'Oh, bless her.'

With it being an emotional night, it suddenly dawned on Rachel that asking Tom to stay over might have been selfish in the circumstances. A big 'need to do better' sign was flashing away in her head. She ought to come clean.

'Look, I'm sorry, Mum, maybe I should have thought . . . but it's just . . . I've asked Tom to stay for tonight. Maybe it's not a good time. He's just nipped home to fetch Mabel, but I can call him, tell him to come across in the morning instead.'

'Don't be so silly, our lass. Tom's more than welcome. And I'm happy to see you two getting on so well. Life's for living, Rachel. Dad wouldn't want us to stop enjoying it.'

'Thanks . . . And yes, you're right; this evening just brings it all home though, doesn't it? Doing the Christmas list and all the Rudolph rituals with Maisy earlier, it felt like he was right there with me.' Rachel had a glint of a tear in her eye. 'It's been an evening full of memories, hasn't it?'

'Ah, yes, all those years of Christmases we had together when you were little. I just think what he's missing out on now, pet. Missing little Maisy growing up when he'd have loved to have seen that. It all seems such a waste. The silly old bugger. Then I get myself a bit emotional and annoyed, and it gets jumbled up like a big fat lump in my heart.' Jill let out a slow sigh. 'Rachel, when your Dad died, something in me died as well. And I know you're feeling a bit uncomfortable about me and Daniel, but these past few weeks – finding that little bit of friendship – I feel like I've come back to life, just a little. It's very early days, and yes, we might just stay as friends, who knows? It'll be small steps, whatever, I'm in no rush at all to get involved with anyone new, but if I ever do, it doesn't mean that I'll ever stop loving your father.'

'I know that and I'm sorry, Mum. I think I've been a bit selfish.'

'It's all right, love. None of this has been easy for any of us. And I'm sorry I didn't tell you about spending a bit of time with Dan. I just didn't know what to make of it myself, I suppose.'

'Oh, it's okay, Mum, I understand. And I miss Dad so much, too.' Rachel headed across and knelt before her mum on the hearthrug, gently taking her hand. 'We're doing all right here though, aren't we?' Rachel was still thoughtful, thinking of the bigger picture; the farm, the Pantry, their family.

'Yes, I think we are, pet. We're managing to hold it all together – and more. Your dad would be proud of the great job you're doing on the farm, and how you've coped with it all.'

'Thanks, Mum. He'd have been proud of you too. All the hard work and energy you've put into the Pudding Pantry and, all of those amazing puddings you've created. Hah, we've even won an award, for goodness' sake – Christmas Pudding of the Year in the *Gazette*! Thanks to good old Granny Ruth and her recipe.'

'Yes, what a year it's been, hey.'

'Absolutely,' Rachel agreed. She took her mum into her arms for a short burst of a hug. 'Love you, Mum.'

'Aw, pet. I love you, too.'

'Well then, shall I pour us a Bailey's Irish Cream, just as a little treat while we go and set out the breakfast table?'

'Now *that*, my girl, sounds a grand idea.'

Rachel and Jill were busy in the kitchen when Tom arrived back twenty minutes later.

'Hey,' he popped his head around the kitchen door, revealing a dusting of white on his coat, 'it's started to snow.'

'Really?' commented Jill.

'Oh, we were so busy setting up in here, we've hardly had the chance to look up.' Rachel glanced at the window. Against the dark of the night was a gentle swirl of snow-flakes, some settling and melting on the pane.

Mabel came dashing in to greet Moss, with a sprinkling of snow on her back, and the dogs circled each other happily.

'Well, come on, ladies. Outside now. It might not last,' ordered Tom. 'And don't worry, it's only the light stuff,' he added seeing the look of concern cross Rachel's face. 'It's nothing like that blizzard.'

'Okay then, let's get the wellies on, Mum. We can finish off here later. We're nearly done, anyhow.'

How wonderful that it was falling on Christmas Eve.

'So, Maisy got her wish, after all.' Rachel smiled. 'I just hope it doesn't melt before morning.'

'I'm not sure there's enough yet to make a snowman for Maisy, mind,' Tom added.

'Oh well. It'll look pretty out there, I'm sure.'

With coats and wellies soon on, they stepped outside into the yard, where there was already a dusting of icing sugar snow on the ground, with more swirling down around them in a hush of magical ice-crystal flakes. Rachel threw her head back and laughed, watching the flakes as they drifted down mesmerisingly, catching on her eyelashes, her nose.

Jill stood watching it fall around her, raising her hands to catch it in her palms. There was something magical about this kind of gentle snow. There was a distant baa from the fields, but the sheep were fine in a light fall like this and Rachel had made sure there was plenty of hay and feed put out for them today. The three of them stood, enjoying the hush that fell all around them along with the snow.

'It's wonderful,' Rachel said happily, glad to be sharing the moment with both Tom and her mother.

'It's pretty, but brrr, it is rather chilly,' added Jill. 'I think I'll get myself back inside.'

Rachel had the feeling that her mum was also trying to give them a little space.

'See you in a minute then, Mum.'

'Okay, Jill,' said Tom.

'I'm glad I've been out and seen it, mind, thanks Tom.'

As the door to the farmhouse closed, the two of them instinctively took a step closer to each other. Rachel watched as a snowflake or two stuck, then melted, on Tom's bottom lip. She couldn't resist kissing him, placing her lips right there where the snowflakes had been, the snow falling all around them, padding softly against their coats, melting in their hair, on their hands.

It was truly a winter wonderland moment, and Rachel didn't want it to end any time soon. They didn't rush, the kiss was long and lingering, and so very heartfelt.

Later that night, after they'd made love, slowly, tenderly and *very* quietly, for fear of waking Maisy or disturbing anyone else in the house, Rachel lay there in her double bed, listening to Tom's steady breathing as he settled to sleep beside her. She felt slightly overwhelmed in a beautiful way; she couldn't even begin to put into words how she felt about him right now. Could she dare to dream even bigger? Might she and Tom have a family of their own one day, a brother or sister for little Maisy? Her heart swelled for him, for what they had together. She had to confess it felt a huge bit like love.

42

'He's been, he's been! The presents are here, Mummy.' Maisy came bowling into Rachel's room at seven the next morning. She tumbled on to the bed to find her mummy's head on one pillow and then Tom's on the other.

'Oh! Hi, Tom.' It was a happy but surprised tone, as Maisy looked and squished her face up. 'What's Tom doing here, Mummy?'

'Well ...' Rachel didn't actually get the chance to try to give her simple explanation (planned in her head last night) about them wanting to be together a bit more, as Maisy had it all worked out for herself within a second. 'Ah, I think Father Christmas sent you, Tom. To stop Mummy being lonely.' Only Maisy could have come up with that one.

'Well yes, maybe that's it, Maisy,' said Rachel.

And so that was it, Tom's arrival was accepted.

'Morning, Maisy. Happy Christmas! And yes, absolutely,' grinned Tom. 'I actually had a little word with the main man himself.'

'*You did*? But no one can see him. Not on Christmas night. Only earlier at those special otter places, like at the castle and things.'

Otter? 'Don't you mean grotto, Maisy?' Rachel queried.
'Otto yes, those.'

'Well, I sent a letter actually. Up my chimney,' added Tom.

'Ooh, we did that too.'

'Merry Christmas, darling.' Rachel bundled her little girl up in her arms with a big kiss.

'Come on then, Mummy. We need to go see what Father Christmas has brought.' Maisy was tugging at her hand.

'Hang on, just let me get my dressing gown on.' Rachel had already put her nightie on in the middle of the night, ready for the dawn landing of an excited five-year-old.

Maisy was suddenly drawn to the bedroom window. 'Yay! It's snowed.' Her voice was filled with wonder. 'We can make a big snowman, Mummy!' Then Maisy squinted her eyes, pressed her nose against the glass, and thrust her hands on her hips, just as Rachel heard the moo of a cow, far too close for comfort. 'Mummy, why are Macduff and the cows outside in the garden? They're making a mess of all the snow.'

'You what?' Rachel was up and out of the bed like a shot, soon standing beside her daughter.

It was still only half light, but the shapes of the cattle were distinct, having a nice plod and chew in Grandma Jill's flower beds beneath the bedroom window. 'Oh no! Oh my! Tom! Gonna need a hand.'

Tom was out of bed in a second and standing in just his boxer shots. Now that would have been a real

Christmas morning treat for Rachel, if there hadn't been a five-year-old in the room, plus a herd of errant cattle stomping all over their garden borders. Why *this* morning of all mornings? Rachel groaned inwardly. Couldn't life give her a break, just this once?

Granny Ruth's voice suddenly burst from the landing. 'Rachel, Ji-ll, the cattle are out!' Her head poked in around the door frame, still in its curlers and net. She'd wanted to look smart with her hair curled for Christmas Day, but hadn't counted on the abrupt awakening. Jill arrived on the scene next, in her dressing gown and slippers.

'Come on, then,' Tom called them to action. 'Let's get this lot rounded up before they cause more damage, or eat something they shouldn't.'

'Hold fire, just one second Tom,' replied Jill with a hint of smile. 'I think I need to get you a boiler suit of Robert's or something else to put on at least.'

'Okey dokey,' he laughed, looking down at his bare torso.

'What about my presents?' Maisy shouted, folding her arms across her chest and sounding most disgruntled.

'They'll still be here when we get back, Maisy,' Rachel appeased, feeling irritated about the delay herself. 'Macduff and his ladies will be making all kinds of trouble if we leave them to it.'

'Don't care.'

Oh dear, this really wasn't the best start to Christmas Day.

Suddenly Jill came up with, 'I think it was Father

Christmas, you know. Well, it's been snowing . . . have you seen? Look. So, I bet the reindeer were cold and hungry and he had to stop to feed them, taking some hay from the cattle shed. He must have been in such a rush he didn't quite click the gate shut properly.'

This was sheer genius. Rachel was impressed.

'Oh, for Rudolph, then?'

'Yes, they'd never make it around the world to all those other children otherwise.'

'Oh, come on then, Grandma. Let's go.'

Jill gave a wink to Rachel over her shoulder, as Maisy was ushered out.

The real explanation, they were soon to find out, was that the straw bed in the cattle shed had layered thickly near to the gate, and given the cows just the height they needed to rub up against and loosen the bolt. It wasn't unheard of, but on Christmas Day? *Really*! It could only happen on a farm!

So, Macduff and his ladies and their now big calves were soon rounded up, with plenty of gentle but firm encouragement and arm waving, by a strange looking army of helpers dressed in pyjamas, dressing gowns and green wellies, plus Tom in his boxer shorts with a borrowed bright-red boiler suit over them. Fifteen minutes later, with all the animals safely back in the cattle shed, and a further helping of hay loaded in for luck, Rachel double-checked the bolt and they headed back to the house to begin Christmas Day anew.

While still in the yard, Rachel spotted a slightly snowy

Tom, dressed head to toe in red, looking like a very sexy and slimmer version of Santa. She burst out laughing.

'What's up with you?' Tom asked, slowing to walk beside her.

They stayed back behind the others, who were already pulling off boots at the farmhouse porch.

'Mummy, come on! It's present time.' Maisy was waving her in, impatiently.

'Won't be a minute, petal.'

'Come on, spill. Or I'll have to snowball you?' Tom whispered at her ear.

'It's just . . . you look like a Skinny Santa in that suit!'

'Well, thanks. I've been called worse. And, of course, I might just have to make all your wishes come true later on,' he added with a rather naughty wink.

'Mum-mee!'

'Let's go, Santa. We can't keep this little girl waiting any longer.'

They strode in to join the others.

'Well then, that was fun and games to start the day, but all's well that ends well, hey? I think this calls for a warming cup of tea and a nice hot chocolate for you, little Maisy.' Jill welcomed them back to the kitchen. 'And then we'll all go and open our Christmas stockings. See if Father Christmas has been good to us?'

'Yay! But hurry, Grandma. I'm ready already.'

They were soon taking their hot drinks through to the living room and the stockings were handed out to all the ladies.

'But where's Tom's?' Maisy suddenly looked concerned.

'Oh, I think Father Christmas has probably left mine at my house. That's where I sent my wishes from.' Tom was thinking quickly, suddenly adding, 'But ah . . . yes, of course, I've got my wish right here, come to think of it. But he couldn't fit Mummy in a stocking, could he?'

'Ah, okay.' With that, Maisy was delving an arm eagerly into her stocking, pulling out sweets, a new book, coloured pens, and her own cooking set with sugar sprinkles, sugar-paste unicorns and polka-dot muffin cases to make her own cupcakes with. Then out came the Santa soft toy mouse that Eve had made which drew a little gasp and an, 'Oh, he's so cute!'.

Rachel found a lovely bottle of perfume in her stocking, that she could never have afforded herself, and some gorgeous chocolate truffles, along with a lottery scratch card. 'Perfect,' she gave Granny Ruth and Jill a warm smile. 'Thank you, Father Christmas.'

Ruth and Jill seemed very pleased with their own little treats, including bubble baths and chocolates from Emma's stall, and there were more gifts that had been wrapped and placed under the tree to open a little later on – much to Maisy's frustration.

'Well, I need to get the turkey into the oven right now, or we won't be eating till midnight at this rate.' Timings had already been delayed with having to round up the escapee cows. 'Then we'll have a bite of breakfast altogether, and after that we can all open our other presents,' said Jill.

'Yes, me and Tom need to pop out on the quad, too, and check the cattle are behaving and get the feed out for the animals.' Farmers didn't get a day off at Christmas!

'Oh-h, even longer until main presents.' Maisy's bottom lip quivered, but Grandma Jill whispered something to her and suddenly she was pronouncing that that was okay and she was happy to stay with Grandma just now. It was awfully warm and cosy there in the kitchen, after all. Rachel caught Maisy giving Grandma a wide-eyed look that suggested they were in cahoots about something . . . What was going on?

Tom jumped on the quad behind Rachel, wrapping his arms around her, and Moss joined them, sitting in his usual place on the back. Mabel, though, had opted to stay by the Aga. The wind was bracing as they sped away up the hill, but they were wrapped up warm in jeans and woollen jumpers, coats, gloves and hats. Tom was sadly no longer in his red boiler suit, though Rachel had suggested he put a towel down it as stuffing in the tummy area and wear it all day to entertain the kids.

After checking the sheep, who were fine apart from one ewe who'd got herself stuck upside down and had got a bit panicked, they slowed at the top of the rise. It was lovely to have some time, even a short while, to themselves. From here they could see both their farms down in the valley with a patchwork of snow-dusted fields around them. The hills showed patches of pale winter green where the snow had already begun to melt in the morning sunlight. There was burnt copper bracken springing from the base of the hedgerows, and the odd dark-green patch of prickly gorse. The scene was panoramic before them, with the sprinkling of snow in the valley glinting in the sunshine, and the hills rolling away in the distance to the grey glimmer of the North Sea.

Rachel turned off the quad's engine. With all the carry-on this morning, they hadn't had chance to even snatch a Christmas kiss and this seemed like the ideal opportunity. She swivelled around on the quad to face her rather handsome passenger. 'Merry Christmas, Tom Watson.'

'Merry Christmas, Rachel Swinton.' He gave her a gorgeous grin.

With that, Rachel raised an arm, to dangle some make-believe mistletoe in the air above them, and moved in for a very much deserved Christmas kiss. It was toe-tinglingly good and warmed all parts of her body. Moss looked on nonchalantly, more interested in a passing crow than the romantic antics taking place before him.

Rachel reluctantly pulled away with a smile, then she turned to rest her back against Tom. He was solid and warm and he wrapped his arms around her.

'I love you.' His words were softly spoken, yet strong at her ear.

'I love you too.' Her words were clear and strong and heartfelt.

Tom's hug became a little tighter. They both looked out across the valley with a sense of peace and calm around them. A brown curlew, distinctive with its long and thin curved beak, cut through the ice-blue sky ahead of them giving its hauntingly beautiful peep. This place made her heart soar, as well as this man beside her.

'Well, I suppose we'd better head back to the family,' said Rachel after a minute or two. 'There'll be one little girl chomping at the bit to open her gifts back at the farmhouse. I'd better get back before she has a meltdown. And then, of course, Mum'll be needing a hand to get the Christmas feast ready for our guests.'

'Hah, yes, of course, and I need to go back and check on my own sheep and cattle. Oh, and there's something else I need to collect and bring back across with me.'

'Ooh, sounds interesting.' Rachel felt a bud of excitement. Was it something for her or a gift for Maisy? That'd be sweet of him?

'Hah, don't get too excited, it's just the starter. I promised your mum I'd bring along a platter of smoked salmon to help out – that was as much as my culinary skills could cope with. But I am bringing a bottle of bubbly and some white wine to go with it, mind.'

'Oh, that's kind, thanks. Can I give you a hand over at your farm at all?'

'No, I'll not be long, assuming all's well. It's just with the farm lads being off today, I'll feel happier having checked everything and putting some more feed out. You get back to Maisy, though; I'll be fine and I'll try to be quick. Oh, and so you know, after lunch, I did promise I'd go and visit my mum and dad.' Tom's parents, who'd had the farm before him, now lived in a hamlet a few miles away. He'd explained he was invited to lunch with the Swintons this year, but he was a loyal son and wanted to spend time with them on Christmas Day too.

'Of course.'

Rachel was soon back home, leaving Tom to nip away. She opened the door to a kitchen full of roasting turkey aromas, but strangely no people.

'Hellooo,' she called out, surprised that no one was about.

A minute or so later, Granny Ruth came down from upstairs. 'Oh, hello lass, I've just finished getting myself ready. What with all the cattle malarkey, I've been plodding around in my dressing gown up till now. Your mum and Maisy are just – just in the yard, letting the chickens out, and yes, checking if there're any fresh eggs.'

'Oh well, the hens haven't been laying much lately. It'll be these short winter days and all the cold weather. They'll be lucky if they find many. Can I get you a cuppa, Granny? I could do with one myself, it's certainly chilly out there.'

'Now that sounds grand, pet. Are you back here on your own? Where's your Tom gone? He is with us for Christmas lunch, isn't he?'

'Oh yes, he's just gone to look in on his own farm. Check that all's well with the animals, so he can then relax for a while.'

'I see. Aye, he's a lovely lad is young Tom. I'm so glad you two have sorted out your differences.'

'Me too.' Rachel smiled. To think, she could have let him slip away, getting all jealous and worked up about Caitlin without stopping to let him explain the truth. She vowed never to take their love for granted again.

'Well, they say the path to love never did run smooth, lass. There's always a few rucks on the way, but where there's a will, there's a way.'

'You're right, Granny. And I'm glad we had our heart-to-heart recently, thank you.'

'I might be old, pet, but I'm not daft. Not yet, anyhow.' She chuckled.

After making a pot of tea, Rachel said, 'Is there anything I can do, do you think? Check on the turkey in the Aga or anything?' Mum seemed to be taking a while fetching the eggs.

'Ach well, I think your mother has it all under control. So I wouldn't open that oven door if I were you. She'll have it all timed to a tee and the temperature just right.'

'Hah, I suppose so. She always was queen of the Christmas dinner. I'd better not interfere. I don't want to be responsible for any turkey disasters – I'd never hear the last of it.'

Jill and Maisy soon arrived back, stamping their feet in the porch, and just two eggs in the basket. They seemed a little flustered, somehow, as though they'd been dashing about.

'Oh, hello love, you're back. Look, just enough eggs

to make my Yorkshire puddings with,' said Jill. The Swinton household had a tradition of serving crispy Yorkshire puddings with their turkey dinner, along with lashings of Grandma Jill's rich and tasty gravy.

'Is there anything I can help with, Mum?' Rachel offered, feeling that she hadn't been pulling her weight in the kitchen today.

'No, it's all in hand. The bird will be ready by two and then it needs to stand a while so that's when I cook the veg and bake my Yorkshires.'

'Well, let me lay the table for you then.' Usually, soon after breakfast on Christmas day, Jill would have it all set up, ready for their dinner, with cutlery, festive napkins, the works, but as yet none of that had been done. Oh well, Rachel mused, it had been a busy morning for them all.

'No need,' Jill tried extra hard to sound nonchalant about it.

Maisy started fidgeting and Ruth gave Jill a knowing glance.

'Okay, what's going on here?'

'Can we tell her Grandma, *please*?' Maisy was now bouncing in the spot.

'Let's go one better and show her, shall we,' replied Jill.

'What are you lot up to, now?' Rachel's interest was piqued.

'It's a surprise!'

'Come on then, shoes back on, Maisy.'

They gathered coats and footwear and headed out the door and across the yard where Jill unlocked the doors to the Pudding Pantry. Hmm . . . Rachel had closed it up last night, thinking they'd not be back in there for a couple of days.

Now what were they up to?

'Go on in,' said Jill with a smile on her face.

Maisy took Rachel's hand and led her through. 'We did it all this morning – and Eve came too.'

'Oh my! Oh, it's wonderful!'

While she'd been out checking her livestock, the Pudding Pantry had been transformed. Two of the tables had been pulled together, and covered with a large white cloth that looked suspiciously like a bedsheet. There was a beautiful floral candle decoration with twists of ivy, pine and holly through it.

'Auntie Eve made the flowers,' Maisy announced. 'And the hanging flags.'

Oh yes, there was festive bunting strung along the back wall with flags of holly print, red and green tartan, and white with a green polka dot – so pretty!

The table was set out for the nine of them with cut glasses and beautifully polished silver knives, forks and spoons.

'The cutlery and glasses were in my cottage, gathering dust. It's about time they got used.' Granny Ruth caught up with them. 'I used to get them out when we had folk around, back when we were still here at the house, but I haven't entertained like that since I moved into the cottage and I think they need to be back at the farm where they belong.'

The fairy lights on the tree were glowing and the chandeliers glinted warmly above the festive table. The log burner had also been lit to take the chill off. How hadn't she seen the smoke from the chimney as she came back to the farmyard? It was cosy and magical – and just right.

'It looks amazing,' Rachel's voice came out slightly choked. 'I can't believe you did all this.'

'So, as you might have guessed by now, we are having our Christmas lunch over here at the Pudding Pantry!' confirmed Jill.

How fitting that was, in this year of converting the barn and making the Pantry dream a reality, with all its trials and tribulations, the highs, lows and special moments that had gone into getting them all this far.

'It's perfect, thank you.' Ooh, she could feel herself welling up.

'Eve helped me this morning too,' explained Jill. 'We had a bit of a rush to do it all.'

'That's lovely of her. And yes, I bet.'

'That's why I was still in my dressing gown and curlers until just before you got back,' Ruth chuckled.

'Oh, and I've made name signs, Mummy – look.' Maisy was brimming with pride.

There were handmade card place names at each setting, decorated with glitter and glue and a festive image for everyone. 'I'm Rudolph, Tom's got Father Christmas, you're the tree and Granny Ruth's the pudding.'

Caroline Roberts

'She chose them all herself. Very fitting,' said Jill.

'*And* I wrote the names on all by myself, too.'

'Ah, I can see that, in your very best handwriting.'

'Grandma told me the spellings.'

'They are really lovely. Well done, Maisy.'

And then something caught Rachel's eye in the glass counter that she was sure she'd left empty yesterday. A wonderful looking Pavlova with whipped cream and all her favourite fruits on, raspberries, strawberries and blueberries.

'Granny Ruth made the rang-er.' This was Maisy's very own word for meringue, finding it hard to say when she was younger. 'And I put the strawberries and things on.'

'Wow, we are going to have such a feast! Thank you, everyone, it looks amazing.'

'Right, well, we'd better get back to the farmhouse,' said Jill. 'I need to get the roast potatoes on next. It won't be that long until our guests start arriving. I'll still cook the roast dinner over there in the Aga, and my plan is to carry it across to serve.'

'Let me give you a hand now, Mum. I'll make the cheese sauce for the leeks, shall I?'

'Yes, that'd be good. Thanks, love.'

'I'm happy you liked your surprise, Mummy,' Maisy chanted, taking Rachel's hand, as they walked back over to the farmhouse. 'It was like when you did the barn for my birthday party.'

'Gosh, yes.' Back in the spring she'd made a birthday surprise for Maisy, setting up the old disused stone barn

386

as a birthday party venue for her little girl. From there, the seed for the Pudding Pantry was sown and the idea had grown. 'And I don't just like it, Maisy, I *love* it.'

Tom arrived at the farmhouse ten minutes later with his platter of smoked salmon slices, sprinkled with black pepper and garnished with lemon slices. He'd also buttered a small mountain of thinly sliced brown bread to accompany it, all wrapped in cling film.

'That looks wonderful, Tom, thank you. I'll pop it in the larder to keep it cool,' said Jill.

'Oh, and I've a little something else.' He pulled a small square gift from his pocket. 'Maisy, this is for you.'

Oh, how thoughtful. Rachel and Tom hadn't yet exchanged gifts, and with this morning being all go, there was still a small pile for Maisy yet to open under the tree.

'Thank you, Tom. Can I open it now, Mummy?'

'Yes, that's fine. Go ahead.'

Maisy unwrapped a small box and carefully unfolded white tissue paper. It was a pretty silver bracelet with butterflies on, very grown-up. Maisy held it out with a big smile. 'Can I put it on?'

Rachel placed it on her wrist.

'Oh, it's lovely, Tom, thank you,' beamed Maisy.

'You'll have to look after it mind, and keep it for special occasions,' said Rachel.

'I will.' She turned her wrist to and fro, so the butterfly wings caught the light.

Caroline Roberts

'Well then, who's a very lucky girl,' said Jill.

'Thank you so much,' Rachel said to Tom.

They went through to open their family gifts next, sitting around the Christmas tree by the crackling fire. Maisy had the largest pile, of course. Rachel had bought her some new clothes and a Christmas DVD and the Twister game was there from Father Christmas, as well as the stocking fillers she'd had earlier. Rachel was relieved that Jake had actually remembered to get his daughter's gift to her on time this year, though the tag looked suspiciously as if it had been written by Chelsea, his girlfriend. But maybe the new woman in his life was helping to keep him in check and reminding him of his fatherly responsibilities. Maisy opened Jake's parcel to find a dress, the correct size for her age, as well as a bead craft set. Maisy went dashing off to try the frock on straight away.

There were some thoughtful presents between the three ladies. The budget had been tight, and they'd all agreed to keep the gifts small this year. Rachel was looking forward to relaxing in her new bubble bath, with a glass of raspberry gin, and she had two new pairs of cosy-warm socks and some new heavy-duty gloves for working in.

Then it was Tom's turn. Rachel's gift to him wasn't the most exciting, she feared, but she'd got him some nice aftershave, and a checked Barbour scarf to go with his waxed coat. She'd also managed to find a humorous mug for his elevenses coffee that read 'Eat Sleep Farm Repeat'.

'These are great, thank you.' He grinned and gave her a hug. 'And now your turn.' He handed her a large box.

'I'll help, Mummy.'

Rachel and Maisy tore open the wrapping to find a pair of sensible, and she had to admit, very nice wellington boots. Hers were getting very worn, and she'd noticed a slight leak that day of the storm, so they would be great. 'Thank you.' Maybe she'd hoped for something slightly more glamorous, but she smiled gratefully, after all, she was going out with a farmer.

'Try them on, go on,' Tom encouraged.

'Ah, okay.' She could see they were the right size from the box.

She pulled a boot out and shoved her foot down in it, then her toes met with something solid. Oh, they must have left one of those scrunched up paper things in there, to keep the shape. She dug a hand in to pull out . . . a smallish square box. Tom began grinning now.

'What's this?'

'Open it and you'll see . . .'

And inside the box, Rachel found a gorgeous watch, practical enough that she could wear it day to day but perfectly lovely. And the card said, 'Time's precious, Rachel . . . and I'd really like to spend more time with you.'

'Oh, Tom, thank you.'

'That's so lovely, Tom,' said Jill.

'Woohoo!' said Maisy, while Granny Ruth looked on with a big smile in her face.

43

With their guests due to arrive any minute, Rachel, Jill, Maisy, Ruth and Tom were all set up in the Pantry just before midday, glasses at the ready for a little festive treat of bubbly.

First up the driveway, with a 'fut fut' of his car engine, was Frank. He arrived at the barn door, dressed smartly in a tweed jacket, shirt and tie, teamed with a pair of beige trousers, merrily wielding a bottle of Harveys Bristol Cream sherry in one hand, which made Ruth smile as it was one of her favourites, and what looked like a familiarly wrapped pudding in the other.

He passed the bottle to Jill, then doffed his cap, saying, 'Hello, and Happy Christmas to all. Thank you so much for having me today.'

'Hello, Frank, Merry Christmas,' replied Jill. 'And you're most welcome.'

'Happy Christmas, Frank.' Rachel gave him a kiss on the cheek.

Maisy came running up too, with a big smile. 'Merry Christmas, Frank.'

'Oh, and I brought something else along. It might seem a bit odd, seeing as it's one I bought from here, but I thought it might help out. I suddenly realised I was never going to eat it all to myself. Oh, and I've some wrapped gifts and a box of chocolates still in the car too.'

The pudding-shaped gift was, in fact, one of their very own Whisky and Orange Christmas Puddings.

Jill gave a big grin. 'You've just made my day, Frank. We ran out of these yesterday, and guess who didn't put one aside?' Jill winked across at Rachel. 'It was far too late to make more, so we didn't have a Christmas pudding left for ourselves in the end. So this is wonderful, thank you.'

'Well, I'm very pleased I brought it now.'

'So, come on in and welcome to our Christmas Pudding Pantry. Can I get anyone a drink? A sherry or a glass of fizz maybe?' Rachel offered.

There were two bottles of prosecco chilling in the fridge, and two more of white burgundy ready to go with the dinner, thanks to Tom.

'A little glass of fizz might just set the day away well,' grinned Frank.

'Sounds a good idea to me. I'll do the honours, Mum,' offered Rachel.

'Thank you, love.'

Granny Ruth began chatting with Frank, whilst Maisy helped gather together Ruth's best wine glasses ready to be filled. She and Amelia were going to have one of the 'special' glasses with some lemonade in.

The cork popped with a merry bang, just as Eve, Amelia and Ben appeared at the Pantry door bearing gifts and grins and apologising for being slightly late.

Rachel wondered then if Jake would actually remember to ring Maisy. It would be a minor miracle, but she knew it would make Maisy's day. Well, she could live in hope. Christmas was a time for miracles, after all. Perhaps she'd send a text message with a thank you for the gift for Maisy to put her in his thoughts, that might stir him to action.

Amelia and Maisy skipped off to the far end of the room to sit beside the sparkly Christmas tree with their special lemonades. Maisy was desperate to tell her friend all about her new toys and clothes. Amelia had brought her favourite gift, a Glow Art set with her, too. So the girls were sitting happily playing, whilst the grown-ups stood talking, sipping their drinks contentedly in the Pantry, with the waft of roast dinner drifting across tantalisingly from the farmhouse.

'Ta dah!' Half an hour later, Christmas dinner was served. The turkey was carried across ceremonially, already carved and sliced and covered with silver foil to keep it warm, along with jugs of gravy, trays of vegetables and roasting tins full of crispy golden potatoes and Yorkshire puddings. There was stuffing, bread sauce and cranberry sauce. The table looked so pretty and festive with the candles flickering gently in Eve's floral centrepiece. There were Christmas crackers to pull, paper hats to put on, along with silly jokes and merriment.

Before they ate, Rachel stood to say a big thank you to Jill, who'd done the majority of the cooking, then she raised her glass to 'friends and family', taking a deep breath as she spoke. There was still, would always be, someone missing from that table, but they had to carry on and make the most of the life they had left without him, and the special group of people here with them today were all helping them to do that. Rachel, Jill and Ruth shared a knowing, loving look, as they raised their glasses silently to Robert too.

And so they settled down to eat, and, despite their sore hearts, there was much chatter and laughter too. The future seemed brighter than it had done for several years and together they were starting to find their silver lining after the darkest of times.

There was a lull after the main course, with no one having room for pudding just yet, and they sat around the festive table, content but too full to move.

Rachel's mobile phone suddenly buzzed to life. 'Oh, excuse me.' She stood up from the table and stood to one side. 'Oh, hi Jake. Merry Christmas.' Wow, so he had remembered.

'Daddy!' Maisy had heard and was up like a shot. She soon took the phone and was chattering away, about her Santa mouse, her Twister game and her bracelet, then she remembered her manners and thanked Jake for the dress. Rachel was pleased to hear that.

Maisy then added, loud and clear for the whole table to hear, 'And Santa put Tom in Mummy's bed.'

There was a splutter from Eve who'd been about to take a sip of prosecco. Frank gave a wink to Rachel along with a big grin, and everyone else looked slightly awkward, particularly Tom. Eve and Ben started snorting and tried to stifle their giggles.

Rachel daren't think what Jake's response to that statement would be. Oh well, at least he knew the full picture now. She didn't want to hide her love with Tom away.

Maisy bulldozed on oblivious. 'Tom's still here, he's the one that gave me the bracelet, and my friend Amelia, and we've all had dinner and there's going to be ice cream and strawberry rang-er pudding in a minute.'

There was a quiet moment, whilst Jake was evidently speaking.

After a few seconds, Maisy replied, 'Yes, okay. Oh, and I do love my dress. Happy Christmas, Daddy! Thank you.' She sounded genuinely happy, bless her. 'Mummy, he wants to talk to you now.'

So, after that very *open* conversation from Maisy, Rachel took the phone. Awkward moment alert. 'Hi, Jake. Yes, yeah we're having a good day thanks.' Rachel could hear chatter in the background down the line and then, 'Yeah – just one minute, Kelvin, I'm on the phone. Go ask your mum.' Suddenly Rachel could picture them there all together – Jake's instant family – while the little girl he had left behind waited for a weekly call if she was lucky. She felt riled, but Rachel was determined not to let it spoil hers or Maisy's day. So she put on a chirpy tone and a smile for Maisy saying, 'Happy Christmas, Jake.' After all, this particular wayward leopard was never going to change his spots. He finished the call, promising to ring Maisy again in a few days' time.

After a wonderful dessert feast of Granny Ruth's award-winning Christmas pudding, with a side portion of Berry Pavlova, a giggle-filled game of charades ensued. That was then followed by Twister, Maisy's all-time favourite. Granny Ruth nearly seized up at one point in her forward crab position during the game, but Rachel and Eve managed to straighten her up, and a further glass of sherry and a sit-down seemed to put her to rights. Moss and Mabel had settled happily together by the log-burning stove, and looked rather loved up, after polishing off a treat of turkey leftovers.

The only cooking disaster of the day was discovered when Jill headed back over to the farmhouse to be met by a slightly smoky aroma – the pigs in blankets were still sitting in the bottom oven of the Aga – she'd totally forgotten about them. Unfortunately, they now looked very like 'pigs in charcoal' but she and Rachel laughed it off. Nobody had noticed they were missing and the rest of the meal had been delicious, after all.

It was time for Tom to head over to his parents' house. Rachel slipped out from the table to see him off. She'd so enjoyed having him here for Christmas Day with them, but totally understood that he needed to spend time with his own family too.

'Thanks for being here with us all today. I've had such a lovely day so far.'

'Me too. It's been brilliant, and as per usual at Primrose Farm, I've eaten far too much. It was thoroughly delicious, mind. Your mum is just *the* best cook. And you're a very close runner-up.'

'I think I'll take that as a compliment.'

Tom then stepped closer to take Rachel in his arms and a rather romantic kiss ensued. The spell was broken by Maisy shouting out to the group inside, 'Ooh, look, Mummy's kissing Tom!' which was followed by warm laughter, and a whoop from Eve.

Tom and Rachel smiled broadly. At least Maisy didn't seem to mind; she was just curious at this newfound public display of affection.

'Can you come back this evening? I'd love you to stay again,' whispered Rachel hopefully, her body already filled with longing for him. *Well, you can't kiss someone like that and not expect a reaction.*

'Yes, I'm sure I can manage that.' Tom was grinning like the cat who'd got the cream.

'I'll see you later, then.'

'Yeah, I'll spend a few hours with Mum and Dad, and then I'll need to go and check on the farm again on my way back over.'

'Okay, that's fine. There's no worry about time.' She felt the weight of her new watch on her wrist. 'Thanks so much for my gift too. It's gorgeous.'

'I'm glad you like it. And thank you for yours, I'll be feeling very cosy in my scarf and smelling super dandy with my new aftershave.'

'Hah yes, better than aroma de sheep or cologne de cow, your usual brand.'

'You, cheeky mare!' He pretended to be affronted but was laughing. 'Right, I'll see you later then . . . when I'll need to severely reprimand you for your insolent comments.'

'Hmm, I look forward to that,' she said teasingly. 'Merry Christmas, Tom.'

'Happy, happy Christmas, Rachel.'

And they sneaked in another Christmas kiss.

'Argh, they're doing it again,' Rachel could hear Maisy's remark from the barn doorway. 'Yuck!' She wasn't so impressed this time.

The festive gathering in the barn dissolved into laughter.

There was that post-Christmas dinner lull and they headed back over to the farmhouse, where Eve, Rachel and Ben cracked on with the washing-up, whilst the girls played with Amelia's new toy and made bead bracelets using Jake's gift. Jill, Ruth and Frank settled in the cosy chairs in the living room by the fire for a well-deserved nap.

At around four, just as it was beginning to get dark, a vehicle rolled up the drive. It was Daniel, who arrived at the porch bearing a bouquet of Christmas flowers. Rachel spotted him out of the kitchen window. He was obviously coming to visit Jill, and Rachel felt that familiar edge of tension. Despite his kind help yesterday, it still just felt strange. Rachel took a deep breath and found a little festive spirit within herself as she called her mum to come through.

'Mum, you've got a guest arrived.'

'Oh?'

'It's Daniel.'

He was already knocking at the door, and she could hardly leave him out in the cold. Rachel gathered a mental olive branch and opened the door with a welcoming smile.

'Merry Christmas, Daniel. Mum's just on her way.'

'Merry Christmas, Rachel. I hope you've all had a lovely day.'

'Yes, we have.'

'Oh, right,' and suddenly Jill was standing there beside Rachel, who moved back politely.

'I hope it's okay to turn up like this. I know it's Christmas Day, but you did say I could call.'

'Of course, yes that's fine. Come on in.'

'For you, Jill. Just a little something. Merry Christmas.' Daniel passed the bouquet across.

'Oh, how lovely. Thank you, Daniel. And, Merry Christmas to you too.' She gave him a friendly peck in the cheek. 'But I think it's *us* who should be getting you flowers after all your help yesterday.'

'Ah, it was no problem.'

'Well, come in then. Did you have a nice time with your mother?'

'Yes, thanks. It was just a quiet day as Mum's getting frailer now, and there was just the two of us. But she did enjoy it. I cooked the full turkey dinner, as you do, and she ate like a horse, which was good to see. She was feeling tired, though, by about three, so I've left her having a snooze.'

'Well then, can I get you a drink of anything? There's some wine on the go, or a cup of tea?'

'A small glass of wine would be lovely. Some red if you have it.'

They had come through to the kitchen and Maisy was soon skipping in to see who the new arrival was. 'Hi Dan, I've got a new bracelet, see?' She thrust her wrist out towards him where there was a glint of delicate silver. 'And a dress.' She gave a twirl.

'Well, you look like a Christmas princess,' he said with a smile. 'So, you're having a good day?'

'A brilliant day!' she beamed, and with that she waltzed back to cosy up with Amelia on the sofa in the lounge, her Christmas DVD now playing.

Rachel looked on as Mum poured out some wine for Daniel and the two of them sat down at the kitchen table, chatting easily over a glass of red each. How could she expect Jill to want to stay on her own for the rest of her life? Of course any new relationship didn't mean that Jill had stopped thinking of, or loving Rachel's dad, her husband. Rachel realised she was being selfish, desperate for them to cling onto their old life – wanting to keep Mum's relationship with Dad sacrosanct. But what she realised now was that it already was. And it always would be.

Yes, maybe it was time they all did a little moving on, whatever form that took. This friendship was developing in very slow and respectful steps. It wasn't like Mum was having an affair – and Dad was gone. That was the honest truth. In fact, watching the pair of them, Rachel realised it was so nice to see Jill smiling again.

'I'll just go on through with the others.' She politely exited, giving them a little space

What a wonderful day it had been. Looking out at all her friends and family, and the joyful mess of presents and food leftover, she felt so grateful for all the special people in her life. That – she thought to herself, also glancing at the picture of her dad on the mantelpiece – was the very best gift of all.

44

Christmas had been everything Rachel had hoped for and so much more. It was the day after Boxing Day and Tom came whizzing across the field on his quad, stopping right beside Rachel who was cracking ice on the water trough. She'd been around the fields where the sheep were, doing the same thing on repeat, to ensure they could still get some fresh water. Her next job was to go and get a trailer load of sugar beet to scatter for the flock; they'd need the extra nutrients in this cold spell.

'Here you are; I've been looking all over for you. I called at the farmhouse, and I've been driving around all your fields. Come on, jump on the back. We need to get going,' Tom announced.

'Why, what's the rush?' Rachel's curiosity was piqued, but she had a lot to do on the farm yet too.

'Now, that would spoil it. Just wait and see.'

'Hmm, very curious.'

'Just something I need to show you,' he added with a grin. 'No time to lose!'

Rachel perched behind him on the quad, wrapping her arms around his waist, breathing in his delicious aftershave scent in the frosty air as they set off. The

December morning blasted chilly around them as they sped towards Tom's farmland, crossing several fields. They seemed to be heading down towards the stream that ran through the valley. There was still a little freezing fog down there and it looked strangely beautiful in the soft glow of the morning light.

'Not far now. I spotted it on my farm checks and just knew I had to show you.' Tantalisingly, he wasn't saying what.

They drove down to the lower pasture, and he pulled to a stop beside the winding stream where there was a copse of trees. The mist hung lightly in the air as the sun tried to break through, in golden-white shafts of light.

'Off we get, just a short walk.'

They headed towards the stream. The overnight frost had been hard, with every blade of grass crunchy under-foot and fronds of bronze bracken blanketed in icy-white crystals.

Tom took her hand and led her towards the stream where he paused and pointed. Just then, a shaft of winter sunlight beamed through the bare branches of the trees on the other side of the bank; some of the smaller trees in the copse stood out in a glisten of magic sparkles. It really was like the fairy glen of Maisy's books; as if each tree and every branch had been touched with an icy wand, making crystal droplets on each tiny twig. The sunlight lit each globe with a spectrum of colours. It was stunning, truly magical – a real winter wonderland.

'Oh, Tom, it's beautiful. Amazing.' Rachel's voice was filled with wonder. She'd worked outside on the land most days since she was seventeen years old, yet she'd never seen anything quite like this.

'I'm so glad it's still here, that it's not melted away yet. I think the mist has kept the temperature down.'

They stood gazing at the sparkling frosty scene – every twig, every blade of grass, every mossy ridge had frost or ice crystals. Nature could be spectacular at times.

'I'll have to take a picture,' said Rachel after gazing, taking it all in for a while. 'Though I don't think my phone camera will do it justice. But I'll have to show Maisy how her Fairy Glen has been made all sparkly and magical.' Little Maisy was at Eve's and Rachel knew the frosty scene couldn't last.

'Yes, she'll love that,' agreed Tom warmly.

Rachel took a few shots, capturing the image as best she could, catching at least some of the coloured sparkle. She looked at Tom. 'Thank you for coming to find me.'

'You're welcome.' He smiled; his dark eyes lit with warmth.

Rachel sighed happily, touched by his thought, that he knew she'd find it beautiful, and that he wanted to share it with her. In fact, it was one of the most romantic things anyone had ever done for her. Simple but stunning, and all totally natural.

What felt totally natural, too, was to turn and kiss this gorgeous man who stood next to her, now holding her hand. She turned, smiled, and moved her head and her lips towards his. He was ready and waiting, welcoming her mouth against his. It was tender, and passionate, and with a myriad of sparkly frosty gems around them, it was a kiss and a moment to remember for all time.

45

That chilled out time between Christmas and New Year was a chance for Rachel to relax, take stock, and spend some precious moments with Maisy, her family and Tom. They had closed the Pudding Pantry for a few days, so there were no baking schedules, and no opening times to adhere to. Yes, the farm animals still needed her care, a farm never stopped after all, but once the feeds and checks were done, that was it, Rachel finally had the luxury of time.

It had stayed frosty with a smattering of snow, just right for country walks, buzzing about on the quad, and having fun with Maisy and Tom.

Tom took the whole family out for a pub lunch, saying that he wanted to treat them as a thank you for making him so welcome all year and for such a wonderful Christmas dinner. Sitting in a country pub by a roaring log fire with Granny Ruth, Jill, Maisy and Tom, a warming steak and ale pie, a half a pint of cider, a view of the hills, and listening in to the local banter, was simple but blissful. And it was so lovely to be looked after, instead of them being the ones bustling about. Maisy was delighted with her fish-finger sandwich and ice-cream dessert. And Granny Ruth, whose appetite had well and truly returned after her illness, enjoyed a hearty lamb hotpot. Yes, it was a time to enjoy life and take a little bit of well-deserved time out.

Mind you, even there in the pub they couldn't stop themselves chattering about plans for the Pantry. They were ready to return with renewed vigour for the beginning of the New Year.

'I'm going to have to come up with a brand-new award-winning recipe for next year, you know, perhaps a Summer Pudding,' commented Ruth. 'After all, I'm not sure we're going to be selling many Christmas puddings for the next six months or more at least.' The old lady chuckled. 'I've got a reputation to live up to now.'

'Well, hang on there, Miss Northumberland Mary Berry, let someone else have a chance in the limelight.' Jill pretended to be affronted. 'I might just have some other pudding delights up my sleeve. Perhaps we could suggest a battle of the sticky toffee puddings next time.'

'Hah, yes,' agreed Rachel, 'I'm sure you'd put up a good fight – and, I could happen to run by the *Gazette* offices with some pudding deliveries once more.'

'Brilliant,' said Tom, enjoying their banter. 'The Pudding Pantry would win every time if I were the judge.'

They all laughed.

'I've been thinking, Mum,' Rachel said, when they'd got back to the farmhouse later that afternoon and were sitting enjoying a pot of tea around the kitchen table.

'We've been tearing ourselves in two trying to do everything and be everything. Yes, we absolutely had to make the most of the build-up in trade for Christmas, but I reckon it'll get quieter again for January and February. Let's work smarter, and make a decision to close the Pantry on say Mondays and Tuesdays.'

They were often quiet days, anyhow, and Tom's earlier warning about her burning herself out had finally come home. These few days, taking a little break, showed her just how precious that breathing space could be . . . for *all* of them.

Jill looked up, listening intently as Rachel carried on. 'I can concentrate on the farm and catch up on any admin work on those days, and you can get a bit of a rest or maybe do some light baking to help prepare for the rest of the week, without having to be up all hours. We need to look after ourselves, as well as the business.'

'Hmm, yes, I see your point. It's been a hectic few months, for sure.'

'Once it gets busier in the spring, then yes, maybe we might need to open say six days a week again, but we can be open-minded and see how it all goes. We need to do well, but we need a bit of balance back in our lives too.'

'That sounds a very good idea, love.' Jill placed her hand reassuringly over Rachel's on the tabletop.

Tom looked across with a smile. 'And, maybe you and me can get a little more time together too.'

'Absolutely.' Rachel grinned.

'And you can take me swimming or to the park, Mummy!' Maisy chipped in.

'Of course.'

A new year already . . . New Year's Eve was only a day away now. A fresh start, a season of change, a time of hope and renewal. Who knew what adventures this year might bring, the happy times, the sad? But whatever it brought, the Swinton ladies would be sure to face it together, united, with open hearts, a sense of pride, some fierce determination and a lot of love.

46

'Rachel, can you come up to the Top Field a minute?' It was Tom on the phone.

It was New Year's Eve and they'd had a bit of a lie-in until eight that morning, with Tom staying over once more, then he said he ought to head across and check on his sheep and cattle. So, what was he doing now, in one of her fields? Perhaps he hadn't realised she'd just been up there herself, putting more hay out. Oh, maybe there was some other issue, perhaps he'd found a weak sheep that was struggling or a break in the fence. Who knew? Every day on the farm brought a new surprise.

'Is everything all right? What are you doing up there? Are the animals okay?'

'Yes, nothing to worry about. Just something I need you to check.'

'Okay. Don't know why you have to be so secretive about it, though,' she grumbled in a low voice.

She'd need to set back off on the quad, so she popped her head into the kitchen to deliver the few eggs she'd just collected from the coop, and to let Jill know where she was heading. Maisy was sitting happily at the kitchen table, playing with her new craft set from Christmas.

'I'm just off to check on the sheep field again, Mum. I'm not sure what's up but Tom needs me. I won't be long, petal,' she added for Maisy's benefit.

'Okay, Mummy. See you later. Say hi to Petie from me.'

'Will do.'

Petie had made a brilliant recovery after his close call in the storm, and was happily back out with the other sheep in that field. She hoped it was nothing to do with him. He was always up to some caper or other. Maisy was concentrating hard, creating a pretty bead necklace, and Grandma Jill was busy at the Aga making homemade soup. Life was back to normal at Primrose Farm and boy, was Rachel glad to see it. After the snowstorm before Christmas, she didn't need any more drama in their lives.

Yet, what Rachel didn't know was that something very dramatic indeed was about to happen.

Arriving at the Top Field five minutes later, some of her sheep were very contentedly eating a trail of feed – that she hadn't put out. What was Tom doing, feeding them for her? They had plenty of hay, after all, and he had his own farm and animals to look after, he didn't need to take on extra work. She could see Tom at the top of the flock, carefully steering the 'snacker' trailer attached to the back of his quad. The rest of the sheep soon moved in to form a shape along its line. A curved line in fact, that joined in a dip between two arches at the top . . . and came all the way down in a 'V' to the bottom. Wow . . . a huge sheep-shaped heart on the hill!

What was he up to now? Rachel couldn't help but grin. The soppy devil.

He drove down to her on his quad with the biggest smile on his face. 'Do you like it?'

'Of course I do, thank you.' She moved forward to give him a hug.

'Ah, hang on. There's something else . . .' He slowly reached inside his waxed jacket, taking something out from the inner pocket. She noticed his hand was trembling a little.

A small navy velvet box was in his palm. And suddenly he was on one knee before her.

He couldn't be, surely . . .?

Rachel felt her heart lodge somewhere in her throat as he looked up, right into her eyes, and started to speak. She felt as though she was in a movie or something. This couldn't be happening. It wasn't her real life.

But the words came loud and clear, if with a lilt of nerves. 'Rachel Swinton, will you marry me?'

The music would be playing in the movie now and the birds singing, with friends and family cheering on in the background. But it was just her and Tom and a snow-dusted field of sheep munching away, blissfully unaware that they had formed a love heart, and that Tom Watson was waiting for her to answer.

Was she ready for this . . . this massive commitment?

She looked out across the valley, taking in the significance of his words. Then she gazed back at Tom, still on one knee before her, and saw the love in his eyes. She thought of the snowstorm and how she had so nearly lost him, saw the hope of all their tomorrows. She knew him well, he knew her, and what they didn't yet know they could explore and learn together.

She nodded, breaking into a grin. 'I will.' Her voice echoed clearly across the valley. 'Of course I will!'

'Yesss!' Tom rose up from his damp, snow-covered knees. 'Phew, that was a long few seconds you had me holding on there.'

Rachel was still feeling stunned, and just stood grinning giddily.

'Woohoo!' Tom shouted across the fields, causing the sheep a brief heads-up stir of alarm, before they settled to their munching again. He lifted Rachel into his strong arms and twirled her around him, making her dizzy with the fields rushing round her like a Primrose Farm kaleidoscope, making her giddy with his love. And she was still a little dazed as he popped her down and gave her the biggest, most beautiful kiss of all, tender and passionate and sexy.

Her husband to be – she rather liked the sound of that! – Tom Watson.

The Twelfth Bake of Christmas

Robert & Jill's Christmas Wedding Cake – A Heart-Shaped
Traditional Christmas Cake baked by Granny Isabel

Rachel stood in the farmhouse sitting room, gazing at the photograph of her mum and dad's wedding day back in 1987. They looked so happy there, stood side by side, Robert's hand placed gently over Jill's, about to cut their wedding cake. Mum looking so pretty and so young, in her traditional white lace frock. Dad looking unusually dapper in a navy, double-breasted suit – a stark change from his usual practical boiler suits for the farm.

The wedding took place the week before Christmas, and money was tight, so Jill's mother, Grandma Isabel, being a canny lady from the Scottish Borders, made a traditional Christmas fruit cake. It was baked into the shape of a heart for them and white-iced, simply yet delicately, with little icing beads all around the base. It made a gorgeous wedding cake for the party of thirty in the Kirkton village hall that day, and any spare was kept back ready for Christmas.

Rachel's own heart swelled and ached just looking at that image. It looked like the perfect day.

A Letter from Caroline

Thank you so much for choosing to read *Christmas at Rachel's Pudding Pantry*. I hope you've enjoyed spending this festive time with the fabulous Swinton family at Primrose Farm. Hopefully you've been curled up with this novel with a mince pie and a bowl of Christmas Pudding to hand!

If you have enjoyed this book, please don't hesitate to get in touch or leave a review. I always love hearing my readers' reactions, and a comment or review also makes a real difference in helping new readers to discover my books for the first time. You'd make this author very happy. 😊

You are welcome to pop along to my Facebook page, Twitter profile or blog page. Please share your news, views, recipe tips and drop by to read all about my favourite puddings and the inspirations behind my writing. It's lovely to make new friends, so keep in touch.

Well, the next book is calling as I'm looking forward to inviting you back to visit Primrose Farm for a wonderful confetti-filled time next summer – so it's back to the writing for me!

Thanks again, and see you soon!

Caroline x

/CarolineRobertsAuthor

@_caroroberts

carolinerobertswriter.blogspot.co.uk

Acknowledgements

Huge thanks to Helen and Johnny Renner and to Jane and Duncan Ord, for showing me around their farms and letting me meet the animals, for providing a cuppa at the farmhouse kitchen table, and answering my many questions about farming life in North Northumberland.

Also, thank you so much to Susan Green of 'The Proof of the Pudding' for welcoming me to her farmhouse, and giving great insight into her fabulous pudding business. I was especially grateful for the Sticky Toffee and Ginger Pudding delights she sent me home with – delicious! All in the name of research, of course!

Friends, Marie and Jenna – thanks for your great recipe tips that inspired some of 'The Twelve Bakes Of Christmas'.

My talented editor, Charlotte Brabbin, a big thank you. Your skills have helped polish this book into what I hope is a little festive gem, and to the whole team at HarperCollins. My lovely agent, Hannah Ferguson, and the team at Hardman & Swainson – thanks so much.

Thanks as always to my wonderful family and friends for all their ongoing support, and to the fabulous Romantic Novelists' Association, especially our Northumberland Chapter, who are always there with writerly advice and friendship, tea and biscuits.

Last but not least, a big hurrah for all my readers and the very supportive book blogging community! My books would be nothing without someone to read and enjoy them. I hope you've had a wonderful time getting to know Rachel, Jill, Ruth and Maisy and spending Christmas with everyone at the Pudding Pantry!

Don't miss the first unforgettable novel in the
Pudding Pantry series

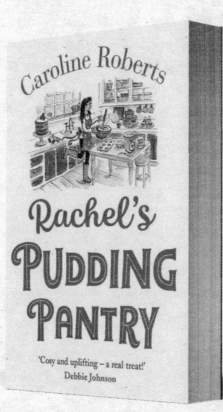

'Family, friendships and fabulous food. The Pudding
Pantry is perfect!' *Sunday Times* bestseller, Heidi Swain

And discover more uplifting and heart-warming romances from Caroline Roberts

Both available to buy now!

Also available to buy now!

KEEP UP WITH

Caroline Roberts

For book news, all the latest gossip, giveaways and gorgeous recipe tips, come and pop by online.

THE PUDDING PANTRY
IS ALWAYS OPEN!